Desire flamed through him as he stood and cupped her face in both hands. Beyond thought, Will bent and pressed his lips to hers, breathing in the mystery of her woman-musk. Then he scooped her in his arms and carried her to the bed in the corner.

Catriona sank back into the softness, floating in an urgency of desire. She clung to his lips, drinking in his kisses, greedy for the whiskey taste of his mouth, his tongue. Fingers fumbled at the front of her bodice, and then his mouth burned kisses down her throat and found her breasts. Passion smoldered low in her belly, a delicious agony of fire, longing to be quenched.

His voice whispered out of the darkness. "Catriona, are you sure?"

A giddy joy, almost laughter, bubbled up in her. "Aye, never more than now . . ."

Books by Stephanie Bartlett

HIGHLAND JADE

HIGHLAND REBEL

HIGHLAND FLAME

Highland Flame

Stephanie Bartlett

BANTAM BOOKS
NEW YORK TORONTO LONDON SYDNEY AUCKLAND

HIGHLAND FLAME

A Bantam Fanfare Book

PUBLISHING HISTORY
Doubleday Loveswept edition published June 1992
Bantam edition/October 1992

ISBN 0-553-29838-0

Published simultaneously in the United States and Canada

Bantam Books are published by Bantam Books, a division of Bantam Doubleday Dell Publishing Group, Inc. Its trademark, consisting of the words "Bantam Books" and the portrayal of a rooster, is Registered in U.S. Patent and Trademark Office and in other countries. Marca Registrada. Bantam Books, 666 Fifth Avenue, New York, New York 10103.

PRINTED IN THE UNITED STATES OF AMERICA

RAD 0 9 8 7 6 5 4 3 2 1

Highland Flame

is lovingly dedicated to my mother,
Sidney Charmaine Bartlett Morrison,
who shared in the sleuthing
and never stopped believing.

Special Thanks

also go to my late teacher, Con Sellers, for loving me enough and for making it all possible; to my best friend and critic, Penny Colvin, for everything we've shared in the last five years; to my agent, Meg Ruley, for going to bat for me; to my editor, Barbara Alpert, for careful attention to detail; to Jane Boley and the staff of the University of Texas at Arlington Special Collections Library, for help and guidance generously offered; to the staff of the Eugene C. Barker Texas History Center in Austin, for preserving our heritage; to my son, Joshua Bartlett Kaine, to my daughter, Ariel Jennie Stultz, and most of all to my husband, Mel Ginsberg, for showing me just how good it can get.

Highland Flame

Chapter 1

Near Arlington, Texas
April 1886

The sweet warm smell of fresh hay followed Catriona Galbraith Macleod as she lifted the tack-room door higher on its sagging rawhide hinges, fitting it into the rough frame and turning the block of wood nailed there to keep it shut. She pulled her tartan shawl around her shoulders, still filled with awe at the miracle of birth. In spite of the difficult midnight delivery, both the foal and the mare seemed fine this morning.

Standing on the stone doorsill, she breathed in the pure crisp air. Sunlight sent long shadows across the sea of grass, tipping each blade with a bead of gold. The prairie spread around her in a giant circle as far as she could see, like a gold tablecloth, featherstitched with red-cedar worm fences and set with wee houses and barns, the cross timbers a dark velvet swath binding one edge.

She sighed. Much as she loved Ian and her new home, she still missed Skye with its towering peaks and the sea lapping at its feet. Homesickness nagged at her. Somehow this flat plain reminded her how big a world she lived in, and how small and alone she was here.

Turning toward the house, she shivered and hurried up the path. It might be spring, but the wind cut through her flannel nightgown and the cold flagstones chilled her bare feet. But despite the discomfort, this was her favorite time of day, when everyone else slept and the whole world was hers alone—so quiet, so peaceful, her morning chores done for the moment. Fresh coffee waited on the back of the kitchen stove, and a clean cloth covered a plate of last night's corn cakes; even the lunch buckets sat ready on the table.

In the distance Ian's prize bull, Old Domino, trumpeted and shambled toward a heifer. So someone else was awake and enjoying the morning. She stopped for a moment to study the now-familiar cattle. How odd they had looked to her when she arrived two years before, with their many shapes and colors, some even with spots, and all as hairless as shorn lambs. So different from the Highland cattle of Skye with their long reddish hair and black horns. But she'd come to admire and love the Texas longhorns for their heartiness, and to share Ian's belief in their importance to the family's future.

She slowed as she reached the farmhouse, stepping out of its long shadow and into the sunlight. Such a fine home, two stories with high ceilings and tall windows in every room. Smooth wooden planking covered the floors, and the kitchen boasted an iron cookstove with a tall black chimney. After dark they could light big oil lamps and read or talk into the night.

She'd have settled for a log cabin, but Ian had said she deserved a real house, no more dirt floors or smoke hanging in the air. Instead, he'd insisted on shipping in lumber for a frame house with weatherboard siding.

But no matter how much she loved the house and loved Ian for building it for her, she knew it had cost more than they could afford. And then there were the windmills he'd built to pump water up from the underground wells. Perhaps if they'd waited until the ranch made more money, Ian wouldn't have needed to work for the railroad. A small cold lump of fear grew in her chest, but she'd promised herself not to say any more about it. Forcing the thought aside, she turned toward her herb garden, examining the rows of plants.

Most of the seeds she'd brought from Scotland hadn't

sprouted at all, and of those that did, only a few lived long enough to bear seed. They didn't belong here any more than she did, but Ian was here, and this was home now. Still, sometimes she longed to walk the moors of her homeland again, gathering the abundance of medicinals hiding amongst the heather. She ran her hand over the fuzzy gray-green leaf of a foxglove, the only one of the biennials to flourish in the dark soil of north central Texas. Soon a double row of pink flowers would cover its spiky stem, and she'd be able to harvest the leaves for a tonic to soothe fevers and strengthen the heart.

If only she knew more about the native plants, she might be able to find substitutes for the remedies she lacked. Not that she had much call for her medicines or much time to visit sick folks since she and Ian came to Texas. Not like Balmeanach, where Mr. Hawthorne might call for her help with an ailing mare, or her brother and his wife might ask for herbs for wee Andrew's cough. She touched the letter in her pocket, listening for the faint crinkle of paper, wishing she could see her nephew while he was still a bairn. She missed the satisfaction of helping people. But the farm was her life now, and Ian and her own wee one; her healing arts weren't needed here. Arlington had a perfectly good doctor, a man who grew up near here with Ian.

A tapping sound from above drew her eyes upward. Ian smiled down at her through the window glass, then laid a forefinger against his puckered lips, the hard muscles of his bare chest outlined in the dim light. With his other hand he motioned her to come up, then disappeared.

The bull bellowed again, and she covered her mouth to keep from laughing. A sweet, tingling warmth swirled low in her belly as she sped on soundless feet around the house and up the stairway into their bedroom.

Panting from the run, she closed the door with a gentle click and tiptoed first to the cradle in the corner. Betsy lay on her back, her tiny rosebud mouth open in deep sleep. Golden-brown curls haloed her wide forehead and ruddy cheeks, and one plump clenched fist lay beside her head on the white blanket. Tenderness clutched at Cat's heart. Her bairn, her daughter. And perhaps another one soon, this time, with luck, a son. She turned toward the bed.

Ian sat against the tall carved headboard, his hands laced behind his head and the coverlet pulled up to his waist. Desire darkened the blue-gray of his eyes, and a smile played across his handsome mouth.

Opening her arms, Cat dropped the tartan shawl to the floor, then bent and grasped the bottom ruffle of her gown and pulled it over her head in one motion. Shivering in the chill air, she posed for a moment, naked, her eyes locked on his, then moved toward him, her hips swaying with each step.

Without a word Ian reached for her, pulling her down atop the warmth of his body. His mouth found hers, and his hands caressed her back and cupped her buttocks, pulling her against his hardness.

Cat melted into him, exploring the smooth planes of his body with her fingers. Her hunger grew as his lips burned a trail down her throat to her breast, drawing a nipple into his mouth, sucking and nibbling at the tender flesh, making her writhe with delight.

She moaned and turned on her side, curling against him. Ian's hand cupped her other breast, then slid down her belly and between her thighs. She gasped at the waves of pleasure spreading through her body. Lifting herself, she straddled him, placing her hands on his shoulders and guiding him inside her. For a long moment she was still, savoring the union of their bodies.

Then his mouth found her breast again and his hands clasped her hips, slowly rocking her to the brink of ecstasy. Her body tensed, eyes closed and head back, and a low cry escaped her lips before she slumped against him.

After a moment Ian chuckled deep in his throat and rolled over on top of her. He kissed her open mouth and bent to nibble her ear, moving into her again in his own rhythm. Wrapping her arms and legs around him, she opened herself as he plunged into her, crying out in his completion.

Arms tight around him, Cat gloried in the weight of his body pressing her into the straw mattress. Her eyes slid shut and she drowsed, floating in the warmth of complete fulfillment until a faint rustling and then a whimper came from the cradle in the corner. Betsy. Such a *Sassenach* name for a Scots bairn, even if she was named for her father's mother.

Ian shifted his weight to his elbows and groaned, then smiled and kissed her. "Morning, wife." His face sobered. "I love you, Catriona. I don't know what I'd ever do without you."

Cat raised her eyebrows and laughed. "Well, dinna think I'd let you try to get on without me, laddie. You're stuck with me now."

Ian snorted and started to pull away, but she locked her arms around him. No matter what she'd promised herself, she had to try again. "I wouldna like to think what my life would be without you, Ian Macleod. And that's why I'm asking you once more not to spike that switch today."

Turning away, Ian stood and pulled his union suit to his waist, slipping his arms into the sleeves and buttoning the front. "Now, Cat, we've already been through this. Don't get yourself in a stew again. I have to, and you know it." The bed sagged as he sat on the edge, pulling on his socks.

Betsy's cry stopped Cat's words. Moving to the cradle, she bent to retrieve her gown and slip it over her head. With shaking fingers she changed Betsy's wet things for dry ones and carried her, still wailing, to the bed. Pulling the quilt over her shoulders, she nestled into the lingering warmth and slid her nipple in the bairn's open mouth.

In the sudden silence she struggled to keep the fear and frustration from her voice. "I dinna know any such thing."

Ian stood to step into his workpants, then bent to tug on his high-heeled boots. "Cat, this strike is as important as the rent boycott on Skye."

Her belly clenched at the memory. "Aye, but on Skye they fought only with sticks. Jim Cutchall and his deputies use guns."

Ian's face twisted into a frown. "The railroads fired a shop steward for going to a union meeting. They've brought in scabs to take our jobs. If we don't keep the trains from moving, we might as well not have a strike."

Cat's jaw tightened. "I can do without the strike better than I can do without you."

Ian slid his arms into his blue cotton shirt and worked the buttons on the cuffs, then turned toward her as he did up the front. His lips set in a thin line. "And are you willing to give up the farm? Because without the union, without this strike, the railroad won't pay me enough to buy seed next year, or pay pickers this year."

Tears burned behind Cat's eyes. "But you and Geordie don't have to be there. You've 'killed' your share of engines. Let someone else take the risks this time."

Color rose in Ian's cheeks, and a muscle twitched beneath his eye as he swept a lock of blond-brown hair off his forehead. When he finally spoke, his voice was cold and dry, like a winter wind. "Even if you could live with a coward for a husband, I couldn't live with myself." His boot heels clicked across the wooden flooring, and he bent to kiss her. "Cat, you know me. I'm no hero. I'll be careful, I promise." He disappeared into the hallway and knocked on Geordie's door.

Catriona sat without moving, waiting for the rhythm of Betsy's mouth on her breast to soothe her, listening until the hoofbeats of the horses softened in the distance. But even then she couldn't free herself of the dread welling up inside her.

Chapter 2

Yawning, Dr. Will Bascom rubbed the sleep from his eyes and snapped the reins of the buggy, urging the horse to a trot. Good thing he was still young enough to survive sleeping on the road, but it was the only way he could make all his house calls in the country and still have time to see patients in town. Now what he needed was a shave and fresh clothes, and a nice big breakfast at the hotel. He gave the horse another slap on its rump with the reins.

Roused from its usual plodding walk, the gelding covered the remaining miles in a short time while Will huddled inside his heavy greatcoat. The cool air tingled his cheeks, driving the last remnants of sleep and dreams from his mind. He found solace in the prairie spreading out around him, the land he'd known as a boy, before the immigrants came and cut it to pieces. Not that he blamed them. Every man had a right to a home of his own.

At the livery he handed the reins to the stable boy, leaving him to unhitch and curry the horse, then walked to the brick building where he kept his second-floor office. He took the narrow steep stairs two at a time and turned the skeleton key in the lock, surprised to find the hallway empty of patients and no messages fluttering from the box beside the door. He let out a noisy sigh. For the first time in weeks he had a few moments for himself.

After stripping to the waist, he broke the ice in the water pitcher and filled a basin, shivering as he scraped the straight razor over his cheeks. By the time he donned a clean shirt and knotted his tie, he was humming an old dance tune. He bounded down the stairs, and his heels clicked along the lank sidewalk, echoing through the empty streets of the still-sleeping town.

Stopping by the newspaper office, he helped himself to the newest edition, leaving behind a nickel. Thank God someone was awake in the hotel kitchen. He ordered steak and eggs and fried potatoes, then sipped a cup of hot black chicory coffee. Other customers straggled in, but it was still early enough and empty enough to quell their voices, only the occasional clatter and clink of tableware disturbing the quiet of the dining room.

He nodded at one or two former patients, but as usual, only those who had paid their bills returned his greeting; the others pretended not to notice, their relationship with him forgotten until the next time they or one of their family members lay at death's door.

He leaned back and opened the newspaper, scanning the news of the railroad strike and glancing at the page of ads. His eye stopped in the help wanted section.

> Wanted: Apprentice typesetter. Room and board and chance to learn news writing. Apply in person at *The World*.

It was about time old Zeke hired a helper. Ever since his Anna died, the old man had been trying to do everything himself, from writing to typesetting to printing. No wonder the pages were riddled with mistakes. Besides, the old man's heart couldn't take the aggravation and long hours.

A shadow fell across his face, and the sharp smell of fresh witch hazel overpowered the lingering aroma of coffee. Opening his eyes, he stared up into a handsome face framed by wavy dark hair. Long-haired Jim Cutchall, the new acting city marshal of Fort Worth and the last man Will wanted to see.

For a moment he considered making an excuse to bolt and run, but restrained himself. "Marshal." He inclined his head in greeting.

The man's narrow lips curved into a smile, twitching his dark mustache upward with a sardonic twist. "Now, Doc, you know better than that. My friends call me Jim." His quiet voice filled the room. Several diners looked up, then quickly away. "Mind if I set a spell?"

Will nodded, irritated by the folksy speech the man affected, meant as it was to disguise Cutchall's true nature behind a mask of simplicity. Most people succumbed to the man's charm, but Will had been immune to it for years. Cutchall was a folk hero from years back, when the Texas Rangers arrested him for murdering homesteaders in New Mexico. Will had never been able to understand why the people of Fort Worth helped him escape, and he damn sure didn't understand why the sheriff made a murderer into a peace officer. Especially now that he was fighting against the strikers. "What can I do for you this morning, Jim?"

The crafty smile froze for a second, then broadened. "Nice little town you got here, Doc. But you know, I think what Arlington needs is a city hospital. Wouldn't you say?"

Will leaned back in his chair and laced his fingers across the front of his vest. He thought of his office, with its scanty furnishings and dim light, and of the pesthouse by the river where they'd carried the worst cases of smallpox during the last epidemic.

Ever since he got his medical license and came home to Texas, he'd dreamed of building a hospital in Arlington like the ones he'd seen back east. Maybe then he wouldn't have to run around the countryside all night and make the rounds in town all day. Of course, Dallas had hospitals, and Tarrant County had a few as well, but they were too far away. And then there were some private ones for certain people, like the Missouri Pacific Hospital for railroad workers in Fort Worth. With its own hospital, Arlington might even be able to attract another doctor, maybe even more than one.

But none of that meant anything to Jim Cutchall. The

man never did anything without some benefit to himself. He wanted something, and until Will knew what that was, it would be a good idea to go slow and keep his cards close to his vest. "Well, I guess I might've thought about a hospital, once or twice. Why'd you ask?"

Cutchall licked his lips and shrugged. "Now, you know I have a lot of friends in Arlington, and I care about what happens here." He rushed on as if he thought Will might not agree. "So when somebody came to me the other day offering money to help build a hospital right here in town, why, I thought of you right away."

Will allowed himself a thin smile. "And who was this someone?"

Cutchall stroked his mustache and grinned. "Can't say, but they seemed real concerned about getting the right kind of man to run it. Said he had to be sure it was someone who upheld the law and didn't align himself with lawbreakers and labor unions."

So, that was the lay of the land. The railroads wanted to keep him from supporting the union men. He wondered just how much bloodshed they expected this afternoon. He'd heard they planned to bring a Missouri Pacific train out of the yard today, and the strikers would do anything they could to stop it. A sour taste filled his mouth. Such a waste, and for what? No man's life was worth a few cents an hour raise. He'd tried to make Ian understand that. He could only hope his friend would listen to reason and stay out of it.

After all, whatever increase they got, the railroads passed it on to the farmers by raising their freight charges. Of course, the railroad owners might be greedy, but they had their own problems, trying to run lines without enough trade to support them. He had no patience with either side, and even less with Cutchall, acting as a messenger boy.

Will clenched his fists and leaned forward, resting one arm on the tablecloth, gritting his teeth, and pitching his voice low, for Cutchall's ears alone. "I'm only going to tell you this once. I don't take sides, and I'm not for sale at any price. I don't give a damn about politics or unions or railroads. I heal the sick and I patch up the wounded no matter who they are or what they believe. And nobody tells me who to treat—not you, and not some railroad bigshot, hospital or no hospital, do you hear me?"

Cutchall's smile froze and his hand strayed toward the holster at his side. For a moment Will held his breath, sure he'd pushed a dangerous man too far. Then Cutchall placed his hands on the tabletop and levered his lanky body out of the chair, his false smile still glued to his face. "Sure thing, Doc. I didn't mean nothing by it."

He backed away, then tugged at the bottom of his waistcoat. "You know, Doc, I always figured you was pretty smart, but now I ain't so sure. This here strike's kindly like a horse race; if you don't back the winner, you got to lose." He rubbed the end of one sleeve over the tin star pinned to his jacket, then fixed Will with his brown-eyed gaze, his smile fading. "When I get done, there ain't gonna be no more union. I aim to end this strike foolishness, and soon." He whirled and strode toward the door.

Geordie squatted beside the steel track, the sharp tang of his own sweat vying with the reek of creosote from the railroad ties in front of him. Although the noon sun warmed his back and pooled dark shadows under him, his fingers ached from the cold of the steel spike he held. The hammer came down, sending a shudder up his arm. He let go and duck-walked along the rail a few inches, setting another spike, grateful to be working with Ian. He'd seen what could happen when a hammer missed its mark, but he knew he could trust his brother-in-law's aim.

The air rang with the sound of steel on steel as Ian drove the spike home. Behind him, two other men worked down the opposite rail toward the junction of the Fort Worth and New Orleans, setting spikes in the switch to keep it turned. That would show the railroad officials not to mess with union men.

The steel rail beside him gave off a deep hum. "Train coming." He squinted up at Ian. "Reckon we better hurry if we want to get away before it gets here."

Ian nodded, his lips quirking up in a thin smile. "We're working as fast as we can." He turned to look behind him at the approaching train. "Granddaddy always told me a thing worth doing was worth doing well." Lifting the huge hammer, he brought it down on the head of the spike.

Geordie sidled a few inches, then held another giant nail in place. His belly clenched as he realized what good targets they made. He'd been expecting trouble ever since the new marshal announced he'd be taking the freight train south. But he'd let himself hope they'd be gone before the lawmen arrived. The hum expanded to a rumble, and the monster grew as it approached, belching black smoke from its stack.

He glanced toward the gully, where six men squatted with Winchesters across their knees. The trainmen didn't stand a chance any more than they had two days before when five hundred men surrounded a train in Fort Worth and pulled all the coupling pins. Being there had reminded him of the day he and Cat had helped rout the Glasgow constables at the Braes. Then, as now, they had right on their side. Sweat trickled down his back under his shirt. Still, no matter how good the odds, the riflemen wouldn't be much protection if the marshal's men shot him from the train.

The chuffing of the steam engine swelled to a roar by the time Ian arced the hammer in its final swing, then shouldered it. Wiping sweat from his palms, Geordie followed the other men off the tracks. There was no way to avoid a fight now.

With a squeal and a cloud of steam, the train slowed to a stop. Five men jumped from the engine. One pointed a six-shooter at Geordie, the mouth of its barrel huge and black.

"You men are under arrest." A tall man with lots of dark hair nodded to one of the other lawmen, his gun never wavering as he pointed it at Ian's chest. "Search them."

In spite of the fear gripping him, a part of Geordie's mind remained calm. He recognized the new marshal by his long hair and the star pinned to his waistcoat. Swallowing, he let his hands rise in surrender, but his fingers itched for a gun. He imagined aiming at the man's head and squeezing the trigger. Tarrant County would be better off without the likes of Long-haired Jim Cutchall.

The marshal jumped back as if he'd heard the unspoken

thought. For a minute he wondered if the man had really been shot. Then he caught the smile spreading across Ian's face as the heavy sledgehammer hit the ground.

Cutchall cocked the six-gun. "Don't give me any excuse to use this."

Geordie held his breath, but Ian's smile never wavered as he slowly raised his hands into the air.

After a long moment Cutchall released the pistol's hammer and turned away, motioning with his gun to another deputy. "Townsend, you keep an eye on these four and get them on board the train." Spurs clinked as the man strode forward and stepped around the black iron grill of the cowcatcher, then stopped between the rails. "All right, you boys." He pointed his six-shooter toward the gully. "Throw up your hands."

Sunlight glinted as half a dozen Winchester barrels rose, all pointing toward the marshal. Color fled from the man's cheeks as he licked his lips and turned to look behind him. "For God's sake, don't shoot." As he shouted the words, he dived behind the switch and fired his six-shooter down the slope.

Rifle shots rang out from across the tracks and behind the pile of railroad ties nearby, catching the deputies in the crossfire. The man called Townsend had been training his gun on Geordie, but now he screamed and fell, clutching his chest.

Geordie dropped to the ground as bullets whined around him.

Cutchall's voice carried above the staccato explosions of gunfire. "Get to cover, men."

Geordie decided it was good advice for an unarmed striker as well. The reek of gunpowder tainted the air as he scooted backward, away from the train.

Three of the deputies crawled toward the engine, leaving bloody stains on the ground behind them. Then, with a roar, the engine came to life. As the wounded men clambered aboard, the brakes released with a sigh of steam, and the train backed away from the junction. Cutchall dashed from behind the switch and raced toward the retreating steam engine. Clutching a railing, the marshal leapt onto the steps and into the cab, then turned and aimed his pistol at Geordie.

He dropped his face against the earth and lay frozen, waiting for the bullet to strike. But just as the gun roared, a shouted word hung in the air. "No!"

The engine picked up speed in reverse, its chuffing softening as it gained distance.

Confused, Geordie raised his head. Just in front of him lay a man, his face turned away and a shock of blond-brown hair pale against the dark wood of a railroad tie. Horror crept up Geordie's spine as he recognized the round-toed boots and the faded denim trousers and realized what Ian had done.

Geordie stood and stumbled toward him. Ian lay on his back, a jagged circle of red pulp in the middle of his chest. Kneeling, he pressed one ear to the mangled shirtfront, straining to hear something, anything besides the beating of his own heart in his ears. At last a faint and distant drumbeat came to him. He climbed to his feet, relief and fear coiling through him. "He's still alive." As the riflemen trudged up the slight rise from the gully and others sidled out from behind the stacks of ties, he shouted, "Pull that buckboard around here. We got to get this man to the doc." As the strikers crowded around him, he ran a hand through his damp hair, then turned to a man he didn't recognize. "It's too far to take him home. See that they take him to the Bon Chance Saloon."

The man nodded. "You going after Cutchall?"

Geordie stood still for a minute, savoring the thought, then shook his head. "No time for that now. I'm going to fetch his wife." He grabbed the reins of the nearest horse. "Just get him to the saloon, and hurry, else it may be too late."

Chapter 3

Catriona placed her palms on the swinging doors in front of her and hesitated, afraid to face the horror waiting inside. Ian was alive; she'd gotten that much from Geordie, but it must be bad to scare him so. She swallowed against the dryness in her mouth. She'd faced hundreds of badly wounded bodies through the years, but never the man she loved. No, Ian would be all right, she had to believe that. Something else must have frighted the lad. Either way, she'd not find out standing there.

She pushed, and the doors swung inward. Although she'd glimpsed the saloon from the street, the interior surprised her by its cleanliness. Stepping inside, she let the doors swing shut behind her and took a deep breath. The raw smell of blood reminded her of a butcher shop as she threaded her way across the wooden floor, scanning the room for Ian. Music and laughter beat at her eardrums, and women paraded around in their underclothes, leaning over men seated at rickety tables. Some of them shot curious glances her way, then turned back to their drinks.

Far in the back, a man bent over a table, the sleeves of his white shirt rolled above his elbows, his forearms spattered with blood. After a moment he straightened, his mouth twisted and his forehead creased. "Damn!" The word exploded from his lips as he wiped his hands on a bar towel, then tossed it in a corner. When he raised his head, she recognized Will Bascom.

Arlington's only doctor had been a friend of Ian's since their schooldays. He'd sat at her table for dinner more than once, although she'd never really gotten to know him as Ian did.

Cat moved forward, pulled by an invisible cord, knowing and refusing to know what she'd find on the table.

Pain lined Ian's handsome face, pale beneath the sun-browned skin. His breath bubbled in and out of his open mouth, and pink spittle clung to his chin. A blood-soaked rag covered half of his bare chest.

Cat touched her fingertips to the edge of the table and looked a question at Will, but she knew his answer even before he shook his head and turned away. A silent scream echoed in her mind, but she forced herself to smile and take her husband's huge rough hand in her own. "Ian love, I'm here."

His fingers closed over hers with surprising strength, and his eyelids flickered open. "Cat." He wheezed, then gave a hollow cough. "Looks like you were right." His lips curved up into a grimace.

"And now's a fine time to decide that." She forced a teasing note into her voice. "Perhaps next time you'll listen."

His gray-blue eyes narrowed. "Sure, next time." He paused, his breath whistling in and out. "I love you, Catriona. I'll always—" He coughed, his fingers crushing hers. Blood trickled from a corner of his mouth, and he lay still. His chest rose, then fell, and his fingers opened. The light faded from his eyes.

As darkness narrowed Cat's vision into a distant pinpoint of light, she realized the screams she heard were her own.

Pinkish water dripped down her forearms as Catriona wrung out the flour-sack towel. Sniffing, she wiped tears from each cheek with the back of one hand, then turned again to the table. The undertaker had tried to persuade her to let him wash and dress the body, but she couldn't bear the thought of a stranger's hands touching Ian.

Instead, she'd agreed to buy a coffin from him, a rough box built of pine boards, brought all the way from East Texas. It lay to one side, its raw smell filling the darkened room. She lifted one lifeless arm, surprised by its weight, and wiped at the cool, rough skin. So big and strong, a blacksmith's hand, but capable of such gentleness. Just yesterday these fingers had caressed her, made her cry out in pleasure. Biting her lip, she swallowed a sob and turned the palm up, scrubbing at brown bloodstains. He must have clutched at his chest after he was hit.

The wound drew her eyes again, a small hole, really, but large enough for a man's life to slip through it. Somehow, she'd known it would come to this. Love and happiness like theirs weren't meant to last. Perhaps she'd always known. The cloth moved up the still forearm, smoothing the blond hairs against the ridged muscles.

Still, it wasn't right to take a man from his wife and child, a young man with years ahead of him. There was something wrong with a world that demanded some men die so other men could be rich. Dipping the rag in the basin again, she twisted the water from it and moved to the end of the table to swab his shoulders. When they were still at the Braes and his body had raged with fever from typhoid, she'd bathed him like this. Almost, she could pretend she was back there, except his skin was cool now instead of hot. And he'd been close to death then, but there was still hope of life. Now there was no hope, for him or for her. A sob forced its way up her tight throat, and she turned away, covering her face with her hands. She flinched at the smell of death clinging to her fingertips as she fought for control.

She couldn't give in, not yet; there was too much to do, too many people who needed her to be strong. Even Ian needed her. This was her last kindness, the last loving act between them. With a shuddering sigh she turned back to her task, sponging at the cords of his neck. A faint roughness of stubble scratched at her fingers. Setting aside the cloth, she reached for the shaving brush and dipped it into the basin, then swirled it around and around on the soap until thick foam coated the bristles. In slow circles she lathered his neck, his cheeks, his upper lip, then stropped the straight razor to a fine edge.

As she scraped the whiskers from his neck and face, she relived every moment of their last morning together. She should have begged him to stay, demanded it, threatened to leave if he insisted on going—anything to keep him home with her, safe. Part of her wanted to believe she could have changed what happened, that she could have made a difference. But she knew he would have gone no matter what she said or did. Lifting the damp cloth, she dabbed away the tiny spots of white lather left by the razor.

His skin gleamed pale and smooth, all traces of pain gone, his eyes closed. He might be sleeping. If only she could wake him as she used to, with a kiss. She bent close, her hair falling across his chin like a curtain. With her eyes closed she pressed her lips against his, the lips she knew so well. But this cool, slack mouth wasn't his any longer. Ian was gone. Pulling back, she gazed down at him. A tear dropped from her face and slid down his cheek. "*Ach*, Laddie, why did you leave and no take me with you?"

Will hesitated, then stepped to the edge of the grave beside Catriona. The early morning sleet and cold rain had washed away bits of black soil, baring the twisted ends of cut roots that choked the straight sides of the deep hole. Sighing, he breathed in the damp, rotten smell of the fresh-turned loam, and reached to take her hand. "Catriona, I—" He tried to hide the pain in his voice, but when she turned to him, he knew she'd heard it.

She gave his hand a squeeze, then slid hers from his grasp. "I know." Tears welled up in her dark blue eyes, and her gaze drifted away to the horizon. Her grief wrapped her in isolation, and he realized she'd forgotten him. He'd wanted to comfort her, but his words could only hurt her more at this point. Perhaps someday—

He made his way to the buggy and clambered up beside Nana, then turned from the wagon seat for one last look at the solitary figure in black, standing beneath the lone post oak. Each time he saw Catriona, she surprised him with her youth, her strength, and her beauty. It was no wonder Ian had loved her so.

Ian. Guilt lanced through him. He should have been able to save the man. If only he'd warned his friend. Or if he'd had a decent place to operate, a hospital.

Nana's voice startled him. "Thee must stop blaming thyself, William." His grandmother knew him so well, it sometimes seemed as though she could read his mind. "Thee could have done no more." The fine wrinkles in her papery skin belied the richness of her voice and the quickness of her eye. She patted his cheek with one withered hand just as she had when he was a gawky kid patching up broken bird wings or dosing a colicky piglet with camomile tea.

But this was no sick farm animal. This was a man who'd been his childhood friend, a man with a wife and child, a man whose life he might have saved. "I could have ridden out and found him, warned him that Cutchall was serious."

Nana's lips drew together like the top of her reticule. "And then what?" As she shook her head, a thin white curl escaped from beneath her shiny black bonnet. "This was Ian; he would have paid thee no mind. Think for a moment, William, think with thy mind instead of thy heart."

Nana was right, as she so often was, and he knew it. But it was so senseless, such a waste. There should have been a way to prevent it. He ached for his own loss. And for hers. He glanced again at the silent figure.

Lewis Price came forward to the graveside and tipped his hat to her, then drove his shovel into the mound of loose earth. Dirt spattered against the lid of the casket.

Catriona turned and trudged toward the house. With each step, heaps of dead grasses gave off sharp, crackling noises, and dry plant stems caught at the hem of her skirt. Betsy shifted against her, moaning and thrashing for a moment. Numb, filled with a hollow ache, she patted the bairn's soft back. At last, with a tremor, the lass sank again into sleep, her body once more a still, dead weight in Cat's arms.

Wiping tears from eyes made raw by hours of weeping,

she cast about for some thought to busy her mind, to keep the sonorous words of the jackleg preacher from echoing again and again in her ears. She didn't even know the man and didn't like him much. But he'd shown up at the graveside, and she hadn't the strength to send him away.

Not that it mattered if anyone spoke at the funeral. Ian could no longer hear or care. He was dead. The knowledge dropped like a stone into the well of her body. No words could make a difference to her now; there was no comfort to be found, only another day to get through, another breath to take.

A part of her had heard the murmured condolences of the other mourners as she nodded and shook their hands, but once she passed, the memory of their words fled, as if they'd said nought at all. She moved alone behind a wall, separating her from life, from all feeling, from all caring.

She paused for a moment where the dry prairie gave way to tilled acres. Wee green points thrust up through the black soil of the field of cottonseed Ian had planted in mid-March. Spring had always been her favorite time of year—until now. She knew she'd never again see the land come to life after winter without remembering Ian's death.

The constant wind stopped for a moment, leaving a stillness filled by the buzzing of bees around a prairie violet. The sharp sweetness of its early blossoms cloyed the air. Sudden anger overwhelmed her, anger at Ian, anger at God, but most of all, anger at Long-haired Jim Cutchall. Someday, he'd get his reward, and when he did, she planned to rejoice. Cat gazed at the small flowered plant hugging the ground, then lifted her foot and set her shoe on its face before she strode on.

At the paling fence she shifted the bairn's weight to her left shoulder and reached for the latch on the gate. A hand covered hers. Flinching away from the touch, Cat whirled. It took her a moment to recognize the small, dapper man with the russet hair and pointy face of a fox. Her eyebrows lifted in surprise.

O. K. Frink owned Arlington's only general store and extended credit to most of Cat's neighbors in exchange for liens against their crops, then charged them double the cash price for buying on time. Most of them went deeper in debt to this man each year. So far she and Ian had managed to avoid the trap, but now, without Ian's railroad salary, she might have to reconsider the man's offer. "What can I do for you, Mr. Frink?"

"Beg pardon, Miz Macleod. I don't wish to appear indelicate by bringing up business in the midst of this sad occasion, but I had a heap of respect for your late husband." He paused, his small, bright eyes shifting toward the house, then toward the fields and pastures. "I know it's only been a short spell since you left Scotland, and you're probably a might homesick. And with your man gone and all, why, I just thought I'd offer you a fair price for your spread, enough should you want to go back home again."

Until that moment she hadn't thought of the future, hadn't thought beyond the funeral. She turned the idea over in her mind. To see Skye once more, to breathe its sweet air, to taste the cool salt breeze against her lips. To go home again.

Betsy squirmed in her arms. *Her* home, aye, but there was the wee bairn to consider, and Geordie and Effie. Her gaze swept across the flat landscape, taking in the fields of cotton and wheat, the cattle grazing in the pasture, and the house—Ian's house, his ranch, his dream.

But how could she live here without him? Suddenly the burden of her loss weighed more than she could bear. She turned to the man. "My apologies, Mr. Frink. I'm very tired. I thank you for your offer, but I can give you no answer today."

The corners of his mouth twitched down, and he stroked his thin reddish mustache with the thumb and forefinger of one hand, then gave a short nod. "I understand, ma'am. You just give it some thought. Rest assured, I will be back."

Geordie hauled on the strap with both hands, feeling it slacken across his shoulders as Sukey slowed at the end of the row. The mule turned a baleful eye over one shoulder and twitched its tail, then dropped its head to crib at some weeds.

Swabbing at his face with a red bandanna, Geordie looked back down the row he'd just plowed. Thinned cotton plants stood in bright green clumps, divided into rows by lines of fresh-turned black soil. The warm weather had brought tall, leafy plants this spring, but the soil could use a good soaking.

He squinted at the sky arched overhead and frowned. No rain clouds today either. All this work to bed the plants for drainage, and they looked to wither and die for lack of water. Unless he ran ditches from the livestock tanks. He shrugged. First things first. Tomorrow he'd get a field crew in to haul the soil around the slender stems to keep the plants from blowing over in the constant wind. That is, if he finished plowing by sundown.

Pulling down on the handles, he tipped the point of the plow out of the soil and let it ride the surface across the raised bed. "Haw, Sukey." He tugged on the near rein and turned left down the next row. Guiding the plow through the tangle of old roots, he strode along the trough created by the double blade.

God, how he hated growing cotton. Even smelly, stupid sheep would be better. But at least the plow was an improvement over the *cashrom* he'd used on Skye. A man could turn only half the acreage with a hand plow. Stubborn as Sukey was, the mule did most of the work, which was a good thing, considering how many times a body had to plow a cotton patch each season. He groaned, thinking of bedding up this patch three more times before it ripened enough to be picked.

Funny, last year he'd enjoyed the fieldwork, learning how to get the most cotton from the soil. He'd been happy to do all the plowing himself, so proud Ian trusted him to do it right.

Misery twisted in his gut—part sadness and loss, part guilt. If he hadn't been so petrified with fear, he could have crawled to cover, and Ian wouldn't have thrown himself in the line of fire to protect him. Of course, some of the deputies fell in the crossfire as well, but he couldn't feel good about that. The wounded men were mostly decent fellas with families. His hands tightened on the handles. The only one who deserved shooting was Jim Cutchall, and he escaped without a scratch.

It wasn't so much having Cutchall fill in as marshal of Fort Worth, but when the man took money from the railroad at the same time, that really griped him. But even killing Cutchall wouldn't bring back the dead. And with Ian gone, he could forget about his own plans.

Pausing, he scanned the field and noted the height of the sun. He'd just have time to finish the last twelve rows before nightfall. He clenched his jaw and clucked to the mule, then returned to his broken thread of thought. He'd helped put Ian in the ground. One way or another, he'd make sure the man's family was taken care of before he gave a thought to his own future.

Chapter 4

May 1886

Cat settled Betsy in the crook of her elbow, letting her shawl cover the front of her dress as she undid the hooks and eased her nipple into the bairn's waiting mouth. "Now, about the haying. How soon do you think we should begin cutting?"

Geordie averted his eyes and buttered a corn cake. "As dry as it is already, I think we can start as soon as the cotton's planted. It'll still need bedding up and hauling, but we can hay in between."

Cat nodded. Thank God for Geordie. With Effie in school all day, there was no one to help do the housework and mind Betsy. She couldn't imagine trying to run the farm without him. Although she wasn't sure how fair it was to the lad. He was nineteen now, time to be thinking about starting a family of his own instead of taking care of his widowed sister. If only Ian had lived.

Pain settled around her heart. It had been almost two months, but each time she thought of him, it hurt as much as those first few days. Mornings were the worst, reaching for him before she was awake. And nights, lying alone in their big bed.

At first she'd thought she wanted to die herself. Only her daughter's need for a mother had kept her alive. She touched the soft, round cheek. Now she realized she had much to live for, people who needed her—her bairn, her brother and sister.

Taking a deep breath, she turned to stare out the kitchen window across the prairie. She didn't know if she'd ever get over Ian's death as long as she stayed here. But if she went back to Skye, his dreams died with him.

A hand touched her shoulder. Effie smiled down at her, her green eyes dancing with mischief. "Here's your coffee, Cat, with fresh cream, just as you like it." The lass settled her slender body into the chair beside her. "Can I hold Betsy now? Is she done eating?"

Geordie cleared his throat and drew his eyebrows down into a frown. "Must you draw attention to it?"

Effie's laugh rang out in the farmhouse kitchen. "Oh, pshaw, Geordie. You know Cat's feeding her under that shawl, just the same as I know it."

"Effie!" Cat tried to sound more shocked than she was, suppressing a giggle. Leave it to her sister to lighten the mood.

At that moment the faint rhythm of hoofbeats echoed up the road. Effie flew to the window, pressing her face against the glass, her feet dancing a little jig. "A rider. Oh, I wonder if he's coming here."

Geordie unfolded from his chair and sauntered over behind Effie to peer through an upper pane. "Looks like Joe Vanzee. What do you suppose he wants?"

Effie's dance stopped, and she turned away from the window. Spots of color came and went in her pale cheeks, and her hands flew to her long copper curls before she bolted from the room.

Cat's mouth went slack for a moment. What was that all about? The lass had been skittish of late. Ian's death had hit them all hard. She shrugged. A thirteen-year-old lassie was entitled to her moods, and Effie had more right than most.

She shifted the bairn to a more comfortable position, willing her to finish sucking and drift into a deeper sleep. Whatever had upset Effie, Cat was relieved the rider wasn't O. K. Frink. The merchant had been by more than once since the funeral to ask again about selling him the farm. Much as she dreaded the visits, she knew it was her own fault for not giving him an answer. Sooner or later, she'd have to make up her mind.

Memories of the craggy peaks of the red Cuillins filled her mind, so real she could feel the cool breeze sweeping down their sides and caressing her skin. God, how she missed the black house where she was born, the ever-present reek of peat smoke hanging in the darkened rooms. Jennet had written condolences about Ian's death, begging her to bring wee Betsy back to Balmeanach.

Life was easier in the Highlands and Islands since the crofting laws passed. She might even be able to rent her own plot of land there. It would be so easy to forget why she and Ian left, so easy to give the furnishing man the answer he wanted and go home to Skye. But she couldna give in just yet. Her jaw set. Frink or no Frink, the decision would just have to wait.

She bent and settled Betsy in her cradle, easing the lass's brown-blond curls from her closed eyes. All the bairns she'd helped into the world, but until she held her own child, she'd never understood a mother's love, the fierce protectiveness.

The hoofbeats galloped ever closer, keeping time with Cat's racing thoughts. Visitors were always welcomed in Texas, as they had always been in Scotland, partly because of strong traditions of hospitality, and partly because they brought word of the outside world.

Any news was better than the usual isolation and loneliness of the prairie, even if it was bad—war, death, disease, injury, politics, freakish weather. But since Ian's death, she hadn't wanted to know about anything except her farm and her family. She wondered what brought Joe this way. She only hoped it wasn't trouble of some kind. She shook herself; it was daft to think a lone rider had to mean disaster.

The closed door muffled Geordie's shouted greeting as the hoofbeats clattered to a stop outside.

Catriona stood in the middle of a sudden pool of stillness until light footfalls clicked down the hall toward her.

Effie had changed into her best dress and shoes, and had pinned her reddish hair high on the crown of her head. She stood pinching her cheeks and biting her lips, a trick someone must have taught her to make them redder.

Cat opened her mouth to say something, then bit her lip and turned away to hide a smile. Let the lass have her moment.

Geordie stuck his head through the open doorway. "I'll go hitch up the buckboard." The stern set of his jaw erased her smile as he ushered their guest into the room, then turned and disappeared toward the barn.

A white-blond forelock all but hid Johann Vanzee's bright blue eyes until he combed it back with one large hand. With his other he clutched an old felt hat to his middle. "It's my baby brother, Pieter. He was trying to help out, what with Pa gone and all. He tried to split some kindling for Ma and like to cut his foot off with Pa's ax." The sound of the lad's labored breathing filled a long moment of silence. "Mama sent me to fetch Doc Bascom, but he's out somewheres. Miz Macleod, folks in town told me you done some doctoring back in Scotland. You got to come right away."

Cat swallowed her surprise. In the two years since she and Ian arrived in Tarrant County, she'd had little call to do any healing except around the farm. Folks here called on Will Bascom when they wanted a doctor. But if he wasn't about—

Calm settled over her as she reached for a pack of clean bandages and boiled cotton thread to put into her bag of herbs. "Did you tie it off to slow the bleeding?"

"Yes'm. And Ma packed it real good with blankets. Can you come?"

Cat nodded and turned to Effie. "There's food in the pantry. You'll have to pack your own lunch and get yourself to school. I'll have to take the wee one with me."

Effie's eyes widened, and her gaze slid toward their guest, then dropped to the floor. In contrast to her usual ready tongue, she nodded and said nothing.

Cat bent and kissed her cheek, then bundled the bairn into her shawl and followed Joe out the kitchen door, giving his shoulder a light pat. "Your brother will be right as rain.

Get home as quick as you can and boil up some clean water. I'll come along behind in the buckboard."

As she stepped onto the porch, Geordie pulled the farm wagon up in front of the steps and jumped out.

Joe bobbed his head at the still-blushing Effie, gave Geordie's hand a quick shake, then ran to his horse and galloped off.

Geordie boosted Cat and Betsy into the high wagon seat, then clambered up beside her. She touched his ruddy cheek with one hand, then gave a quick wave to Effie as he shook the reins and clucked to the horse.

Glad for her brother's silence as the wagon jounced down the rutted road, Cat searched her memory for everything she'd learned from Victor about deep cuts. In return for showing him her herbal lore, the Crofting Commission doctor had taught her many things—about men as well as about medicine. She recalled his face, so serious as he bent to kiss her, spilling wild rosehips in the bracken at their feet. She wondered how he fared in London and if he ever married his heiress after all. If only he were here to guide her now.

The lad could be crippled for life or bleed to death if the wound was too deep. A lump rose in her throat. What if she had to amputate? Her arms tightened around Betsy and she shuddered, but she knew she'd do whatever she must to save the lad's life. Thank God it wasn't far to the Vanzee farm. Not that it was much of a farm, but that wasn't the Vanzees' fault really.

Until they left Amsterdam, Hilda and Axel Vanzee had seldom even visited the countryside. They were city folk, born and raised. Axel was a cabinetmaker, and his father before him. Why they'd given it all up, she'd never understood.

Like so many others, they'd been fooled by railroad brochures that promised a Garden of Eden in north central Texas. She'd heard the stories often enough at meetings of the Farmers Alliance. Granted, the soil was rich, but without water and farm machinery, it was only good for grazing cattle and growing a little cotton.

At least she and Ian had known what they faced, had

been able to plan for the sudden shifts of weather that marked Ian's birthplace, although it had left her no cash in reserve. Still, she was better off than most; she had water.

But even if there hadn't been a drought, people like the Vanzees had little or no money to buy seeds and supplies. And if they did manage to raise a crop without drowning in debt to the furnishing man, the railroads—the same ones who sold them the land—charged so much for freight to get their goods to market that they rarely had enough left to last until the next year.

After two years of starvation and debt, Axel had taken a job with a cabinetmaker in Dallas, leaving Hilda and the boys to manage alone during the week. Cat's mouth twisted in bitterness. Some paradise it had turned out to be, where fathers had to leave their families in order to feed them, and wee lads maimed themselves trying to be men.

Chapter 5

As Geordie slowed the wagon to turn into the narrow drive to the farmhouse, Cat's pity changed to anger against the rich and powerful men who tricked these simple people into thinking they were ranchers. Lean cattle lined the split-rail fences, grazing the already cropped grass, their bloated bellies and dull eyes a sign of Axel's ignorance more than lack of care.

Scrawny chickens pecked in the dust of the kitchen yard, scattering as he pulled the buckboard to a stop. After a moment a shy lad of seven or eight scampered out the kitchen door and held the horse while Geordie helped her alight from the wagon. What was this one's name? Hans? As he helped Geordie unhitch the horse, she noticed his feet were bare and muddy, and the trousers he wore had been patched several times.

Hilda scurried out the kitchen door, her gray hair straggling from her crown of braids, her square face flushed and her hands fluttering from the worn cuffs of her shirtwaist dress. Always difficult to understand, her fractured English was now beyond Cat's ability or patience.

Snuggling her bairn against her, Cat pushed past the distraught mother and into the kitchen. It was clean and bare, its sole decoration a painting of windmills hanging on one wall. Cat moved toward a woodstove in the corner, the only spot of warmth in the damp, chill room. A tall blond girl came through a far door carrying a large teakettle. It took Cat a moment to recognize Effie's friend, Amalia, though everyone called her Molly.

Sweet-faced and quiet, Molly had always been one of Cat's favorites among the children from the nearby farms. But in the months since the girl had left school, Cat had seldom seen her. Now she realized Molly had blossomed into a young woman. After all, she must be fifteen by now. The girl set the cast iron kettle on the stove to heat. Good. Joe had remembered.

A thin smile barely hiding her concern, Molly came toward her. "Miz Macleod, thanks for coming." She twisted her hands in her apron. "We're all so worried about Pieter. Can you help him?"

"That I canna say until I've seen him." Betsy squirmed in her arms, and Cat uncovered the bairn's sweet face. "Ach, now, and what am I to do with you?"

"Oh, Miz Macleod, I'd just love to mind her for you." Molly's eyes sparkled and her cheeks flushed as she reached for the squirming bundle.

"Well, that's all right, then. Thanks." Cat settled the bairn in the young woman's arms. "Now, could someone take me to wee Pieter?"

Hilda blinked. "*Ja.*" She turned and bustled through an archway into a well-lighted parlor where Joe sat holding the hand of a small boy. Better and better.

She smiled at Joe, then sank down beside the small body on the settle and took one white hand in hers. It was still warm; he probably hadn't lost too much blood, then. "Pieter, I am Mrs. Macleod. Do you remember me?"

Round eyes flickered open, and a faint smile played over the pinched mouth. "Yeth, you're Betsy's ma."

The slight lisp tugged at Cat's heart, and she smiled down at him. "I've come to look at your foot, to make it better."

Two very white teeth sank into the lad's lower lip, but he nodded.

"I may have to hurt you to make you better. You may

want to cry, and that's all right, but try not to be frightened of me, all right?"

Again, the quick nod. "I'm big. I won't cry." The wide blue eyes closed.

If only she had something to make him sleep. Perhaps he'd be lucky and pass out from the pain. Turning back the bottom edge of the quilt, she unwound the cocoon of blankets around the slender leg. "Joe, please take your ma to the kitchen and keep her out of here. If you've got any whiskey, give her a taste, then bring the bottle to me. And a basin of boiled water."

Inside the nest of cloth, blood barely oozed from the small foot. That might mean the cut hadn't opened a vein. A leather belt wound around his calf to slow the bleeding. Joe again? But in spite of his fast thinking, gore covered the slender limb. Cat closed her eyes for a moment, fighting her queasy stomach. After years of treating sickness and injury without a qualm, it was carrying Betsy that first made her react to the sight of blood. When she opened her eyes, a basin and a bottle had appeared, but she was alone again in the room with her small patient.

Digging into her bag, she brought out the packet of clean cloths and dipped one in the clean, warm water, then began to sponge the area of the wound. "Pieter, can you feel my hand?" She wiggled each toe.

"Yeth, it tickles."

Another good sign. With most of the blood removed, she could see the size of the gash. Only a few inches long, but the foot was so tiny it cut across most of it. Lifting his leg, she turned the wound toward the light, letting the edges fall open. Layers of yellow and white, oozing clear pink water. Skin, fat, but the muscle lay smooth and whole. A clean cut, with no sign of an open vein. Knots in Cat's shoulders and back eased. "Your foot will be as good as new, Pieter." Relief echoed back in her own ears. "This will burn."

Cat pulled the cork from the whiskey with her teeth, and after scrubbing her hands with a splash of the amber liquid, clamped one hand around the lad's foot and poured the alcohol into the gaping wound.

The small foot twitched, and Pieter drew in his breath with a hiss, but his eyes stayed closed and he made no other sound. She bit her lip. *Sometimes you must hurt in order to heal.* She repeated Gran's words in her mind as she set the wee foot back on the blankets and fished out a curved needle. She forced herself to smile down at her patient. "You *are* a brave lad, Pieter."

Again the pinched lips curved upward.

Cat doused the needle in whiskey, then struck a sulphur match and waited until the blue flame died before threading the eye with heavy cotton twist. She lifted her voice. "Joe, could you please come here?"

After a moment the door opened, and his earnest, square face appeared. "Yes'm?"

"I need you to hold his foot steady."

Joe's fair skin lost all its color, and his Adam's apple bobbed twice, but he stepped inside, closing the door and following her instructions.

Cat's jaw tightened, and she forced herself not to focus on anything but the wound. She hated hurting anybody, especially an innocent bairn. Working fast, but taking care to do it right, Cat stitched the inner layer of fat together, then closed the outer layer of skin with one continuous thread. In a week she'd pull the thread from the outside, leaving the inner layers whole.

After tying a solid knot, she let herself glance at Pieter's face, waxy white against the pillow. A big tear lay like a crystal on his pale lashes, then slid down one round cheek.

"Laddie, your foot is all sewn up like a Christmas goose. I'll let you look at it in a minute. But first I have to take Joe's belt off your leg and give it back so his pants dinna fall down."

Pieter's thin baby lips parted and a chuckle bubbled out.

Cat's jaw relaxed a wee bit. "It will hurt, so you must be brave for a few more minutes, and then it will begin to feel much better, all right?"

His small pink tongue swiped at his pale lips, then he bobbed his head in agreement.

Cat nodded for Joe to release his grip on the lad's foot, then bent to unbuckle the wide belt, loosening it bit by bit.

Again the indrawn hissing breath, this time with a strangled sob.

"Pieter, I need you to move your foot up and down for me."

His lips drew back, showing white teeth gritted together. The foot extended, then flexed.

"Now around and around."

The small foot, its color easing from blue to pink, made a slow circle.

"That's fine, Pieter. Now you must promise me to stay in bed for a whole week and not to try to walk until I come back and take the sewing out."

The blue eyes flickered open. "I promith. Can I thee it now?"

Laughing, Cat nodded. As he examined the row of stitches, she set out packets of herbs, adding a pinch of this and a pinch of that—lobelia for inflammation, golden seal for bleeding, comfrey to knit the skin together, wild woodbine to help him rest. After binding the foot in clean rags and removing the bloody swaddling, Cat left Pieter with his brother and went in search of the lad's mother.

In the kitchen she found Molly bouncing the wee bairn on her knee. Betsy's baby laughter filled the room, and Geordie hovered nearby, his eyes wide and his smile soft. So, a lassie had finally caught her brother's eye.

The girl's mother bustled into the room, her pale eyebrows knitting at the young people. Her mouth puckered, then opened.

But Cat stepped between, holding a packet of herbs in a twist of paper. "Here, Mrs. Vanzee. Make a tea from this and give him a cup each day. I'll be back in a week."

"My boy, my baby, his foot will heal?" Hilda's words were slower, more careful.

"Yes, he'll be fine, but you must remember to give him the tea each day, and feed him lots of meat and bread. And don't let him out of bed, you *ken*—you understand?"

"*Ja.*" The woman gave her gray head a vigorous nod.

Cat turned to gather her things, but Joe's voice stopped her.

He stepped through the door from the parlor into the

kitchen. "Miz Macleod, we can't afford much, but we have a little money saved." One hand plunged into the pocket of his denim pants.

Cat glanced at Hilda's face and started to refuse, but the lad who'd held her horse burst through the kitchen door. "Buggy coming. It's Doc Bascom." He turned and ran out again, slamming the door behind him.

Hilda placed her hand on Joe's arm, pushing the money back into his pocket. "We wait for the doctor."

"But Ma—"

Hilda let loose a string of foreign words that silenced her son, then turned and smiled up at Cat. "You make my Pieter some tea before you go, *ja?*" It was more a command than a question.

Anger raged through Cat's body, but she held it in check. "If you like."

Hands shaking, she measured the herbs into a large teapot, then filled it with boiling water.

Geordie touched her shoulder. "Maybe we should just leave."

She nodded. "Maybe." After all, she'd been about to refuse the money anyway. But she went on making the tea. There was something about the look on Hilda's face that brought out all her stubbornness. On Skye she'd seldom taken money for healing; instead, folks offered her whatever they could spare, a *stirk* or a *braxy* ewe, sometimes a kitten, or a dozen eggs.

At first she'd hated the idea of gaining from other people's misfortunes, especially people who could ill afford it. Later she'd been pleased to see their gratitude in their gifts, once she realized she didn't cause their problems or ask them to come to her. Now it was almost a point of pride; did these people think she ought to work for naught?

"Cat." Geordie's voice pulled at her, his discomfort evident in his flushed cheeks and downturned mouth.

She squeezed his hand. "Dinna *fash* yerself, laddie. I'll not shame you haggling over my fee. But we canna leave without seeing Will."

She realized it was true; it would be rude to leave just as Will Bascom arrived. After all, he'd been Ian's friend, and he'd done his best to save her husband's life. It wasn't fair to keep avoiding him.

Just as she finished filling a cup with herb tea and setting it to cool, a buggy pulled up out front, and the doctor followed Hans into the kitchen. He looked the same as she remembered, tall and lean, dressed all in black, with a mane of auburn hair and unsettling gray-green eyes. A most attractive man.

After nodding a greeting to her, he turned to Hilda. "I'm sorry it took me so long to get here, but I was all the way up to Grapevine on another call." She'd forgotten the warmth of his voice, with its soft, slow accent, and he looked younger than he had the last time she'd really looked at him, that day at the saloon. The day Ian died. She looked away, the memory of him leaning over Ian threatening to suffocate her.

"Joe fetched the widow Macleod, and she fixed him up already." Hilda's voice held a note of apology.

Cat gritted her teeth.

"Miz Macleod, it's a pleasure to see you again." When he smiled, his eyes crinkled at the corners.

Cat forced herself to smile back as she murmured a response, grateful for his formality in front of her neighbors. If only she could keep him from bringing up the past. It was hard enough being in the same room with him, but she knew if she tried to talk about Ian, her throat would close up and she'd burst into tears.

He rubbed his hands together and surveyed the room. "As long as I'm here, you don't mind if I take a look at your handiwork and ask a few questions, do you?"

She swallowed her surprise and nodded. "Of course not." She supposed it was only reasonable. After all, he had no way of knowing her or her work, and he was a real doctor, while she was only a folk healer. Still, as she followed him into the parlor, she couldn't help but wonder how he'd like it if she visited his patients to double-check his work. As he tousled Pieter's hair and undid the bandages she'd fastened minutes before, she answered his questions about the wound and how she'd treated it.

At last he retied the bandages and stood. "Catriona, you do fine work. Can I ask where you learned it?"

His question surprised her, but she was not ashamed of her knowledge, or of how she acquired it. "Most of my healing lore I got at my gran's knee, as she did from her own grandmother. But some I learned from a British doctor before I left Scotland to come here."

Surprise lit his face, and something like approval. "They taught you well. I'm surprised Ia—no one ever mentioned it." He chucked Pieter under the chin. "Thanks for letting me horn in." As he brushed past her, his hand lit on her shoulder for a moment, warming her skin through the thin cloth of her dress. Then he was gone.

She took a deep breath and let it out, disturbed by her response to his touch but warmed by his kind words and his understanding. Somehow today had softened the painful memories a wee bit. She turned to her patient and patted his hand. "You must rest now, Pieter. I'll bring you some tea with honey, and after you drink it, I want you to take a nap."

Two lines appeared between his blond brows. "I don't take naps anymore. I'm big."

Cat smiled down at him. "Of course you are, but these naps are not for you, they're for your foot. It's very tired. So will you do it for your foot?"

His brow smoothed. "All right. My foot *does* feel tired." His heavy eyelids drooped.

As she entered the kitchen, Joe and Hilda stopped talking and turned toward her. Joe's cheeks were flushed and his mother's mouth turned down. Molly and Geordie stood together, their eyes turned away from the scene and each other.

Will stepped out of the shadows, slipping his arms into his black greatcoat. "As I was saying, Miz Vanzee, I couldn't possibly take a fee for the house call since Miz Macleod did all the work."

Joe tugged himself free of his mother and strode toward Cat, thrusting a wad of bills into her hands. "Miz Macleod, we're beholden to you. I know Pa would want you to have this." He shot a glance at his mother, who turned her back.

Cat's hand closed around the greenbacks with a faint reluctance. She didn't want charity, even from an old friend, but she'd earned the fee, and she needed it. Pressing her lips together, she loosened the strings of her reticule and dropped the bills inside.

Joe strode across the puncheon floor and shook Will's hand. "Much obliged to you for coming, Doc."

"You're mighty welcome, son." His eyes crinkled and his lips turned up as he turned to Cat, clasping her cold hand in his warm one. A thrill ran up her arm. "It was a real pleasure, Miz Macleod." He tipped his hat. "And I hope I see you again. Soon."

Chapter 6

Will fought his way up from sleep, away from the images haunting his dreams—an endless sea of faceless patients, all holding up their arms in supplication, crying out for help. The smell of death filled his nostrils, and the rope cut into his wrists as he struggled to free his bloodstained hands.

Groaning, he sat up in the stuffy darkness of his office. The terror melted away as he rubbed his face, breathing in the sharp medicine smells. Damn! He so seldom had a chance to rest, and when he did manage to fall asleep, nightmares plagued him.

The dream, of course, was familiar, one that had haunted him since his first days at medical school, when his first patients died despite his best efforts. For months he'd dreamed it night after night, but gradually over the years the images had faded. That is, until the blasted union workers decided to strike, and the local lawmen signed on the railroad payrolls.

Until Ian—for a moment he was there again in the saloon, his fingers slimy with his friend's blood, probing for the bullet deep in the man's chest, knowing it was hopeless, knowing this man he'd grown up with was about to die and there was nothing he could do to prevent it.

He clenched his fists, anger flaring through his grief. The

man was a fool, letting Cutchall shoot him down, leaving his wife and child at the mercy of the crop-lien system. And for what? The strike had failed, breaking the back of the railroad union.

He flexed his fingers and rubbed his face. If only that were the end. But it was just a matter of time before some other unfortunates reared up and fought for their rights. This time it would probably be the small farmers who'd strike back. And he'd be there to patch them up when they did.

Noise exploded from the door, someone's fist pounding on the brittle wood. "Doc, wake up."

"Keep your shirt on." He pulled on his trousers, tucking in the tail of his nightshirt. "What time is it?" He raised his voice to penetrate the thin walls as he stumbled across the floor and fumbled with the skeleton key.

"Ten to three." Lewis Price's wide mouth quirked upward as the door swung open. "A coupla cowpunchers shot each other up real bad at the saloon." His brown eyes twinkled, and his black hair fuzzed behind his head like a halo—hardly the usual melancholy image of an undertaker.

Will couldn't help returning the puckish smile. Lewis was a good friend, the only other person who understood the frightful exhilaration of touching mortality every day. He envied the man sometimes; Lewis never lost sleep over his clients, because by the time he got them, they were past hope. "Melva Lee again?"

The round face stilled for a moment. "Yep. Promised herself to one, then the other, then stepped out of the way and let 'em go at it. She's a bad one."

Will slid his arms into the sleeves of his jacket. "Yup. So, customers for me, or for you?" It would be unlike Lewis to seek him out in the middle of a cold night just to sign death certificates, but he had to ask.

"One apiece. The young one's mine. Name of Foster." He snorted. "Not even old enough to shave. Didn't stand a chance. But the kid lasted long enough to plug a few into old Quincy." His voice held a grudging note of respect.

Will groaned. He hadn't known the kid, but he knew the man who'd been shot, the town drunk, or one of them, just an old cowboy left behind when the cattle drives moved west. He ran errands and carried messages for folks, earning just enough to keep himself in rotgut. Yvette sometimes let him sleep in the kitchen when the weather turned cold.

"Got the body over to the house. I'll pick up the certificate later." He turned away.

Will shrugged on his heavy greatcoat and grabbed his medical bag. "I'll bring it around. Maybe you could rustle me up some breakfast."

Lewis smiled back at him over one shoulder. "Sure thing, Doc." His stubby hand covered a yawn. "You come by whenever you finish up. I won't get any more sleep tonight anyhow."

Will followed the chubby figure down the steep, narrow stairs, saying good-bye on the street before he turned toward town, picking his way among dried wagon ruts by the light of a summer moon.

Despite the hour, light and noise spilled into the street from Madame Yvette's Saloon as he mounted the steps to the plank sidewalk and pushed through the swinging doors. The notes of a tinkly piano underscored the sounds of glasses clinking against bottles and loud voices raised in laughter and conversation. As he crossed the room toward the stairway, smells of sweat and beer and cheap whiskey washed past him.

Trailing one hand against the gilded red wallpaper, he mounted the stairs, his boots sinking into the thick carpet runner. Not for the first time he marveled at Yvette's flamboyant taste in furnishings, so different from her personal style. He turned at the first landing and stopped.

Melva Lee Hornsby posed at the head of the stairs, one hand on her ample waist, a feather boa draped over her bare shoulders. "Howdy, Doc!" Her deep voice rasped across his ear. Tossing her brassy blond curls, she started down the steps, her wide hips swaying from side to side, her bare thighs wobbling at each step. "Thought you might turn up." Pouting her red-stained lips, she stopped two steps above him and bent forward just enough to expose her plump bosom. "Too bad about Quincy and the kid. I feel just awful!"

Looking into her wide eyes, Will loaded all the sarcasm

he could manage into his voice. "Why, Melva Lee, I can tell that just by looking at you."

The whore's mouth opened, then snapped shut. With a scowl she flounced past him down the stairs without another word.

Glad to be rid of her, he hurried up the last flight of steps, clutching his bag. Quincy was a tough old fool, but even he deserved prompt treatment. Will paused on the top step and wondered where Yvette had stashed his patient. Noises coming from behind the row of closed doors hinted at the activities of the occupants, but gave no clue to Quincy's location.

He shook his head, remembering the teaching hospitals back east, with their rows of clean beds and the operating theater and its galleries for students. Sometimes he wondered why he ever came back to Texas. But he knew—it was in his blood. In a way he loved the wildness, even as he despised the senseless bloodshed. There was a freedom here that he hadn't seen anywhere else, an individuality, a spirit of independence in the people. He shrugged. Besides, if he wasn't here, who'd patch up the gunslingers and the whores?

After a moment Yvette emerged from a room at the far end of the hall, beckoning to him, her beautiful face dark with concern. The sight of her always soothed him, like fine music or a French masterpiece. He drank in the splendor of the chestnut hair framing her delicate face, and the lines of her narrow figure, as always encased from head to toe in black silk.

And why is it you mourn? he'd asked her when they first met.

For my lost innocence. Although she smiled as she gave him her answer, he knew some truth must lie behind the jest. He couldn't imagine what she'd lived through before she left New Orleans, but whatever it was, she made it clear to her customers that although her girls could all be bought, the madam was not available at any price.

Now, as she ushered him through the door, she stood on tiptoe and pressed her soft lips to his cheek. The sweet, sharp smell of violets surrounded him for a moment. "I am so happy to see you. I thought the old man would die before you arrived, *cher*." The softness of her Cajun accent warmed him.

He smiled. "Don't you worry, sugar. He's too mean to die, isn't that right, Quincy?"

As he stepped close to the bed, the odor gagged him for a minute. The man must not have bathed in a year, and the reek of cheap whiskey added to the stench.

"God-a-mighty, Doc, you took your sweet time getting here." The leathery skin around the old cowboy's eyes crinkled and his near-toothless mouth split into a grin, forming a canyon between his stubbled cheeks. "That little son of a bitch tried to shoot my balls off, begging your pardon, Miss Yvette. My gut hurts real bad."

"I'll wager it does at that." Setting his bag on the bedside table, he opened it and handed Yvette a pair of scissors. "Cut his pants away."

The old man sputtered. "But, Doc, them's the only pants I got. What am I gonna wear?"

Yvette paused, the blades open in her slender hand.

Will closed his bag with a click and lifted it from the table. "Fine, wear them to your own funeral."

"Wait!" Quincy's face paled. "Okay, okay, cut them." He took a long pull from the bottle in his hand and closed his eyes.

Yvette bent over the wounded man, slitting the heavy blue denim from ankle to waist. As she sawed at the thick waistband, he reached down, pulling the cloth taut on both sides of the blades. At last the material gave way and she handed the scissors back to him.

But when he tried to remove the cut cloth, Quincy grabbed the shreds of his clothing. "Good God, Doc. It was bad enough you cut off my pants, but I won't have no woman looking at my privates."

Bending close to the old man, Yvette whispered something Will couldn't hear.

Quincy's color rose in his unshaven cheeks, and he gave a high, squealing giggle as he moved his hands to his sides.

Without another word Yvette removed the blood-soaked denim, then cleansed the area of the wound with alcohol, revealing a short, deep furrow in the flesh. Dark blood oozed from the wound.

Will forgot everything then but the job in front of him. For long moments he probed, following the path of the bullet, sliding his fingers through the intestines and sniffing the air for the telltale odor of punctured bowel.

At last he dropped the bullet into a brass spitoon with a tiny ping. "Done." He poured alcohol inside the tunnel of flesh, ignoring Quincy's indrawn breath. Except for an occasional pull at his bottle of red-eye, the man hadn't moved or made a sound during the operation. Most Texans, both the natives and immigrants, seemed to think it was cowardly to show pain. With ether in short supply, it made surgery a little easier. Will stitched the wound closed and bandaged it with clean cloth. "Quincy, you're a right lucky fella."

The cowboy snorted and pulled at the bottle again. "Luck like this I can do without." After a moment he raised his hand in a lazy salute. "Much obliged, Doc."

"I think you've had enough, Quincy. What you need now is some shut-eye." He reached for a sheet to cover the man.

"*Non*. He cannot stay here." Yvette's soft mouth firmed into a straight line. "This is not a hospital."

Will sighed and rubbed his eyes, suddenly very tired. "Okay. You're right. Send some boys up to carry him to my office. And take that bottle away from him."

"But, Doc!" Quincy levered himself up on one elbow, then his face contorted and he fell panting back onto the mattress. His breath sighed out and his eyes closed. After a short silence he lapsed into a snore.

Will looked across the bed, smiling into Yvette's eyes. "Thanks for all the help." He bent to pack his instruments. "What would I do without you?"

Irony tinged her delicate laugh. "You do not need me, *cher*. What you need is another doctor, or at least a nurse." She paused, then moved around the bed and touched his arm. "Is there no one in Tarrant County who knows enough of healing to be a real help to you?"

He started to shake his head, but then he remembered

the Vanzee boy and Catriona's handiwork. She could probably use the money, and with the skills she already had, she'd make a fine assistant. If only he had a real hospital where he could train her. Still, it was a good idea. He nodded at Yvette. "You just might have something there, sugar."

Chapter 7

Catriona set aside the pen and leaned back in the hard wooden chair, closing her eyes against the flickering light of the lamp. The bitter smell of ink and burning kerosene blended with the sweetness of the night air. Numbers and letters chased each other inside her eyelids, pages of the ledger in Ian's bold hand and the last few entries in her own spidery script.

She rubbed her forehead. Too many ifs—if the water in the wells held until the drought ended, if the price of jute bagging didn't jump any higher, if the value of cotton didn't drop too much at market time. She should have enough to buy supplies for the coming year without going into debt. When he wasn't badgering her to sell the farm to him, O. K. Frink kept offering her credit against next year's crop.

If only she could give in to temptation and sell him the farm and go back to Skye. She closed her eyes, picturing the shoreline of Raasay across the sound from Balmeanach. Then she could give up worrying about all this—crops, supplies, everything. With a sigh she opened her eyes and stared at the ledger again. Not yet. She couldn't give up yet.

She picked up the pen again and considered. Accepting Frink's offer of credit would mean she'd have to pay interest for the full year, even on things she bought just before harvest, and his time prices were twice as high as cash. Many of her neighbors worked and worked but sank deeper in debt to the furnishing man each year. She had no intention of joining them.

Too bad she couldn't hold her cotton, store the bales in the barn or somewhere until prices rose again in the winter and spring. Of course, the barn was already full of hay, tough prairie grass dried and piled high in the loft. It was the only thing that had saved Ian's herd during last winter's blizzards.

Most of the ranchers didn't go to the trouble of haying, letting the cattle graze through the winter, and they had lost many head for lack of feed. Cat was glad Ian had listened to her. On Skye they cut every scrap of grass they could and tossed it over walls and hedgerows to dry. And here the grass stretched to the horizon in every direction, free for the cutting.

Grass was the only thing that didn't cost money here. Sure, neighbors helped one another out with building barns or shucking corn, working together as they had in Scotland, but pickers and drovers had to be paid. She was lucky not to have to pay a foreman. Since Ian was killed, Geordie had worked for room and board and some pocket money, but it couldn't last. Sometime soon she'd have to pay him what he was worth or lose him.

That was the real reason she couldn't store her cotton; she needed the money, and soon. Without Ian's railroad wages, there was only enough cash to last through harvest time. And if she could have afforded to wait, she'd have a hard time selling the bales on her own. Some of the folks in Tarrant County had tried cotton bulking in years past, but the buyers always seemed to find enough individual farmers who'd sell their cotton at lower prices. Bulking would work only if everyone banded together and if they bulked so much cotton the buyers couldn't ignore them.

She sighed. No, come September, every cotton farmer in the South would dump his whole crop on the market at once and drive prices down, maybe even below nine cents a pound. And she'd have to join them. Not much profit when it cost eight cents a pound to raise it.

Cat rose and walked to the window, staring out at the

moonlit fields. Unlike some of her neighbors, she at least had a crop to sell, thanks to Ian and his windmills.

The old-timers had laughed when he drilled wells and put up the big-bladed machines to pump the water into the livestock tanks. "Plenty of rainwater for crops and livestock, boy. Don't need no fancy doodads to farm 'round here." He hadn't said much, but just kept working.

Of course, that was before the drought. The old-timers stopped laughing when the hot sun seared the prairie brown, withering cotton fields and pastures alike, drying out kitchen gardens and weakening cattle. She knew she was lucky to have good water, and plenty of it. Ian had been right, even if he hadn't lived to see it.

Swallowing against the lump in her throat, she trudged back to the table and lowered herself onto the chair. Damn him, why did he have to die? Tears threatened to spill onto the ledger, but she dashed them from her eyes and bent to the books again.

If they were very careful, she might be able to make it, especially if she accepted Doc Bascom's offer of work. It rankled a little that he wanted to train her to do things his way, but she knew he could teach her some things about medicine. He just didn't realize yet that she could teach him as well.

But if she took the job, she wouldn't have to sell Ian's cattle. She'd grown to love the beasts, and it cost little enough to keep the herd. Besides, the price of beef dropped more every month, and she'd be damned if she'd take a loss because the Texas & Pacific Railroad charged such high freight rates. As it was, meat buyers in the East could ship beef in from Wyoming or Montana at half the cost. At least the family had meat and milk in plenty.

Cat wiped the metal nib on the blotter, then replaced the cap on the inkwell and tested the figures on the page for dryness. She tensed at the sound of a footfall on the porch, then relaxed as she recognized her brother's tread. By the time he clicked the door shut, she had a cup of hot coffee waiting for him on the table.

"Cat, I'm glad you're still up. I—" He turned a ladder-back chair around and straddled it, his eyes sparkling and his cheeks flushed. "I need some advice."

Smiling, Cat leaned forward, her forearms resting one atop the other along the near edge of the table. "So, you finally noticed how wise I am after all these years, then."

Leaning back, he wiped his palms on his thighs, a gesture so like Ian it wrenched her heart. "I'm serious." His mouth straightened, but his eyes still danced.

"All right, then, out with it." Cat forced the smile from her mouth. Probably a lassie, and about time too.

"You know Mr. Timmerman over at *The World?*"

Surprised, Cat nodded. Everyone knew the editor of the town's only newspaper.

Geordie leaned forward, his fingers clutching the table's edge. "Well, he offered me a job." A grin widened his mouth, and his words tumbled out in a rush. "Just typesetting at first, but he says I can try my hand at writing if I've a mind to. He said I could live here and ride into town each day to work."

Cat forced her smile to stay in place. "Aye, and what did you tell him?" She knew what his answer must be, how long he'd hoped for just such a chance, but she had to ask, to give herself time to swallow her concern.

Geordie's brow furrowed. "Well, ah, that's the problem. I mean, if I take this job, who's going to run the ranch?"

Drawing her lips together, Cat nodded, letting sarcasm taint her words. "So, you're that important I canna get along without you?" It was true, but she had to make him believe otherwise.

Confusion slackened his mouth for a moment, then he pressed his lips together. "You think I should take the job."

"A man would be a fool not to, and I dinna like to think my own brother's a fool. We'll manage somehow." That was true as well, although finding the money to pay a foreman would take some doing. Perhaps she should reconsider O. K. Frink's offer of credit. Or maybe she should give up and sell out, move into town. Or go back to Skye. Homesickness filled her for a long moment. It would be so easy.

Geordie pushed himself up, dismounting the chair with a swing of his leg. He stood, rocking heel-to-toe for a moment.

"I mentioned to Joe Vanzee that you might need a foreman. He said he'd be willing to work for board and extra food he could take home to his mama. He's coming by tomorrow to talk to you."

She thought of Joe holding out the money to pay her for healing his brother. The knots in her shoulders loosened, and her mouth slid into a smile on its own. "And you were that sure of my answer?" She hoped the Vanzees liked milk and beef.

Geordie lifted his shoulders, but red crept up from his collar and onto his cheeks. "If you'd said no, I'd have tried to talk you into it. But I would've taken the job either way." He bent and touched his lips to her forehead as he strode past her, and then he was gone up the stairs, the clacking of his boot heels echoing above her head.

A sad tenderness filled her, a bittersweet acceptance of another change in her life. No matter what she decided about the farm, yesterday was gone. Her bonnie wee brother was no longer a lad, but a man with his own life to lead, his own way to make. Levering herself up, she bent to close the ledger, then lifted the lamp to light her way up the dark stairs to her cold and lonely bed.

But even the soothing rhythm of Betsy's mouth at her breast had failed to lull Catriona to sleep. Now, across the room, the soft sighing of the wee bairn's even breath whispered in the still darkness.

Envying her daughter's warm, forgetful ease, Cat lay wide awake. Her body cried out for rest, tired in every bone, but peace wouldn't come again tonight. After an eternity of half dreams, chasing her worries in an endless circle, she sat up in the big bed and struck a match to light a tallow candle.

The reek of sulphur and hot fat tinged the air, and the sudden sphere of yellow light darkened the corners of the bedroom as she fitted the glass chimney onto its holder. Smooth floorboards chilled her bare feet as she tiptoed to the cradle.

Like ripe wheat twined about wild roses, Betsy's blond curls glistened, framing her soft cheeks and her wee bud of a mouth. Brown lashes fringed her closed eyes in perfect half-circles. Her body lay open, *canny* arms and legs wide, surrendered to the haven of sleep. All the riches of a summer afternoon in one bonny package, like the day she was conceived.

Cat turned away, fighting down the pain of the joyful memory. Clenching her jaw, she forced her feet to carry her to the brass-bound steamer trunk in the corner. It was time —time to stop living in the past, to get on with her life. Kneeling, she set the candle on the windowsill and raised the heavy lid. She lifted out the tall Stetson, setting it to one side. Then the round-toed boots, their high heels clacking together as they touched the floor.

Leather chaps, union suits, work pants, shirts—she stacked them all in neat piles around her on the floor. She knew she should give them away, or cut them down for Geordie, or make something from them. They weren't fancy enough for quilt pieces or soft enough for baby clothes. But the important thing was to use them, anything but letting them molder in a trunk.

Reaching into the chest one last time, her hand scraped the paper-lined bottom and closed around cold metal. The watch. She pulled it into the light and flipped up the lid. The face stared back at her, two black hands frozen in position, silent. She knew what this had meant to Ian, the watch his grandfather had given him. Her trembling fingers found the stem, turning the ridged edges. After only a few turns the hair-thin second hand swept around, and the gears inside purred with a quiet ticking.

She cradled it in her hand a moment as the warmth of her skin replaced the metallic chill, then clicked the lid closed and set it beside the candle. A sudden urge to hurry seized her, and she scooped the clothing into her arms. Holding the bulk with her chin, she leaned into the trunk.

Her breath caught in her throat, and she dropped the bundle, then retrieved a workshirt and pressed it to her face. Tears wet the worn fabric as she breathed in, savoring the scent of leather and sage, the smell of Ian's body locked into the cloth.

Sobs forced their way up her aching throat, and finally she surrendered. Slumping against the chest, she let the grief take her. As the tears slowed at last, she lifted her head, her body aching from exhaustion and cold.

She smoothed the shirt and lay it atop the others in the trunk. There was time yet. She set the boots and the tall hat inside, nestling the pocket watch beside them. Plenty of time to worry about this later. She levered herself up against the chest's brass-bound lip.

Darkness closed around her, and distant voices whispered in her ears. She reached for the wall and held herself up until the dizziness passed and her vision cleared. Faint knowledge stirred deep within her as she turned to stare out the window, where a thin crescent of new moon glimmered low in the night sky. Her face chilled, then warmed as she counted back over the days and weeks.

Bittersweet joy bubbled up in her, and she knew. Ian had given her one last bit of himself before he died, and he hadn't even known. Her hand strayed to her belly. A bairn, a son this time, she was sure.

Snuffing the candle, Cat made her way back to bed. All her doubts and fears had fled in the silvery moonlight. Suddenly the world made sense again. She knew now what she'd been waiting for. And she knew what she must do.

Chapter 8

Geordie rubbed his nose with the back of one hand, wishing the kerosene smell of the ink didn't make his eyes water. With stained fingertips he reached for a lowercase *n*, sliding it in beside the *o*, and wondered if this Violet Weston was his old schoolmarm. Must be; there couldn't be more than one. Somehow he'd never thought of his teacher getting married.

He fished a period out of the box and slid some blanks into place at the end of the line. He'd like to see her expression when old Pruneface saw his by-line. *If* Zeke ever gave him a chance to write anything. So far, all he'd done was set type and sort it. Still, he liked knowing the news before the paper came out. And the money helped at home. He pushed down the twinge of guilt. Joe was doing just fine running the farm. And Cat had insisted he take this job.

Reaching for the next piece of copy, he sidled around the layout board and grabbed a capital **V** to start the headline. Looked like Village Creek was the place to be on Independence Day. Wiping his hand on his apron, he turned the page to get a better look at the doings listed there. Picnic, swimming, dancing, fireworks. Boy, he couldn't wait for Sunday to arrive.

As he slid the type into place one by one, his mind

wandered. Maybe he could get away from his family for a while and spend some time alone with Molly, maybe take a walk down the creek a piece. He could just picture her sitting on the bank, dangling her feet in the water, her yellow hair shining in the sun, lifting the hem of a new dress—

"George, you mind telling me what a *throud* is?" Zeke squinted through his bifocals, the lines of his face twisted into a scowl. He held up a piece of newsprint with several red circles.

Shame replaced his glow of happiness as Geordie took the sheet in one hand. "Drouth. I got it backward."

Zeke snorted. "And damn near every third word on the page."

A heavy hand came down on his shoulder, and a chuckle sounded in his ear. "Never mind, boy. I was worse'n this when I first started. But I got to get this paper out yet this week." Taking off his eyeglasses, the old man polished the lenses with a red kerchief. "Tell you what, son. I'll finish up here. In the meantime, I want you to run over to the hotel. There's a couple over there just came in on the stage from Llano Estacado, and they're telling horror stories about dry creekbeds and dying cattle. You go see if you can make sense of it."

Geordie stood for a minute, wondering if he heard right. "You mean you want me to write a story?"

The old man puckered his lips and cocked his head, then nodded. "Yup, I reckon that's just what I mean. Now, git on over there and bring me something worth printing."

He pulled the apron over his head and hung it on the wall, then started for the door at a run.

"Uh, son, you might should wash those hands first. And take a look in the mirror at your face." Zeke chuckled.

Let him laugh. A story, his own story. He scrubbed the black stains, wiping his hands on a rag and frowning at the smear of ink across his nose. "I'll do you proud, Mr. Timmerman. You won't regret this, you'll see." He grabbed a notebook and pencil, then turned in the doorway. "And thanks."

• • •

Will savored the rich taste and smiled up at Catriona. "You know you make the best cup of coffee in Tarrant County?" He couldn't resist flirting with her a bit.

Light danced in her dark blue eyes as she lifted the spatterware pot from the woodstove and carried it to the table. "And someone in Dallas County makes a better?" She cocked her head in a way that always stirred a fire deep inside him.

"Well, not that I've tasted, but—" He sipped again to cover his chagrin, his thumb rubbing the smooth warm surface of the cup. She could always turn his words inside out. "Would you settle for the best in Texas, or should I tell you it's the best in the world?"

Her tinkling laugh filled the cool, dark kitchen. "No, the county will do. But would you have me credit that you rode all the way out here just to praise my coffee, then?"

"No, I came to ask you again if you'd come to work for me as my assistant." His gaze locked with hers. "I need you, Cat. The country's filling up, and there's more sickness than one man can treat."

Her face sobered as she refilled their cups and returned the pot to the back of the stove. "*Ach*, then, you'll want an answer tonight. I'll be right back." She stepped through the doorway and was gone.

He set the cup down, sliding it back and forth on the smooth tabletop, remembering the meals he'd shared with Ian and his family in this room. What would the man have said about his wife working? Sadness washed through him. Catriona would never consider it if Ian were alive. And she could still say no. But he did need her help. And he knew she could use the money too.

Quiet footsteps echoed in the hall, and Geordie and Effie followed Cat into the room, surprise and curiosity lighting their faces as they greeted him and settled around the table.

Cat sank onto a chair opposite him and smiled, her hands clasping the heavy white mug. "Well, now, I need your help to make some decisions today." She drew a deep breath and stared into the cup. "But first I must give you some news." She cleared her throat. "I'm carrying Ian's child."

Will's sadness twisted into pity for a moment, until Cat lifted her face.

Her eyes glowed and a smile trembled on her lips. "So, Doctor, do you still crave my help?"

Will hesitated. He hadn't planned on a pregnant assistant. And it might not be fair to her; the long hours and hard work tired him, and he wasn't in a delicate condition. "Can you manage?"

Her eyes sparkled again. "Oh, aye, I bedded up cotton when I was carrying Betsy."

A chair scraped back from the table as Geordie stood, turning his face toward the open door. In the dim light Cat could see his furrowed brow and the stain of red rising in his cheeks. She bit her lip, wishing she could take back her hasty words. Keeping her voice soft, she reached to touch his hand. "Sorry, lad, I dinna mean to shame you with my woman's talk, but now I must have your help."

He nodded, but didn't shift his gaze.

Effie squirmed in her chair, a smile curving her lips and her eyes wide with excitement. "And mine, Cat?"

"Aye, lassie, and especially yours." She placed her palms flat on the table. "Dr. Bascom has asked me to work for him in town." She turned toward Will and gave him a smile. "And I'd like to tell him yes, but I'll need you both. Geordie, can you work at the paper and still have time to see that Joe runs things right on the farm?"

Again Geordie nodded.

"There's a canny lad. And, Effie, now that you're out of school, I'll need you to mind Betsy every day and help keep house."

Color drained from the lass's face and her smile dissolved.

"Dinna fear, you'll do a lovely job. Betsy likes to stay with you, and now that she drinks from a cup, you'll have no trouble." Of course, the lass couldna manage it all alone, but she'd thought of that as well. "Do you think your friend Molly might like a job helping you?"

Effie jumped up and ran around the table to throw her arms around Cat's neck. "Oh, yes. May I ride over and ask her?"

"Aye." Her lips twitched as she struggled to hide her smile. "And you might ask your brother to drive you."

Geordie turned and stared at her for a moment, then set his hat on his head and strode toward the door. "Let's go."

Effie gathered her shawl from a hook and ran after him.

Laughing, Cat rose and walked to the window to watch them go, but she sobered at the sight of a lone horseman approaching. Frink again. Well, this time she had an answer for him. As he pulled up by the porch, she remembered she already had company. "Excuse me a moment, Will."

His eyebrows knotted, but his lips and eyes smiled at her as he nodded and sipped his coffee.

Stepping out onto the porch, Cat tasted dust on the hot, dry wind. So many farmers suffered from the drought already, and the summer had just begun. If they didn't get rain, many would lose their crops and have to take leins against next year's cotton. And Frink would grow fat from cheating them.

The small man swung down from his horse and beat his felt hat against his leg. Dust clouded the air around him and clung to his expensive suit and his rust-colored hair. He wiped his thin red mustache with a square of white linen and gave a half bow. "Miz Macleod, why, you look right pretty today."

Gritting her teeth, Cat forced herself to smile at him, hiding both her irritation and her growing sadness. In her mind she said her final good-bye to Skye, knowing she might never see it again. "Mr. Frink, let's not dally. You've come to ask me again if you might buy my farm. And after all your patience, I must disappoint you. I dinna wish to sell."

Frink's mouth opened, then snapped shut. He tugged at his waistcoat and cleared his throat. "Now, Miz Macleod, I offered you more than the place was worth to begin with. Everybody 'round here's losing money on their grain crops 'cause of this dry spell. You'll just end up losing the farm anyway, and then you'll have nothing to show for the last two years."

Cat clenched her hands on the porch railing and let the smile slip from her face. She knew what he said was possible, but she wouldn't give him the satisfaction of admitting it.

"*Ach*, man, there's where you're wrong. I have no intention of losing my land, now or later."

Frink's smile faded. "Be reasonable. You can't run this place, a woman alone."

"Aye, but that's just what I intend to do. Good day to you, Mr. Frink." She crossed her arms over her chest and met his gaze.

His mustache twitched as he swung back up into the saddle. He sat for a moment, then shook his head and gave a noisy sigh. "Have it your way, then. I can wait." He jerked the reins, turning his mount toward the road, then dug his spurs into the animal's sides. The wind carried away the clouds of dust as he galloped away.

Cat stood alone, her answer still on her lips. "I dinna think so. Better the sheriff's auction than sell to the likes of you."

A footfall beside her reminded her again of Will's strength. Her spirit leaned toward his, taking comfort from his presence. Now more than ever she needed him—his friendship and his offer of work, and maybe something more as well. She turned to him with a smile, her heart lighter than it had been for weeks. "So, what time shall I report to work tomorrow, boss?"

Chapter 9

July 1886

Catriona leaned back, the bark of the willow tree pressing into her back through the thin muslin of her Mother Hubbard dress. Deep shade cooled the sweat on her face and beneath her arms as she closed her eyes.

Breathing in, she willed her stomach to settle as the fresh air cleansed the smoke of burning fat from her nostrils. The smell of barbecue usually sharpened her appetite, but in her condition even the most pleasant of smells made her queasy. A smile touched her lips as her hand stole to her growing belly.

Gentle sounds of water running over rocks in the creek bed muffled the clink of horseshoes and the cries of competitors in a nearby grove. It dizzied her to see so many people gathered at Village Creek to celebrate Independence Day this year. Living alone on the empty plains so much of the time, she'd forgotten how much noise a crowd of people could make. At least the men had gone easy on the whiskey so far, but it was not yet noon. Plenty of time for them to grow rowdy as the afternoon lengthened and the dry heat parched their throats.

Voices grew louder, moving toward her from the picnic grounds. Opening her eyes, Cat drew her knees up and wrapped her arms around her shins as a group of men passed close beside the willow, deep in argument.

She recognized Axel Vanzee, Molly and Joe's father, by the shock of white-blond hair and pale blue eyes. He must be home from Dallas to spend the holiday with his family.

Cat had to strain to understand his words, his accent thickened by anger. "*Nein*, it is wrong, I say." He pounded one fist into his palm. "To strike, to boycott is to break the law. The Alliance must keep to its business and stay out of politics." He crossed his arms over his chest and glared at the men one by one.

"But don't you see? Strikes and boycotts are our only weapon against the monopolies." Lewis Price kept his voice calm, but a light shone in his eyes.

Cat leaned her chin on her knees. She hadn't seen the mortician since Ian's funeral. What did an undertaker care about such things?

Price perched on a boulder facing Vanzee, tugging at one knee of his trousers. "It's not just the railroads. The manufacturers who buy your cotton and make your plows and your wagons control how much they pay you and how much goods cost."

The others formed a jagged circle around the two men, some nodding and murmuring among themselves. An old man stepped into the circle, then pulled a red kerchief from his pocket and mopped the dome of his bald head. No mistaking Mr. Timmerman, the owner of *The World* and Geordie's boss. Silence reigned, a sign of respect no doubt, as he rubbed the lenses of his spectacles and re-hooked them over his ears. "Now, let me get this straight, Lewis. You say the Alliance has to be more than a business concern."

Price nodded, pulling a long stalk of prairie grass and tucking the soft green root end between his back teeth. "Got to. It's the only way."

Vanzee spat in the grass at his feet. "And I say those who strike and boycott are no better than criminals."

Overcome with rage, Cat jumped to her feet.

A dozen pairs of eyes turned toward her. Price stood, tugging his waistcoat straight. "Miz Macleod. What an unexpected pleasure." He glanced behind him at the other men. "We, uh, didn't know you was there. Sorry to disturb you."

Heat rose to Cat's cheeks, but she couldn't let Axel Vanzee's words stand unchallenged. "Aye, I didna mean to overhear." She sought Axel's eyes, but he turned his face away. "But I canna just walk away now. My husband died in the railroad strike, and you all know Ian was no criminal." She searched each face in turn.

Only Vanzee refused to meet her gaze. Price nodded his encouragement.

Cat's voice shook with anger and grief. "He died fighting for a better life for his family. Isn't that what we all left the old world for?" She took a breath to steady herself.

"Back home in Scotland I fought side by side with the women and bairns of my village when the constables came to take away our men. And what was their crime?"

She lifted her chin. "They couldna pay the unfair rents the landlords demanded. It was not until we all stood together and refused to pay our rents that the government heard our cries. We had to break the law in order to change it." Tears slid down her cheeks and thickened her voice. "I would hate to think Ian died for nought."

Silence lengthened as the men looked at one another, then away. Someone cleared his throat.

Then a young voice broke the stillness. "Cat, where are you?" Effie's coppery curls bobbed as she sidled through the standing men. "One of the Ransom boys got hit in the arm with a horseshoe." She wrinkled her nose. "Blood everywhere. Doc Bascom's calling for you."

Concern for the injured lad replaced Cat's relief at being rescued from an awkward situation. "You'll excuse me, gentlemen." She placed a hand on her younger sister's shoulder. "Show me where he is."

Will tucked the corners of the bandage under the knot to hold it all in place. He glanced at the boy's injured right arm, then his dirty face. "Now then, Jasper. Mind you, keep that covered until it heals over and we can take the stitches out."

Catriona turned from packing sutures and catgut back into his bag. "Aye, and no swimming, do you *ken?*"

The dark eyes shifted away, and a scowl turned down the corners of the child's mouth. "But—" His eyes turned toward his father, and he swallowed, then nodded. "Yes sir, Doc. Miz Macleod. Whatever you say." With grimy fingernails he scratched his freckled nose.

The elder Ransom gave the boy's narrow right shoulder a rough shove. "Mind your manners, youngun."

Will hated to think about what treatment the boy got at home. Luke Ransom was the kind of man who wanted folks to think he was lenient with his wife and kids, but Will knew better, having patched up Rosie after more than one of Luke's drunken rages.

The boy stared at his father, confusion and fear crumpling his small forehead.

Will gritted his teeth as Ransom tapped his son on the head, a none-too-gentle blow. "Tell him thanks, you fool." Hardness edged his voice and shone in his eyes.

"Uh, much obliged, Doc. Ma'am." He held out his grimy left hand to Will for an awkward handshake, but stopped short of touching Cat.

"Me too, Doc." Luke's grin showed a gap and the blackened stump of a rotten tooth. "Much obliged." His smile edged toward a leer as he gave a half-bow in Catriona's direction. "We're beholden, Miz Macleod, me and mine."

Cat gave a short nod, then busied herself with the medical supplies once more.

Will was glad she hadn't wasted a smile on the man. "Give my best to Rosie." About all Rose Ransom had in the world was the love and respect of her friends, but there was precious little they could do to help her. Especially since she claimed to love the lout. *Women—*

"I'll tell her, Doc." Ransom clamped one hand on the boy's hurt wrist, ignoring the child's hiss of pain, and dragged him toward the clearing where the whiskey barrels stood.

"What an awful man." Catriona's words startled him.

Will couldn't remember ever having heard her say anything bad about anyone. "Always was, man and boy. We all grew up together, but Ian had even less use for Luke than I did back then."

Catriona's face clouded and she dropped her gaze.

He chewed his lip. What kind of fool was he, mentioning her dead husband, just saying his name out like that? "Cat, I'm sorry, I—I just didn't think."

Cat lifted her face, a smile trembling on her lips and her eyes shiny with unshed tears. "No, dinna *fash* yourself." She touched his hand, sending a thrill of warmth up his arm. "I'd like to hear."

He captured her hand and tucked it under his elbow. "Let's find a shady spot." He led her toward the willow trees lining the banks of Village Creek. "We were the class scoundrels, the three of us—the bane of any teacher's existence. Luke was mean clear through, same as he is today, picking fights, hurting people. But Ian and I were after excitement, anything to break the monotony of Mr. Turley's lessons." A smile twitched his lips at a sudden memory.

Cat tugged his arm, an answering smile curving her lips. "Come then, now, you must tell me."

"One day Ian drew a picture of Mr. Turley on one side of his double slate, and on the other side a picture of Mr. Kelly, who always ate more than his share at every fish fry. They were both fat, as his matching verse pointed out. The teacher grabbed the slate out of Ian's hand and read it aloud."

Will stopped, closing his eyes as he searched for the exact words. "Good Professor Turley/And fish-eating Mr. Kelly—/ It's hard indeed to tell/ Which has the larger belly."

Cat giggled, covering her mouth with her hand. "Poor man."

Will nodded. "Ian was sorry later."

Cat cocked her head, her dark hair brushing the white ruffles at her shoulder. "What happened?"

Will kicked at a clump of grass in the path. "Turley got fed up with Luke one day and tried to paddle him. Luke beat him near senseless with his bare fists, then tried to finish him off with a big rock. Turley never came back to school, but then, neither did Luke. Ian and I were glad to see the last of him."

He walked on in silence, wishing the conversation had taken a brighter turn. Stopping under a willow, he slipped off his jacket and spread it over the gnarled roots. "Madam." With an exaggerated bow, he gestured for Cat to sit.

She sank down and arranged her skirts around her ankles, then smiled up at him and patted the ground. "I'd like to hear more about you two lads—you and Ian."

He settled beside her and shrugged. "Not much to tell really—just the usual escapades. Tying a skunk to the bell rope. Putting a cow in the belfry. But our best was the night we hoisted a buggy clear up onto the schoolhouse roof. You should've seen the teacher's face come morning."

Catriona's tinkling laugh blended with the music of the creek.

Will hadn't heard her laugh like that since before Ian died. It was all he could do not to reach out, put his arms around her, hold her close.

She turned her face toward the far side of the creek, her eyes shining in the cool shade of the willow. "I envy you, knowing him then."

Will leaned over and plucked a gray-green leaf from a trailing branch. Of course, it was Ian she was interested in, his memory she longed for. Tearing the leaf into tiny pieces, he wondered if she could ever feel half so much for him.

A hot wind, carrying the scent of parched earth, tugged at Cat's skirts as she alit from the buckboard. On the horizon the sun glared, shooting reddish-orange arrows of light across the prairie, but even the coming darkness did little to ease the dry heat of the air. At times like this she missed Skye the most, with its cool, fresh breezes. And rain greening the moors.

She reached up for Betsy and swung the toddler to the ground, then held tight to the wee hand as they made their way across the slick, dry grass to the door of the old Grange hall.

The Grange had once boasted thousands of members among the farmers of Texas, but with the failure of their programs and their leaders' refusal to fight for legislative reform, many of the members had switched to the Farmers Alliance. When she and Ian first arrived, they had joined in the hope that the farmers might band together to fight the railroads and the merchants. But so far they'd done little but talk. Since Ian's death, she'd heard of other meetings as folks banded together to talk about the low grain yields and the drought, but she hadn't been able to bring herself to attend.

Cat made her slow way up the aisle, letting Betsy set their pace and nodding at acquaintances in the crowded room. Even some town folk attended, including the undertaker, Lewis Price, and even an old broken-down cowboy named Quincy. Kerosene lamps sent flickering light against the walls, and a roar of voices filled the stuffy air. After the hard work and isolation of farm life on the prairie, any meeting became a social event. It was a shame the young people hadn't come, but in a way she'd been relieved when they decided to stay home.

Effie and Molly had made some excuse to stay at the farm for the evening. Cat suspected it had something to do with two strapping lads without shirts pitching hay in the cooler evening air. They could do worse, she supposed.

Joe was a good worker, as Effie'd taken great pains to point out. But although poor Geordie tried to show an interest in Molly, between the newspaper and the farmwork, he'd little enough time to think of anything else.

Not that she had much time herself, now that she worked for Will every day. And after work she did the day's baking and cooked dishes for Molly to take to the threshing bees at nearby farms. If she wanted help from her neighbors, she had to offer it in return. So tonight's long ride alone with Betsy in the buckboard and the prospect of listening to other folks talk all evening came as a welcome relief.

She sank down on a bench and pulled Betsy onto her knee, grateful for her loose-fitting Mother Hubbard dress. Although her waist had only just begun to thicken, many of the older women could spot a pregnancy right away, sometimes even before the woman knew herself. Much as she liked her neighbors, she didn't think she could bear their pity or their suspicions when they found out she was with child again.

Betsy squirmed and fussed to get down, but finally Cat draped her shawl over one shoulder and let the wee lassie suckle. The bairn fell asleep just as the meeting began. During the opening rituals, Cat's mind drifted back over her day. Up at dawn, she hurried through the morning chores until Molly arrived to help Effie with the bairn, then drove into town with Geordie to Will's office. The hours had been a blur of injury and illness, from a colicky baby to a haying accident to an old man with sunstroke. As she watched Will work, she gained new respect for him, even when she didn't agree with his treatments.

Sometimes she wanted to suggest an herbal tisane or poultice, but she bit her tongue. Better to wait until he asked. It wasn't that he looked down on herbal remedies; it was more that he knew his own methods and trusted them. Besides, her stock of herbs dwindled more each year, especially with the dry heat of this year's drought. As long as her herbs were the only thing affected.

She glanced around. Between the livestock killed during last winter's blizzards and the wheat and cotton ruined by too much sun and too little rain this summer, many of the people in this room would go into debt for the first time this year. Thank God for Ian and his windmills, and his good sense in cutting enough hay to feed the herds last winter. She missed him so much sometimes.

It was some small comfort, knowing how proud he'd be of the way they were getting on without him. At least their crops and cattle would make it, even if her herb garden gave back little for the water she lavished on it. What she needed was someone to show her how to use the native plants, but so far no one could tell her much. Maybe it was just as well she was learning another type of healing from Will each day. And the extra money might keep them out of debt for another year.

With a sigh she slid her nipple from Betsy's mouth and fastened the front of her dress, then arranged her shawl over the sleeping bairn and turned her attention back to the meeting.

At last the chairman had called for new business, and some man was talking about electing a delegate to the state convention in Cleburne the following month. Then another man stood and argued against sending anyone and against the Alliance getting involved in politics, especially after the losses from the Knights of Labor strike.

As the man sat down, Cat stood, easing Betsy up onto her shoulder. "Mr. Chairman." People around her turned to stare up at her. Although women were equal members of the Alliance, the men seemed to do most of the talking. Up until tonight she'd been happy to let them. But this time she wouldn't keep quiet, not when so much was at stake.

Ted Driscoll nodded at her. "The chair recognizes Miz Macleod."

Voices buzzed around her, and her knees wobbled, but she lifted her chin. "You all know me." She turned her head, taking in the people on both sides. "This man told us we all lost so much in the strike." Her voice shook, but she clasped Betsy to her and forced herself to continue. "But I say to you that I lost more than most. I lost my husband, the father of my children. And Texas lost a good man."

The woman beside her gasped, her gaze running up and down Cat's body before she turned to whisper to the woman on her other side. A wave of murmuring rose up and crested over her.

Cat's cheeks warmed and she chewed her lip. So much for keeping the bairn a secret. But this went beyond her personal comfort or the pettiness of local gossip. She clenched her jaw, remembering the nights on the Isle of Skye when she spoke to the crofters, encouraging them to withhold their rents until they got fair treatment. Ian had been right; this cause was just as important. "This same man would have you give up, quit because you lost this one battle."

She took a deep breath. "My husband may be dead, but his dream lives on. If we give up now, he will have died for nought, and his dream will die too. The railroads and the bankers and the merchants will get richer, and we'll all get poorer and deeper in debt." The hall fell silent for a moment. "Is that what we want? I for one say no."

Voices boiled up around her as she sank back down to the bench, suddenly exhausted. In the front of the hall a gavel banged, and at last the crowd quieted. From a far corner one voice rose above the others. "I nominate Catriona Macleod to represent our alliance at the state convention in Cleburne."

Again the gavel rang out and Driscoll's voice shouted for quiet. "Do I hear a second?"

A chorus rose up, their words tripping over one another, all seconding her nomination. An avalanche of ayes answered the chairman's call for a voice vote. Though they shouted, those opposed were too few. With a low rumble of mutters a handful of men and women sidled down the aisles and out the open double doors.

Cat sat holding Betsy, too shocked to move or speak as Driscoll pounded the gavel again for quiet and called for donations to pay expenses for the trip. What in the world had she gotten herself into this time?

Chapter 10

August 1886

Will signaled for Catriona to sit up, then turned away, pouring fresh water into the basin from the pitcher atop the highboy. He plunged his shaking hands into the lukewarm liquid. Whatever was the matter with him? He'd examined many attractive women before, but never had he lost his objectivity so completely. Seeing her partially unclothed and in her own bed had unnerved him, and touching her silky skin had lit a fire in his veins.

"Well then, what's the diagnosis, Doctor?" The rich melody of Cat's voice only deepened his desire for her.

He cleared his throat, then answered without looking in her direction, focusing instead on drying with a clean floursack towel. "Offhand, I'd say you're with child, Miz Macleod. Due around Christmas or thereabouts." He tried to keep his voice light and teasing despite his struggle with his own feelings.

"And the bairn, it's well?" Concern edged into Cat's question.

This time he had to look, force himself to smile reassurance at her. It wasn't fair to worry her because he couldn't control his base desires. "From what I can tell, everything is fine."

Relief loosened the tension in her face before she tipped

her head as her slim fingers worked small buttons into the buttonholes on her bodice. "Then it's safe to travel?"

He shrugged. "Should be." A grin tugged at the corners of his mouth. "You planning a long wagon ride, say into Fort Worth, or maybe even Dallas?"

Her lips narrowed into a straight line, and she lifted her chin, tossing her dark hair back over her shoulders. "To Cleburne on the train. The local alliance elected me as their delegate to the state convention."

"But—" He stopped to make sense of his reactions. Better to go slow. After all, he had no say in what she did. "Who'll take care of the farm, and what about Betsy?"

Cat swung her feet over the side of the bed and slid to the floor, clinging with one hand to the high headboard as she stood. "My daughter will manage without me for a few days. As for the farm, I'll leave it to the same four who mind things while I work for you."

He cursed himself for not having more control as his voice grew louder. "And what about that, what about my patients?"

Something blazed behind the deep blue of Cat's eyes. "They must do without me a short while as well, then. Thank you for your concern, and your advice, Doctor." She held out her hand in a gesture of dismissal.

He clasped her fingers, noting the hidden strength beneath the smooth softness, and wished for an excuse to prolong the touch. Instead, he nodded and released her hand. "My pleasure." He gathered his bag and his hat and turned toward the door. "See that you eat well and get plenty of rest."

As he made his way down the narrow stairs, a question echoed in his mind. *And what about me? How will I manage without you?*

Dizzy and nauseated by the close heat and stifling odors of the Pullman car, Cat eased toward the window. After several tries, she finally wrenched the glass open and gulped in fresh dry air. She settled back on the worn seat, her gaze held by the brown fields rushing by. She'd heard the stories from

West Texas of barbed wire fences downed and cattlemen driving their herds east in search of water, of settlers forced to give up their land and leave the state. It was bad enough in Tarrant County, but it could always be worse. And Johnson County didn't look to be faring much better.

The wind shifted for a moment, drawing sooty smoke from the engine into the car. Cat coughed, then pulled out a kerchief to cover her mouth and nose. After a moment the wind shifted again, carrying the smoke with it. Somewhere behind her a baby cried. Even though she knew it wasn't Betsy, her nipples tingled as her milk let down. She was glad she'd bound her corsets tight, even though she had trouble breathing. At least her breasts wouldn't get as sore, but she didn't expect to be truly comfortable again until she got home and nursed her bairn.

She questioned once more her wisdom in agreeing to go to Cleburne. The Alliance could have picked a better delegate, or at least a more eager one. And she could have stayed with her family and her work. After all, she had enough to keep her busy at home.

And she couldn't help but wonder how Will was getting on. Ida's bairn was due any day. But that was nonsense. He'd managed without her for years. Still, he had seemed a little cool and distant when she told him she would be gone a few days. Perhaps he disapproved of a woman mixing in politics, especially a pregnant widow. She wasn't sure she approved herself, for that matter. But more than likely he had something else on his mind.

After all, Yvette would be there to help him. They seemed to be old and dear friends, perhaps old lovers if the town gossips had the right of it. A shame they never married, although she wasn't surprised. The doctor might consider himself too good for a madam. Or maybe Yvette did hate men, and that's why she never sold herself.

Cat shuddered inside. It would be a better world if no woman sold herself ever. But perhaps some of them had no other choice. At least Yvette seemed to really care about her girls, protecting them and checking them for disease on a regular basis. They could be worse off, she supposed.

Another gust of smoke curled in through the window.

She could be worse off herself, though she wasn't sure how. It was only a little more than forty miles from the farm to Cleburne. Maybe she should have driven the buckboard down after all, but that would have taken days instead of hours.

The chuffing of the engine decreased as it labored up a gradual slope. Nearing the top, the train slowed to a halt. The crowded car buzzed with voices as Cat peered out the dirty window, trying to see what had caused the delay. It hadn't been that many years since Black Bart stopped trains all over Texas and robbed passengers of their valuables, shooting anyone who resisted. Unable to see ought but dry grass and scrubby trees, she leaned back and closed her eyes, waiting for whatever came. Lord knew, she hadn't much to steal. Nor did her fellow passengers, by their looks. And there were no fancy private cars with this train.

At last a conductor appeared. He raised white-gloved hands and shouted for attention. "Ladies and gents, no need to be alarmed. There's a cow lying down on the tracks ahead, and with this grade, we don't have enough steam to blow the whistle and keep going at the same time." At that moment the steam whistle sounded, and the conductor passed on through the car amid hoots and catcalls. After several more loud shrieks from the engine, the train finally jerked to a start again, with passengers cheering and laughing. But Cat didn't think it was funny.

The big railroad tycoons bought up rail lines, raised rates as high as possible, then kept the profits and moved on. They left behind a husk, unable to provide decent service or to pay wage increases to their workers. She'd hated the idea of paying for her fare, seeing Alliance dollars go to the man who owned the Katy Line. Jay Gould caused the Knights of Labor strike, and as far as she was concerned, he was just as much responsible for Ian's death as Long-haired Jim Cutchall.

God, how she missed Ian. He would have understood why she had to go to Cleburne. The child inside her belly stirred. She crossed her arms over her thickening middle. This convention might be her only chance to help make a better life for herself, and for their children.

• • •

The room stank of whiskey and sweat, with a thin overlay of cheap perfume. "For God's sake, Yvette, can't you open a window?" Will turned back to the girl on the bed. "There now, Ida, you rest a minute." He leaned her back on the ruffled bolster. "It won't be much longer and you'll be able to hold the little darling in your arms."

Tears filled her red-rimmed eyes. "You loco or something, Doc? What do I want with the little bastard? It's not like I didn't try to get rid of it." She wiped her nose on the back of one hand. "I'm only paying the piper 'cause I got no other choice, but that's no reason to insult me with all that shit about being a loving mother."

Will sighed and lifted her wrapper, pressing his ear to her swollen belly until he heard a faint ticking, like a pocket watch wrapped in cotton lint. At least the little beggar was still alive. Not that the life ahead of it was any great boon.

If only Cat were here instead of off playing politics in Cleburne, she could talk to the woman. She'd know what to say. He stood and poured water from a pitcher into a wash basin, then scrubbed his hands and doused them with whiskey.

"Hey, save some of that for me." Ida managed a dogged grin. "I'm the one in labor here." Her smile froze into a grimace and she writhed and groaned. "It hurts, Doc, God, it hurts! Give me a drink, damn you."

"You've had enough. Any more and it could hurt the child." He stoppered the glass bottle and shoved it out of her reach on the bedside table.

"As if I care. Let it die." She lay back, panting, her puffy face shiny with sweat. "Let me die too, while you're at it." Tears traced dark lines through the powder beneath her eyes, and she turned her face away.

He sighed as Yvette moved to the bed, her black taffeta hissing against the satin coverlet when she sat beside the weeping girl. "There, there, *chérie*. You cannot mean that. Just think what fun we will have, dressing your *petit enfant* and wheeling him around town. Why, he shall be the best-dressed child in Arlington, *non?*"

At least Yvette was here. Will couldn't remember how he used to manage alone. He concentrated on threading some boiled cotton twist through a suture and setting it to one side in case the opening tore.

Ida groaned and squirmed for a long moment, then gave a harsh sob. "I don't care about that. It hurts; it's going to tear me apart. I want to die."

He turned to the sad creature on the bed. She couldn't have been more than eighteen, but she looked older, aged by whiskey and opium and hard use. Her face bore faint scars from the beatings she took before she came to the Bon Chance. He got few calls to patch up split lips or broken noses here, although a time or two he'd signed death certificates for men who'd ignored Yvette's rules about not hitting the whores. It was enough to keep most of the customers in line.

Yvette took the girl's face in her hands. "You must not say that anymore. You must live, or else who shall take care of your child? Now you be good, and I shall give you another drink very soon. *Eh bien?*"

The frowsy head nodded. "Okay."

He lifted the sheet to check her progress, wondering again what could make a woman choose this life. Many reasons, he supposed, as many as there were fallen women. Good, she was dilated fully.

"Ida." He bent toward her, suppressing his desire to gag at the stench of her breath. "With the next pain I want you to push. Do you hear me?"

She nodded, then groaned and struggled to sit, her body tensed as she bared her teeth and furrowed her brow. After a moment she fell back like a marionette whose strings had been cut.

He examined her and nodded. "Very good. Only one or two more like that." Perhaps all the whiskey had relaxed her, or perhaps this was not her first, as she claimed. Although what she hoped to gain by such a lie he could only guess.

With two more pushes he was able to deliver the head. Lifting the tiny chin slightly, he scooped mucus from the child's mouth with his fingers and signaled with his head to Yvette. "Get a blanket ready."

Eyes wide, the madam shrugged, then shook her head. Her lips paled and she turned away, gagging.

Damn the woman. As if she hadn't seen her share of births. And damn Catriona, too, for not being here when he needed her help.

Ida groaned and heaved herself upright. The veins stood out in her neck, and her breath came in a great hiss between her teeth.

Will eased one shoulder down and out, then the other, and the purple-blue body slid onto the sheets. Hooking his fingers between the tiny ankles, Will lifted the baby upside down and patted the narrow back. With a honking sound the baby took a breath, then let out a low wail, his face a mask of agony.

Ida fell back with a sigh, and Will smiled at her. "Here's your son." He nestled the squalling boy in the crook of his mother's arm.

The girl stared down at the scowling face, then ran one finger over the matted dark curls. "Well, I never." Her face lit with pleasure, suddenly pretty in spite of all she'd been through. "Ain't he a beauty?"

Nodding, Will busied himself with the cord and afterbirth. Yvette touched his shoulder, then handed him a soft shawl, and he tucked it around the tiny body. He kept his voice low. "You can send Lewis home. We won't be needing his services today."

Ida opened the top of her gown and with expert fingers slid a nipple into the tiny, searching mouth. The baby's cries turned to grunts of pleasure, and the new mother chuckled deep in her throat. She turned, her eyes shining, looking closer to her age than he'd ever seen her. "God, Doc, I'm awful sorry for the way I acted before. Could we, uh, just forget them things I said?"

Will turned away, sliding his hands into the basin of water and smiling to himself. "What things were those, Ida?"

"You know—oh, I get it. Thanks, Doc."

Shaking the water from his hands, he took the towel Yvette held out.

"*Oui*, I am sorry too." Her hand lay for a moment on his bare forearm, as light as a butterfly. "If you needed her so much, why did you not tell her so? Then perhaps she would not have gone."

Her words sank deep, sending out ripples like a rock dropped in a pond. "Why? Well, that's a good question, sugar. I reckon I just figured it out this minute myself."

Chapter 11

Excitement coursed through her as the grievance committee mounted the platform and the president banged the gavel for order. After four days of listening to debates between those who saw the Alliance as a business organization and those who saw political action as the only hope of improving the farmers' lot, Cat was ready for the delegates to reach a consensus about something, anything. From the mutterings of the others surrounding her, it sounded as if they felt the same way. Besides electing new officers, about the only concrete thing the delegates had decided so far was to replace the *Rural Citizen* with the *Southern Mercury* as the official Alliance newspaper.

The chairman cleared his throat, and a tense hush fell over the delegates. "We, the Committee for the Good of the Order, hereby demand such legislation—" A storm of protest from the crowd drowned the man's next words. Surprised by the strong language of the committee report, Cat struggled to make out the rest of his sentence but caught only what sounded like "shameful abuses" and "arrogant capitalists."

At the sound of the gavel the crowd quieted. The committee chairman continued, listing more than a dozen demands, including legal recognition of labor unions and cooperatives, railroad regulation, and land reform. Muttering began anew as the man read number seventeen, requiring the Alliance president to press these demands on the state and national legislatures.

Cat clenched her fists in an agony of excitement. At last someone was trying to do something about the problems of the poor people. If only the delegates could agree, they could band together and make it work. The Alliance boasted seventy thousand members in Texas, enough voters that the government would have to pay attention.

"Mr. President!" Voices called from around the room, each shouting louder than the one before. Cat struggled to follow the debate, finally gathering that the committee had chosen to address the grievances with demands because requests made to the legislature in the past had been ignored. The argument raged on around Cat until she grew dizzy from the heat and the press of bodies. At last the committee succeeded in calling for a vote over the protests of the conservatives. When the recording secretary called the roll of delegates, Cat shouted out a lusty "aye." In a tense moment the secretary announced the tally: The Texas State Farmers Alliance had adopted the committee's demands by a vote of ninety-two to seventy-nine.

The shouts of victory met with angry cries, and men and women sidled down the rows, seeking a way out. One old fellow stopped in front of Cat and shook his finger in her face. "Mark my words, young woman. Politics will be the downfall of the Alliance, just as it was of the Grange. It'll split the membership in two, and we'll all end up worse off than before."

Cat stared after him, her mouth open, then shook her head. He might be right, but they had to try.

Joe shaded his eyes from the noontime sun, his hands giving off the faint smell of leather. Yep, those were buzzards circling near the pasture where the herd grazed. He kneed the gelding into a gallop, hoping to find a dead jackrabbit or coyote or some such. Anything but one of Miz Macleod's cattle.

The wind dried his sweaty shirt, whipped his hair out of his face, and knocked his hat off his head. He let the John B. trail behind him, the bonnet string under his chin keeping it from blowing away altogether as he pressed his cheek against the gray's neck. If he wasn't so worried, he'd enjoy the freedom of skimming across the prairie at top speed. This must be what it was like to be an eagle, soaring above the ground.

He raced toward the carcass, following the birds of prey as they glided downward in a tighter and tighter spiral. Pulling up on the reins, he brought the horse to a standstill, scattering the scavengers in a flurry of long black wings. The buzzards settled nearby, their small yellow eyes fastened on him and their red necks gleaming in the harsh sunlight.

He shifted his eyes from the disgusting birds to their dinner, his belly twisting at the sight. A spring calf, or what was left of it. Dried reddish manure coated its tail and hind legs. He shaded his eyes and studied the backsides of the other cattle grazing nearby. More of the same. He knew what that meant. Just his luck when he'd only been there a month to have the herd come down with the red dysentery, and when the boss lady was gone, to boot. He only hoped she wouldn't blame him.

No, Miz Macleod wasn't that sort at all, and if she was here, she'd cure the dysentery if anybody could. He'd never forget how she sewed Pieter's foot darn near back onto his leg. He grabbed the coil of rope from his saddle and tied it around the dead animal's back legs, then wound the other end around his saddle horn. Might as well tow it back toward the barn as leave it for the buzzards. They'd make the other animals nervous, and he didn't need that. He'd have to get a shovel and dig a pit to bury it.

Swinging into the saddle, he kneed the gelding into a trot, then glanced behind at the sound of wings flapping. The buzzards rose like a black cloud, following him in high, lazy circles. He must look like the angel of death riding through all this dry prairie grass with such an escort. He just hoped Miz Macleod got back before he had to bury any more.

• • •

Heat radiated through the black broadcloth of Will's suit as Catriona rested her hands atop his shoulders, aware of the strong muscles beneath the cloth. She turned her eyes away as his hands clasped her waist and he lifted her from the buggy, setting her on her feet near the steps to the back porch. At last the uncomfortable ride was at an end. She only hoped he'd say his farewells and be off soon.

She smoothed her skirts and gave Effie a quick kiss and hug. Nodding a greeting to Molly, she gathered Betsy up in her arms, murmuring pleasantries about the trip and listening to the news of all that had gone on during her absence.

But her mind kept returning to Will. He stood to one side, hat in hand, his face as stony as it had remained during the long, silent drive.

She'd been so happy to see him as she stepped down onto the platform at the Arlington depot. And when he admitted how much he'd missed her, how much he needed her help, she was pleased. Even his embarrassing insistence on examining her at his office had flattered her. But when he asked her to promise she'd quit working for the Alliance and concentrate on working for him, at least until the bairn came, she told him it was no concern of his and she'd find her own way home.

She'd finally given in and let him drive her home, but they hadn't spoken two words each the whole way. She turned toward him, offering her hand. "Thank you again for the ride, Doctor."

He gave her a half-bow. "My pleasure, Miz Macleod."

Effie crinkled her brow, her face turning from one to the other. "Won't you come inside for a cup of coffee? I made it myself."

Damn the lass and her good manners! Still, she couldn't be inhospitable.

Will curled the brim of his black hat in his fingers. "No, I've patients waiting." His eyes sought Cat's.

She gritted her teeth and forced herself to smile. "Please, do come in, just for one cup." She gestured toward the kitchen door.

Will smiled. "Well, just for a few minutes."

With her free hand Cat lifted her skirts to clear the bottom step, but the sound of hoofbeats stopped her.

Effie ran up onto the porch and shaded her eyes against the bright sunlight. "It's Joe, riding fast. He must've seen your buggy."

The awkward pause lengthened as the horse and rider galloped closer. At last Joe reined in his mount in a swirl of dust and tipped his hat. "Boy, am I glad you're back, Miz Macleod. We've got trouble."

Cat stepped closer to look at the calf draped over Joe's saddle. "Aye, so I see." She smoothed the animal's rough coat with one hand. "Poor wee mite. How many more?"

Joe shrugged. "Maybe a dozen—maybe more."

A wave of fatigue rolled over Cat. "Go back out and drive the herd closer in. Cut out the affected calves and put them in the closest holding pen." As he wheeled and clattered away, she turned to her sister. "Effie, you fill the washtub with fresh water and get it boiling." Handing Betsy over, she smiled at Joe's sister. "Molly, you mind the bairn while I go to the stillroom for the herbs I need." A hand closed over her upper arm.

Concern clouded Will's gray-green eyes. "You've just had a long, hard journey. Let Joe handle it. You ought to rest, if not for your own sake, for the sake of the child you're carrying."

Clenching her jaw, she shook off his touch. "Aye, and I must do this for the sake of the child as well. You know the red dysentery could cut my herd in half. Joe's done all he knows how to." She shook her head. "No, this is my farm and my job. I'll take my ease when my work is done, and not before."

Will raked his auburn hair back from his forehead. "Well, I guess I could stay."

Cat snorted. "And do what? You've no more experience with sick cattle than Joe, or less." She drew herself up, and made her voice cool and polite. "I thank you for your kind offer, but we'll manage this ourselves."

Will's eyes blazed and his mouth tightened to a thin line, but he said nothing, just settled his hat on his head and climbed back into the buggy. But instead of clucking to the horse, he leaned back in the seat, propping his feet on the dash and crossing his arms over his broad chest.

Regret wrenched at her, and she cursed her sharp tongue. The last thing she'd wanted to do was argue with Will. But after a moment she sighed and rolled up her sleeves. Let him sit there, then. She'd worry about Will Bascom later. Right now she didn't have time.

She turned to Effie and Molly, who stood staring at her with their eyes wide. "Let's get to work, then."

Chapter 12

September 1886

Geordie leaned the pitchfork against the back of the wagon seat and jumped down from the flatbed. Rubbing his hands over his faded workpants first, he accepted the glass of lemonade from Molly. "Much obliged." The cool tart liquid eased his dry throat, and the honey-sweetness lingered on his tongue.

Joe vaulted down to take the other glass. "Thanks, sis."

As Molly wiped her hands on her apron, the slanting rays of the lowering sun turned her blond hair into a halo. She tilted her face up toward the loft. "Looks like you boys are almost finished here. Shall I bring your supper, or would you like to eat at the table for a change?"

Joe grunted, tipping the glass up to empty it, then wiped his mouth on his sleeve. "We'll be up directly we finish." His eyes met Geordie's, and his cheeks darkened. "That is, if it's all right with you."

Geordie shrugged. "Suits me." He savored the last swallow of lemonade, then handed the empty glass to Molly. "That was right good." A grin tugged at his mouth, but he turned away to hide it. She'd think he was loco if he didn't watch out. He clambered into the wagon and hefted the pitchfork, then stopped as a flash of pink caught his eye. The back of Molly's skirt flared from her slender waist, swaying with each graceful step she took toward the house. Clenching the wooden handle in his hands, he imagined caressing the smooth, rounded flesh beneath the yards of calico.

At the scraping of Joe's pitchfork against the wagon bed, Geordie jumped, then turned back to pitching hay. Except for the scraping and swishing of the two forks in the hay and the whining of mosquitoes, the barn fell silent. That was one of the things he liked about working with Joe. The man knew when to talk and when to keep quiet. He almost wished he had more time to spend on the farm, instead of riding home from the paper in the late afternoon and working until sundown. Especially with the sweet inducement of Molly's company.

But he loved the smell of the ink, the excitement of tracking down leads for a story, seeing his words in print. It didn't pay much, but Zeke was turning more and more of the reporting over to him. And someday he'd be able to make a difference in the world just the way the Edinburgh reporters rallied the people of Scotland behind the Crofters' Rebellion.

He sneezed at the hay dust and chaff tickling his nose, and he scratched at a fresh mosquito bite. Instead of the dry heat eliminating the pesty insects this year, they seemed to thrive in the sluggish streams and stagnant ponds. He wiped the sweat trickling into his eyes. It seemed hotter inside the barn than outside even at sunset and beneath the shingled roof.

Still, in spite of the discomfort, his body fell into the rhythm of the work, bending to scoop the dried grass onto the fork, then stretching up to send it high into the loft for winter fodder. But his mind returned again and again to the waking dream of Molly in his arms, all pink and white perfection, until the last golden forkful arced through the air into the sweltering darkness above.

He hung his fork on a nail in the rafters, then climbed over the back of the seat to drive the wagon outside. He knew Joe would climb the ladder and shift the hay to the back of the loft to make room for more. Cat insisted they lay up as much hay as they could get their hands on, just in case this winter was as bad as last. Joe didn't act overly impressed with the plan, but as usual, their foreman didn't offer any opinion. And Cat had been right about so many things, especially the way she treated the red dysentery, adding herbs to the calves' food. They'd lost only a few head.

Too bad his sister didn't handle her own affairs with as much wisdom. Any fool could see she loved Will and he loved her. But instead of owning up to it, they spent all their time arguing. If he ever got up the nerve to tell Molly how he felt about her, he'd never argue with her, no matter what.

After stabling the horse, Geordie wandered to the corner of the barn, where he could get a clear view of the entire farm. The wind dried the sweat on his body but did nothing to cool him. In the pasture the longhorns grazed the tough brown prairie grass, and the stubble in the shorn wheat fields glistened gold in the fierce sunlight. Clouds of white clung to the delicate stalks of the cotton plants. And the snap beans and other truck in the kitchen garden waited to be picked and preserved for winter. Fishing a bandanna from his back pocket, he wiped his face, then turned at the sound of the big barn doors swinging shut.

Joe dropped the bar in place and shaded his eyes with one hand, then waved and started toward the house.

Geordie hurried to catch up to him, falling into step on the dusty path. "Say, when are you planning on picking the rest of that cotton?"

"Next week." Although his voice was calm, the two words came from between tight lips.

Poor lad must be tired and hot. He'd been working all day, not just an hour or two. He shoved his hands into his trouser pockets. "So you plan to burn the stubble in the wheat fields or plow it under come spring?"

Joe slowed, then stopped and faced him. "I'll do whatever you and Miz Macleod say, just like I always do."

Geordie frowned. "Look, I just asked what you planned. I trust your judgment."

"Then why all the questions? Do you just not trust me, or do you think I'm stupid?" Joe's eyes glittered in the reddish light, and his face darkened.

"Now wait a minute." He placed his hand on the other man's forearm.

Joe shook it off. "Fire me if you want to, but this has been sticking in my craw since I started this job. Look around you." His hands swept out to encompass the land around them. "Folks all over are selling up and moving away because of the drouth. You got one of the best small farms in the county, plenty of water, healthy livestock—everything a man could want. And what do you do with it?" He crossed his arms over his chest. "You hire me to work it for you so's you can run off to town and play at being a newspaperman." With one rawboned hand, he swept his white-blond forelock off his face. "And then you and your sister hover over me like a heifer with her first calf." His hands dropped to his sides, and his jaw worked. "If you don't trust me to run the place, just say so, and I'll leave so's you can get somebody better."

He opened his mouth, then closed it and licked his lips. "I *do* trust you, Joe. I was, uh, just trying to help out. You know, keep an eye on things?" He shrugged. "I wasn't trying to crowd you."

Joe pressed thumb and forefinger against the bridge of his nose. "Look, I'm sorry. It's just—are you sure you'd rather work in town?"

Geordie held up his hands in surrender. "I'm sure. The job is yours for as long as you want it. I only wish we could pay you a real wage."

"Naw, don't worry about that." He flipped the thought away with one hand. "My ma's tickled with the food and milk we bring home." Joe started up the path again, then stopped. "I'm beholden to you, but I still can't fathom why you don't want to run the place yourself." With a shrug he turned and trudged on.

He stood for a moment, then followed Joe up the path, trying to think of a way to explain. The place wasn't really his, and never would be; it belonged to Cat, and to her children. Besides, he wasn't a farmer. He was a reporter, and a damn good one. And someday he'd be the best. Maybe then he could go to Molly's father—

Up ahead, the screen door squeaked open, then banged shut. Molly stood on the porch with Betsy straddling one hip, the last rays of the sun outlining their two blond heads like twin beacons.

As he stopped in the path and raised his hand to wave, Joe's words came back to him. *Everything a man could want.* If only he could offer her what she deserved.

Cat looked up at the sound of boot heels on the stairway. "Did you find him?"

Geordie stood panting in the open doorway. "Aye. He's right behind me in the buggy. How is she?" His fingers crab-walked the edges of his hat brim, and his shoulders heaved with each breath.

"The same." She wrung cool water from a damp cloth, then laid it over Molly's forehead. "Sometimes I wish we'd get those newfangled telephones like they have in Dallas. Especially with all the sickness. Did Joe get back from telling his mother?"

"Not yet." He stepped closer, his dark hair falling forward as he bent over the sick girl. "What do you think is wrong with her?"

Cat sighed as she squeezed the water from another cloth and sponged at the lass's arms. "A fever of some kind. More than likely, the same as the others." She studied his profile, surprised by the depth of his concern. "There's nought more you can do, lad. Best get yourself back to town. We can manage without you better than Mr. Timmerman."

He opened his mouth, then closed it and nodded. Without another word he left the room, his boot heels echoing down the hall.

Effie sidled through the doorway and hovered near the shuttered window. "Is the doctor coming?"

Cat nodded. "Aye. Where's Betsy?"

"Sleeping." Her slim hand smoothed the golden curls fanned out across the pillow. "Will she be all right, Cat?"

"That I canna say, but we'll do our best by her." She lifted the cloth from the lass's forehead and bent close to the flushed face. "Molly." She tapped the soft cheek. "Can you hear me, lass?"

Pale blue eyes fluttered open. "Stephen?"

Effie gasped and her cheeks crimsoned.

"And who might this Stephen be, then?" Cat kept her voice light, unwilling to force her sister to betray a confidence. "A lad from school?"

After chewing her lip for a moment, Effie turned her eyes to the window, running her finger back and forth on the sill. "I don't know his last name."

Molly's cracked lips curved into a smile, and a few nonsense words tumbled out.

Still keeping her tone easy, Cat placed a fresh cloth on the girl's fevered brow. "What else?"

Effie faced the window, eyes downcast. "She won't tell me anything."

It was hard to believe; those two confided everything to each other. But it was just as hard to believe her sister would lie, even out of loyalty. "I *ken.*" She wrung water from another cloth. "Handsome, is he, then?"

Effie shrugged. "I've never seen him." She turned her green eyes toward Cat at last. "I'm so afraid she'll get hurt. You won't tell her mama?"

Cat shook her head. Tell Hilda Vanzee her delirious daughter called out for some mysterious stranger? Not likely. The woman was difficult enough. "Her secret is safe with me." In some ways it was just as well Molly had decided to spend the night with Effie. Who knew how her mother might have reacted had she fallen ill in her own bed? She only hoped the lass knew what she was about.

A giggle rose from the bed. "Of course I love you, Stephen." Then her voice trailed off. A sob from the corner drew Cat's gaze to Effie's tear-stained face.

"Dinna *greit*, lassie. I'll do my best." She handed a dry cloth to her sister. "Now wipe your eyes and get yourself to the kitchen and start some breakfast for Joe. He'll be back anytime now, and the doctor might be grateful for a bite as well. Off you go."

Wiping her eyes, the lass nodded and rushed from the room, her footsteps muffled by another slow, familiar tread in the hall.

Cat smoothed her apron across the small dome of her belly and stepped to the doorway to greet Will. Relief eased her taut muscles as she smiled a greeting. At least the strain of their disagreement about the Alliance had dissolved in the forced closeness of their work.

Sunlight from the open doorway hid his face and outlined his body, emphasizing his drooping shoulders and heavy steps. He must have come right from a full night of house calls, and she knew he hadn't a moment's rest the day before. It was all the two of them could do to keep up with the regular patients most days. And now with this fever—tenderness and respect for this man overwhelmed her for a moment.

Reaching the end of the hall, he turned toward her, and light spilled over his smiling mouth and darkened the shadows beneath his red-rimmed eyes. "So, Doctor, what's your diagnosis?" His teasing tone couldn't disguise the fatigue roughening his voice.

Any other time she'd have risen to his challenge with a *canny* phrase, but concern for both the doctor and the patient sobered her. "The same fever, if I'm no mistaken." She took his hat and helped him from the long cotton duster, both covered with grit from the dry roads.

He sighed and stepped toward the bed. "At least we think we know what it is. A doctor from Galveston calls it dengue. Folks around here call it breakbone. It's prevalent in the tropics, but he's never seen it this far north of the Gulf Coast. We've got cases springing up every day. Must be the bad air from all the stagnant water around." Rolling up his sleeves, he rinsed his hands in the basin of water.

Cat held out a dry flour-sack towel. "Then how does he say to treat it?"

Will took the cloth, rubbing his hands and wrists, then dropping it on the table. "Treat the symptoms, keep them comfortable. Most of the patients will get a rash on the fourth day and reach crisis on the fifth." He pressed his palm to Molly's forehead, then bent and placed an ear against her chest.

The lass tossed her head, loosing a string of babble that trailed off to a whimper. Her eyes opened, and her face twisted in agony. "My arms, my knees. It hurts. Somebody please make it stop."

Will smoothed Molly's damp hair from her face. "Hush now. You'll be better soon."

The tenderness in his voice touched Cat. Sometimes he'd seemed so distant, as if his patients' pain didn't touch him. Or perhaps that's how she wished to see him, so she could deny her feelings as well. Her fingers twitched with a desire to stroke his face, smooth out the tired lines in his forehead.

When Will straightened up, compassion etched his handsome features. He opened his black leather satchel and rummaged inside. "I just hope my supply of laudanum holds out." He stopped and faced her, his eyes locking on hers. "All we can do is let the disease run its course." His voice held a hollow note. "And pray this outbreak doesn't grow into an epidemic."

Chapter 13

October 1886

Catriona cradled her middle as she squatted in the tall buffalo grass to dig the snakeroot. She turned to Will's grandmother. "Mrs. Bascom, I wish I'd asked you about healing herbs earlier in the year, when everything was in bloom. It would be so much easier if we could see the color of the flowers." Inside her belly the bairn rolled from one side to the other like a ship in a storm. Getting up and down would have been easier in the spring as well.

As the old woman sank to her knees, she leaned her weight on Cat's shoulder. "Thee may call me Nana, as William does. The medicine is said to be stronger if it's gathered in the autumn." She patted Cat's shoulder. "Thee'll see, there are plenty of herbs close by."

Cat smiled as she prodded with her digging stick to loosen the dirt around the base of the plant. She liked Will's grandmother, and the older woman's knowledge of native plant lore was invaluable, especially with Will's supply of regular medicines dwindling. Worming her hand into the tangle of threadlike grass roots, she traced the finger-thick tuber several inches into the rich black soil. Even under the layer of sod the earth was warm and dry to the touch after so many months without rain.

She curled her fingers around the slippery root and

rocked back on her heels, using her weight to lift the plant from its anchor beneath the ground. With a snap the root yielded, and Catriona threw her free hand behind her to keep from falling.

"Thee has done well. This will relieve fever, pain, and many other complaints." Nana took the treasure, twisting loose the tough, dry stem and tossing it aside before she set the snakelike root in the basket.

At least the plant lived up to its name. She only hoped it lived up to its reputation; Will's store of laudanum was almost gone. She struggled to lever herself up, then bent to lift Nana to her feet as well.

The old woman swayed, the breath rasping in her throat a moment before her hooded eyes sought Cat's. "It is good thee has decided to help my William. He needs thee." Releasing her hold, the woman turned away, her frail body gliding over the rugged ground. "Come. I saw more snakeroot over this way."

Cat dusted her palms together, wondering what Will might have said about her to his grandmother. She caught the handle of the basket in one hand and the digging stick in the other, and followed the old woman across the open pasture.

Effie tugged the book out of the glare of the noonday sun and into the shade thrown by her sunbonnet, then shifted on the hard wagon seat. She wrinkled her nose as the horse lifted his tail right in front of her and dropped a mess into the dusty street. Embarrassed, she looked around to see if anyone had noticed, then pressed her nostrils together with thumb and forefinger and shrugged. After all, no one in town seemed to pay any mind to such things. People dumped everything into the streets, including what was in their chamber pots. She knew by tomorrow morning no one would be able to tell what Dobbin had done the day before. After all, the streets were full of horses who did their business wherever they happened to be. The farm smells were fresh by comparison.

Still, she wished Cat would hurry up, even if Madame

Yvette did have three cases of breakbone fever upstairs at the Bon Chance. She glanced up at the gaudy front of the saloon and the tall windows of the second floor. A pale face disappeared behind the dark red drapes. Why would anyone up there be looking out at her? For a moment she wondered just what went on up there, what kind of women lived in such a place.

But all she was really interested in was getting home and talking to Molly, and maybe even saying a few words to Joe. Not that he ever said much in return, or even acted like he heard her. Someday—

She sighed. At least, with the fever going around, Cat had left Betsy at home with Molly when they came in to get supplies. Much as she loved her baby niece, it was good to get away from her once in a while. In fact, it would have been a nice trip if Doc hadn't sent them over here so he could drive out to some farm clear the other direction. Darn this fever anyhow. But at least they were nice to each other again now. She'd never fight with Joe like that, she was sure. Her life would be just like this girl Pamela in the novel she was reading. After lots of romance, she'd settle down and have a nice family with Joe. She turned back to the book nestled on her lap. Until then she knew she'd go crazy if she didn't have her books to read.

"Effie!" Cat's voice startled her.

She tipped her head back, squinting in the bright sunlight. "Aye?"

"Bring me more snakeroot. It's in the cloth bag under the seat. Come up the back stairs." The window rattled closed.

"But—" Go up there? By herself? She slammed her book closed on the wooden seat. Why did things like this happen to her anyhow? Twisting in the seat, she dug underneath until her hand grazed the rough cloth of the herb bag stashed there. She tugged it up and slung it over her shoulder, then clambered down over the wheel and onto the wooden plank sidewalk, stepping around a gob of spit as she headed for the alley between the saloon and the hardware store.

Effie hurried along the narrow canyon between brick

walls, shivering in the sudden chill and almost blinded by the deep shade. Her stomach churned at the stench of rotting food and worse. At least in the streets the sun and wind dried things out and blew the worst smells away.

She paused at the foot of the rickety wooden stairs and chewed her bottom lip. Paint peeled from the warped siding, and dark mold crept up the posts from the damp ground.

A pale face surrounded by stringy dark hair appeared in the doorway to the second floor. "You Effie?" Could this be the same face she glimpsed from out front?

Effie swallowed and nodded.

A smile lit the face, making it almost pretty. The girl stepped onto the landing above. A young baby straddled her hip. "Ida. C'mon up. Miz Macleod's waiting."

Might as well get it over with. Effie scrambled up the stairs, the heavy bag bouncing against her back.

Ida gestured with her head. "Down this-a-way." She turned and walked through the door and headed down the hall.

Effie followed in silence, her eyes roving the velvet-covered walls. She'd never seen paintings of ladies in their altogether before. Wait till she told Molly. She frowned down at her own scrawny form, wondering if she'd ever look that round, then stopped just short of running into her guide. Better pay attention.

"Y'ever been in a whorehouse before?" Ida cocked her head, then kissed the top of the baby's fuzzy head.

Effie shook her head, then smiled at the baby, noticing for the first time how clean and plump the bairn looked.

"His name's Arthur. Wanna hold him?" Ida held the boy out toward her.

"Thanks. Is he yours?" Effie breathed in the sweet, clean baby smell and cuddled the plump body against her.

"Yup." Ida touched the tip of one finger to the child's button nose. "Isn't he something?"

"Lovely." She bit into her lip, wondering how a girl so young could already be a mother. Besides, she'd always thought sporting women were old and ugly. It chilled something deep inside to think of some old cowpuncher doing things to this girl. She forced the thought away. Best find out where Cat was. "Maybe we should get this stuff to my sister. She needs it bad, more than likely."

"Sure. Let me take that bag." Ida slipped the drawstring from Effie's shoulder and slung it over her own, then strode down the hall, her voice trailing behind her. "I just ain't in too much of a hurry, seeing as how it's for Melva Lee."

Effie followed, holding the baby tight in her arms. "Why's that? Don't you like her?"

Ida snorted. "Don't nobody *like* Melva Lee. But it ain't that. It's just, you know—justice—to see her hurting for once, after she's hurt so many other folks."

Effie walked in silence, unable to think of anything to say.

A moment later Ida stopped again and pointed to an open door. "She's in here." She stepped to the threshold and held out the cloth sack. "Here you be, Miz Macleod. Your sister's out here in the hall."

Cat's muffled voice thanked her, then a stream of swear words erupted from somewhere inside the room.

"Nice, ain't it? Real pretty and ladylike. That's just like Melva Lee—cussing at a person for trying to help her." Her mouth curling in disgust, Ida shrugged and turned toward Effie. Her eyes narrowed with interest. "I seen you in the wagon before, reading. You like books?"

Effie smiled. "Books are practically my life."

Little Arthur squawked, and Ida reached out to take him. "Huh. If that don't beat all. Miss Yvette, she's got shelves of them."

Catriona emerged from the room, closing the door behind her with a thud. Her arm went around Effie's shoulders. "Thank you, Ida, for all your help today."

"Anytime, Miz Macleod." Ida waggled the baby's hand. "Say good-bye, Arthur." Then she turned and was gone.

Catriona's eyes held a tinge of sadness as she smiled down at Effie and gave her shoulders a squeeze. "Now then, my brave lassie, let's get you home."

The clean smell of sawdust mixed with the tang of sweat in the hot, dry air. Resting the water jug against one hip, Cat stopped beneath a lone tree and wiped her forehead with the back of her free hand. Voices rose above the ringing of hammers and axes and the humming rasp of saws, shouting directions and requests with good humor.

She enjoyed working with other folks for a common goal, and it was a good chance to visit with neighbors. Barn raisings and threshing parties always reminded her of work parties at Balmeanach. Sadness still welled up in her whenever she thought of Skye, but she knew she could never go home. No, Scotland wasn't home anymore; Texas was her home now, and her children's home as well.

She smoothed one hand over her bulging belly. She'd caught some disapproving looks from some of the other women, and she knew many of them would have stayed home in this condition. But her work didn't end because she carried Ian's child in her belly, so why should she deny herself a bit of fun?

Slinging the jug over her shoulder once more, Cat headed toward the men hewing the rooftree. The sun was hot for October, and working so hard, the men would be parched.

Sunlight glistened on bare arms and chests, and sweat matted and darkened the men's hair. She didn't recognize any of them, but the one with his back to her looked familiar somehow. She stopped a safe distance away as he swung the ax with precision, chipping out a smooth notch.

"All right, water!" One of the men took the heavy jug from her and tipped it up to his lips with both hands to drink deep, then splashed some over his head and face before handing it on.

The man with the ax set it aside and turned gray-green eyes toward her.

With a start she recognized Will. No wonder he looked familiar, but she'd never noticed he had such wide shoulders or such powerful arms. Men did look different without their clothes. A tingling deep in her belly surprised her and brought a wave of heat to her face.

He scowled at her, wiping his face on a red kerchief as he strode toward her. "Catriona, what in the world are you doing here?" He pitched his voice beneath the playful laughter and teasing of the other men.

She smiled up at him, determined not to argue and spoil the day. "Dinna scold me, Will Bascom. I canna stand to be idle while others are working."

His expression softened, but concern still edged his voice. "But that jug is too heavy for you to be hauling around in the sun. Do you want to bring on early labor?"

She sighed, then shook her head. Nice as it might be to have it over with and hold her bairn in her arms, she knew children born too soon often sickened and died. She couldn't bear to lose this bairn, this last symbol of Ian's love.

One of the men jostled in front of Will and handed the jug back to Cat with mumbled thanks.

She laughed, hoisting it with one hand. "It's no great weight now the water's gone."

Will reached out and took the empty jug from her hand. "I'll carry it as far as the creek, and then you'll sit in the shade and rest a bit."

Cat rolled her eyes in pretended despair. "Aye, Doctor, whatever you say."

This time he laughed with her. "I deserve a break anyhow. Especially since these greedy-guts didn't leave me a drop." He turned to the men as he shrugged on a blue chambray shirt. "Can you spare me a while, boys?"

Their good-natured hoots and catcalls echoed after Catriona as she followed him through the tall grass toward the line of trees marking the creek. She couldn't get over how different he looked today until she realized she'd never seen him wear anything but his black suit before. Somehow, dressed in work clothes, he seemed younger, more attractive.

She bit her lip as another wave of warmth surged through her. At least she could be grateful he couldn't hear her thoughts. She'd be mortified if he knew her feelings, especially since he couldn't return them. No man could be interested in a pregnant widow, a woman carrying another man's child. Whatever was the matter with her today, thinking such thoughts?

Shade dappled Will's shoulders as he reached the stand of willows. Pushing through the curtain of gray-green branches, he knelt on the bank, filling the jug, then lying flat to drink from the gurgling creek.

Cat settled downstream a bit and stripped off her shoes and stockings to ease her feet into the cool flow. They were lucky to find this much shade and clean water. She wondered if they'd ever see rain again.

Will sat up, wiping his mouth on his sleeve, and smiled at her. "I've been meaning to thank you for your help with the breakbone fever. You and Nana and your snakeroot really helped make a parcel of folks more comfortable." He plucked a tall blade of grass and tucked it in one corner of his mouth, then leaned back with his palms flat on the ground behind him. "It's good to see you here. Too many women stay home when they're with child, as if it's something to be ashamed of. I think a pregnant woman is one of nature's most beautiful creations."

Warmth rose in Cat's cheeks, and she turned to look downstream, her mind racing to find an answer, any answer at all. At last she faced Will again, unable to stand the silence any longer. "I—I couldna miss a barn raising. They remind me so of home."

Will brought his hands up and wrapped his arms around his knees, bringing his face closer to hers. "And just where is home?"

On safe ground again, Cat let her thoughts wander back across the wide Atlantic. "The Isle of Skye in the west of Scotland, in a wee village called Balmeanach. It was a hard life, but the people worked together, sang together. They made working a pleasure by sharing it with one another."

Will pulled the blade of grass from his lips and arced it like a small spear into the creek. "Why did you leave?"

Cat straightened her knees, holding her dripping feet above the rushing water. "Many reasons, really. Ian wanted to come home to Texas."

"So what kept you here after he died?"

Cat shot a quick look at him, but Will's face held a gentle question instead of an accusation. She wondered how much to tell him, what he would think if he knew the whole truth. But what could she gain by keeping such a secret? He was nothing more to her than a friend, after all. "I helped organize a rent strike against the laird, the man who owned all the land we farmed. When he found out, he offered to pay my passage if I'd leave Scotland and never return."

Will nodded. "Mighty considerate of him."

"Aye." The word sat sour on Cat's tongue.

His brow furrowed. "How come he didn't just send you to jail?"

"Even he couldna send his own bastard daughter to the gaol."

Will's eyes widened and he nodded again, but he didn't say anything else.

Cat pulled on her shoes and struggled to her feet. "We'd best take the water back. There are more thirsty men waiting." She reached for the full jug.

Will grabbed for the handle, then let it go and pulled himself up. "Reckon you're right. I'd best go see about that rooftree."

Disappointment weighed heavy in Cat's chest as she watched him walk away across the strip of prairie. So it did make a difference, even in America, even to a man like Will. If only she'd kept her own council. He need never have known, unless—but she realized now how impossible it was, that half-dream of being more to him than a friend's widow, an assistant in his medical practice. Setting her jaw, she slung the heavy jug over her shoulder and started back through the tall grass.

She'd no time for such nonsense in her life now.

Chapter 14

Catriona paused in the doorway of Frink's general store to let her eyes adjust to the dim interior after the brightness of the noonday sun outside. Competing smells engulfed her—molasses, tobacco, kerosene, coffee. All the things folks couldn't grow or make for themselves. She seldom came into town anymore, especially in her condition, but she couldn't put it off much longer.

O. K. Frink hurried forward from the bowels of the store, a green apron tied around his narrow waist. "Why, Miz Macleod, what a downright pleasure to see you. I don't believe you've been in since last July." His thin lips curved up at the ends, but the smile never reached his eyes. "What can I get you?"

Cat pulled a list from her reticule and ticked off each item.

Frink piled the bags and jars on the counter, moving with surprising speed among the crowded shelves. "Anything else?" He blinked his small eyes, and the tip of his tongue swiped at his thin lips.

Cat folded the list and pushed it into her drawstring bag. "No, that's it. What do I owe you, then?"

He pulled a stub of a pencil from behind his ear and

scratched at a slip of paper. "That'll be seven dollars and fifty-five cents." He shoved the slip toward her.

She glanced down, then looked into his eyes. "There must be some mistake. Those are time prices." She pulled folded greenbacks from her bag. "I pay in cash, as always."

He licked his lips and stared at the paper without a word.

Cat tapped her foot on the wooden flooring. "I can always cross the street and get my things from Mr. Ditto." She turned toward the door. "Good day to you, then." She flung the words over her shoulder.

"Wait."

She turned back. "Aye?"

Sweat peppered his high forehead. "You're right. I don't know what I was thinking of." His fingers flew over the scrap of paper. "That's two dollars and fifty-five cents."

She peeled three one-dollar bills from the folding money and laid it on the counter, then held out her hand.

He counted silver into her palm, then his fingers closed around hers. "Miz Macleod, I worry about you, a woman alone and in your condition, especially with all the ill feelings about this Alliance business."

She jerked her wrist from his sweaty grasp. "You've no need to concern yourself on my account, Mr. Frink." She gathered up her purchases, fitting them into her string bag.

His small eyes glistened and he licked his lips. "Still and all, any time you want to sell your land or put a lien on next year's crop, I'm your man. It don't hurt none to remember who your friends are."

She turned away, letting irony edge her voice. "Aye, I'll keep that in mind."

Geordie had never seen so many people in one place before in his life, all in their fanciest clothes. At least the heat hadn't drenched them in sweat and dust yet. His stomach growled as he breathed in the smells of fried chicken and corn on the cob from a nearby food booth. Must be near noon. He squinted at the sun, then stopped to pull his pocket watch from his waistcoat.

Voices eddied around him as he replaced the timepiece

and threaded his way through the crowd toward the main gate. So far, the first day of the first Dallas State Fair looked to be a success, in spite of the governor's opening address. Nothing but political hot air—enough to fill Professor Brayton's balloon. He'd have to make sure he didn't miss the first ascension, with the man swinging beneath the big air bag on a trapeze. Maybe he could even get an interview with the man. Imagine crossing the English Channel and the Indian Ocean in midair, and now the man was here in Texas.

He checked his pocket for his notebook and lead pencil. He'd need them to write the stories Zeke wanted. Fingering his press pass, he marveled again at his good luck. It must be the Dallas papers picking up his article about the dengue fever. That and the alternate Alliance charter were his biggest stories so far. And now, for the next seven days, it was his job to see and do everything the fair offered, then ride back to Arlington in the evenings and write it up.

Of course, some of it was bound to be boring, reporting all the premiums and who won them, but think of all the exciting things he could write up as well. And today he could share it with Molly. A tingle warmed his middle at the thought. They had to find a way to persuade her parents to let them go off for a while, even if they had to have Joe and Effie along.

He slid the schedule from his pocket as he walked, wondering if she'd want to see the Indian dancers. He hoped she wouldn't be interested in the judging of the jams and jellies later in the afternoon. The names of the winners would be posted, and he could copy them down later for the article. As he sidestepped a family with a picnic basket, the wind picked up, carrying a hint of manure from the barns. Maybe they should wander through the stock exhibit instead. After the high-stakes trotting stallions, they'd have to decide between the baseball game and the bicyclists.

And he did want to show her the view from the observatory in the Exposition Building before the sun went down. From there a body could see the countryside for thirty miles in any direction. He was glad she hadn't been with him the first time. He must have looked like a hayseed, walking around, gawking at the size of the place. Well, he'd let her choose; today was her day, and anything she wanted was fine with him.

At the gate he hung back, brushing his suit and smoothing his hair. He pulled himself back to a slow walk as he avoided the incoming tide of fairgoers. It wouldn't do to appear too eager. Standing behind one of the ticket-takers, he glanced at his pocket watch, then rocked back on his heels. If only he could make himself as calm as he hoped he looked.

A girl with long blond hair appeared for a moment in the midst of the throng. He craned his neck, suddenly afraid she wouldn't see him and pass on by. He caught sight of the golden curls again, but the face was not Molly's. Heat crept up his neck to his cheeks and he clenched his fists. *Try not to make a fool of yourself, man.*

A hand gripped his shoulder, and he turned, ready to fight.

Joe grinned at him. "Nothing like sneaking up on you in a crowd."

He forced a laugh and shoved his hands in his pockets. "About time you showed up. Where's everybody else?" His eyes scanned the crowd for Molly.

Effie peered around Joe's shoulder, her green eyes glinting and a smile twitching her lips. "I thought you were going to punch him, for a minute." She turned and glanced over her shoulder. "I do wish the others would hurry."

Joe put one hand on Effie's shoulder and cuffed Geordie's arm with the other. "You two stay put. I'll go see what's holding them up."

As soon as he was out of earshot, Geordie turned to Effie. "Where's Molly? Why isn't she with you?"

Her brow furrowed. "She told her mama she felt poorly and wanted to stay home, but don't worry. You and I and Joe will have a great time." Her fingers smoothed his lapels, as gentle as her voice. "Now, I don't want you to act like somebody shot your dog. Have a little pride."

As the meaning of her words sank in, disappointment weighted his chest like a stone. His throat tightened and he clenched his jaw. There must be some way he could salvage something from this day. If only he didn't have to work; he didn't give a fig for the fair without Molly to share it with him.

Effie's eyes caught his, and she dropped her voice. "And don't even think about going to see her. It'd just get you both in trouble."

"Mind your own business, baby sister." He brushed her hands from the front of his coat and turned to watch Joe emerge from the crowd, a huge basket over his arm. Following behind him came his mother and father and the other children. And behind them he caught sight of Cat's dark curls and Betsy's light ones.

Just how much of an idiot did Effie think he was? He knew how improper it would be for a young man to spend time alone with an unmarried girl. And he would never do anything to compromise Molly's virtue.

Chapter 15

December 1886

Catriona pulled the oven door down and bent to peer at the traditional Scottish Christmas pastries. The rich smell of dried fruits and nuts surrounded her as she tapped the pastry crusts of the "black buns." Using a dishtowel for a hot pad, she pulled the flat pan from the oven. The golden half-moons bubbled with dark juices as she set them aside to cool and closed the cookstove door.

As she straightened, a deep ache began low in her back, spreading like an iron band around her huge belly. She breathed out through her nose and glanced at the clock. Still ten minutes apart. After two weeks she was sick of false labor. She hadn't had any with Betsy, but it wasn't uncommon with a second bairn. Or it could mean the beginning of a difficult birth. She pushed the thought away. The child wasn't due for another week, and she'd had no bloody show. This would likely subside, as it had before. Until her waters broke, she refused to believe she was in labor at all. Not that she wouldn't give anything to be done with carrying this bairn, to hold him in her arms at last. But there was certainly no reason to spoil Christmas dinner with worry.

She lifted the lid from the heavy skillet and tested the frying chicken with a fork, savoring the rich odor as the grease sizzled and popped. It was a good mixture of holiday dishes, some Scottish and some Texan—the best of both. It wouldn't be long now until they could all sit down around the table together.

Nana Bascom's voice sounded at her elbow. "Time to check the sweet potato pudding, if thee might kindly open the door?" The spicy-sweet smell of cinnamon and vanilla rose from the grated yellow-orange mess in the heavy iron skillet. An unlikely sweet, but one she'd come to enjoy.

Cat couldn't help but smile as she did what the old woman asked. She was glad she'd invited Will and his grandmother to join the family. It could have been a bleak holiday, but it was easier somehow with guests to entertain. And she knew they'd have been alone, just the two of them, the only ones still alive of their family.

A squeal of laughter punctuated the low rumble of men's voices coming from the parlor. Betsy must be entertaining the grown-ups with her antics again, making her new rag doll dance. So sweet of Nana to spend her time sewing the wee clothes and to crochet a soft new shawl for Cat. To say nothing of the watch chain for Geordie and the hair combs for Effie. She chewed her lip, wishing she could have given store bought gifts this year. But they were lucky to have food to put on the table.

Not all her neighbors were so lucky. She wished she'd had more to spare for the gift baskets the churches delivered to the poor. She could understand when some people refused the gifts out of pride, but if her bairns were crying from cold and hunger— But they weren't, thanks to the windmills and a full hayloft. Thanks to Ian. God, how she missed him still, especially today.

She sighed. At last this year was almost over, and with it all the hardships. It had started with blizzards and starving cattle and was ending with drought and failed crops. And in between lay murder and epidemic. The coming year had to prove happier for them all.

She turned her thoughts away, lifting the top from the butter crock and measuring out enough for a batch of shortbread. As she set the wooden paddle aside, another pain gripped her belly. She gasped, then bit her lip. Her eyes sought the face of the clock. Seven minutes. Still, it might mean nothing. One day they'd gotten down to three minutes apart, then stopped. The band around her middle loosened, and she reached for the wooden circle to cover the butter crock again.

The oven door clanged shut and a sizzling skillet settled on the highboy beside her, its heat radiating out to warm her skin. Nana's gnarled hand covered hers. "Thee is in labor?" Gentleness lit her blue-green eyes, and all the lines in her face turned down in sympathy.

Cat shook her head. "I dinna think so." She kept her voice light. "Only false pains, and not the first of those."

"And has thee told thy doctor?" Nana's lips pursed, and she cocked her head to one side.

"There's naught to tell just yet." She covered the butter and set it inside the cupboard. "Dinner's ready. Shall we call everyone to the table?"

Nana's heavy eyelids narrowed, but she nodded. "As thee wishes." The old woman turned to the stove, lifting fried chicken onto a platter.

Cat waddled through the door and steadied herself against the wall for a moment, breathing in the chill air of the stairwell, suddenly so tired she could barely move. Once they got dinner out of the way, she would sit down for the rest of the afternoon. She only hoped the Vanzees would change their minds about stopping by on their way home from church. She sighed. Even if they did stop, she could just let Effie and Nana act as hostesses.

Inside her belly, a pair of heels drummed a tattoo far to one side. She frowned. His feet should be under her rib cage by now and his head pointing straight down. She shrugged. There was still plenty of time for him to turn. A shiver wreathed her shoulders and she trudged to the parlor door.

Betsy ran to her, pressing her wee face into the folds of her skirt, shrieking with laughter as she clasped her arms around Cat's knees. "Mama, Mama."

She reached a hand down to tousle the shiny blond curls. "Come, lassie, everyone." She caught her daughter's wee hand. "Time for dinner."

She followed the others toward the kitchen, stopping

outside the doorway as another pain gripped her. When it eased, she forced a smile onto her face and took her seat.

From Ian's place at the head of the table, Will smiled at her over the steaming dishes. As the conversation eddied around her, she toyed with bits of food on her plate, unable to eat. Memories of the year before haunted her. Ian holding his daughter in his arms, his eyes shining with pride and love as he looked at her, talking of his dreams for the family, for the years to come. How could she sit here, surrounded by loved ones, while he lay alone in the ground out under the post oak?

The faces around her smiled and talked of the cotton crop and when the drought might end. At last Will stood and lifted his glass filled with homemade loganberry wine. "To friends and family, those here and those who've gone before." His eyes locked on Cat's.

He understood, almost as if he read her mind. Of course, he must miss Ian as well. How could she be so selfish to forget that others besides her had loved her husband? She levered herself up from her chair and lifted her glass.

A sharp cramp started low in her belly and spread upward like a girdle of fire. The glass dropped from her fingers, its dark liquid pooling on the polished wood. As the pain increased, she rested the palms of her hands flat on the tabletop. Something tight burst between her legs, and warmth cascaded down her thighs, staining her skirts and covering her feet with pinkish water.

Something cool and damp pressed itself against her forehead. Catriona forced her eyes open, blinking in the bright light of the kerosene lamp. Its faint oily smell blended with the familiar fresh-earth odor of birthing.

Will's face swam above her. His lips curved in a gentle smile, but his eyes narrowed with concern. "Catriona, I've got to try to turn the baby again right after the next pain. It may hurt." His smile faded, and he placed his hands on either side of her face. "Do you understand?"

She tried to lift her hand to touch his cheek, to ease his worry, but her hand weighed too much. "Aye." She licked at her dry lips. "Dinna *fash* yourself, laddie." Her eyelids closed themselves, and she floated for a moment, for eternity.

And then the pain began again in the small of her back. Her eyes opened. She waited for it to build, taking shallow sips of air through her mouth, her eyes fastened on the hands of the clock. The small hand pointed at the Roman numeral two, and the long hand clicked once, twice before the pressure ebbed away and was gone. She'd thought Betsy's birth so difficult alone here with Ian, and both of them scared to death. But those memories seemed like a lazy summer's day by comparison.

Will stood over her again, smearing his hands with something yellow. Butter. She'd used it herself to prevent infection during delivery. But what was he doing here? Where was Ian? Memory returned in a painful flood. Ian was gone, dead. And Will was trying to turn the baby. Yes, he'd tried before, but the womb hadn't been open enough.

He leaned forward, placing one hand on the counterpane beside her. This time a different kind of pain entered her, the steady pressure of his hand moving up the birth canal. The few times she'd been forced to do this to other women, she'd never guessed how much it hurt. *Please let him be quick about it.* A moan escaped her. Will turned his eyes away from her face, and she bit into her lower lip to keep herself silent. Why make it any harder for him?

With his free hand he pressed into the huge dome of her belly, his fingers molding her flesh. At last his hand settled in one spot. He must have found the bairn's head. Pulling with a steady pressure against his other hand, he brought his forearm down across her belly. Slowly, the child within her shifted, an inch, two. Will smiled down at her, beads of sweat dotting his forehead.

Then the belt of pain tightened around her once more. She drew in a deep breath and closed her eyes, letting the agony carry her to the pinnacle and down the other side. As the pain relinquished its hold at last, a great weariness spread through her body. She would never survive; she was too exhausted even to raise her voice above a whisper. "Let us go, Will. Let Ian call us home."

A hand clamped under her chin. "Look at me." She

opened her eyes, shocked at the harsh tone. She'd never heard him speak to anyone that way before. "How dare you quit on me?" Will's face contorted, tears threatening to spill from his eyes. "You can't give up. I won't let you. Do you understand?" Beneath the command lay a plea.

She found herself nodding, her chin still cupped in his hand.

His grip loosened, and he lay his arm against her belly once more.

Forcing herself to relax, she bit her lip against the strangeness of the sensation. As the pressure increased, her belly swelled away from the onslaught of Will's arm, rising to a point on one side. Like a wave pulling back and curling over itself onto a rocky shore, the bulk inside her rotated, settling far down between her legs. Even before Will lifted his arm, another pain captured her.

As it subsided, Will withdrew his hand, wiping the shiny gore on a towel before he patted her shoulder. "You did just fine. The baby's head is down. With the next pain you can push." His gentle words matched the tremor of a smile touching his lips. Then his brows drew together. "Catriona, about what I said—"

She held up one hand. "You dinna need to say it, laddie. You were right."

He turned his face away. "But I—"

She drew in a sharp breath as a new pain encircled her, even stronger than the one before. His words hung forgotten in the air as she struggled up, propping herself on her elbows, giving in to the undeniable need to bear down. As it ebbed, she flopped back onto the pillows.

She closed her eyes, sliding away into the welcoming darkness. Too soon she had to struggle up again, pushing with all her might before she slipped into the brief, quiet space between. Twice, three times her body commanded her, then released her.

Will's voice filtered through her weariness. "The head is out. Just one more."

Closing her eyes tight, Catriona pulled herself upright and gave a final push, then fell back, panting, onto the bed. From a distance came a faint mewling cry. The bairn, at last.

She lifted her head from the pillows, her weariness suddenly gone.

Will smiled down at her, the corners of his gray-green eyes crinkling. "A boy!" With gentle movements he held up the wee body for her to see, then curled the bairn onto her bare middle and covered them both with a blanket.

Cat reached down, resting her hands on the small back, the warmth of the damp body radiating through the coverlet. She caressed the black hair plastered to his crown. "Hullo, laddie."

A wee red face turned toward her, and a pair of dark eyes fastened on her face. After a moment the bairn blinked, then his face screwed up in a yawn.

Heat spread across the skin of Cat's belly and down her sides. It took her a moment to realize what had happened, but then laughter bubbled up inside her. "So, lad, you'd christen your mum before she can christen you."

Will's gentle voice sobered her. "Catriona, you have to push once more for the afterbirth." He smiled down at her. "Can you do it?"

She squinted her eyes and focused on the lax muscles. One last push.

After a moment he spoke again. "Whoa! You were very brave. And you have a fine son."

Son. The word echoed through her mind. A son—Ian's son, no longer nestled safe beneath her ribs. Now he was separate, his own person. Her last physical link with Ian was broken. She had lost him forever. Black grief welled up in her, and the tears began to flow as she whispered his name.

Will leaned back against the tufted upholstery of the seat, searching for a comfortable position for his aching back. The black leather of the buggy's top gave off a tealike odor in the cool, dry predawn air. Even now in the midst of winter, not so much as a drop of morning dew moistened the land. How much longer until this dry spell ended?

Switching the reins to his right hand, he reached across and tucked the carriage robe around Nana. Still, at least it wasn't cold and wet or frozen. This was bad enough. No telling how this long night would affect her, but he couldn't have left Catriona in labor even long enough to take his frail old grandmother home. And the stubborn old woman refused to let Geordie drive her.

He smiled. Nana would give him a tongue-lashing if she even heard him call her old or frail. She might think she was invulnerable, but he knew better. He'd lost too many elderly folks to pneumonia and influenza during the blizzards a year before. Well, at least he could keep her warm and dry, and she was getting a little rest now on the long drive home.

If only he could rest. The gelding knew the way without any coaxing, probably eager for its own stall and a pail of oats. But every time Will closed his eyes, he relived the terror of those few minutes when he saw Catriona slipping away from him.

Somehow, after the barn raising, he'd thought she was strong enough to face anything. Imagine, a woman leading a rebellion against her own father. What she must have gone through as a child, and then being forced to leave her home and start again in a new land. He'd been so humbled by her bravery, he couldn't think what to say, couldn't keep himself from admitting how he felt about her, so he'd taken the coward's way and said nothing.

And then today he'd realized how fragile her strength was, how close she came to just giving up. Her voice rang again in his mind. *Let me go.* How could he explain to her the effect of those words on him?

It wasn't just the concern of a doctor trying to save the life of a patient. He knew now, if he was honest with himself. He could no more have let her go than he could will himself to stop breathing. He didn't do any of it for her. It was for himself, because he couldn't face the thought of a world without her.

And she still grieved for her dead husband. Now he'd have to face her, and after the way he'd treated her, he wouldn't blame her if she never wanted to see him again. But he needed to see her, to be with her. He only hoped she'd forget everything in the excitement of her new son. A boy. Ian would be so proud. Dropping the reins, he rubbed his face with both hands.

A gentle hand squeezed his elbow. Nana's paper-dry voice whispered into the chill wind. "Does thee wish to talk about it?"

He glanced at her wrinkled face, dim in the gray light of false dawn. "I almost lost her, Nana. And the baby."

The grayed head bobbed in agreement. "But thee didn't."

The silence between them hung heavy with her unspoken question. At last he forced the words from his aching throat. "I—I think I'm falling in love with her."

"Good. She is a fine woman, a good match for thee, William."

Words leapt from his mouth, forced out by fear and longing. "She still loves her husband's memory." He choked on the thought. "He was my friend."

She squeezed his arm again, then patted his hand. "I know it is difficult now. But if thee is patient, it will all come around right." The clopping of the horse's hooves filled the quiet as he struggled to convince himself of the truth of her words. "Love is not always easy, but it is almost always worth waiting for."

Chapter 16

January 1887

Geordie poked his head through the depot door and wrinkled his nose at the usual reek of stale cigars in the dusty air. "Hey, Sam, papers come in yet?"

A stogie clenched in his teeth, the man behind the ticket counter answered without looking up from his dime novel. "Yup. On the last train through." With slow movements he slapped a stack of newspapers onto the counter and turned back to his book.

Geordie scooped up the pile of newsprint, breathing in the carbon smell of the black ink. Leaning on the counter, he glanced at the open page. *Buffalo Bill Cody*. "That's a good one. You get to the part where he's in the loft?"

The man grunted.

"Thanks, Sam." Clutching the thick bundle of papers under one arm, Geordie strode out the door, his boot heels making hollow thuds on the wooden platform and the stairs. He crossed the tracks, stepping over the steel rails and setting his feet between the square ties to avoid coating his boot soles in creosote. Even in January the sun was hot enough to turn the black coating to a sticky liquid.

The wind whipped dust into the air as he reached the covered sidewalk in front of the restaurant. Damn, but he'd be glad when it finally rained again, if it ever did. No telling what would happen when the growers started burning the cotton stalks. Just what folks around here needed—a prairie fire, and no water to put it out. He shrugged and hurried past the grocery and the drugstore on the corner of Main and Centre. Disasters made good copy.

If only Arlington had a little more of her own news. Not much happened here beyond a church social or choir practice, maybe a revival meeting or a picnic. When the Alliance had voted to send Cat to the new state convention this month in Waco, it was the biggest news story since the fair and the epidemic last October.

He still couldn't decide whether to be proud, worried, or envious. Anyway, there was one good thing about it. With Cat gone, Molly would have to stay over to take care of the babies. A week alone with Molly. Maybe he'd get up the nerve to talk with her, even if it was only about the weather. At least that would be a start. Of course they wouldn't really be alone anyway. Effie would be there, and Joe.

Maybe he should go to Waco with Cat to protect her. Of course, she'd never admit she needed protection, but he'd heard some loose talk around town about the merchants making trouble for the Alliance. And it would give him an excuse to cover the alliance news. Not that Zeke could afford to give him the week off. The old man depended on him to do most of the writing now. And there was no money to pay his expenses, even if he could take the time.

That was why so much of what *The World* printed came from other papers like the ones in his arms. He'd been halfway hoping the papers wouldn't be at the depot. He was tired of summarizing other reporters' stories, especially this late in the day.

He'd been trying all week to get home early, before Molly left for the day. Not that it would do him any good. He might as well be deaf and dumb for all the brilliant things he could think of to say around her. He dodged a slow-moving carriage as he crossed Main Street.

Sometimes he almost wished she'd fall for some other fella so he could give up trying to find a way to tell her how much he loved her. He skirted the back of a horse tied to a hitching post, as much to avoid stepping in the fresh road apple behind it as to keep from getting kicked. He banged the papers against his side as he passed the row of stores lining Centre Street. Maybe it was just as well. If he was here writing stories, he couldn't be sitting at home tongue-tied, making a fool of himself.

He trotted down the steps and crossed the narrow alley, then slowed as he mounted the risers to the wooden platform fronting the print shop, not wanting the editor to think of him as a kid. He ducked in the open doorway and settled in a chair behind the desk, calling to let Zeke know he was back as he leafed through the papers and scanned the headlines.

The old man appeared in the doorway, wiping his hands on an already blackened rag. "Anything we can use?" His wire-framed glasses rested low on his nose, and thin white hair stood up like a halo around the shiny dome of his bald head. "We still got a hole on page one, and we could use some fillers in the back."

Geordie pulled the front section of *The Daily News* from the stack and bent over it. "An earthquake in Galveston yesterday." He set it aside and picked up a daily from the East Coast, frowning at the date. Almost a week old. "Wait, here's something. Congressman John Reagan of Texas today lent his support to the establishment of an Interstate Commerce Commission." He folded the page to a more convenient width and leaned back, tapping the paper against the desktop. "You know what that means. Railroad regulation. And about time too."

Zeke tucked the rag into the pocket of his stained leather apron and hiked one hip onto the corner of the desk. "Tell me about it. What's your opinion?"

Geordie took a minute to organize his thoughts, then listed the pros and cons of the proposed legislation and how it would affect the people of Arlington. He ended with his endorsement of the bill, provided it outlawed pooling and fixed equal freight charges for long and short hauls.

Zeke stood. "Good. Write it just like you said it." He turned toward the door to the composing room. "We'll run it on page two. It's about time you tried your hand at an editorial." He turned back, tilting his head down so his eyes met

Geordie's over the tops of his eyeglasses. "Think you can do it?"

Geordie clenched his fists, clamping down the excitement in his voice. He didn't want to give Zeke cause to regret his decision. "Yes, sir. You bet I can."

Catriona tugged a corner of the shawl around the bairn's face to keep the lamplight out of his eyes. He peered up at her around the curve of her breast as his cheeks worked in and out, his mouth clamped tight to her nipple. With one finger she stroked the silken hair at his temple, so black against the white of his skin.

Her son looked as much like her as her daughter looked like Ian. She leaned back, pressing her heels against the floor to start the rocker, savoring her contentment. Somehow, holding the bairn in her arms at last, it was easier to think of Ian without pain.

The tears she shed the day Duncan was born had cleansed a festering wound. Much as she still missed him, and much as she hated the men responsible for his death, now she could remember the good times without crying. She'd never love anyone that way again, but at least she could look toward a satisfying future without him now.

And she had her two bairns, Betsy after Ian's mother, and Duncan after Ian's father. They'd picked the name when she was carrying Betsy, and it suited the wee lad in her arms. Almost, he could have been a Macdonald, he looked so much like her own father, who hadn't changed a whit in the years she'd been gone from Skye. That much she could read in the letters Fergus and Jennet wrote. Their rebellion continued, with crofters taking back deer parks from absent lairds and ladies, rebuilding black houses empty since the clearances of '51. And in the middle of it all, her father, the Laird Macdonald, safe and well fed at Armadale Castle while his people eked out a meager living.

The bairn squirmed in her arms, and she forced herself to let the old anger go. No sense souring her milk and walking the floor all night because of the likes of Rory Macdonald. He was part of another life, and she'd been a different person then, a mere lass with more grit than brains. She was a woman now, and a mother, with her children to look after.

A knock at the door startled her. She flipped a corner of the shawl over her bare breast, hoping some stranger hadn't lost his way. What would a body think, seeing her in her nightclothes in the kitchen. "Who's there?"

Duncan jumped at her words, his arms and legs stiffening as he lost hold of her breast. With an angry-sounding squawk, he rooted his nose against her until she slid one hand under the shawl and guided her nipple into his mouth, patting his wee backside with her free hand. Cat couldn't help but smile when he grunted and smacked his lips, then settled again, a precious weight in her arms.

The door swung open and Will stuck his head inside. "May I?"

Relief mixed with pleased excitement at the sight of his handsome face. For a moment her pulse raced, and she took a calming breath, chiding herself for behaving like a schoolgirl. "Aye, come in." She leaned back into the rocking chair once more. "Pull up a seat."

He set his hat on the table and moved a straight-backed chair so he could face her. "I hope you don't mind." He pinched the fabric above the knees of his trousers as he sank down with a sigh, his face pale and lined with fatigue. "I had a house call near here, and I saw the light as I drove by."

"You should know you'll always find a welcome here." Duncan's mouth released her nipple, and with one hand under the shawl she drew the top of her nightgown closed.

Odd how shy she was with Will, silly when she thought about it. The man was a doctor; he'd seen a hundred women without their clothing. Besides, she'd shared the second most intimate experience in life with him—childbirth. The sight of her naked breast wouldn't interest him in the least. Still, she fastened the buttons with one hand before she lifted the covering from Duncan's sleeping face.

Will leaned forward, resting his elbows on his knees, his hands dangling in the space between. "A mighty fine-looking boy, Catriona." His lips quirked up in a smile and his eyes twinkled. "Takes after his mother."

Cat flushed and groped for something to say. "Aye, and

his granddad as well." She touched the black down of the bairn's head. "A wee Macdonald, eh, laddie?" Her father's face swam before her for a moment, and then was gone.

Will raised his eyebrows, then shrugged. "Filling out fast too."

"He eats all the time." Warmth stole into her cheeks after the words tumbled out of her mouth. She dropped her gaze, struggling to find something less embarrassing to discuss. "How are things at the office?"

"Busy. I really could use your help as soon as you're able." His gentle voice coaxed her to look up again.

"When I get back from Waco, I'll be ready to work."

Will's mouth hardened and his eyes narrowed. "Geordie told me the Alliance made you a delegate again, but I couldn't believe you'd actually go."

"And why shouldn't I?" Cat tried to keep the sudden anger from her voice. She chewed her lip, fighting the emptiness of fear and regret. He couldn't truly disapprove this time; he just didn't understand how important this meeting was.

He leaned back and crossed his arms over his chest. "I could think of a dozen reasons, but let me ask you a question instead."

Cat gave a curt nod, her anger cooling into determination. "Aye, ask."

"Just what do you expect to accomplish? Your enemies are too powerful. Do you think men like O. K. Frink are going to back down? Remember how the strike ended."

Anger welled up in her, and she leaned forward, clutching the bairn to her chest. "How dare you mention the strike to me! I know better than anyone what we lost that day. You may not care whether Ian's death counts for anything, but I dinna intend to let it go, to lie down and let life roll over me, no matter what you or anyone else thinks."

Will stood and paced across the floor. He faced the darkened window as the angry silence between them grew. At last, when he spoke, weariness weighted his words. "And what about Duncan?" He turned and combed one hand straight back through his auburn hair. "I suppose you'll leave him here to risk drinking cow's milk from a bottle, or maybe you plan to take him along." His sudden sarcasm bordered on cruelty. "That'll make you popular at the convention, carrying around a squalling baby."

Cat glanced down at the bairn sleeping in her arms. He was right; it would be hard on the wee laddie, but even as small as he was, Duncan was first a Macleod. "If it's your business, which it is not, Effie will go with me to Waco and tend both bairns."

Will strode toward her, stopping behind his chair and resting both hands on its back. "You're forgetting your work, the people who need you."

Cat shook her head. "Can you no see? I have to go, as much for them as for myself. This convention is a way to improve all our lives. If I can make any difference in the world, I have no choice but to try."

Effie leaned over the laundry basket and settled Duncan atop the folded blanket serving as a mattress. His eyes moved from left to right beneath his almost transparent eyelids, and his chin quivered as he suckled an invisible breast. Must be dreaming of food, the clever little mite. It wouldn't be much longer now until his mama returned to the hotel to feed him dinner.

She walked to the window, wondering if she dare take the children for a stroll to the drugstore on the corner, maybe buy herself a sarsaparilla. Goodness knew, she had little enough else to do, cooped up in this boring hotel room all day long. Duncan slept most of the time, and Betsy sat on the rug in the winter sunshine, hugging her rag doll or looking at her favorite book.

That left plenty of time to daydream about Joe. She wondered what he was doing right now. Probably not thinking of her. She knelt in the sunlight and rested her forearms on the windowsill, wishing she'd stayed home. Cat could have asked Molly to come along. She rested her forehead on her arms.

The trip had sounded so exciting at first. She'd never been to Waco before. She'd expected a city like Dallas, or even Fort Worth, but it was just a spot where three rail lines crossed the Brazos River. Even if it did have two opera houses, that did her no good at all. She couldn't go to one with the children or by herself. And Cat would likely be too tired to go anywhere after the first day of the convention.

A wail from across the room roused her. With a sigh she pushed herself up and hurried to the basket, then lifted the bairn into her arms and slipped her little finger into his greedy mouth.

Everybody else got to do exciting things. Geordie was always chasing after stories, and Joe got to ride around herding cattle all the time, and Molly was back at the farm cooking and doing for them both. And Cat was off at the convention where all kinds of stuff must be happening, speeches and the like, important men making important decisions. And here she was, stuck taking care of a squalling baby.

Tension hung in the air as Cat sidled through the rows of delegates seated on straight-back chairs. Ever since the Cleburne convention, the Alliance membership had been divided over the political nature of the Cleburne demands. Before the end of August, members of the state leadership went so far as to form another Alliance, and in October the state had issued them a charter. Now, in January, both factions had agreed to come together in Waco to try to resolve their differences. The convention resembled two armed camps in an uneasy truce.

At last she found a vacant seat near the side door. She hated climbing over people when she had to sneak out to feed Duncan every few hours. Not that anyone had paid any attention during the chaotic session the day before.

After the chairman had opened the floor to discussion by asking the dissenting faction for a statement of objections to the Cleburne demands, he'd done nothing but answer questions and listen to motions until it was time to adjourn late in the afternoon. She hoped they'd get further today. If they couldn't reconcile their differences, there would be no more Farmers Alliance. Couldn't these pigheaded fools understand they had to stick together to get anywhere against the merchants and the railroads?

As she settled onto a hard chair, the sound of a gavel split the air, quelling the angry mutterings of the five hundred delegates.

C. W. Macune strode across the platform, his square body encased in a dark suit, and a high white collar and dark tie surrounding his thick neck.

Cat admired the way his dark hair lay in perfect order and his heavy mustache curved in a smooth arc above his mouth as he called the meeting to order as acting president. There was something about this man that made people want to follow him.

He took the gavel and held it aloft as he turned his wide, handsome face toward the crowd. "The chair recognizes no man until the delegates have heard the objectives of this meeting and have elected a temporary chairman for this convention."

A roar rose up around her. Voices called out all at once, the sense of individual words and sentences lost in a babble of protest. At last, after repeated cracks of the gavel, the delegates quieted. Macune had decided to take control. Now maybe they could get something done.

Macune listed his reasons for calling the convention, hitting hard at the need for farmers to stand united to fight for economic reforms. A few of the men and women around Cat nodded as he outlined the problems of the recent past and the present situation. By the time he began to describe his recommendations for the future, five hundred pairs of eyes turned toward him and a listening silence fell over the room.

The acting president called for the formation of a national Alliance to build an even stronger base for economic action. Cat's own excitement grew as he outlined the need for an Alliance Exchange, explaining the advantages of buying supplies directly and brokering their own cotton and wheat. This was what the farmers of Texas needed to ensure a decent living from their land.

She was not surprised when Macune finished his address amid wild applause, nor when he again called for the election of a temporary chairman and was elected by a unanimous voice vote without any other nominations. The first item on his agenda was the election of a board of directors.

As men and women stood to call out nominations for the twenty-five positions, Cat scanned the delegates nearby. Faces that moments before had reflected anger and mistrust now glowed with hope.

She turned again to the man on the platform. Somehow, by focusing on the future, C. W. Macune had managed to work a miracle. He'd healed the breach and reunited the Alliance. Seeing this almost made up for all she'd endured in the past. Furnishing men like O. K. Frink could make all the trouble they wanted. Now, with the farmers all standing together, there was nothing they couldn't accomplish.

Chapter 17

February 1887

The smell of sawdust from the floor of the big top had never failed to excite him even as he grew older. But today he had more reason than ever before. Keeping his eyes to the front, Geordie inched closer to Molly on the hard wooden bench. The warmth of her body and the faint scent of rose petals called out to him. He glanced at her, savoring the shine of her hair so close beside his shoulder. When she turned and smiled up at him, his heart turned over with joy.

He still couldn't believe his luck, getting free tickets to cover the Barnum show for Zeke. And instead of having to wait until Saturday, Mrs. Vanzee had said they might go during the week, just the four of them. And the crowded benches meant Joe and Effie had to sit in front. It was all just too good to be true.

Molly's hand touched his as she pointed at the high-wire act in the far ring. A woman climbed onto the small platform, her costume exposing an indecent but enticing amount of her plump body.

Geordie's cheeks warmed as he traced the outline of the ankles and calves covered only by white tights, wondering what Molly's limbs looked like beneath her long skirts. The woman walked the wire with apparent ease, frontward, backward, until she reached the center. Teetering there, she opened a pink parasol and held it high over her head for a moment, then stretched both arms out and lifted one foot. She hung there, suspended in space, then stepped lightly to the far end of the wire amid huge applause.

A puff of cool air drew Geordie's attention down and back to the bottom of the tent wall. A brief glimmer of torchlight from outside silhouetted the shape of a boy or a small man on all fours before it went dark again. Somebody without the price of admission, poor soul, but if he wasn't quieter, he'd get caught and thrown out.

A minute later, in the midst of a clown skit, a body shot out from beneath a bench in the front row and ran to the center ring, shouting over the music of the circus band. At first he thought the boy was one of the clowns, just part of the act. Geordie strained to catch the words, something about a shooting. The boy turned their way, cupping his hands around his mouth. "Luke Stout shot and killed Jim Cutchall."

My God, now, that was some news. The man who killed Ian, dead by the hand of a notorious gambler. He allowed himself a moment of satisfaction. Men climbed to their feet, their angry voices drowning out the circus music. Far away to his right, a voice rose above the others. "What are we waiting for? Let's get Luke Stout." Voices throughout the big top echoed the words, and men struggled down from the high benches and streamed out the doors, shouting and shooting their pistols in the air.

Geordie stood. He'd like to shake the man's hand, but he knew the world wouldn't lose much if the crowd lynched Luke Stout. Either way, this story was news, and he had to cover it.

Molly jumped up beside him, her hand clutching at his sleeve and her face pale. Her eyes rolled back in her head, and without a word she crumpled forward into his arms.

Geordie crouched in the doorway of the shooting gallery, rubbing the damp blood between his fingertips. The faint smell of gunpowder still hung in the air, but it might have been a cow they shot here instead of a man for all he could tell now. He pushed himself up and wandered out onto the plank sidewalk. Not much to see really, considering a man had died there only hours before, just a pool of blood staining the wood and a few bullet holes.

For the hundredth time he wished he hadn't let Joe talk him into staying and covering the story. He'd followed the angry crowd, expecting to see frontier justice at work. But by the time the mob arrived at the jailhouse, Stout was safe behind bars with armed deputies standing guard everywhere. Pretty soon the people dispersed; the days of lynching parties in Fort Worth were over for good.

An old man sidled over to him. "You from the paper?"

Geordie nodded. He'd seen this type before, news hounds, always ready to tell their version of what happened, even if they'd been blocks away at the time. "What can I do for you?"

The old man's eyes narrowed. "Well, I could sure use a nickel to buy a beer."

Without a word Geordie turned away in disgust. This one was even worse than the usual, not even pretending to have a story before he asked for money.

A grubby hand clamped on his arm, and the dirty, unshaven face pushed into his. "I seen the whole thing. Hiding over yonder in the alley." He pointed with a shaking hand. "There was a passle of reporters before, but I didn't like the looks of any of them. But I'll tell you, if you'll stand me to a beer." His toothless mouth spasmed into a hopeful grin.

Geordie considered. The old man might be telling the truth. And he might have already spilled his version to anyone who'd listen. Or, more than likely, he'd tried to sell his story to more than one, and they'd turned him down. But it could be worth a nickel to hear what the man said. "Okay, tell me your story first. If I like it, I'll buy you a drink."

The old man rubbed his hands together, then drew himself up. "Cutchall and Bull was standing there." He pointed to a spot just past the gallery. "And Luke was over yonder, in the doorway to the Elephant.

"Luke, he was smiling and he says, 'Howdy, Jim. Bull.' Then he tips his hat. 'I'm obliged to you for meeting with me like this.' And he pulls his coat back and slides his thumbs into the armholes of his vest like this." The old man demonstrated. "Then he says, 'But what I got to say is private.'

"So the marshal turns to Bull and says, 'It's okay. Why don't you go inside and buy yourself a beer?' Then Bull shrugs and walks away, and once he's gone, Luke says, 'So, Jim. I hear tell you want a bigger percentage of the take from the keno tables.'

"Well, Jim doesn't answer right away, and I can tell he's thinking about the rumors going around about him calling Earp and Masterson down from Dodge City to help him out. Everybody knows how Luke refused to carry a gun in Leadville so the other gunslingers would leave him alone. Luke, he was fast with a gun, but not fast enough to go up against the likes of Cutchall alone."

The old man paused and cocked his head, but Geordie just nodded for him to continue. He'd heard this much, or some variation of it, before from other witnesses.

"So finally Jim, he says, 'Well, now that you mention it, I have been thinking of upping my cut.' And then he crosses his arms over his chest and leans against a post.

"Luke smiles real sweet and says, 'You know, you're an ungrateful son of a bitch, Jim. I proved what kind of friend I am to you. Don't you remember how I gave you the money for your trip to New Mexico so you could clear your name?' "

Geordie tugged his notebook from his pocket and flipped it open. Somehow, what the old man said held a ring of truth. Maybe he'd just better take some notes.

"Then Jim smiles back and says, 'I ain't forgot. But I've heard some things lately to make a body wonder just how good a friend you are.'

"So Luke says, 'And I've heard rumors about you, too, but I don't pay attention to what I hear.'

"Then Jim drops his hands and I think Luke's a goner, but Jim just hitches up his trousers and spits into the street. He says, 'Well, maybe you should pay attention. If you want to keep the Elephant open, I gotta have more money to keep the politicians off my back.' He smiles again, real arrogant-like. 'And a little extra for my own trouble.'

"Then Luke gives him a nod. 'I'll go along with you this time, Jim. But someday you're gonna push me too far.'

"Jim just throws back his head and laughs. He says, 'And someday we're all gonna be dead and buried too. I'll take my chances.' He crosses in front of Luke toward the saloon and says, 'Now I could use me a drink.' And he turns his back.

"Luke pulls a gun from the waistband of his pants and fires, just like that." The old man paused.

Geordie swallowed against the sudden dryness in his throat. "But that's cold-blooded murder, shooting a man in the back." Even if Cutchall did kill Ian the same way, that didn't make it right for Luke Stout to gun him down like a dog.

The old man lifted a hand. "Wait, there's more. The bullet catches poor Jim in the right shoulder and spins him around. He just grabs at his shoulder with his left hand—he's right-handed, see? So he can't even go for his own gun. And he just looks Luke in the eye and says, 'Shoot, Luke, or give up your gun.'

"Luke says, 'Good-bye, Jim,' and shoots him again twice in the chest. Throws him clean across the threshold of the shooting gallery, half in and half out the door.

"Then Luke runs over and takes a pistol out of the marshal's back pocket and puts it in Jim's bloody right hand, then backs away a piece and fires two more shots in the air for good measure.

"Somebody come running out of the saloon about then, saying 'God-a-mighty. What happened?'

"So Luke, he says, 'I went to adjust my vest, and I guess he thought I was gonna draw on him, so he went for it. His gun musta stuck, or else I'd be dead.' "

Geordie flipped his notebook closed. "So did you tell the sheriff your story?"

The old man squinted. "Tried to, but who's gonna listen to a crazy old coot like me?" He gave a high-pitched cackle and held out his hand. "Well, partner, I kept my part of the deal, so where's my drinking money?"

Geordie dug a nickel out of his pocket and placed it in the old man's shaky grasp. "Thanks for telling me."

The man nodded once, then shuffled away toward the saloon.

Geordie slid his notebook back into his pocket. He'd like to print up the old man's story, but he had no way of knowing if it was true or not. And no way to find out. He hardly thought Luke Stout was gonna admit to shooting a man in the back. And Long-haired Jim Cutchall wasn't talking. All this time and energy for nothing, hardly even enough for a news brief.

He sighed, wishing he'd gone with Effie and Joe to take Molly to the doctor's office in Arlington instead of staying in Fort Worth. Tenderness swept over him as he remembered her bravery, insisting she was all right and didn't need a doctor. If she came to any harm, he didn't know what he'd do.

Chapter 18

Will plunged his hands into the basin of hot water, then reached for the soap, scrubbing his hands hard. Poor kid. How had she gotten into this mess? But he knew. There was only one way, after all.

Without looking up, he spoke in his most comforting voice. "You may sit up now and arrange your clothing." He reached for a clean towel and took his time drying his hands and rolling down his sleeves.

When he turned, she was sitting on the edge of the bed, ankles crossed and hands folded in her lap, looking even younger than her fifteen years. What kind of man took advantage of a young girl? Unless it was a boy her age. Only one way to find out.

He scooted a chair up to the bedside so he could face her and leaned his elbows on his knees. "So, how are you feeling now?"

Pink flooded her pale cheeks, and she dropped her gaze. "Fine, except for dying of shame."

"Now, now. There's no shame between a doctor and his patient." Will kept his tone gentle. "And the dizziness?"

"All gone. I'm fine now." Her eyes lifted to his, asking him to agree. "I just stood up too fast."

His smile faded. Surely she must know, or at least suspect. "And why do you think you fainted?"

She turned away, twisting her reticule between her fingers. "It must have been the crowd and all the excitement. It's just a case of the vapors, isn't it?"

"Molly." He took her hand and waited until her eyes met his. "You're with child. When was your last monthly?"

Her lips paled. "December. But I've never been all that regular." She swallowed. "Are you sure, Doc?"

He nodded. "Who's the father?"

Her small white teeth pressed into her lower lip, and she shook her head.

Will leaned back, crossing his arms. He hadn't expected it to be easy. "Is it Geordie?"

Her eyebrows lifted and her eyes widened. "Good gracious, no."

"Then who? You can trust me. I won't tell anyone." He let his voice harden the slightest bit. "If you want my help, you have to confide in me."

Her eyes flashed. "You can't help me, Doc. Nobody can. Now I can't say any more." She rose from the bed and extended her hand, suddenly older than her years. "I'm much obliged."

Weariness settled over him as he unfolded from the chair and took her small, soft hand in his. "Are you sure you don't want me to talk to the man, or at least help you tell your parents?"

A smile bloomed on her sweet young face, but it never reached the sadness of her eyes. "That's a mighty fine offer, but it wouldn't do any good. He's not in a position to help me either." Her hand touched his cheek. "You understand what I mean, don't you?"

Will nodded. He'd heard the story all too often. He knew exactly what she meant.

Joe wrinkled his nose at the strong smell of cow manure and urine as he lifted the pitchfork full of bedding, tossing it into the wagon. He still thought Miz Macleod was a little bit crazy, insisting he save the stuff and plow it into the dirt before he planted. She said it made the plants grow better and they always did it in Scotland.

'Course, everybody knew the soil around here was the richest in Texas, not like some of the played-out dirt in Virginia or Kentucky, where folks had been farming for a hundred years or better. Still, she was the boss, and right smart, leastways for a woman.

He wished his own mama was more like her. She seemed to think farming was a matter of tossing out some seeds and waiting for food to grow. He did the best he could after he went home at night, but he was only one man. Even with what Papa made working in Dallas, they'd have a hard time of it without the food Miz Macleod sent home with him and Molly every day.

Molly sure had acted funny earlier that morning, upset-like. He wondered what she was up to, wanting to talk to Mama alone. Probably just some woman thing.

Anyhow, he wished she'd hurry up and get here so's everybody else would leave for work. Miz Macleod was so busy this morning she hadn't even offered him breakfast like usual. But he'd talk Molly into fixing him something good, side meat and grits and eggs, maybe. His belly knotted at the thought. He wrinkled his nose and thrust the tines of the pitchfork into another manure-filled pile of old hay.

Cat settled Betsy into her high chair and forced herself to smile at the lass. It wasn't fair to take out her frustration on an innocent bairn. She spooned porridge into a bowl and added top milk and molasses. As she ferried the first bite toward her daughter's wee mouth, a small hand darted out, grabbing the spoon and slinging oatmeal across the table.

"No." Surprise raised her voice and gave it an edge.

Betsy's face puckered, her lower lip curling out and down.

"Hush now, it's all right." She unwrapped the wee fingers from the handle of the baby spoon and filled it again, careful to avoid the bairn's grasp as she managed to put the food into Betsy's open mouth. "There's a *canny* lass."

Hoofbeats echoed up the road, and Cat jumped to her

feet. That had to be Molly at last. She ran to the window, ignoring Betsy's squawks. Against the morning sky, Will's buggy skimmed down the road toward the farm. Damn.

She hurried back to Betsy, shoveling porridge into the bairn's mouth, then stacking dirty dishes and wiping up spilled food in between bites. It wasn't until his boot heels thudded up the steps to the back porch that she realized she hadn't dressed her hair yet that day. After wiping her hands on her apron, she finger-combed her curls back from her face and went to answer his quiet rap on the door.

Will smiled down at her, a twinkle warming his gray-green eyes. "Is everything okay here?" Instead of appreciating his usual tidy appearance, she found herself annoyed by it today. His crisp auburn hair smoothed back from his forehead in perfect waves, his skin glowed, and his clothing looked smooth and clean.

She swept her hands down her front and spread them out to encompass the whole room in her gesture. "You can see for yourself."

Betsy chose that moment to laugh, dribbling porridge down her chin and slapping her hands in the mess on the tray.

Will chuckled, then turned it into a cough as he stepped across the threshold and closed the door behind him. "Can I help?"

Cat shook her head, smiling in spite of herself. "Coffee?"

He held up his hands. "I'll get it if you'll tell me what's going on. When you didn't come in, I got worried, so I canceled my morning appointments and drove out to make sure everything was all right."

Grabbing a wet cloth, she mopped up the spilled porridge, talking over her shoulder. "*Ach*, it's Molly. She told her brother she had to stay a bit this morning and talk with their mother, but wouldn't tell him why." She held another spoonful up to Betsy's mouth, but the lass pressed her lips tight together and turned her head away. "Fine, then. Starve." She muttered the words under her breath as she dropped the spoon in the bowl and carried it to the dry sink.

"What was that?" Will settled in a chair across the table.

"*Nought*. But you'd do better to stay out of the range of my daughter's spoon." She dipped the sticky cloth in a basin of water, then wrung it almost dry and went to work on Betsy. The bairn's loud squawks made it impossible to talk until every trace of porridge was gone from the wee face and hands. "There now." She settled the lass on her feet and watched her toddle to Will and hold up her hands.

His smile softened as he reached down and picked her up. He settled her on his lap, tugging his timepiece from his watch pocket and placing it in her pudgy hand.

Swallowing against a sudden tenderness, she turned away and busied herself scraping dishes. "I sent Geordie to the Vanzees' to fetch Molly, and he's been gone the better part of an hour." At his silence, she glanced over her shoulder. "You wouldn't know anything about this, would you?"

A red stain crept into his cheeks and he dropped his gaze. "I—"

Duncan's wail split the air. Cat hurried to the cradle and lifted the bairn in her arms, then settled into her rocker. She unbuttoned the front of her dress, thinking only of quieting him as she thrust her nipple into his mouth. She raised her eyes to meet Will's, and not sure what she read there, she dropped them again and tugged the front of her dress closed, covering as much of her breast as possible. Wishing she'd grabbed a shawl as well, she cast about for the lost thread of their conversation. Oh, aye—Molly. "You were saying?"

Hoofbeats cut through the awkward silence. Will stood and carried Betsy to the window. "It's Geordie."

"Is Molly with him?" She tightened her lips in irritation, wishing he'd not force her to drag each word from him this way.

He shook his head, keeping his face toward the window.

After another uncomfortable silence, Geordie bounded through the door, his brown hair blown around his face and his breath coming in gasps. "Miz Vanzee wouldn't talk to me in English. She just kept yelling these foreign words and slamming things around the kitchen. Then little Pieter told me she locked Molly in her room."

Geordie dropped into a chair and struggled to catch his breath. "She wouldn't let me see her." His voice broke, and he swallowed. "Finally she said to tell you Molly can't work for us anymore, and she said we were to blame for her daughter's shame."

Chapter 19

March 1887

Catriona set her foot on the back of the shovel and used the weight of her body to force the sharp edge through the matted tangle of dead grass. A *cashrom* would have been easier, although she had no special love for the crooked footplow common in her homeland. Pressing down and back on the handle, she levered the wedge of soil up and over, a black pyramid shot with threadlike white roots. Still, she had no other choice; the small herb garden lay too close to the house for the horse-drawn plow. Besides, it was too small to bother Geordie or Joe about. She set the shovel and dug in again.

And with Molly gone, she couldn't work with Will, so at least this way she could begin to cultivate more medicinal herbs to replace the ones she'd used during the epidemic. She turned another wedge of earth. By autumn she'd need fresh supplies of all her standard remedies, not that many of the seeds from Scotland had grown well here. If only she knew what other native plants to gather besides snakeroot.

A pair of feet appeared in front of her, just beyond the churned earth. Even as she jumped back at the unexpected intrusion, Cat noted the soft leather shoes, moccasins Ian had called them when he made her a pair for Christmas so many years before. But beaded flowers covered the toes of these, and the stitching showed great skill. Her gaze traveled up the cloth squaw dress and apron, past the long plaits of dark hair shot with gray, to intense dark eyes set in a sunburned face, lined but ageless. Cat gripped the handle of the shovel. "*Ach*, you startled me."

"My mother teach me to walk quiet long time ago. I sneak up on deer and rabbits." The woman crossed her arms over her wide chest and stood, her broad face unreadable, not offering any more explanation.

Cat wiped her palms on her apron, then held out her hand and introduced herself.

The woman took her hand and pumped it up and down twice, then let go. "My name Sanapia. White doctor send me to take care of babies."

"Dr. Bascom sent you?"

Sanapia nodded.

What on earth was Will thinking of? He knew better than to think she'd leave her children with just anyone, no matter how much she wanted to get back to work with him. Maybe he was tired of waiting. After all, it had been three long weeks since Molly's mother locked her up.

And in that time no one had seen the lass step foot outside her home, and Hilda turned callers away at the door. When Cat had asked Joe about it, he just looked away and shrugged. Of course, Will might know, but he wasn't talking either. She didn't know what might persuade Hilda to let the lass return, but Cat hadn't given up hope yet.

Still, she did need help with the bairns now. She put her hands on her hips and considered, guessing the woman before her was at least half Comanche. Not that she held ought against the Indians. She'd never really seen many; they were all on reservations long before she arrived in Arlington. But she'd always sympathized with them, being kicked off their land by more powerful men. It reminded her of the clearances on Skye before she was born. The thought brought a wave of homesickness. If only she could be there for an hour— With a sigh she forced her mind back to the woman before her.

It couldna hurt to ask her a bit about herself. "And what experience have you with children, then?"

Something flickered behind the stony face. "Have seven babies of my own."

Cat nodded and smiled, urging the woman to continue. "And where are they now?"

Dark lashes veiled the woman's eyes as her gaze dropped to the ground. "All dead. Husband too. Family too. Only Sanapia now."

Regret and sympathy tugged at Cat. She might have guessed. So many bairns died here—too many. She realized she'd made her decision; if Will had sent this Sanapia to her, he must trust her, and Cat found herself trusting the woman as well. At the least, she looked clean and healthy and strong, which was more than she could say for the other women who'd offered to watch the bairns. "I canna pay you, just your meals."

Sanapia shook her head. "Eats and bed."

She supposed she could put a cot in the kitchen for her. It might be good having someone there at night, in case Will needed her to go on a house call with him. She sighed. At this point she couldn't afford to say no. "All right. We'll give it a try."

Breathing in the honey smell of Duncan's skin, Effie sank down in the rocker in the open doorway. The constant wind did little to cool a person, but it did dry the sweat on her face. She settled the child against her arm with as much air between them as possible and fingered the woolen soaker over the baby's diaper. A little damp, but not likely to leak through. She smiled; maybe she ought to lift the baby's white cotton gown and let the wind dry his pants.

Duncan squirmed closer until his small dark head rested against her breast. A deep contentment settled within Effie as she rocked and hummed a soft tune. When the baby's eyelids fluttered down, she added words, her tongue sliding over the Gaelic lyrics with ease. She had no idea where she learned the lullaby; it seemed she'd always known it. Perhaps her mother had sung it to Catriona and Cat to her when she was small. Poor Cat didn't sing much anymore. Maybe she missed Ian. It was sad to think of their love ending so soon.

But then, it happened to lots of women. After all, Sanapia was a widow too, and none of her children survived the smallpox epidemic. People died, or left, or fell out of love. She wondered if that would happen to her.

No, she had to believe there was something better. She leaned down and kissed Duncan's dark curls. And she knew what she wanted—a home and family, and a husband who worked hard and made friends easily, like Joe. No, not like Joe—she wanted Joe himself, not an imitation.

Duncan stirred in her arms, so she sang another verse as she settled the sleeping child on a trundle bed in the corner. A faint scraping sound came from the porch, but she ignored it. The wind was always kicking up leaves and twigs. The last words of the song hung in the air.

"Miss Effie?"

She whirled toward the door. It took her a moment to place the young woman hesitating in the kitchen doorway, "Ida?"

The girl's unpainted cheeks reddened. "I hope you don't mind me coming to see you like this."

Effie went to her and took her hand. "Of course not. Please sit here." She pointed to a chair. "What a surprise. Can I get you something?"

Shaking her head, Ida settled herself on the ladder-back chair, letting the skirt of her brown gingham dress fall to her ankles. A simple straw hat trimmed with ribbon rosebuds and feathers covered her dark hair, and careful ringlets hung over her ears.

Effie sat beside the girl, wondering at the purpose of the visit. It was no small thing to ride all the way to the farm from Arlington. She smiled, surprised by her own pleasure at the unexpected visit, and pleased by the obvious care the girl had taken with her appearance. The way Ida was dressed, Effie almost hadn't recognized her. Why, looking at her now, she'd never guess Ida was one of Yvette's girls. She was almost pretty, not at all like her usual frowsy self. "You look so nice today. Is that a new dress?"

Ida chuckled and raised one eyebrow. "A big change, eh?"

Effie cleared her throat. "I didn't mean—"

The girl flipped the thought away with one gloved hand. "Naw, I know. I just like to look respectable sometimes." Her face sobered. "Truth is, I come to ask you a favor, like."

Effie clasped her hands, resting them in her lap. "Go on, then, ask." Please let it be something easy, so she wouldn't have to say no.

Ida dropped her gaze, toying with a beaded bag in her lap. "Well, when I was little, my mama used to read to me from the Bible, and I thought it was the most wonderful thing in the world, to be able to read." She paused, her eyes still cast down. "But Pa, he didn't cotton to it, so she didn't never teach me."

Effie touched Ida's hand. "So you'd like me to read to you from the Bible sometimes?"

Ida lifted her eyes and her shoulders heaved as she drew a deep breath. "No, well, yes, sort of." She shook her head. "What I mean is, when I seen you in your wagon that day, well, I decided I wanted to learn to read. I'd be real honored if you'd teach me. I could even pay you a little."

Effie chewed her lip and stared at her hands. That would take time, and there was so much to do on the farm now that Molly was gone, even with Sanapia's help. What would Cat say? And more important, what would Joe think? She knew he didn't approve of Madame Yvette's girls. But she was so lonely, and it would be fun to have some company again. And some money of her own, to spend as she pleased. Besides, she hated to say no to any woman who wanted to better herself.

She turned to Ida and smiled. "Okay, you've got a deal."

Ida's eyes widened. "You mean it? Gosh, when can we start?"

Effie glanced at the sleeping baby, then rose and fetched the Bible off the shelf. "How about right now?"

Chapter 20

April 1887

Will held the kerosene lamp high as he leaned over the head of the bed. The man's chest rose and fell, but his slack-jawed stare showed no response to the light. An ugly bruise smudged one side of his forehead, its purplish surface streaked with brown scratches. "How did this happen?"

"He was letting the herd into the lower pasture two days ago, and some of them must have smelled water in the creek bed. Anyhow, they stampeded, I reckon." The thin voice quavered. "My boy found him on the ground, passed out. We drug him up here to the house and put him to bed."

Will set the lamp on a homemade table and turned to face the wife. "But why did you wait so long to send for me?"

The narrow face crumpled, and the woman twisted her chapped hands together. "I kept hoping he'd come out of it by himself. We can't pay you much as it is."

Will nodded and turned back to the patient, examining the bones of the skull for swellings or soft spots. He'd guessed at their poverty when he saw the scraggly cattle in the pasture and the dry grass cropped too close to the dusty soil.

At least the two children looked healthy and clean, even if their clothes sported patches. And the father ate enough to keep his strength, but the mother must have starved herself to make more for everyone else. He'd seen it again and again in the last year. Most of the small farmers and ranchers lived from hand to mouth with no money in reserve against a poor year. And the furnishing man only gave so much credit after one crop failure.

Damn this drought. They probably had limited drinking water too, and what they did have was more than likely contaminated, or soon would be. It was a wonder they weren't all sick or dead already. He wondered what kept them here. Enough folks had cleared out, gone north in search of easier lands to farm, although farmers everywhere faced the same risks. So many ways to lose everything, it hardly seemed worth the trouble.

Maybe Catriona had the right of it with her Farmers Alliance after all. There had to be a better way of life for farmers, and maybe they'd only find it through legislation. He regretted their argument before her trip to Waco, although he still wished she'd stay out of the political battles. He'd been trying to protect her, keep her safe, but he had no right to tell her what to do. And in a way, he had to respect her spirit, her courage. A smile twitched at the corners of his mouth. She always could get a rise out of him, maybe because he cared so much.

Anyhow, he was thankful she was finally back at work, although he'd been surprised when she hired Sanapia. Nana had been right about those two getting along. He only wished he'd stopped tonight and brought Cat along on this call. And not just because he liked having her beside him; he could use another pair of hands for the surgery, and this woman didn't look to be strong enough to be much help. "Bring me a basin of boiled water and some soap. And another lamp."

A hand touched his arm. "Is he gonna be all right, Doc?" The woman's eyes pleaded with him. She was pretty enough, or would be if she had a little more meat on her bones. With the farm, she might attract another good man to help her raise her children. Just as Catriona could. After all, Cat was a damned fine-looking woman with a much better farm.

He squirmed at the thought, then straightened up. "I can't say for sure. I'm gonna try something I've only read about. With surgery he might get well, or he might live a long time without ever coming around at all." He imagined himself lying here, soiling himself, his mindless body a burden to those he loved—given the choice, Will knew he'd rather be dead. But it wasn't up to him to decide for anyone else. He shrugged. "Without surgery he'll die, and soon. You do understand?"

The woman nodded, a smile trembling on her lips. "We're grateful for whatever you can do." She bustled away, returning with a lantern and a steaming basin.

He shrugged off his jacket and rolled up his shirt-sleeves. "How about a bucket?" Scalp incisions always bled, and he hated to stain the floor. He arranged the limp body across the bed.

She nodded and fetched one, paling as he set it under her husband's head and finished laying out his tools.

"Does he have a straight razor?"

She scurried off again. Good. Keep her too busy to think about what he planned to do.

He trimmed the dark hair as close as he could with scissors, then lathered it with the warm water and a lump of gray soap. He tested the blade when she handed it to him, then scraped away the hair above the bruise. As he expected, the purple smudge extended back from the hairline several inches. After scrubbing his hands, he lifted a scalpel and made a long cut, opening the flesh to the bone. The body jerked once, then lay still again.

He didn't even look up at the woman's indrawn breath. "Stay or go as you please, but keep quiet." With a clean cloth he mopped the blood from the incision. Not even a hairline fracture; the pressure was inside the skull, just as he'd thought. He picked up the bone drill.

He'd never used one before, and he could only guess how gruesome he looked to this woman as he set the bit against her husband's head and turned the handle. Sweat trickled down his sides and chilled his face. It took him a few tries to keep the metal from slipping on the smooth surface of the bone, but at last the bit dug in and yellow-white powder spun up out of the hole.

He cranked the handle until the drill pushed through

the hard bone and into soft tissue, then he reversed the handle and wound the bit out. Black blood oozed from the hole. He tugged the man's shoulders toward him until the head tipped over the edge of the mattress. He'd made the hole as far back as he could, hoping gravity would drain the wound without requiring suction. After several minutes the fluid lightened to a clear yellow and slowed to a trickle.

Will eased the body back onto the bed and sponged the opening clean. With boiled cotton thread he stitched the edges of the cut together and tied a bandage in place.

The man's wife shuffled forward from a corner, her eyes wide and her face gray.

Will shrugged in answer to her unspoken question. "It may be a while before he comes around, if he ever does."

She nodded and helped him tug the body the right way in the bed, then tucked the worn blankets around the limp form.

Will cleaned his hands and wiped down his instruments before packing them in his leather satchel. Weariness ached in every corner of his body as he followed the woman out to the kitchen.

She faced him, squaring her shoulders and lifting her chin. "How much do we owe you, Doc?"

He debated. Too much and they couldn't pay, too little and she'd suspect charity. "Two dollars."

He must have guessed right, because her face brightened as she lifted the lid from a sugar bowl and counted out silver and copper coins. "There you be, and—" She turned at a faint sound from the bedroom.

A rusty voice croaked out one word. "Thelma?"

The woman flew from the room.

After a moment Will followed her.

She knelt beside the bed, her body racked with sobs, trying to explain what had happened.

What Will wouldn't give to see such naked devotion on Cat's face. He moved to the bed, testing the man's arms and legs for any signs of paralysis. Relief eased the tension in his neck and shoulders. The man showed some weakness, but no more than normal for someone who'd been bedridden and lost quite a bit of blood.

A weak hand gripped his arm. "So, Doc, tell me the truth. How bad off am I?"

Will retrieved his bag from the floor and straightened. "You'll have to take it easy, stay in bed another week or two." With a twinge of envy he smiled down at the young couple, their hands clasped tight together. "After that we'll see."

The woman leaned over and threw her arms around her husband, then jumped to her feet and turned to Will, her smile shining through her tears. She took his hand and raised herself on tiptoe to kiss his cheek. "Thank you."

The cool smell of damp earth rose up from the ditch as Geordie strode through the cotton patch. After a near-sleepless night, he was relieved to be up and outside early, closing the water gates. So far the system of ditches and dams worked fine, but he still wondered if they shouldn't have waited for the rain like everybody else. What if the rain didn't come again this year, where would they be?

The expensive seed was in the ground now, and there was no turning back. He wasn't sure they could last a whole season without rain. What if the wells dried up too?

And some of the neighbors wanted him to share what water they had, but he knew there wasn't enough. He'd hated saying no to neighbors. And although he'd offered to help dig wells and build windmills, there were bound to be some hard feelings. Most folks couldn't afford to invest in equipment this year after last year's crops failed.

A shadow fell across the rows of tiny green shoots. For a minute he couldn't figure out the cause. It had been that long since he'd seen clouds like the ones spreading across the horizon to the west. He shrugged, refusing to let himself hope. He'd seen a few clouds in the last year, but none had done him any good.

As he made his way toward the next dam, his thoughts, as always, drifted to Molly, like a tongue to a sore tooth. At first he'd just been angry when Hilda refused to let him see her. And now, after a few months of not seeing her, of missing her and worrying about her, he had to be honest with himself; he loved her and wanted to marry her, no matter what shame she'd brought to her family. He refused to believe she could have done anything so terrible, no matter how her mother babbled.

He was going to ask her, first chance he got. If she said no, all he had to lose was his pride, and that seemed a small enough thing to risk for a lifetime of love and happiness. And he intended to make her happy, if she'd give him the chance. But first he had to get her away from her mother, and he had no idea how to go about doing that.

Something wet landed on his head. Thinking it was a bird dropping, he reached a hand to his hair in disgust. But then a host of big drops splashed to the ground around his feet, and he finally looked up. Pale gray covered the dome of the sky, and little black clouds flew under the top layer. A year ago he'd have said that meant a long rain. The raindrops drummed the ground, gathering speed and volume.

He whirled around, laughing, then jumped high, his fist punching the air above his head. "Rain, by God! It's raining." He ran toward the barn, relishing the water soaking his clothes as he readied his horse. In minutes he had his foot in the stirrup, swinging himself into the saddle. He dug his boot heels into the gelding's side and raced down the lane, his horse's hooves splashing in the deepening puddles. The end of an eighteen-month drought. He had to get to the newspaper office; this was the biggest news story in weeks.

Chapter 21

June 1887

Heat rushed out the open oven door as Catriona bent and gave the top of each layer cake a gentle touch in the center. Pleased with the results, she padded her hands with a folded flour-sack towel and lifted first one, then the other of the cakes, setting them to cool near the open window, the expensive smells of sugar and eggs and butter blending with the perfume of early summer flowers.

Outside, yellow and red and purple dotted the green ripples of tall prairie grass. Thank God for the rain, three inches that first day and steady on since then. Everything flourished again, outside the house and inside. Hard to believe it was two years since Betsy's birth, since Ian laid the wee red-faced bairn in her arms. If only he were here today to see her, to see how clever and beautiful she'd grown. A familiar ache crept into her chest and settled behind her eyes, but she wouldn't give in to it today. A birthday should be a happy time.

"Mmm, smells good." Geordie's hand reached across her shoulder toward the cake.

Cat slapped it away and turned, smiling up at her brother.

He stuck out his lower lip. "Aww, Cat." His words

whined out through downturned lips. "I just wanted a smidgen."

She drew her eyebrows down and pressed her lips together, trying to look stern. "You must wait with everybody else."

Hanging his head in mock despair, he shuffled back to the table and settled himself to read the newspaper. It had been a long time since she'd seen him so happy. Not since the day Hilda shut Molly away. Before, she'd dismissed his feelings for the lass as puppy love, but she realized that awful day how wrong she'd been. He really loved the lass as a man loves a woman. To see him play like a child again lightened her own heavy heart.

Cat cocked her head and studied the picture before her, savoring the moment and storing it away to look at again and again in the long loneliness of night, like a tintype in an album of memories. Geordie, her wee brother all grown up to a handsome man, a successful journalist.

Effie sat beside him, looking her fourteen years for a change, her copper hair loose on her shoulders. So young to work so hard, barely older than the bairns she cared for each day and doing a good job of it as well.

And in her sister's lap sat Duncan, half a year old and big for his age. His hair and eyes were her own, so like her real father, or her cousin Malcolm and his wee Rory. If she could trust her cousin's last letter, her father was keeping true to his word to leave them both in peace. And no matter how she longed to go home, she must remember that they depended on her to keep her word and never return to Skye.

She smiled down at her son, glad that he took after her in looks. It would be so hard to see Ian each time she looked at him, although his manner was like his father's, calm and quiet. Effie cuddled the lad close, tickling him under the chin until he squirmed and squealed with delight.

Upstairs, Betsy chattered, her high, sweet voice punctuated by Sanapia's deeper tones. Cat wondered again how she'd ever managed without the Indian woman. Sanapia's calm know-how eased all their lives, and the wisdom of her words drew confidences from Geordie and Effie. Cat even found herself opening up to the woman, sharing her fears and worries.

And then there was the woman's boundless energy. Already today Sanapia had bathed and changed the baby and managed to get Betsy in and out of the tub as well. Now she was getting the lass dressed in her new party frock. Cat could concentrate on the cake, knowing Betsy would emerge scrubbed and polished, every curl, every button, every bow in perfect order.

Effie looked up from her game with Duncan. "Need some help?"

Cat shook her head. "You rest. Besides, holding the bairn *is* helping." She moved to the sideboard, testing the thickened flour and milk to see if it was cool enough.

Effie's voice trailed after her. "How many guests are we expecting?"

Lifting the lid from the butter crock, Cat ladled a teacup full and added the yellow lump to a bowl of precious white cane sugar and creamed the two together. "Will is bringing Nana, and I invited the Vanzees. Joe said for sure he'd be here."

The legs of Effie's chair scraped the floor as she pushed back her chair. "Here, Uncle George. Hold your nephew awhile." She dumped the lad in the midst of the newspaper and ran from the room.

Geordie dropped the pages and caught the bairn under the arms, lifting him high in the air. His eyes met Cat's, and his face split into a grin. "Poor Joe. He'd best keep his wits about him. I fancy our Effie's set her cap."

Cat chuckled as she added vanilla extract to the fluffy mixture in the bowl. The lass would come back in a few minutes with her hair done up high, wearing her best red bombazine dress, just that month cut down from one of Nana Bascom's. For all the good it would do her. She stirred the cooked flour and milk into the bowl, then hurried to the windowsill to turn the cakes out of their pans, praying they wouldn't stick.

Joe never showed the slightest interest in Effie. He was kind and considerate, but he always talked to her as he did his younger brother. Cat knew it infuriated her sister to be treated as a grown-up by everyone except the one man who counted. She returned to the sideboard and dug in the wooden spoon, beating the thick mixture together.

After several minutes Cat's arm grew weary, and she stopped to rest a moment. Sighing, she glanced at her reflection in the mirror above the sideboard. She wiped her hands on her apron and reached up to tuck in a straggling curl, wondering if Will would like her new hairstyle. She frowned at herself and turned back to beating the icing. What an odd thing to think about.

After all, the two of them were only friends. It hardly mattered to him how she dressed or wore her hair as long as she did her job. True, she did enjoy working with him, being with him most every day. And she found herself especially looking forward to seeing him today, but that was as much for the bairns as for herself. Or was it? She forced the question aside, and with it the glow bubbling inside her.

Betsy and Duncan were lucky to have people like Will and Nana in their lives. Texas wasn't like Skye, where families stayed close. Why, except for her brother and sister, the Bascoms were all the family her bairns knew. She lifted the spoon. A stiff peak formed in the fluffy whiteness, the same consistency as whipped cream. Just right.

She shook a finger at her brother. "Stay out of my icing, then." Stepping close, she gave Duncan a gentle tap on the chin with one finger. "And you as well, my lad."

He cooed up at her and clutched her hand, his dark blue eyes a mirror of her own.

For a moment she longed to swing him up and hold him to her breast, but that wouldn't get the cake iced. She planted a kiss on his forehead and untangled his fingers from a strand of her hair.

The cakes both tested cool to her fingertips as she brushed the loose crumbs from the tops and sides.

Effie's heels clicked down the hallway, and she swooped into the kitchen, plucking Duncan from Geordie's arms. "Well?"

Cat bit her lip to keep from smiling as she examined her sister's appearance. "You'll do." She slid the first layer onto a cake plate dotted with icing to hold it in place, then scooped a dollop of fluffy white into the middle of the round layer and smoothed it out to the edge all around.

"You'll do? That's all?" She tapped one toe against the hardwood floor and turned to Geordie. "And what do you say?"

With careful fingers Cat eased the top layer from the rack and settled it in place.

Geordie leaned back in his chair and crossed his arms over his chest, letting his gaze travel up and down, his lips pursed together. "Aye. Cat has the right of it." He let his careful American speech slip back into Scots. "You'll do in a pinch." His eyes twinkled, and he grinned.

With her free hand Effie aimed a blow at his head, but he ducked. "You're both cruel." The lilt of her voice belied the anger of her words. She cuddled the bairn against her shoulder. "Well, at least Duncan loves me."

Cat turned away to hide her smile, spreading icing over the top and down the sides of both layers.

At the sound of hoofbeats Effie danced to the window, Duncan still clasped in her arms. Her face beamed her welcome as Joe and Pieter stepped through the kitchen door.

"Effie, Geordie, Miz Macleod." Joe tipped his hat to each in turn. "My mama asked me to give you her apologies." Spots of color appeared in each of his handsome cheeks. "She was feeling too poorly to come, so she sent me and Pieter. I—I hope you understand."

"Aye." The taste of the word soured on her tongue. She knew Hilda Vanzee still blamed her for whatever had happened with Molly. She worried about the lass, cooped up in that farmhouse so long with only her mother's curses for company. Still, she knew there was nought any of them could do for her.

But Cat wasn't about to let anything spoil the day. She forced a smile to her lips. "And we're grateful she could spare you. We'll have to be sure to remember to send her some cake." She squatted beside the smaller lad. "So, Pieter, and how is the foot?" She asked him each time they met, a special wee ritual they shared.

"Still fine. Wanna see?" Without waiting for an answer,

he launched into a shuffling dance, designed to show how well his once-injured foot could move.

Cat clapped her hands in appreciation. "And could you drink a root beer after all that? I made it myself last winter."

His pale blue eyes widened. "Yes, please." Somehow his voice sounded different, older. It took her a minute to understand. He'd lost his lisp. Another wee one growing up. "How about you, Joe?"

"Yes'm. Thank you." Without a glance at Effie he strode to the table and dropped into a chair next to Geordie.

Effie hugged Duncan and settled herself in the rocker, her stiff smile and high color the only signs of her disappointment.

There was nothing anybody could do but let them work it out for themselves. Cat hurried to the pantry, grabbing an earthenware pitcher and turning the tap on the keg to fill it with root beer.

When she returned, Sanapia stood in the doorway, dark and erect. And in the middle of the floor, Betsy held out the edges of her skirt, eager to show off her new pink dress. Golden curls shimmered around her face as she toddled to each guest, expecting and receiving their adoration. If only Ian could see her.

Sighing, Cat set the pitcher in the center of the table and opened the top of the breakfront to get her best company glasses. And why not? Her daughter's birthday was a special occasion.

When she turned back with her hands full of glassware, Will and Nana stood in the doorway. Her heart lifted as Betsy squealed and toddled toward them amid all the greetings.

Will held up his hands. "Wait. We brought a very special surprise for everyone." He stepped to one side of the doorway, and Nana stepped to the other, her wrinkled face glowing.

Into the space between stood Molly.

Cat froze for a moment, unable to believe the miracle before her. No one had been able to see Molly since last February.

Now here she stood, dressed in an old Mother Hubbard

dress and her best bonnet. Her face was fuller, and the loose dress couldn't quite hide her heavier breasts or the dome of her belly.

So that was the shame Hilda had screamed about. Just what did Hilda think it would help by locking her up in her condition? The truth would be known sooner or later. And why blame the Macleods for it, or was it rather the Galbraiths? She shot a glance at Geordie, unable to keep the question from her mind. But the grayish tinge of his face was all the answer she needed. If he were the father, he'd at least have suspected. No, her brother had no part in this, more's the pity. He'd have made the lass a good husband.

Cat turned back to their surprise guest. She looked a bit different, but Cat knew she was still the same, still the Molly they all loved, no matter what she'd been through.

A smile twitched the corners of Molly's mouth. "Well, may I come in?"

Geordie took a deep breath and wiped his sweaty palms on his trousers, then forced himself to cross the room to Molly. "May I sit with you?" He'd wanted to talk to her all through the party, ever since he saw her standing in the doorway. Even if—well, sure it hurt, knowing she'd been with someone else instead of him. But he knew he still loved her, no matter what.

Molly nodded, a smile trembling on her lips as she patted the chair beside her. "I'd like that."

He settled on the hard seat, then leaned forward, resting his elbows on his widespread knees, his clasped hands drooping between. "So, how've you been?" Heat flooded his cheeks. How could he ask such a stupid question? As if he couldn't see for himself.

She sighed. "Tolerable, considering." She smoothed her dress over her belly. "I heard you that day, arguing with Mama." Her fingertips brushed the back of his hand. "I tried and tried to tell her it wasn't you, but she just wouldn't believe me. I would've apologized sooner, but . . ." Her voice trailed off.

Geordie looked away and nodded. "We kept asking what

happened, but those who knew weren't telling." He cleared his throat, trying to think of something to say, to fill the silence that lay between them. "So how'd you get her to let you come today?"

Molly's eyes sparkled, and she cupped one hand over her mouth to cover a giggle. "She didn't let me. I heard Joe begging her to let me come to Betsy's party, but she just kept telling him no." Her pretty mouth twisted for a moment, but then she rushed on. "After he and Pieter left, I heard her snoring in her room. So I climbed out the window and walked real fast to the road, and Doc and Miz Bascom picked me up." Her mouth trembled. "She's gonna be real put out at me when I go back."

Geordie clenched the seat of the wooden chair with both hands and tried to keep his voice calm. "Then don't go."

Her eyes widened. "What?"

The frightened whisper somehow gave him courage. "Don't go home. Stay here with us."

Her brown lashes curtained the blue of her eyes as she shook her head. "No, I couldn't. Then folks would think it really was you."

He shrugged. "So let them. What do we care?"

Unshed tears glistened in her eyes. "It wouldn't be fair to you."

He leaned over and took her hand, breathing in the honey smell of her. "Marry me. Let me take care of you and the baby." His voice trembled. "I love you, no matter what you did."

She tipped her head to one side. "You really mean it, don't you? You really do love me."

He nodded, his eyes drinking in the beauty of her face.

Her words came very slowly, as if she chose them and placed them just so, like beads on a string. "It won't be easy, you know. Folks can be very unforgiving around here."

Warmth stole through him. She was going to say yes. Molly was going to agree to marry him.

Her small white teeth bit into her bottom lip. "Just one thing I want you to know—the baby's father, I loved him.

And I think he loved me, but he's, well, he's not free to marry."

"Poor man." He could understand how a man could lose himself with Molly, could refuse to think beyond the joy of holding her, touching her. Although it was torture to think of her in another man's arms, he couldn't hate this mysterious stranger. In fact, he ought to be grateful the man wasn't free, or she'd likely be married already.

He glanced around the room at the other guests, then shrugged and slid to one knee in front of her chair, still clasping her hands in his. He didn't care who saw, who knew. He pitched his voice louder, so all the room would hear. "Amalia Vanzee, will you marry me?"

Voices hushed, and the room filled with shocked silence. A grin tugged at Geordie's mouth and he couldn't keep the old Scots lilt from his whisper. "This time you must answer me, lassie, for I *willna* ask you thrice."

Molly's eyes shone, and pink tinged her cheeks, but her eyes never left his. "I'd be proud to."

Chapter 22

Will smoothed the front of his waistcoat, grateful to be outside in whatever relief the twilight offered from the heat. Butter-yellow light glowed from the windows of the farmhouse, competing with the last rays of the sunset. A roar of chair-scraping and lowered voices echoed through the kitchen door. Not a bad turnout, considering.

At least under the circumstances, Molly might be spared the *chivaree*. He chuckled at some of his memories of wedding-night forays in his youth, blackening his face and wearing his clothes backward, demanding drinks and making noise with the best of them.

A bit of a wind carried the sweet scent of wildflowers to him, pressing his best suit against his body and drying the sweat on the back of his neck. One thing was certain, Molly had picked a beautiful day for her wedding.

Not that any day would be a bad day to see these two young people joined together. He never thought Hilda would agree, but she'd waded right into the thick of the plans as if a pregnant bride was a common thing, which, come to think of it, it might be. He ought to know.

Will fingered his collar and wondered how much longer he'd have to wait. He had patients who needed him; he couldn't hang around here all day. Maybe agreeing to give the bride away hadn't been such a good idea. After all, the girl had a father in Dallas. She never would have asked him if Axel had been able to come home. And she was probably grateful to him for keeping her secret so long.

The minister was a replacement too. The same jack-leg preacher who showed up at Ian's funeral. Will hadn't cared much for the fellow then, but at least he hadn't sniffed and turned away like the regular parson. But if Molly didn't hurry up, all the guests would get up and leave.

He stood on tiptoe and peeked through the parlor window. In a back corner he made out Yvette's black dress and a few of her girls in their Sunday finest. She'd even cleaned up old Quincy and dragged him along as an escort. Leave it to Molly to invite them, and Cat to agree, in spite of the decent women of the town. Not that Molly hadn't given them plenty to talk about already, the old biddies.

Although it didn't seem to faze the groom. Geordie was already in his place, hands clasped in front of him, his hair slicked back, and a dazed smile on his face. Joe stood beside him, his fair skin scrubbed bright red beneath his white-blond hair. At least that was fitting, the bride's brother acting as best man.

Lewis Price caught Will's eye and gave him a wink, looking more like a riverboat gambler than an undertaker in his ruffled white shirt and fancy jacket. Will settled back on his heels. No sense letting Hilda catch him peeping through the window. He'd had about as much of her bossing as he could stand at the rehearsal.

He paced to the back of the building again, peering in the open kitchen door. Sometimes womenfolk took an inordinate amount of time getting ready for social events.

Molly must be glad to have her freedom. He hoped her gratitude might turn to love for Geordie after a while. He was a good man and deserved to be happy. He wondered if he'd be able to marry Cat, knowing she didn't love him.

Catriona would be glad of the girl's help, no doubt, at least until the new baby came. Another mouth for Cat to feed. He worried about her, trying to take care of everyone, run a home, and work long hours with him. She ought to have some time to take it easy. But he needed her, depended on her. And not just for her help or her healing skills. He found himself confiding in her about himself and his life, as well as his dream of building a hospital in Arlington. And while they worked, she confided in him about how much she missed Ian and how much she wanted to make the farm a success.

Not that the extra work seemed to be harming her. And she surely looked healthy, with her shining hair and bright eyes. It was a pity a woman like her slept alone every night. He couldn't imagine her staying that way for long. The image of her with another man flashed through his mind, a bolt of lightning from a clear sky. His fists clenched and his body stiffened for a moment. Then the rage bled away, leaving his mouth dry.

He shoved his hands into his pockets to stifle the trembling and turned to pace toward the front of the farmhouse. Not for the first time, he realized he was jealous. Jealous of the wife of his best friend. No, not wife—*widow*. He stopped, his feet scuffing the gritty soil of the dooryard. Perhaps that was why he'd hired her, so he could be with her all the time, keep her from seeing other men.

A door opened and closed, and he forced his thoughts away from Catriona as light footsteps came down the kitchen steps toward him. Molly smiled as she slipped her hand through the crook of the arm he offered. She'd made good use of her time. Crocheted lace adorned the front of her loose white dress, and her hair swept up from her temples in graceful waves. Her cheeks glowed so pink, for a moment he wondered if she'd borrowed some paint from one of Yvette's girls, until she reached up gloved hands and pinched them with her fingertips. He'd never realized before how attractive a woman Molly truly was.

He patted her gloved hand and guided her to the front of the farmhouse and up the steps. The voices inside the parlor hushed and a sea of faces turned toward them. A fiddle sang out, its plaintive voice filling the still air. Sweat dampened his sides beneath his shirt as he strode with her through the front doorway and into the parlor, matching his pace to hers.

When they reached the minister, Geordie stepped forward, surprise and delight coloring his features. So Molly's husband-to-be hadn't realized what a looker she was either. Better that kind of surprise than the other direction; he certainly didn't look to be disappointed. Molly released Will's arm and stepped up to the altar with her groom.

As the minister spoke the familiar words, Will stepped back and slid into the front pew beside Catriona, aware of the faint scent of honey and sunshine rising from her. He glanced at her and then away, struck by how fragile she suddenly seemed, so vulnerable, such easy prey for any man. Desire and guilt twisted together in him. He owed it to his dead friend to protect her, not to let her be influenced by any needs but her own—not even his. He would have to be strong enough to wait and let her come to him.

Molly's soft voice filled the farmhouse in response to the minister's question. "I will."

Will made his own vow as the bride's words echoed inside his head.

A shaft of early morning touched her closed eyelids, turning the cool darkness to glowing red. Molly stretched, enjoying the softness of the mattress beneath her and the warmth of Geordie's naked body so close beside hers. The faint smell of him lingered on her skin, and she kept her eyes closed, breathing it in. Her mind skipped back like a child at play, touching down for a moment at each precious memory of the day before.

Turning her head, she drank in the sight of her husband's face, so peaceful in sleep, almost childlike. She longed to hold his head against her bosom, but she didn't want to wake him. Instead, she wanted to enjoy her memories a bit longer. Now, where had she been? Oh, yes, after the guests had finally left, Geordie had led her to his room, *their* room now. Then he took her in his arms, looked her right in the eye, and said the words she'd waited to hear. "I love you,

Mrs. Galbraith." She squirmed with delight at the memory, knowing how lucky she was.

His eyes had widened when he pulled her down onto the bed and she didn't resist, when she returned his kisses and pressed herself against him, her hands exploring his body.

Even in the beginning with Stephen it had never been so wonderful. She'd loved him, but she'd never taken much physical pleasure from their coupling. And once she'd told him about their baby, well, it was best not to think on that now.

Instead, her thoughts turned back to Geordie, her face warming at the memory of her new husband's hands and mouth exploring her body, the waves of pleasure he called forth with his passion. No one had ever told her how wonderful it could be between a man and a woman.

If only she'd known sooner that it was really Geordie she wanted, loved, before she wasted herself on another woman's husband. God, what a fool she'd been! But there was no going back, and somehow it had worked out better than she'd ever hoped—better than she deserved.

She glanced at Geordie's handsome profile, his heavy dark hair curling around his wide forehead, the sensuality of his gentle mouth, so relaxed and vulnerable in sleep. She loved being with him, now more than ever, and not just in bed; they'd always been friends, sharing the same interests in books and new ideas. And now that she knew he loved her, and she'd proven her love to him, no one could ever part them. Now their souls would be joined together for always.

Cradling the dome of her belly, she slid from the high bed and tiptoed across the thick rag rug to the chest of drawers where a plain water pitcher stood. After filling the china basin half full, she found a clean handkerchief in the top drawer and used it for a washcloth, giving herself a thorough spit bath. When he awoke, if her new husband wanted her again, she'd be ready, all fresh and clean.

Shivering in the chill air, she realized she was too excited to keep still much longer, and if she stayed, Geordie would wake. Tenderness warmed her as she glanced at him, so peaceful in his sleep. With quiet movements she slipped on her undergarments and loose dress. Sitting on the floor, she slid her feet into an old pair of soft boots, then faced the mirror, searching her face for any sign of the change in her. The same plump blond girl stared back at her as when she dressed in her wedding gown the afternoon before.

She tiptoed to the bed, a new sense of her own power rising up as she stared down at the sleeping man. Even if it didn't show on the outside yet, she knew what it was to be a woman now, even more surely than the day she first got her curse, or the day Doc told her she carried Stephen's child. To give such pleasure to another human being, and to get so much in return— It was almost more joy than a body could bear.

With her fingertips she traced the smooth line of his jaw, then bent to kiss one corner of his mouth. He stirred and mumbled something, then rolled away from her, pulling the coverlet to his ears.

A smile tugged at her lips as she tiptoed out, easing the door closed without a sound. "Sweet dreams." Her soft murmur echoed in the quiet hallway. The whole family was sleeping late after the excitement of the wedding the day before, so she slipped down the stairs and out the side door.

She strolled toward the barn, still musing on the mysteries Geordie had shown her. For years she'd watched stallions mounting mares, bulls covering cows, even the barn cat rolling on the ground surrounded by toms. And always she'd wondered what drove them to couple. She'd never guessed at the magic, the deep joy, the satisfaction of sharing herself with the man she loved. It was all so much more than the simple getting of offspring.

Her steps slowed, and her thoughts darted this way and that in guilt and pain. Her child. She was carrying another man's child. How could Geordie ever forgive that? She could barely stand to think of what she'd done, what she was asking of this man who loved her. To raise another man's child as his own, to let everyone in the county believe it was his. Taking a deep breath, she told herself to calm down, that it would be all right. Geordie loved her. He'd said so, shown her how much.

For a moment she imagined herself holding a baby in her arms, Geordie's baby. She would be so happy to be carrying his child. And if anyone did, he deserved a son of his own. As soon as possible after this baby was born, they'd try for another, one of their own. And in the meantime, well, she'd just have to find as many ways as she could to make it up to him.

Chapter 23

July 1887

As Geordie settled himself on a bench at a makeshift table, the clamor of voices around him filled him with as much excitement as the smells of roast meats and fresh-baked bread filled him with hunger. One of the cooks had told him they'd baked fourteen thousand loaves and roasted several hundred animals to feed the throng of anti-prohibitionists. Workers passed among the tables carrying platters heaped with food. He hoped there'd be enough for everybody. Some placed the number of folks on the grounds as high as twenty thousand, the biggest rally of its kind ever seen in Texas. And he was here to report it.

It was a grand day. The only way it could be better was to have Molly with him to share the excitement. He sighed as he helped himself to fried chicken and corn on the cob. But he knew it was better for her to stay home and rest, especially now that she got tired so easily.

It didn't seem to matter how often he told her to take it easy. She still insisted on working too hard, probably from some wrong-headed notion of making it up to him for not being the father of her baby.

Hell, he didn't care who she'd slept with before, now that she was his wife. That baby was what finally brought them together. Without it, she might never have married him. And now more than ever before he knew how empty his life would have been if somehow she hadn't said yes.

If only she could have watched the parade that morning. What a sight that had been, first the Texas veterans, all now in their sixties and seventies, leading the parade. The crowds gave them a rousing cheer as they passed. And then came the hundreds of voters from all over the state, black groups and white groups side by side, holding their bright banners in the air. He'd seen Arlington's own undertaker, Lewis Price, and that old reprobate Quincy, marching side by side.

He bit into a cob of buttered corn, the sweet juices wetting his chin. The people of Texas could be proud of the way they treated their black voters. Why, they even had one for a speaker, a man named Melvin Wade. Of course, he spoke to the black audience over on the other side, where they sat eating their dinners. After cleaning the last kernels from the cob, Geordie set it aside and bit into a chicken leg, savoring the crispy skin and the tender meat inside.

Voices hushed around him as the chairman introduced the next speaker. "Gentlemen, I give you a native Texan, a fearless officer, a true democrat—the attorney general of the state of Texas, James Stephen Hogg."

Shouts and applause accompanied the tall, heavy man as he mounted the steps to the podium. "I have a letter here in my hand for you from Governor Ross." He shucked his coat and held up a sheet of paper as his voice boomed out over the crowd.

Politicians always amazed Geordie with their volume, even one with such a broad chest and obvious lung power. He wiped his hands on a coarse linen napkin and dug his notebook out of his pocket to note the letter's contents, wondering if Ross had made a mistake by sending someone else to give this speech. After all, the state capital wasn't that far from Fort Worth. Maybe the governor hadn't realized just how many voters would show up today. If so, he wasn't alone in underestimating the anti-prohibitionist movement in Texas.

Hogg held up his hands for silence and read from the paper in his hands. "I rejoice in your movement and have faith and hope in your triumphant success in an uncompromising antagonism to every policy inculcating the idea that the people of Texas have fallen so low in their private lives or public morals that justifies such a paternal or protective spirit, or the notion that society cannot prosper without at every turn being watched by the state."

Geordie smiled as he scribbled his notes. Sounded just like Ross's rhetoric, although the way this fellow read it, it almost seemed to make some kind of sense. He turned his attention back to the broad figure on the grandstand. The man had set the letter aside and was using the power of his voice to woo the crowd, calling for a sound defeat of the prohibition amendment at the polls.

After today's parade, the prohibitionists themselves had conceded defeat, even before the elections. Geordie glanced at the rapt faces around him.

Hogg paused to sip a glass of lemonade.

A voice called out from the crowd. "So, Mr. Hogg, how about the railroads?"

Hogg hooked his thumbs through his suspenders and cocked his head. "Well, sir, as I see it, the fight is on, and I may get the worst of it." Even at this distance Geordie could see the wide grin stretched across the man's face. "But one thing is certain, somebody else will get a little disfigured in the fray."

This attorney general bore watching. Not only was the fellow a fine speaker, but he'd started out as a newspaper publisher before studying law. Without a doubt, James Stephen Hogg had a bright future in Texas politics.

Effie picked up another carrot from the dry sink. Yellow-orange juice stained her fingertips, making them dry and sticky. Seemed as if she'd scraped and sliced ten pounds of the things, but at least she was almost done. Then she could go on to another chore.

Threshing days always went the same. Up early to fix a big breakfast, then no more than get that cleaned up and it was time to start dinner. From then until noon, the whole house smelled of chicken boiling on the stove, and the steam made the hot kitchen unbearable.

She was so sick of making and eating chicken pie, she could scream. This must be the tenth threshing party they'd been to this month, and every woman cooked the same dish the same way. At least this one was at home.

She and Molly used to sneak away to her room when the older women weren't looking. She never used to hate the harvest then. It always reminded her of Skye. In Scotland, the crofters did all their jobs together. Here, although sometimes the menfolk helped each other rounding up stray cattle and branding new calves, harvest time was the only part of the year when folks pitched in and helped one another.

To think, she actually used to look forward to threshing season so she could spend time with her best friend. Those days were gone for good, with Molly sick abed. None of the others were near her age. They all sat or stood in groups of three or four, gossiping about babies and menfolk until she thought she'd scream. And after the baby came, Molly'd be one of *them*.

Almost enough to make a body wish she was back in school, with lots of other things to think about. Almost, but not quite. Although October was only weeks away, she knew she wasn't ready to begin again yet. She picked up the last carrot and set the edge of the knife against its skin. She wondered what her friend was doing at that moment, upstairs in bed. Probably reading a book.

Mrs. Hale's voice rose above the murmur. "Well, isn't it obvious now why Hilda locked her up?"

Effie bit her lip and set the carrot on the cutting board, giving it a chop that sent one of the orange disks flying.

Mrs. Anderson nodded, her voice dropping to a confidential level, but still loud enough so Effie couldn't help but overhear. "Should have locked her up sooner, if you ask me."

Mrs. Hale's eyes shone as she leaned over the cake she was icing. "Why, I'm not surprised it happened. After all, they were practically living here together in sin all those months."

Effie gave the carrot another vicious whack. Didn't they realize she was right here, listening to every word?

Mrs. Anderson frowned. "Do you really think so? And

him so successful at the newspaper and all. Why, I heard one of those New York papers bought one of his stories and printed it. You'd think he'd have married her right away, before she started to show."

Effie scooped the pile of orange circles into a bowl and stood. She'd heard all she cared to.

Mrs. Hale tilted her head to one side. "Maybe he has his reasons. For all we know, he might not *be* the father." She turned and smiled as Effie stooped to pick up a fallen slice of carrot. "Oh, hello, dear. We were just talking about your new sister-in-law. How is the poor thing doing? We're so sorry she isn't feeling well today."

Of course they were sorry. If Molly'd been downstairs they could have tortured her directly instead of just gossiping about her behind her back. She took a deep breath and forced herself to smile. They were stupid and thoughtless, but they meant no harm. Their own lives must be boring compared to Molly's, or even her own. And much as she'd like to take them to task, she knew Molly needed all the goodwill she could get. "Well, she keeps her spirits up as best she can. She reads books to improve her mind." She cast about for something else to say as they goggled at her, but she knew she had to get away or she'd scream. "Would you excuse me, please?"

She set the bowl of sliced carrots on the sideboard and grabbed a half-bushel of peas. "If you want me, I'll be on the porch shelling these."

Cat looked up from a steaming pot and smiled, her hand continuing to make circles with the wooden spoon. Sweat glistened on her face, and black tendrils curled at her temples. "Aye, I'd join you if I could. It should be a wee bit cooler outside." Her eyes darted toward the two gossips across the room. "And a bit quieter as well."

Effie touched Cat's shoulder in gratitude, then turned and wrestled the basket out the screen door and around the corner, where she could get a clear view of the steam engine and the men working. She narrowed her eyes against the glare, letting her gaze roam over the small figures until she picked him out.

Joe's bare arms bulged in the sunlight. Damn him anyhow. She couldn't decide whether to love him or hate him. Of course, every time she tried to hate him, he'd do something so sweet she couldn't stay mad. If he'd just stop treating her like a kid. She ought to quit wasting her time fixing herself up for him. She dropped down into an old rocker and set the basket between her feet. Why, today he hadn't even noticed her new dress. The man was just plain ignorant.

But then, who was she to talk? She never even stopped to wonder who might be the father of Molly's child. She'd been so startled when she found out, she never thought to ask. She picked up a pea pod and pressed the narrow sides together. Could the old biddies in the kitchen be right? What if it wasn't Geordie's child? She had a hard time imagining her brother in a compromising situation with any woman, let alone with Molly. But if it wasn't his child, why would he marry her? She had to admit, he'd always been crazy about the girl, but Molly never seemed interested.

She dropped the opened pod back into the basket and lifted her gaze to the threshing crew again, picking out Joe's tall, lean frame and shock of white-blond hair. Would she be strong enough to resist her passion for him if he ever stopped treating her like a little sister? She shivered in spite of the heat, a delicious chill promising unknown pleasures.

There was so much she still didn't understand about men and women. It confused her, trying to figure out why some women seemed to like *it* and some didn't. She knew folks divided women into good and bad by whether they liked it or not. But somehow it seemed backward to her. If men liked it, then a woman who liked it too ought to be a good woman, but everyone said they were bad. She wished she could ask if Molly liked it with Geordie. She twisted her face at the disgusting thought. And what about Cat—had she liked it with Ian, did she miss it? And did she want to do it with Will?

A peal of laughter echoed from inside the kitchen. Enough nonsense. Better get these vegetables ready before they closed the pies and put them in to bake. She reached again for the pea pod she'd dropped, stripping the shiny green seeds from their shell, letting them fall into the hammock of cloth between her spread knees. Still, she hated to let those gossips talk about her brother and her best friend that way.

Sighing, she reached for another pea pod, her hands working of their own accord. There was nothing she could do but wait and hope Molly's baby looked like Geordie.

Catriona leaned forward in the straight-back chair, breathing in the masculine odors of leather and tobacco. She knew she was the only woman in the City Exchange Building today, but she was determined not to let it keep her from getting the information she wanted. If it bothered the stodgy men of the exchange, so be it; she wasn't about to cater to them. She glanced beside her at Will, his face smooth and still, only his eyes warm as his gaze met hers. Hoping he understood, she turned her attention to the man across the desk. "Mr. Macune, could you explain to me in more detail how the cotton is sold?"

C. W. Macune was even more charming in person than she'd remembered, and being an Alliance man, he likely saw nothing unusual in a woman concerning herself with farm business, particularly a widow woman. His broad, handsome face came alive with good humor. "Why, Miz Macleod, I'd be honored to explain while I show you the sample room." He rose and gave a half-bow. "And you, Doctor, would you care to see it as well?"

Cat gave Will a grateful smile as he agreed and got to his feet, his lean body elegant in his black suit. She always felt a little flush of pride walking beside such a fine-looking man. She allowed him to match strides with the state chairman, following along behind as Macune described his plans. She found herself enjoying the outing even more than she'd expected, although she was almost certain Will had little real interest in the workings of the cotton market. It was lovely to share something with him besides medicine and family concerns. And to be honest with herself, she enjoyed showing off in an area she understood better than he.

"When a county business agent gets together twenty-five samples, he sends them here. We'll lay them out on tables like these so the buyers can come and inspect the quality and bid on the stored bales." Macune paused to allow Cat's slow steps to bring her abreast of them in the high-ceilinged room. Wee bits of cotton lint floated in a shaft of sunshine from a skylight. "And it may be possible to thus provide county agents with accurate information about market values, allowing them to sell at an equitable price to local buyers as well, without the cotton ever leaving their county warehouse to come here."

Cat nodded. "So when do we begin?"

His eyes twinkled at her, and his mustache, normally turned down at the ends, spread across his face as he smiled. "We'll wait for approval of the delegates at the convention in Waco next month. I trust you'll be there representing your local alliance?"

"I haven't made up my mind as yet." Molly's baby was due about that time. She glanced sidelong at Will, remembering the words they'd already exchanged about it. Her desires pulled her both ways, wanting to stay with him and be with Molly when her time came, but at the same time feeling duty bound to go. "But I am considering it. Have you found any help for the farmers in the crop-lien system?"

Macune sobered. "I've done a great deal of thinking on the subject. I'll unveil my plans at the convention."

"All the more reason to consider attending." She glanced again at Will, wondering at his unusual silence.

Will stood a little apart, his eyes narrowed in concentration, his gaze fixed on a blank wall. Sometimes when she looked at him, it struck her anew just how handsome he was, and she found herself drawn to him, almost against her will.

Macune cleared his throat. "Would you excuse me, please? Urgent business calls." He made the same half-bow as before, then captured her hand and gave it a warm squeeze. "Thank you for coming, Miz Macleod. Your questions are welcome, and your interest is appreciated."

"As are your answers, Mr. Macune." Her cheeks warmed as she slid her hand from his grasp.

The state chairman turned to Will, holding out his hand. "Doctor."

Will blinked, then shook the man's hand, murmuring a polite phrase.

Macune hurried away, raising his hand in greeting as he neared another group of visitors.

"Can you bear to drag yourself away, then, lad?" She smiled to take the sting from her words.

Will laughed. "I wouldn't make much of an actor, now, would I?"

She shook her head, pleased with how the day had gone and wondering if she should go to Waco again in a month. Slipping her hand through the crook of his arm, she clung to him, the hard warmth of his forearm sending thrills of pleasure through her. He guided her down the stairs to the outside and placed his warm, strong hands on her waist as he helped her into the buggy. Without a sound he clucked to the horse, and they jerked into motion, threading their way through the traffic in the streets.

As they reached the edge of town, she leaned over and touched his arm, putting all her gratitude into her voice. "Thank you for taking me. It meant that much to me, knowing we dinna agree on the Alliance."

He turned toward her, the corners of his eyes crinkling. "Happy to do it. I know how important it is to you, even if I still have some reservations." His smile slid away again, and they rode in silence for a few moments before he turned to her again. "How is Molly today?"

A chill crept over her. She'd never heard quite that tone in his voice before. "About the same as yesterday. Why?"

"Have you noticed how her hands and feet have swollen way beyond the usual? I was hoping you'd have an herbal remedy." He kept his face forward, his knuckles white as he gripped the reins.

She considered, searching her memory for anything helpful. "I never saw this on Skye. Just how serious is it?"

His jaw set, and for a moment she thought he wouldn't answer at all. "If it goes into toxemia, well— Let's just say it could be dangerous to the mother as well as the child."

Chapter 24

September 1887

The clean smell of fresh-turned soil rose around Joe as he tamped down the loose dirt with the back of the shovel, then trod over the makeshift grave with his boots to pack it even more. Didn't want the coyotes to come sniffing around the herd and take it into their narrow heads to help themselves.

He wiped his hands on his chaps, leaving sticky pink smears. He hated messing with unborn calves, funny little hairless, unfinished-looking things. But he had to bury them to keep the placenta smell from getting the other in-calf cows to dropping theirs early. He'd already cut out the mother and isolated her so she wouldn't cause the others to abort. He'd seen it run through a herd like a prairie fire.

Miz Macleod would likely be upset about losing the calf. She loved critters, and she had a real knack with them too. And the herd was important to her. She'd told him how it had been her dead husband's dream. You had to admire a woman who kept on going no matter how hard it got. 'Course, the whole family was that way. Look at little Effie, just a kid herself and taking on so much of her sister's work with the kids and the house. And Geordie, working his way up to reporter.

Too bad Molly wasn't more like them. But now she was

feeling so poorly and all, it seemed like God was punishing her for giving in to fleshly temptations. He'd never make that mistake himself.

Swinging back up into the saddle, he turned Paint toward the farmhouse so he could tell Miz Macleod. She knew how to cure such things. Too bad she couldn't do more for Molly. He'd been relieved when his sister married Geordie, although he suspected the baby didn't belong to her new husband. If he knew who the varmint was, he'd give him a good whipping for getting an innocent young girl in a family way, then leaving her like that. But he reckoned none of that mattered now she was married. He just hoped his little sister would be okay.

Cat pressed the needle through the thick layers of the quilt with one hand and retrieved it with the other, trying not to think about the spontaneous abortion running through her herd. She was grateful to Joe for acting so fast, separating the gravid cows from the ones who'd already dropped their young too soon. She only hoped the herbal infusion and the richer feed could strengthen the remaining cows and preserve their calves.

"So, Miz Macleod, just how does this new joint-note plan work exactly?" Nelda Hale's smile creased her sagging cheeks but never reached her eyes.

Cat pushed the needle through from the underside, checking to make sure she kept the stitch small and tight as she considered her answer. "Simple, really. Each member figures what supplies he needs for the coming year." She smiled at the woman, reminding herself how important it was to get as much support as possible if Macune's new plan was to work—even from old busybodies like Mrs. Hale. "Then they tally all the lists up and make a joint note for everybody in that Alliance, promising a portion of next year's crops as security." She plied her needle through the many layers of cloth, pleased that the afternoon's quilting bee gave her a chance to explain.

"Do tell." Nelda's eyes narrowed, and she leaned forward a bit. "What then?"

Cat's voice continued. "Then they send the note and the list of supplies on to the Exchange. Mr. Macune uses the notes to borrow money from the banks to pay for the supplies." She glanced at the other quilters seated around the large wooden frame. For a moment she felt like the quilt, held in place and pierced by all their eyes. "The farmers get their supplies at cost, then when they sell their crops in the fall, they pay off the notes, Macune pays off the banks, and everybody is happy."

Minnie Anderson's whiny voice pitched in. "Everybody but the merchants."

Cat snorted. "Those leeches. Serves them right."

Mrs. Anderson's fingers stopped moving and she leaned back in her chair. "Still, they stand to lose money, and that makes them dangerous."

"Aye, and so were the constables from Glasgow when they attacked my village on Skye, but we dinna let that stop us." Cat unclenched her hands and set the needle to the quilt cover again.

"And they near killed you, from what I hear tell." Mrs. Anderson licked her wrinkled lips and lowered her eyes to the needle in her hands.

Cat knew by now when to change the subject. Many of these women, hard as their lives might have been, would rather suffer in silence than risk losing their men. And after losing Ian, she could hardly blame them. But she knew the farmers would get no relief without standing together, fighting for their cause. If she couldn't convince them one way, she'd try another. "Geordie tells me there's to be a new Alliance factory at Marble Falls."

The women expressed their surprise and interest as Catriona went on, emphasizing the positive role of the Alliance in their lives. As she was finishing up, the thundering of a horse's hooves drowned out her voice.

Nelda Hale stood and craned her neck out the window into the darkness. "It looks like your brother, Catriona, and he's riding fast." That could mean only one thing—Will needed Cat's help, and he'd sent Geordie to fetch her. A shiver tiptoed up her spine.

She wound her thread around two fingers and pinned the

small skein to the quilt top, then rose and hurried to the open door.

Geordie reined in, then slid from the horse's back, leaving it stamping and blowing, its sides stained with sweat. Her brother mounted the steps in two bounds, then grabbed her elbow and tugged her out onto the porch. "You can ride behind me. It's faster than the buckboard. Doc said to bring you as fast as I could."

Cat leaned away, her heart pounding, and pulled her elbow from his grasp. "Slow yourself down a bit, laddie, and tell me what this is about."

Geordie clenched his fists, then drew himself up and took a deep breath. "It's Molly. The baby's on its way."

Cool fresh air swirled around Will as the door opened behind him, making him realize how stale the room had grown. "Let's get that window open."

Geordie jumped up and fumbled at the casement.

Catriona's cool hand touched his shoulder. "Well?" She glanced at the figure on the bed, then turned her face to his, her blue eyes unreadable in the dim light.

Relief lightened his words. "Five minutes apart."

The window screeched open behind him. A rush of hot air stirred in the room and Geordie sidled over, his helpless hands shoved into his back pockets. "Will she be all right, Doc?"

God, how he hated questions like this one. At least Catriona never asked him for answers he didn't have. Maybe because she understood. "I don't know of any reason why not." Actually, he could think of several, but there was no sense in worrying him too. "You wait downstairs, son. We'll let you know."

The young man nodded, brows furrowed, then left, closing the door behind him.

Catriona stood with her back to him, unpacking the instruments from his bag and laying them out on a clean white cloth atop the dresser without being asked. Sometimes it seemed she read his mind.

He moved back to the bedside and gazed down at Molly.

Even with reddish splotches mottling her puffy face and her closed eyes sunk into dark-smudged sockets, she was still beautiful. In spite of the heat, she clutched the bedclothes around her neck with swollen fingers.

"Molly?"

Her eyelids fluttered open. "Hey, Doc." Weariness and pain thickened her voice.

A shadow fell across the bed from the other side. Cat bent down and smoothed the lank hair from the girl's forehead. "How are you getting on, then?" The gentle warmth of her voice always soothed him as much as it did the patients.

Molly licked her chapped lips. "Okay, I guess." She clung to Catriona's hand. "You'll stay with me, won't you, Cat?"

"Of course. Now we must let the doctor find how you're progressing, all right?"

The girl nodded and closed her eyes as Cat turned back the blankets and lifted the girl's knees into position, making a tent between them of the white gown.

He poured fresh water into the basin and scrubbed his hands, drying them on a clean towel before examining the neck of the womb. "Two fingers." Not bad for a first labor. He nodded to Cat to rearrange the bedclothes as he washed and dried his hands again. "You're coming along nicely. It won't be long now."

The girl grunted and clutched at the sheets. A sheen of sweat covered her upper lip, and she gave a long groan, almost a sob, before she quieted.

He sat on the edge of the bed and took her hand as her eyelids flickered up. "Any other pain anywhere?"

She narrowed her eyes. "Just a bad headache, and I'm having trouble seeing."

Sweat dampened his armpits and his mouth dried. He patted her hand, then released it and stood. "Try not to think about it, okay? Just close your eyes and rest between the pains."

He opened the door and beckoned for Catriona to join him in the hall.

She touched Molly's hand. "I'll be just outside. You'll

call me if you need me, then?" At the girl's nod, she came around the bed through the doorway.

He closed the door behind him. "I don't like the sound of this. It could be severe edema."

Cat's face paled. "Can you do anything?"

"We've got to speed her labor along by breaking the bag of waters." He ran a hand back through his hair.

Her brows drew together. "But will a dry labor not be harder on her?"

He nodded. "It's a risk, but otherwise—" He left the words hanging in the air and opened the door.

A gasp and a low moan from the bed announced another labor pain.

Cat hurried to ready the girl. "Molly, the doctor is going to help you. He'll break your water, and then the bairn will come much faster, you *ken?*"

Will removed the long hook from the top of the dresser and seated himself on the bed. With the fingers of one hand he pushed against the opening of the womb, making a bubble of water to protect the baby's head. Then, with his other hand, he guided the sharp instrument inside, hooking the tough membrane and giving a tug.

Molly moaned.

Water and blood gushed out between her legs, staining his hands and turning the sheets pink.

Her moan grew to a cry and she clutched her head in both hands, then subsided, whimpering as Cat mopped her face with a damp cloth.

"Can you not give her something for the headache, at the least?" Cat's dark blue eyes begged him.

Shaking his head, he pushed himself up from the bed. He set the bloody instrument atop the dresser and rinsed his hands in fresh water. "The only thing that might dull the pain is opium, and it's too risky. We don't even know what causes edema, or what might make it worse."

The corners of her mouth turned down. She came across the floor to him, her voice pitched low. "What about snakeroot?"

He shook his head. "It probably wouldn't help, and it may even harm her or the child." He placed his hands on her shoulders. "Cat, don't you think I want to make it easier for her? I'm doing everything I can."

A sigh escaped her lips, and she dropped her gaze. "Aye, I know you are. It's just, well, she's family now."

He lifted her chin with one hand. "Hey, I'm fond of her too, don't forget."

Her eyes caught and held him for a moment before he dropped his hands and turned back to the patient. He stopped and gripped the foot of the bed.

Molly's eyelids fluttered open, showing nothing but white. Her arms and legs stiffened, then jerked in great spasms, twisting the bedding around her.

Cat pulled on his arm. "What is it, what's happening to her?"

"It's the edema, throwing her into fits. That's why I wanted to hurry her labor along." A weariness sank into his bones.

Molly's body quieted, and her eyes opened. "I feel sick." She gagged.

Cat ran to the bed and helped the girl onto her side.

Vomit spewed from her mouth onto the blankets, filling the air with its sour tang. She began to cry.

Will grabbed dry towels and a damp cloth, bending to help clean the mess as best he could. "It's all right." He dabbed the cloth beneath the girl's haunted eyes. "It's over now. Lie back and rest."

Cat settled the girl back onto the pillows. "What about something to calm her fits?"

Will considered. The convulsions stood to harm mother and child more than any medicine might. "You have something in mind?"

"Skullcap, or selfheal." She picked up the vomit-covered cloths and piled them in a corner. "I've tissanes of each in my bag."

He shrugged. "Try both." He bent his head, placing his ear against the girl's chest. Her heart raced and fluttered. "Let's just hope she's strong enough when the time comes to push this baby out."

Chapter 25

Cat braced her arms around Molly's middle, letting the lass lean back against her shoulder. The muscles in her back burned from supporting the extra weight, and her breasts ached with the need to feed her bairn. Effie had brought Duncan in for her to nurse several times during the long ordeal.

More than twenty-four hours since Will fetched her from the ranch, a full night and day watching Molly's torture—labor pains every five minutes, and every half hour another fit, more vomiting. Thank God it was almost over.

The last rays of the setting sun shadowed Will's face, darkening the smudges beneath his eyes and deepening the lines on either side of his mouth. "Come on, one more push. You can do it."

The belly beneath Cat's forearms hardened, and a loud groan filled her ear as Molly bore down.

Will bent over the foot of the bed, his sleeves rolled to his elbows and his hands deep in the **V** between Molly's bent knees. "Atta girl, Molly. Atta girl. There. All done. You lie back and rest now."

Cat eased Molly back onto the pillows and wiped the lass's damp face.

Will lifted the still, blue form by its feet, patting the narrow back. He cleared the mouth with his fingers and patted again. His eyes met Cat's and he shook his head, then lay the limp body to one side.

Poor lass, to go through so much, and for naught. Cat walked to the end of the bed and covered the wee lad with a cloth, then touched Will's shoulder. She'd seen him lose patients before. It never got any easier.

He turned his face away and sniffed. "All right now, Molly, we gotta deliver the afterbirth." His voice held a gentle authority. "Give me just a little push." He lay his forearm across her still-rounded belly and pressed down.

Molly moaned, pushing herself up on her elbows, her face contorted. The afterbirth slid into Will's outstretched hand, and she fell back, panting, her eyes closed. "My baby —is it okay? I didn't hear it cry."

Tears swelled in Cat's eyes. She questioned Will with her eyes. At his nod she bent her mouth to the lass's ear. "Molly, your wee bairn, he didna make it. He's gone."

The lass's eyelids flew open wide and her mouth twisted open. "No. Oh, no." Her eyes rolled back, and she stiffened, her arms and legs twitching and flailing. A great gush of bright red blood stained the sheets.

Will moved to the side of the bed and bent over her. "Hold her as still as you can. We've got to stop the bleeding." He pressed both hands into the lass's belly.

Cat reached for Molly's hands, holding them down against the mattress. It took all her strength to keep the lass pinned to the bed. After a moment the twitching eased and the rigid muscles softened again. Cat released her.

Molly opened her eyes. "Tell Geordie—" She gasped, then continued, her voice the whisper of wind through dry branches. "Tell him I always loved him, even before—" Her face twisted into a grimace and her body tensed and jerked for long moments. At last the fit subsided, and she lay unmoving against the pillows, her eyes closed, her jaw slack.

Cat stood, frozen, a numbing curtain of grief covering her mind, unable, unwilling, to believe another life was fading.

Will grabbed the lass's delicate shoulders. "We're losing her." He shook the limp frame, a child worrying a rag doll. "Dammit, Molly, you can't give up." He let go and pressed his ear to her chest. After an eternity of minutes, he straightened and walked, gray-faced, to the darkening window.

Cat lifted the tiny, cold body from the foot of the bed and nestled the lad in his mother's still-warm arms, straightening Molly's legs and smoothing her gown. Tossing back the coverlet, she drew the sheet over the two bodies, covering the lovely, quiet face and the golden curls spread across the pillow.

She moved to the window, quiet noises of the farm drifting past her into the still room. Downstairs, voices murmured, a low rumble of concern, even the bairns subdued in the quiet house. Outside, the sounds of life. Inside, only blood and death and silence. Oh, God! What was she going to say to her brother?

Will's finger stroked her cheek. "Come on. I'll help you tell the family."

Will hesitated at the foot of the steps to his office, breathing in the dusty sweetness of the autumn twilight. Catriona hadn't wanted to leave Geordie, but the lad rode off alone into the prairie. Will had insisted on driving Catriona into Arlington to the mortician. Knowing how she'd acted when Ian died, he was surprised when she agreed. And now Lewis Price was on his way out to the farm to see to the bodies.

Will knew he ought to go on to the livery, get the buggy, and drive Catriona home as he'd promised. But somehow he just couldn't bear the thought of leaving her there and driving back to town alone. As they stood together on the plank sidewalk, the weight of her hand on his arm was his only link to life, to sanity. She understood his sense of loss as no one else ever could. He cleared his throat and turned to her. "I—would you be insulted if I suggested stopping at the office for a few minutes? I keep a bottle of whiskey there, and I think we could both use a drink."

Her lovely face turned up toward his, drawn and pale

from their long ordeal, but marked by an odd calm. "Aye, I could use a taste at that."

He guided her up the steep steps and unlocked the door, fumbling inside for a lamp and a match. Air warmed by the afternoon sun surrounded him with familiar scents of leather and carbolic as the wick caught and a circle of light flared around them. Carrying the lamp, he led the way into his private office. He set the light on a corner of the desk and pulled up an armchair for Catriona.

She dropped into it with a delicate sigh, leaning her head against the high back and closing her eyes.

He seated himself in the desk chair, then delved in the bottom desk drawer for the flask. The cork rolled to a stop on the thick green blotter, and he poured an inch of the brownish liquor in the only glass and set it in front of Cat. He tipped the bottle to his lips, savoring the trail of fire burning all the way to his belly.

But even that couldn't erase the image of Molly stretched across the bed she'd shared with Geordie, a child dying giving birth to another child. What kind of world was it where such things could happen?

He stood and paced to the window, seeing but not seeing the molten gold of the sunset spreading across the horizon, drawing starry darkness down after it. Sudden frustration surged through him at the senselessness and waste, at his own helplessness. All his skill hadn't saved her. There was just too much he didn't know. He pitched the flask with all his might against the wall. It crashed, showering fragments of glass and drops of whiskey onto the wooden floor. "Goddammit, I shouldn't have let them die!"

Catriona turned her tear-stained face, eyes wide and her mouth open. After a moment her lips set in a grim line and her eyes narrowed. "And who would you be to decide that? God himself? Face it, man, you couldna save them. No one could."

Her words arrowed into him, through all the scars, the years of armor, opening all the wounds anew. Tears burned a trail of acid down his face. And now he must add shame, the shame of showing his impotence before this woman, the woman he cared more about than anyone else in the world. He sank down into the chair and turned his face away, unwilling to look into her accusing eyes.

Then suddenly her arms were around him, pressing his face to the soft warmth of her bosom. Her kindness dissolved what was left of his calm. He pressed against her, letting the tears flow, losing himself in his grief. Nothing would bring back Molly or her son, or Ian, or a host of others he'd lost through the years. He'd become a doctor to save lives, without ever counting the cost of those he failed to save.

Catriona was right—he was only a man, not a god. He'd done his best, all he could do, and it was time to stop carrying around the ghosts of those who'd died in his care. At last, after he'd spent the grief of years, the tears stopped and he sat for a moment, enjoying a deep sense of peace.

Then a slow awareness returned. He held a woman in his arms, a woman he'd dreamed of holding, a woman he loved. Without loosening his arms he leaned back in her embrace and turned his face up toward hers.

Tears jeweled her dark lashes, and her soft lips trembled, but something more than pain or compassion hid in her dark blue eyes.

Desire flamed through him as he stood and cupped her face in both hands. Beyond thought, he bent and pressed his lips to hers, breathing in the mystery of her woman-musk.

With a soft groan she wound her arms around his neck, and he drew her to him, marveling at the softness of her breasts, her belly, her thighs pressing against him. With a sigh he released her, then scooped her in his arms and carried her to the cot in the corner.

The narrow bed protested at the weight pressing down on it. Catriona sank back into the softness, floating in an urgency of desire. She clung to his lips, drinking in his kisses, greedy for the whiskey taste of his mouth, his tongue. Fingers fumbled at the front of her bodice, and then his mouth burned kisses down her throat and found her breasts, suckling at her nipples, teasing them to aching hardness.

Passion smoldered low in her belly, a delicious agony of fire longing to be quenched. She lifted her hips, pushing her belly against the hardness of him, wanting the weight of his naked body pressing down on hers.

One hand molded her skirt to her hips and down her thigh, then lifted the hem up around her waist. A smooth palm caressed her skin, sending a warm tingle up her spine. A voice whispered out of the darkness. "Catriona, are you sure?"

A giddy joy, almost laughter, bubbled up in her. "Aye, never more than now."

His lips brushed hers, and then he pushed away and stood beside the bed.

Her heart pounded, and her mind formed words her mouth couldn't speak. *No, don't leave, don't stop, not now.* And then she realized what he meant to do as he shrugged out of first his coat, then his shirt.

As he loosened the front of his trousers, she struggled to her feet, unhooking her skirt and letting it pool on the floor at her feet. Sliding her arms from the open bodice, she let it fall and stepped out of her summer union suit. She shivered, naked in the cool air.

Warm hands reached, touched, caressed, and finally drew her close. Body melted against body, thigh to thigh, belly to belly. She slid her arms around his neck, savoring the silken texture of his skin as she lifted her mouth to his.

His hands cupping her buttocks, he lifted her, pulling her tight against him. She hooked her legs around his waist, and he carried her to the desk, his lips never leaving hers as his hardness pressed hot against her soft flesh.

Hunger possessed her as he set her on the edge of the desktop and ran the tips of his fingers over her back, her breasts, her belly. As he touched the hidden desire between her thighs, she moaned, then gasped with pleasure as he guided himself inside her.

She pressed her face against his shoulder, abandoning herself to the rhythm of his body merging with hers. All the hidden longing of the last year welled up in her, cresting and overflowing in a long sob of passion satisfied. As she melted against him in one last fluttering moan, he stiffened and thrust inside, filling her. She clung to him, holding him against her as he shuddered and gave a quiet groan.

His lips sought hers in a gentle communion as he lifted her and carried her to the cot once more and stretched his body beside hers. Pulling her buttocks against him, he curled around her, one spoon nestled against another, whispering her name. "Catriona, I love you."

Chapter 26

Cat settled back in the desk chair, the swishing of her skirts the only sound in the quiet kitchen. A vase of fading roses filled the air with their sad fragrance. Any other time, she would enjoy this early morning hour before the farm awoke.

But today she could not shake the weight of her grief. The loss of Molly left a hole in her heart, the gap of a missing tooth in an otherwise perfect smile. Nothing had hurt so much in years, not since Ian's death.

At least Molly had known some pleasure, some of the gentleness of love. True, the girl had paid a price for her short-lived happiness, the heavy toll extracted by the narrow minds of a small Texas town.

She leaned forward, setting her elbows on the tabletop and pressing the heels of her hands against her closed eyes. If only she could cry as Effie had, wailing and sobbing into the night. The lass mourned Molly as a sister. And she mourned her like a daughter.

Restless, she stood and paced the room, trying to think of something to keep her busy, to occupy her mind. She'd sent out the funeral announcements, heavy white paper edged in black. And ordered the flowers, and extra food for the mourners to eat afterward. Lewis Price had spent all night laying Molly and the bairn out in the parlor. When he finished at sunrise, Molly looked as beautiful as a bride dressed in a fine white dress, her wee son nestled in her arms, all ready for friends and family to view.

Catriona wondered who might appear. No one had heard a word from Hilda since the wedding, almost as if once Molly married, she was no longer any of Hilda's concern.

She glanced out the window toward the pin oak where Ian lay buried. Geordie chose a spot nearby for his wife and son to rest. She closed her eyes, conjuring up the loving moments they'd all shared over the summer, but the thoughts just deepened her sadness. At least she was sure Molly had been happy here, happier even than at home with her family.

She forced her eyes open again and moved to the window, leaning against the smooth casement, her hands trembling on the sill. Ribbons of yellow sunlight spread across the empty prairie; it must be nearing six o'clock. A cock crowed in the yard, and somewhere in a distant pasture a cow lowed, calling its calf to suck. A buggy pulled down the lane toward the small cemetery under the oak. Must be Lewis, come with the grave diggers.

She turned away, busying herself with preparations for breakfast, but Molly filled her thoughts—and Geordie. How could her sweet brother survive this blow? *Think. Think of something else, something pleasant, ordinary.*

A gentle tapping shivered the window in the kitchen door. Cat whirled, then rushed to open it. A woman hesitated in the doorway, her head and face covered by a heavy shawl.

Cat stiffened. She wasn't dressed for company. Still, she couldn't turn anyone away. "Can I help you, then?"

The woman's hands shook as she pushed the shawl back, revealing a crown of gray braids. "*Ja.*" Red rimmed the pale blue eyes and lines scored the broad face. Hilda Vanzee. "Could I see her, my Molly, and the little one, just for a moment?" Her voice broke and she wiped her wet cheeks, her eyes begging for compassion. "Is that too much to ask, to kiss my baby good-bye?"

Tears welled up in Cat's eyes and threatened to close her

throat. Where had the woman been during Molly's last weeks? A lass needed her mother then. But keeping Hilda away from the bodies helped no one, least of all Molly, who was beyond help or pain. She gestured toward the door to the parlor. "Aye. Come, I'll show you the way."

Geordie slid his hat from his head and stepped into the cool, dim silence. Banks of roses and wildflowers masked the faint scent of dust and decay in the front parlor. Fear and pain hollowed him as he stepped toward the shiny white coffin in the center of the room. Cat's voice echoed in his mind, repeating Molly's last words, words meant for him.

He stopped, his fingers resting on a smooth brass handle. The undertaker had driven into Dallas to find the best coffin money could buy. Pulling his gaze up from the enameled sides, he gasped. In a few short hours he'd forgotten just how beautiful she was.

She lay there, her blond curls arranged on a white satin pillow, her brown lashes resting on her pink and white cheeks and her mouth curved in a soft smile. And there, clasped in her arms, lay her tiny bairn, the cause of all this pain and death. His chest swelled with a painful tenderness. *Poor wee mite. You dinna ask to be born.*

Cat had dressed Molly all in white, in her bridal gown, the same dress she'd worn not long ago at their wedding. Lace ruffles gathered around her neck and covered her shoulders and her bosom. As he stared down at her, it almost seemed as if her chest lifted the least bit. His mind reeled. It was all a mistake. She was asleep, not dead. Any fool could see that. He reached out a hand to stroke her cheek, then recoiled. Cold and hard, not warm and soft. The last of his hope withered and died.

Dead. She was really dead. He would never see her eyes open again, never hear her laugh, never hold her body close again.

Her last words rang in his mind. They'd shared so much in these few months. And now it was over, gone forever, never to come again. If only he'd stayed beside her instead of leaving her alone with Cat and Will.

He spun on his heel and stared out the dusty windows, not seeing anything but the memory of pain contorting his wife's face. He knew he couldn't have saved her, but he could have been there beside her, heard the last words she'd said. But did she really mean them? He sighed; he'd never know.

What he did know was that he'd never love again as he'd loved her—still did love her. Bending over the casket, he brushed his lips across hers, then turned and walked out into the bright autumn sunshine.

Effie climbed from the carriage, leaving Geordie and Will to help the others alight. She walked to the far side of Ian's grave, where a new pit yawned in the sod. A heap of black soil dried nearby, its odor of fresh-turned earth clashing with the dry scents of dust and prairie grass on the wind. A pale blue sky arched overhead, trimmed at the edges of the horizon with a smudge of black.

Drawn up beside the square-edged hole stood the hearse, the white coffin inside gleaming in the noonday sun. She dabbed her damp eyes, already aching from too many tears, and turned away from the painful brightness.

Buckboards and black carriages clogged the lane all the way to the main road, and droves of dark-clad mourners made their solemn way to the pin oak to pay their last respects to Molly. She sighed. Something about a girl dying young and pretty and under slightly scandalous circumstances just made folks turn out for funerals. And the warm weather didn't hurt.

Not that most folks hadn't liked Molly as much as Effie did. But their respects would have meant so much more to the lass while she lived. Might have taken some of the sting from the shame.

Geordie came to stand on her right, hands clasped in front of him, his left hand loose around his right wrist. An odd calm glowed in his face instead of the agony of grief she'd expected. She'd never understand her brother.

At least his grief didn't intrude on her own. She had

enough trouble with her own tears and sobs, especially with all these people gathering around.

Cat squeezed her elbow as she slid into place on Effie's left, and Will and Nana stepped up to the graveside just beyond. They hadn't abandoned Molly when she needed their friendship either.

Joe appeared across the open grave, tall and handsome in his new black suit, guiding his mother across the dry grass like a child, or an old woman. Axel followed a few paces behind, his younger sons on either side.

A dark shape glided to the narrow end of the deep rectangle, Yvette with several of her girls in tow, all in respectable black, their faces scrubbed clean of paint. Even old man Quincy looked somewhat sober. The Hales, the Andersons, so many who'd been cruel or thoughtless when Molly was alive. She closed her eyes, suddenly too tired to look at the crowd.

Wind whispered through the branches of the pin oak, covering the soft murmurings of the crowd. She glanced back toward Joe, unable as always to keep her eyes from seeking him, even for a few moments. But even his presence did nothing to lift her pain today. Molly, her best friend in the whole world, gone, dead. How would she live without her?

Chapter 27

October 1887

Cat hung the lantern on a hook above Bossy's stall and patted the cow's side. "Sooo." Bending, she stroked the swollen udder, giving one teat a gentle squeeze.

Bossy lowed and sidestepped toward her, pushing Cat against the side of the stall.

"All right, then." She leaned her shoulder against the hairy hide, breathing in the warm smells of milk and manure until the cow stepped the other way. Free again, Cat pulled a jar from the pocket of her wrapper and wiped some of the cooling salve on the milk bag. "If only you had a calf to keep your milk flowing."

At least she hadn't drunk any of Bossy's last milk. All she needed was to get the milk sickness herself, and then where would Duncan be? The wee lad liked to eat, that was certain, crawling over and holding his arms up whenever she sat down. Which wasn't often enough lately.

She sighed and put the jar back into her wrapper pocket, then reached her arms high and stretched. Something dribbled onto her head. She reached up and pulled a handful of straw from her hair, then glanced at the loft above her. Must be a puff of wind, or a field mouse building a nest. She'd have Joe look in the morning.

She reached one hand up for the lantern. More straw

spilled onto her head, glowing in the yellow light as it drifted to the dirt floor. "What the—?" She bent forward and dusted the dry grass from her head, then made her way to the ladder. Better leave the lantern. No sense taking a chance on a fire. Besides, it shed enough light hanging down below. She should be able to see, even in the loft.

She kicked off her old brogans and hung her wrapper over a convenient nail, then stood for a moment, hands on her hips, trying to figure how to hold up the hem of her nightgown and use both hands to climb the ladder. Finally, she shrugged and knotted the loose material on one side, leaving her lower legs bare. When she grabbed the handrails and stepped onto the first rung, another shower of straw surrounded her, filling the air with dust and chaff. She sneezed, then wiped her nose on her sleeve and pulled herself up the ladder, emerging into the warm, sweet-smelling darkness of the loft.

She swiveled her head, unable to make out anything except the dim outlines of mounded straw. As she pulled herself up and stepped onto the floor, a board creaked, and something crackled and whispered in the straw behind her. Before she could turn, a pair of arms clamped around her, pulling her down into the scratchy softness.

Fear froze her belly and she struck out, kicking and struggling against her attacker. She twisted her head, trying to see his face. At last her elbow connected with something soft, and a groan sounded in her ear. She pushed out of his grasp and skittered away. Her breath wheezed in and out and her heart pounded, the sound filling her ears in the quiet darkness.

"Cat?" It took a moment for the voice to register.

She crawled back toward the ladder, relief warring with her irritation. "Will Bascom, it would serve you right if I'd shoved you down out of this loft on your head. What are you doing up here, besides trying to scare me to death?"

Laughing, he caught her wrist and pulled her down on top of him. "Figured you'd be out to check on Bossy before you turned in. I finished my night rounds early, so I sneaked in here and waited for you."

Passion awaits you...
Step into the magical world of

Enjoy Kay Hooper's *"Larger Than Life"*!
Not for sale anywhere, this exclusive
novel is yours to keep–FREE–
no matter what!

Detach and affix this stamp to the
reply card and mail at once!

SEE DETAILS INSIDE...

Her anger ebbed at the hard warmth of his body beneath hers. "But where's the buggy?"

"Over yonder under some trees. We have to protect your reputation now, you know." His arms slid around her waist, and his hands caressed her back through the thin cotton of her gown. "I had to see you."

The words stirred a longing deep inside her, but she fought to keep it from her voice. "And now that you've seen me?" Let him worry a bit, especially after tricking her like that.

His hands stopped their gentle circling. "I reckon I could leave—"

Her fingers found his lips. "Hush." She silenced him with a kiss, its urgency answering any doubts.

Will's lips parted, letting her savor the sweetness of his tongue. She shivered as his hands slid down her back, and eased the knotted hem of her gown up to her waist. Cupping her bare buttocks, he pulled her against him, his hard heat pressing into her belly.

Her own hunger dizzied her. She traced his handsome cheeks with her mouth, the day's stubble bruising her lips. She nuzzled the skin of his neck and licked the hollow beneath his ear.

His hands slid lower, slipping between the backs of her thighs, nudging her legs apart.

She sat up, straddling him, the wool of his trousers rough against her inner thighs and bits of straw scratching her knees and calves. With trembling fingers she struggled to undo his shirt buttons, at last exposing his chest to her exploring fingers.

She delighted in the swirls of hair, a silky pelt covering the hard planes of his muscles, the tiny beads of his erect nipples. Her fingers trailed lower, across his belly to the waist of his trousers, worrying the buttons apart until she could slide one hand inside, encircling the smooth, hard shaft.

Will gasped, moving his hands up the outsides of her thighs to her waist, tugging the hem of her gown upward.

Her breath grew ragged. She withdrew her hand and grabbed the hem of her gown, slipping it over her head in one motion. She spread it across the straw beside Will and rolled over onto it. Lying on her back, she held her hungry arms up to him.

He stood over her for a moment, shrugging off his shirt and easing out of his trousers. Kneeling between her legs, he brushed his open palms across her nipples until she moaned, then leaned forward to touch her mouth with his, a teasing, haunting kiss. He cupped her breasts with his hands, sucking first one and then the other.

His tongue trailed fire down her belly. He dropped his face between her thighs, his tongue sending waves of pleasure coursing through her.

She arched against him, reveling in the sweet sensation of his touch. At last she could wait no more. She reached for him, pulled him atop her, her lips seeking his.

With gentle, demanding hands, she guided him inside her. Her fingertips clutched at his buttocks, pressing deep into his soft flesh as she rose to meet him. Each thrust carried her higher, farther, fiercer, until molten gold filled her veins, and she exploded with pleasure.

With one final thrust Will cried out, then sank atop her, gasping.

Overcome with sudden tenderness, Cat tightened her arms around his chest and held him close, drifting in a glow of satisfied desire.

Too soon he rolled off her and lay stretched across the straw, his body just touching hers.

Sweat cooled on her skin and bits of straw poked sharp ends into her back through the cotton of her gown. Soon she would have to stir, to move, sit, stand, but not yet.

Will raised himself on one elbow, tracing lines across her belly with a piece of straw.

Cat turned her face, arching her neck to kiss his shoulder. "I'll miss you."

He chuckled. "Why? I'm not going anywhere."

"Aye? Well, I must. The convention's but a week away." She closed her eyes. "Have you ever been to Shreveport?"

The straw lifted from her belly, and the weight of Will's head pressed against her shoulder. "So you're still planning to go. I thought you'd change your mind." His words hung heavy in the air between them.

She rolled toward him. "And why would I do that?" Her eyes sought his, but his face lay in shadow.

"Cat, you know how I feel about this. I still think it isn't worth the risks."

She swallowed her impatience. She didn't want to argue, but she had to make him understand. "Can you not see we're winning? The Exchange is overflowing with samples. They got top price from a factory in England for one lot of fifteen hundred bales. And using joint notes, the farmers can get out from under the crop liens and buy their supplies at a fair price."

He sighed. "And what about the cotton agents and furnishing men you're putting out of business? Don't you see, they'll have to fight back any way they can. And I don't want you in the middle of the battle." He rolled toward her. "Is that so wrong, to want you to be safe? I know how important this is to you now, but once we're married—"

"Once we're what?" Cat sat up, wrapping her arms around her bare knees. A sick chill tightened her belly.

Will's hand tugged at her shoulder, trying to turn her toward him. "Married. Cat, I love you. I just thought—"

She shrugged off his hand. "*Aye*, I know what you thought, that I'd be happy to give up the fight and become your wife." She stood and retrieved her gown, sliding it over her head, her back still to him. "But I'm not your wife, and even if I was—" She stopped, chewing her lip.

The coolness of his voice chilled her. "Go on. If you were?"

She faced him, her arms crossed over her breasts. "I'm no man's property, never was, never could be. Ian—Ian understood that. I thought you did as well."

He climbed to his feet and stepped into his trousers, doing up the buttons in the heavy silence. At last he looked at her. "You're right, Catriona. You're not my wife. And I'm not Ian, and I never will be." He ran his hand through his hair, then bent and picked up his shirt. "Look, I think I'd better go."

Cat bit her lip. A yawning pit opened inside her. "Aye, perhaps you'd better."

He opened his mouth, then closed it and shook his head. He swung onto the ladder and sank out of sight, his boots clattering down the wooden rungs.

She stood, unmoving, as his boot heels thudded across the floor below. Only after the barn door creaked open and closed again did she sink back down into the straw. Silent tears leaked from her eyes and dropped onto her folded hands.

The sound of many voices mingled with the clattering of dinnerware in the long hall. Effie breathed in the appetizing aromas of fried chicken, corn, and other special dishes set out at one end. Half the folks at the meeting came because of the pot-luck dinner beforehand, especially bachelors like Lewis Price, and even that old drunk Quincy. Everybody knew the best cooks in the county belonged to the Farmers Alliance.

She set her plate on the checkered tablecloth and lifted her skirts to step over the long bench, settling herself beside Violet Weston—Violet Williams now. It was nice how she insisted Effie call her Vi now, and easier than remembering her married name. Silly how women had to change their names when they married but men didn't. She hadn't visited with her old teacher for quite a while, as the baby in the woman's arms reminded her. "Good to see you. Isn't he a handsome lad though?"

"Thanks. I think he takes after his pa." Vi scooted the heavy bundle higher on her lap as two small hands reached toward the table. "He keeps wanting to eat from my plate, even though he hasn't any teeth yet." A serenity glowed from her mentor's face, making Vi look younger than her years.

Lifting her fork, Effie popped a piece of barbecue into her mouth, savoring the tart-sweet flavor of the tender meat. Not that Vi was that many years her senior. After all, if Molly had lived, she'd have a baby about this age. The image came to her again of the wee body nestled in the girl's arms, so tiny and perfect.

Molly had been little more than a year older. It could as easily have been Effie lying in the casket, her own child in her arms. And much as she enjoyed her niece and nephew and the children of her friends, she had to admit she hungered for a baby of her own. A girl with her copper curls and green eyes, or maybe a boy like Joe, with white-blond hair and blue eyes.

The idea prompted warm stirrings in her body. Sometimes she couldn't stop the thoughts of Molly in bed with Geordie. It must have been a powerful urge to make a decent girl forget herself. That is, if Geordie really was the father, but she guessed she'd never know now. She'd never dream of asking him, and he wasn't about to volunteer it. Not that it mattered anymore.

She glanced down the table at Joe, seated on the other side next to Geordie, laughing and telling stories with Vi's husband. In her mind, Joe's large, rough hands caressed her bare skin, stroking her breasts, her belly, dipping down between her thighs.

When Vi touched her hand, Effie jumped. "What? I'm sorry. I—I must have been daydreaming."

"I asked if you might hold little Reuben for me for a spell. Are you all right?" She tilted her head to one side.

Effie's cheeks warmed. "Of course." She held out her hands for the baby, enjoying the softness of his small body cuddled against her. Her gaze strayed to Joe again.

Violet's eyes flickered in his direction, then back at her. "So that's how it is." Her lips spread into a teasing smile. "I wondered what ailed you. Does he know you're sweet on him?"

Heat seared her cheeks, and she tipped her face down toward the baby. "No!" The whispered word exploded from her mouth.

Vi giggled. "Well, why don't you let him know?"

"You mean just tell him? I couldn't." Effie gulped.

This time Vi laughed aloud. "Might not be such a bad idea at that, but no, I was thinking of a little coquetting, some sparking."

"I've tried, but he just ignores me." She rubbed the baby's back with one hand, biting off her quiet words. "He treats me like a kid sister. I get so mad at him sometimes."

Vi narrowed her eyes and bit into a piece of fried chicken. "He seems to get on well with your brother."

Effie sighed. "They're good friends." Not that it helped her much. "He's our foreman at the farm."

Vi leaned closer. "Maybe you should confide in your brother. He might be able to think of a way to help you."

She shook her head. What an idea. "I couldn't do that. He'd never understand."

Her friend's shoulders lifted, then dropped. "Okay, but how long are you willing to wait for him to figure it out? If he ever does." Vi set the chicken aside, then lifted a steaming cup of chicory coffee to her lips and sipped. "Of course, if you don't go after him, someone else may."

Effie's chest tightened at the thought of Joe with another girl. "Maybe you're right. After all, what's a brother for?"

Catriona sank down on a chair and sipped a cup of punch, enjoying the cool tartness of the fruit juices. People swirled around her in a colorful mob, all talking and enjoying refreshments during a break from committee meetings.

So far, the convention had gone well, a testament to C. W. Macune's ability to unify factions just as he'd done in Waco in January. This time he'd pulled together the Texas Farmers Alliance, the Louisiana Farmers Union, the Arkansas Agricultural Wheel, and a number of smaller farm organizations to form a national alliance.

She wondered again how he managed to get them all on the same side. In addition to his personal charm, it must be his vision of political and economic possibilities for farmers. She found it impossible not to get excited when he outlined his plans for the future of farmers in the United States.

A body settled in the chair beside her. She glanced up into Macune's smiling face. Her cheeks warmed as if she'd been caught gossiping about him. Nonsense. He couldn't read her thoughts. "Mr. President."

"It's a pleasure to see you here, Miz Macleod." His broad

shoulders heaved as he chuckled. "But call me Charles, please."

"If you'll call me Catriona." She sipped her punch, wondering what to say next.

"So, Catriona, how did your cotton crop fare this year?" His chair creaked as he leaned back.

She rested the cup on her knee, grateful he chose a question she could answer. "We've no cause to complain, and the exchange got us a fair price. But then, you know that."

"Actually, I don't. We processed hundreds of bales, but all in numbered lots. We only know the county of origin. Helps keep us from showing favoritism." He rested his hands on his knees. "And what did you think of my opening address? Your candid opinion, now."

She smiled. "It impressed me so much, I memorized it." She closed her eyes. "This is indeed an auspicious occasion. It is the first session of this body; and this body is the first organization of real cotton growers inaugurated on a plan calculated to assist the poor man."

This time he laughed aloud. "Stop. You do the words more justice than I ever could."

Warmth flooded Cat's cheeks again. "A poor imitation. You were wonderful."

His broad face sobered. "Much as I appreciate the praise, I had another reason for asking. I understand you're no stranger to the podium yourself."

She chewed her lip, not sure what he meant.

He tilted his head to one side. "Some of your fellow delegates tell me you used to give speeches on Skye during the rent strikes."

Cat blinked. "Aye, but I'm no speechmaker. I only spoke what was in my heart, and the people listened."

"And ended by forcing Her Majesty's government to pass new laws to protect the crofters." He smoothed his mustache with the flat of his thumbnail. "Quite an accomplishment, speechmaker or no."

"But you canna think that I alone—"

He leaned toward her. "Of course not, but without you, or someone like you, they might not have succeeded. Good speakers are born, not trained, and the farmers of the United States can't afford to waste your talents."

His voice dropped almost to a whisper. "This afternoon I will outline our new education program. Many of these farmers are new to this country and don't understand the rights and responsibilities of being citizens. The only way we can hope to make permanent changes in our way of life is by educating our membership. And we need lecturers who can hold an audience—people like you, Catriona."

She tried to keep her excitement in check. A chance to really contribute, to make a difference again. But she was no young lass free to roam the countryside. Even on Skye she'd had problems getting away. "But even if I knew enough to make a speech, I have two wee bairns and a farm of my own, and other work as well."

"As for what you know, I think you understand more than you give yourself credit for. Besides, what you don't know we could teach you. And of course we'd pay for your expenses and your time." He touched her hand. "Don't give me an answer now, unless you mean to say yes. But will you at least consider it?"

She found herself nodding. "Aye, I'll give it some thought."

Chapter 28

December 1887

Even before Will stepped across the threshold, the harsh, high-pitched wheeze told him everything. He kept his eyes on the patient, unable to meet Catriona's gaze or risk a look at Sanapia, standing totem-still in the corner.

Early morning sunlight streamed through the window, haloing the blond head where it lay on the white pillowcase. The face might have been Ian's at this age. He knelt beside the bed, taking the soft, tiny hand in his. "Betsy, may I look at your throat, sweetheart?"

She nodded and opened her mouth, the fetid smell of her breath surrounding him.

With gentle fingers he turned her face into the sunlight. "Can you say *aah* for me?" He pressed down on her tongue with his index finger. The yellow-green spots covering her tonsils confirmed all his fears. The thick, gray false membrane had already begun to form.

Diphtheria. Putrid sore throat, *morbus strangulatoris*. And he'd lost two patients to it already this week, watching them strangle as their air passages closed, their necks disfigured by swelling. The thought of this little one gasping for air sickened him. And worse yet, the thought of Lewis laying out this tiny body— He'd tried every procedure known, from painting the throat to cutting the membrane inside, and even opening a hole in the windpipe from the outside. But every operation risked still more swelling, and none offered much hope.

He smiled down at the sweet face. "Good girl." He stroked her cheek, noting the low-grade fever. She couldn't be more than two and a half years old, square in the middle of the most dangerous age range.

He stood and strode to the dresser, washing his hands in the fluted basin. Every winter he faced the same enemies. This, and whooping cough, pneumonia, and in the summer smallpox and typhoid. And not one useful thing he could do against any of them. Of course, some lived, but more from their own strength than his cure. Not that he didn't save lives, patching up bullet wounds and cuts. But not enough. It would never be enough until he could save them all.

After all these years he ought to be used to this feeling of helplessness. It was always the same as the first time, when his parents lay bleeding in front of the burned-out cabin. *God's will*, Nana had said when she brought him back to Arlington. *They died for their faith, teaching the ways of peace to the heathen Indians*. It was then he'd decided to become a doctor, to fight violence in his own way, a way even God couldn't object to.

"Will?" Cat's voice quavered.

He turned, forcing himself to use a brisk, businesslike tone. "You must keep her flat in bed for at least twelve days and give her lots of fluids." He paused. "And watch to see the membrane doesn't close her throat."

"It's the same, then? What the wee Tidwell lad died from?"

He looked at her then and nodded, wishing he could take her in his arms, comfort her somehow. First Ian, then Molly, and now this. But he was as helpless to breach the distance between them as he was to offer her assurances about Betsy's recovery.

Since the night in the loft, she'd been cool, working beside him but never offering anything beyond her duties as his nurse. Not that he blamed her, after that stupid remark about marrying her. It was obvious she still loved Ian, not him.

He'd wanted her to love him, wanted it so much, and she seemed so loving, so passionate. But then, she was passionate about everything—her children, her work, that damned Farmers Alliance. And she wasn't the first lonely widow to turn to another man for comfort. After all, it had been more than a year since Ian's death. He'd mistaken her warmth for love, when it must have been loneliness, or worse yet, pity. After all, she'd come to him in his weakness, crying because he couldn't save Molly.

He'd wanted to apologize a hundred times since then, but couldn't bring himself to try for fear she'd think he only wanted to seduce her again. His pride couldn't take another beating. No, things were better as they were, for everyone involved.

She stepped closer, tipping her lovely face up to his. Tears glistened in her dark blue eyes, and her soft mouth trembled. "Is there nothing you can do?"

Something wrenched in his chest. He longed to touch her, take her shoulders in both hands, but instead he clenched his fists and kept them at his sides. "Believe me, I wish there were. We can only let the fever take its course. And hope."

Catriona ladled the hot chicken broth into a bowl and set it on the tray, her belly clenching at the rich smell. The very thought of food revolted her ever since Will's visit. She had no appetite, not while her baby lay there so ill, perhaps dying, although Sanapia kept telling her she must eat to keep up her strength.

The Indian woman never faltered, going about her chores without complaint, eating and drinking and sleeping as if nothing had happened. Yet when she was with Betsy, the tenderness in the woman's every touch showed how much she loved the bairn in her own way.

Perhaps Cat would be better off with some of Sanapia's calm acceptance, if that's what it was. She didn't know what they'd do if one of them couldn't keep things going. She lifted a clean spoon from the dresser drawer and added it to the tray, along with a clean, soft cloth from the rag bag. Liquids, Will had said, very hot or very cold.

She lifted the tray, frowning as her hands quivered. Perhaps Sanapia was right. Once she got Betsy to eat some of this broth, she'd force herself to eat a bowl as well.

She paced into the hall, keeping the tray level as she mounted the stairs. Puzzled, she stopped on the top step. She could swear she hadn't closed the door to Betsy's room. She shrugged and set the tray on the hall table and twisted the knob, swinging the door wide. Cat froze in horror and confusion.

Sanapia bent over the bairn, holding a small dish in one hand and pushing the other in Betsy's open mouth. A persistent gagging sound came from the still form on the bed.

Cat uttered an inarticulate cry of pain and rage, the sound of a mother bear protecting a cub. She rushed into the room and dragged the woman away from her child. "Are you mad, then? What are you doing?" She gave the heavy body a shove and bent over the bairn. "Betsy honey, are you all right? How does your throat feel?"

The bairn stared up at her. "Better, Mama." One wee hand patted her cheek. " 'Napia said so."

Reassured, at least for the moment, Cat straightened and turned.

Sanapia stood in a corner, still and erect, arms crossed over her fringed bodice. On the floor lay remnants of the small bowl and its contents, bits of thick paste and slivers of crockery spattered everywhere.

Cat knelt, touching one finger to the goo and lifting it first to her nose, then her tongue. She didn't recognize the bitter taste. Her voice quavered. "What is this, and what were you doing with it?"

Sanapia gave no sign of hearing for a moment. When she spoke, her face remained a stony mask. "*Bekwinatsu*. To open her throat."

Cat stood, then sank down on the bed beside the sick child, shame replacing her anger. "Do you mean this is medicine, and you were trying to help her?"

The woman nodded, her long gray braids bobbing

against crossed arms. "Swelling medicine. I poke baby's throat, make her breathe."

"But why—?" She stopped, knowing the answer. The woman had been afraid to tell her, afraid to share the knowledge, afraid of not being allowed to help the wee bairn. And was she so wrong? "I—" She stroked Betsy's cheek, then looked into Sanapia's eyes. "I'm sorry. I thought you were hurting her."

Sanapia's face softened almost to a smile. "Is good to protect babies. I was a fierce mother too."

Through her relief, an excitement built in Catriona. "But where did you get this medicine, and how did you know it would help?"

The woman paced to the window, her moccasins noiseless on the wooden floor. "I get it out there." She pointed toward the brown expanse of the prairie. "I see many medicines growing. You can't see." She turned to Cat, drawing herself up, her features glowing with pride. "My grandmother was Comanche Eagle Doctor. She teaches me."

All this time, the herb lore she needed was right here under her own roof. "Sanapia, many children are ill, like Betsy. If I go with you, will you show me the plants and teach me to make this swelling medicine?" Her heart pounded, fearing the woman would refuse.

The thin lips pursed together and the proud face turned once more toward the window. At last she nodded. "I will teach you."

Chapter 29

March 1888

Geordie slid the blade of his pocket knife into the soil, hacking at the threadlike tangle already intertwined with the crumbly black earth. As he lifted the circle of sod, dry brown grass crackled in his hands, giving off a scent of dust and decay. With gentle fingers he placed the fragile plant in the hole, pressing dirt around the ball of roots. Brushing his palms together, he climbed to his feet and stepped back to admire the results.

The lavender of the wild pansies dipped and swayed in the breeze, a living bouquet sheltered by the wooden headstone of Molly's grave. Later he'd bring roses and lilies, but for today this was enough. The first flowers of a new spring. How she would have welcomed them after the cold and deadly winter.

He bent to retrieve his jacket from the grass, shivering in the chill wind. Seven months. So much time had passed. An eternity; a day. Sometimes he found himself laughing, enjoying life, forgetting for a moment or an hour or a day. And then she would rise up in his mind, the echo of her voice, her scent, the tilt of her head, and he would long for her touch, her warm body in his arms. But no matter how he tried, he couldn't keep her in his mind every minute, not the way he'd like.

Shrugging into his jacket, he turned toward the larger mound of Ian's grave. More than once he'd wondered how the man would have fared if Catriona had died and he'd stayed behind. He could almost hear his brother-in-law's advice, something about getting on with his life. Easy words to say.

Even Cat hadn't been able to let go of the past entirely. She'd found someone to love, if he was any judge, but something held her back from giving her whole heart. Maybe someday she'd be ready to really live again, but even then a part of her would stay in this hole in the ground.

And a part of him would lay buried here beside Molly. Maybe some people had only one great love inside them, but maybe one was enough. He turned back to the smaller mound, its crown of pansies fluttering like small flags. Nothing so special, only a clump of tiny wildflowers. But if Molly was somewhere near, at least she'd know he hadn't forgotten.

The wind carried a faint scent of smoke on the cool morning air. Catriona shielded her eyes with one hand. There, on the horizon, somebody burning cotton stalks, no doubt. Must be the Garrisons. They always took their time getting their fields cleared for planting.

And Sanapia took hers gathering herbs. The woman paced ahead of her, her moccasins soundless in the crackling brown grass, a basket slung over one arm. All at once she stopped and set the basket down. Facing the morning sun, she knelt in front of a spindly green plant, murmuring to it.

Cat edged closer but still couldn't make out the words, although she recognized the plant as some kind of milkweed.

Sanapia lifted her broad face, her dark eyes flickering over Cat's. "This *bekwinatsu*. I tell it I'm coming to take it away. I say I need you to help the childrens that got closed throats." Speaking more words in her own language, she pulled a strip of dark green calico from her basket and tied it to one of the plant's narrow branches. "I tell it I'm going to give it something in return."

Cat nodded, sympathizing with the woman's respect for

the natural world. On Skye she'd made small offerings to the fairies herself more than once.

Using a digging stick, Sanapia pushed the dirt and tangled roots away from the stem. At last she eased the medicinal herb from the ground and removed the root, laying the rest of the plant across the hole, the green cloth still trailing from one branch. She held out the long, whitish root. "This make good liniment for bruises, bone breaks, pains here." She pointed to her belly, then placed the root in the basket and heaved herself to her feet. "And paste for poking throats."

Cat stared at the plant, memorizing its shape and color, in case she ever had to find it again on her own. Hard to believe such a common plant saved so many lives. They'd been lucky to only lose two, although every death took its toll, on her and on Will.

Sanapia touched her shoulder. "You miss white doctor." It was not a question.

Cat looked up into the dark eyes, startled as always by the woman's perceptions. Color crept into her cheeks as she nodded. "What should I do, Sanapia?"

The Indian woman shook her head. "White peoples live backwards." She squatted beside Cat, pulling a twig from a tangle of grass and drawing a circle in the sandy soil. She touched a point at the bottom of the figure. "This south, the place of the heart." She touched the stick to the left of the circle. "This west, the place of the hand." The corners of her eyes wrinkled as she squinted at Cat. "Indian give with heart, hold with hand. White man hold with heart, give with hand. Mix up."

She leaned forward again, placing the tip of her makeshift pointer at the top of the circle. "This north, the place of the head. Over here east, the place of the spirit." She touched a spot on the right. "Indian listens with head, follows spirit. White man sit in church, listens with spirit, but follows what in here." She touched one stained fingertip to her temple. "Backwards." She dropped the stick and levered herself up to stand. "You listen with head and decide with spirit, you no have to ask me."

The thought of being with Will brought back the aching

loss, a constant companion these last weeks. He'd been distant, never even trying to touch her since the night in the loft, as if they'd never been lovers at all. Maybe Sanapia was right. Part of her wished she'd agreed to his proposal. After all, she did want to marry him. But no, his actions spoke clearer than words. If she wouldn't be owned, he wanted no part of her. And that price was too high, even for love.

Sanapia hailed her from across a sea of brown grass. Another healing plant. Excitement bubbled in her as she gazed across the sweeping prairie. How many other medicines grew up out of this black soil?

She patted the cloth bag slung over her shoulder, its meager contents feather-light against her body. With her few hardy transplants and native plants to replace the ones that wouldn't grow, it would soon be full again.

And maybe she'd find something better or different, even something that could have saved Molly and her baby. Sadness weighed on her. If only she'd found out about the Indian woman's knowledge sooner. But there was no going back. All she could do was learn as much as possible, so when it happened again— If Sanapia knew of a cure, Cat would find it.

The pungent smell of ink hung in the warm spring air. Geordie pushed himself up from the desk and made his way into the pressroom, carrying his latest story in his hand.

Zeke bent over a table, his gnarled hands black with ink or grease. Despite his white hair and stooped shoulders, the man never seemed to tire of tinkering with his press or setting type.

"Here's the copy you wanted." Geordie held out the sheet of paper.

The old man grunted and pushed his wire-frame glasses higher on his face, leaving black streaks on his nose. "What's this about again?" His fingers smudged the edges of the paper as he held it up.

"Jim Hogg. Remember, we talked about his record with the railroads?" Ever since that anti-prohibition rally, Geordie had kept an eye out for stories about the attorney general, and he liked what he read. "He got the MKT to repair their lines by threatening to revoke their charter. And he made the Santa Fe reopen their Texas office instead of trying to run things from out of state."

Zeke peered over the top of his glasses. "So he enforces the law. Ain't that his job?"

"Well, I hear tell he's getting ready to file an anti-monopoly suit against the Texas Traffic Association for fixing rates, and the Fort Worth Board of Trade just voted to endorse the lower rates of the FWD city railway." He usually respected Zeke's opinions about things, but couldn't the old man see what was right in front of him? "We've finally got the railroads on the run, and Hogg's at least part of the reason. He's a comer, I tell you."

Zeke set the sheet of paper aside and unhooked his glasses from behind each ear, then settled one hip atop a rickety table. "Hogg is right smart, I admit. Smart enough to know the farmers have the votes but the merchants have the money." He snorted. "By fighting the railroads, he gets credit for helping everybody without losing anything." He laced his fingers over his leather apron. "But when it comes down to the farmers against the merchants, whose side do you think he'll take?"

Geordie scratched his nose. He hadn't thought of that. "But that's what the Exchange is all about, getting a fair deal for the Alliance members, so the merchants don't suck them dry."

Zeke pursed his lips and nodded. "Ever ask yourself why the Grange co-ops failed?"

He shook his head.

Zeke shrugged. "You go taking money out of a man's pocket even if he's cheating you, or maybe especially if he's cheating you, and you got to expect him to kick up a fuss about it." He held up the paper. "I got some time before I have to set this. Sure you don't want to add anything or change it?"

He hesitated, hooking his thumbs in the waist of his trousers. He hated to disagree with his boss; he respected the man's opinions. After all, Zeke was the editor and owner, and besides, he'd always encouraged Geordie to write the truth, no matter whose toes he had to step on. He shook his head again. "Nope. I reckon no matter what his reasons, Hogg did us all a favor, and he deserves credit for that much."

Zeke smiled. "It stands as is, then, boy. I like a man who knows his own mind."

Catriona bent forward, trying to grab Duncan as the lad squealed and trotted away among a forest of adult legs. With the meeting over, the children romped around the hall, dodging underfoot as their parents packed up the dishes and whatever remained of the food. Cat straightened, a fist on each hip. At least she wasn't the only mother here chasing a child. "Duncan Fergus Macleod, you come back here."

A puckish face haloed in dark curls peered around the leg of a table, then disappeared into the crowd again.

If she weren't so angry, Cat would have had to laugh. She edged among the other members, hoping Duncan didn't knock anyone down or end up with a pot of food over his head. At last she reached an open space in time to see the toddler chugging across the shiny wood floor toward a group of men. "Duncan!"

The smiling face turned toward her again, and at that moment the wee lad knocked into a pair of trouser-covered legs.

Wide hands caught him, lifting his chubby body up against a dressy black jacket. Charles Macune's smile tilted up the ends of his heavy mustache and crinkled the skin around his eyes. "Whoa there, partner. Where you going in such a hurry?"

Duncan tipped his wide-eyed face up and giggled, one fist pressed against his lower lip.

Cat hurried over. "I'm sorry, Mr. Macune."

"Charlie, remember? It's a pleasure to see you again, Miss Mac—Catriona. And is this *canny* lad your own?" He bounced Duncan on his arm.

"Aye." Cat reached for her son. "And a right headstrong one he is at that. I shudder to think what he'll be in a year."

Duncan turned his face away and cuddled closer to

Charlie the way he used to cling to Will before their disagreement. Wee fingers reached out to stroke the stiff, dark hairs of the man's mustache. Perhaps the lad blamed Will for not spending time with the family, or it could be the child reflected her own distance from him.

With his free hand Charlie patted Duncan's back through his gingham shirt.

Cat dropped her arms to her sides again. "He seems to like you."

His eyes twinkled. "Kids and dogs can always sense a soft heart."

The wistfulness in his voice tugged Cat's mouth into a smile. "So tell me, then, how are you getting on at the Exchange?"

"Dandy." His body swayed from side to side and he lowered his voice as Duncan leaned his head against the broad shoulder. "So far this year we've ordered and delivered fifty barrels of molasses, several carloads of tobacco, and a thousand brand-new farm wagons, all at a savings of forty percent over the time prices of the furnishing men."

Cat laced her fingers together and dropped her clasped hands against her skirts, searching for a polite answer to such pleasant news. "And the joint notes?"

Charlie's smile faded. His thick brows drew together and he inclined his head toward hers, his voice quiet in the noisy room. "Well, we've quite a few in hand, more than enough to cover our purchases. But the truth is, I'm a bit concerned. I had planned to sell the notes to local banks, or use them for collateral for a bank loan for operating capital."

Cat pressed her fingers together. "And the banks refused?"

He nodded. "Not only in Dallas, but Houston, Galveston, and New Orleans as well. They said it was against state law."

Anger tightened Cat's voice. "The merchants couldn't have anything to do with this, could they?"

One corner of his mouth quirked up and his brows lifted. "Why, ma'am, how could you think such a thing?"

Cat laughed at this unexpected wit, then sobered again. "But what will you do?"

He tilted his head, his face serious again. "Well, as of now, our creditors are willing to carry us until October, and by then the farmers can buy their notes back, once we sell their cotton for a decent price." He glanced at the sleepy face resting on his shoulder and rubbed the plump back, his own face a study of tenderness. "But I'd rest a lot easier if the board hadn't voted to invest in our own building in Dallas. I tried to talk sense to them, but they're dead set on it. One hundred feet by one hundred fifty feet, and four stories high, at a cost of forty-five thousand dollars."

Cat blinked, as awed by the dimensions as the amount of money. "But don't you need the space for all the supplies and the cotton?"

"So the board tells me, but we managed without it this year." He sighed. "This building is too big. It'll only ever be fit for a warehouse. And the expense will put too much strain on our credit."

"What can you do?" Cat reached for the now-sleeping toddler, transferring the warm, limp weight onto her own shoulder.

"Hope and pray our creditors don't panic before we can pay them." Charlie's hand touched Duncan's black curls for a moment, then dropped to his side. "We may have to go to the membership for pledges. That's where you could help us out by lecturing."

Cat bit her lip. She wanted more than anything to offer her help to this man. But she knew she couldn't. Whether he realized it or not, Will Bascom needed her, and not just in his medical practice. She couldn't walk away from him or their patients. "I'm sorry, but I have to decline."

Charlie's mustache drooped, but he nodded. "If you change your mind, will you let me know?"

Cat smiled up at him. "Aye, and gladly."

Chapter 30

April 1888

Joe wiped raindrops from his eyes and squinted against the harsh yellow-gray light coming through the black thunderclouds as his horse zigzagged to cut off a stray. Grabbing his hat by the brim and leaning down from the saddle, he hazed it in the steer's eyes, turning the skittish animal back toward the herd.

Between rumbles of distant thunder he caught the sound of Miz Macleod's voice shouting as her horse bunched the cattle together. Lightning flashed, leaving a picture of her in his mind. Black curls streamed out behind her as she clung to the horse's neck. The cow pony wheeled and headed the herd toward the corral.

He'd been shocked when she insisted they bring the cattle in from the range before the storm hit, and even more so when she appeared in a pair of old denim trousers belted at the waist with a length of rope. And when she swung into the saddle astride, he didn't know what to think.

But it turned out she knew what she was doing, letting the cow pony have its head. Hell, she rode as good as most men, better than some.

Water drizzled down the back of his neck under the collar of his slicker. He jammed his hat down on his head and urged his horse forward, following the last of the stragglers as they joined the main herd. If the rain kept coming like this, the creeks were sure to rise over their banks. He'd best help Miz Macleod get these critters corralled and get himself home to check on Mama and Pieter and Hans before it got too dark.

Moving against the tide of theatergoers heading toward the lobby for intermission, Geordie followed the dapper little man toward the stage. What a chance! Even though the incessant drumming of rain on the tin roof had drowned her melodious voice, and she flinched at each flash of lightning, Lily Langtry hadn't disappointed the opening-night crowd at the opera house in Dallas.

Nobody claimed any great talent for the famous English actress, but few disputed her uncommon beauty. Say, that wasn't bad. Stopping in his tracks, he pulled his notebook from his pocket and jotted down the words. He might use them later, when he wrote the story. Nights like this made him love newspaper work.

Stuffing the notebook back into his pocket, he hurried to catch up with his guide. He didn't know the man's name or his relationship to the acting troupe or the opera house. The fellow had just walked up and offered him an interview with the star for a price. He'd been surprised when the man actually met him in the aisle at intermission, especially since he'd refused to pay the money before the interview. He stopped in front of a curtained opening, wondering what had become of the little fellow in his Fancy Dan suit. A hand reached between the curtains, closing on his wrist and pulling him through the doorway.

As the curtains dropped behind him, he breathed the backstage smells of sweat and greasepaint filling the semidarkness. Too bad Molly couldn't be here. She'd talked of meeting Mrs. Langtry since the first day they met. But instead of saddening him, the thought just made him feel closer to his lost love.

"This way." The man clipped his words like a Sassenach. Maybe he was from England too.

Geordie followed him, climbing the short flight of stairs,

emerging into sudden chaos. With the curtain down, workmen scurried around the darkened stage, changing the set, shouting, and cursing at one another. In a back corner Mrs. Langtry's leading man, Mr. Coghlin, lounged against a wall, laughing and talking to a young woman still wearing face paint and parts of a costume. The actor held a smoking cigarette in one hand and took a pull from a small glass bottle with the other.

Geordie edged away from the noise and activity, following the little Englishman toward the row of dressing room doors. Several of them stood open, and men and women wandered in and out in various stages of undress. Keeping his eyes to the front, he hurried along, reviewing the first act in his mind.

So far, except for Mrs. Langtry, the play had little to recommend it. Even the orchestra's fitful music flickered in and out of tune. The only real moment of drama came when the woman playing Mrs. Beck fainted during a brilliant flash of lightning. And the Jersey Lily herself didn't perform as much as she posed in her beautiful costumes and recited her lines. Of course she'd struck enough different attitudes to show her famous figure off to advantage and to turn the men in the audience to quivering jelly, himself included.

A woman burst from a doorway just in front of him, and he had to jump back to keep from running into her. As she brushed past, reeking of alcohol, her face an angry mask, he recognized her. The hapless Miss Russell, the one who'd fainted. The footlights and greasepaint had been kind to her, making her prettier and younger onstage than off. He glanced after her, then turned back to his search.

The last door bore a five-pointed star. His pulse quickened as the Englishman rapped his knuckles against the rough wood.

"Enter." There was no mistaking the voice calling from inside.

The man motioned for him to wait. From behind the door voices rose and fell for a few minutes. At last the door opened again and the little man held out his open palm.

Geordie dropped the agreed price into the outstretched hand.

The man smiled, tossed the coin, and caught it, then tipped his hat and motioned Geordie inside before he disappeared.

After wiping his sweaty palm on his trouser leg, Geordie stepped inside. Baskets of hot-house lilies perfumed the air with their honey-sweetness, framing the lovely creature seated in their midst. Mrs. Langtry half reclined in an overstuffed armchair, an open silk robe revealing the front of her corset and chemise. Dark curls cascaded over her bare shoulders as she leaned her head against the chair's brocaded back and turned her melting blue eyes toward him. "Yes?"

Geordie closed his open mouth and swallowed. "Uh, Mrs. Langtry, I represent the local press, and I, uh, was hoping maybe you'd answer a few questions?"

The perfect mouth pulled into a pout. "And I'd so hoped for a suitor, or at the least an admirer." Her large hands hung over the arms of the chair, empty and limp.

"But I am." The words tumbled from his mouth. "That is, I mean—" His cheeks flamed as he strangled to a stop.

She laughed, a low, soft chuckle. "There, there. I was having you on." She lifted one hand in a languid gesture. "Do shut the door."

He hurried to comply, then perched on the edge of a rickety chair and pulled his notebook from his pocket. He couldn't believe his luck. "So what do you think of Texas?"

She lifted her hands, propping her elbows against the chair's arms and pressing the fingertips of one hand against those of the other. "This is my first visit here." Her lips curving upward, she turned her face toward the mirror in front of her. "I am surprised beyond measure and somewhat ashamed to confess to you the ideas I had about Texas." Her eyes flickered toward him and away. "I was led to believe you people were all savages." She chuckled again. "I even left my diamonds in New Orleans for fear they'd be stolen by train robbers."

His lead pencil scratched across the page. "And now?"

"Now I see that I and my possessions are quite as safe in Texas as anywhere." She laced her long, narrow fingers together. "I daresay you have as many cultivated and refined people, and as many pretty women, as any state in the Union."

He hesitated, not wanting to ask about the dreadful performance and unable to think of anything else to ask. He hadn't expected to get as far as her dressing room, let alone persuade her to talk to him. "And what is your favorite place in Texas so far?"

Her eyes closed, the dark, heavy lashes a contrast to the rose and cream of her complexion. "I am particularly struck with San Antonio, and Dallas as well, of course. San Antonio has such a colorful history, and of course here you have such a business push, such growth and prosperity to be seen on all hands."

The scratching of his pencil and the insistent rhythm of the rain filled the silence. He cast about for something else to ask. Lightning flashed outside, and thunder rolled.

Her eyes flickered open and she turned her beautiful face to him once again. "No more questions? Then I'll ask you one." Her smile broadened. "Your accent doesn't sound to be pure Texas. Are you from England?"

"Scotland. The Isle of Skye."

Her smile dimmed, but she leaned toward him. "Ah. And do you miss it?"

He shrugged. "Sometimes. The sea, the mountains, the rain. But not the lairds, and not the hardships."

She nodded, but didn't speak.

After a moment he cleared his throat. "And do you ever miss Jersey?"

Her eyes locked on his, the clear blue misted with tears. "Yes, yes, I do."

The door swung inward, and the little man's face appeared in the opening. "Five minutes." He swung the door wide.

The actress rose and paced behind a screen in the corner. "You will excuse me, won't you? I must change for the next act."

He jumped to his feet. "I can't thank you enough, Mrs. Langtry. You've no idea how much this meant to me."

Her eyes crinkled over the top of the screen. "I've some idea, I suppose. I do hope you enjoy the rest of the play."

"Yes'm. I will." And that was a promise he knew he'd keep.

As Will fought to control the buggy racing along the muddy track, a flash of lightning left behind a ghost picture of the dark, wet countryside around him. Wind whipped his face, driving drops of water like bullets into his eyes and eddying the high spoked wheels against the sides of the deep ruts.

In the next flash he caught sight of Nana's wrinkled face, her eyes wide and one gnarled hand gripping the edge of the tufted leather seat. If only he could have spared her this nightmare ride. But he couldn't risk leaving her at home. The old farmhouse they lived in stood too near the bend in the creek. During the last flood it had overflowed its banks, and water had filled the root cellar. And after today's downpour, even Nana herself said she'd never seen the branch rise this fast, and she'd lived hereabouts longer than any of the other old-timers.

No, he'd been right to insist she go with him to the Macleod farm. The ground wasn't much higher there, or anywhere else nearby, for that matter. But it was farther from any of the streams meandering across the prairie. Nana would be safe, if he could get her there.

And Cat's house was closer to town. Of course if the rain kept falling, Arlington would soon be cut off, surrounded by the Trinity River three miles to the north, Rush Creek three miles to the west, and Allum Branch three miles south. Once the bridges went, they'd be trapped until the waters receded. He wondered if the Texas and Pacific tracks would wash out to the east or the west.

Clenching his jaw, he slapped the reins across the horse's rump. But none of that mattered as much to him as his real reason for taking his grandmother to Catriona. He had to make sure they were safe, and the best way was to keep them together—both of the women he loved. The thought of Cat in danger convinced him of that; no matter how distant she acted or how stubborn, he loved her, would always love her.

He only hoped she was at home, minding her children, instead of off with that Indian woman picking weeds. No, even Cat wouldn't have ventured far from home in this weather, unless they went out before the storm started. The image of her struggling through waist-high prairie grass in this deluge paralyzed him. He had to hurry.

A dark outline loomed in the road ahead. The bridge at last. He drove straight toward it without slowing, praying it would hold until they crossed it. Every time the water rose, this rickety span pulled loose from its mooring and floated downstream to the next bend. The residents complained, but each time the county threw it back together with as little time and money as possible. This time he'd see they dug the pilings down to bedrock himself. That is, if he managed to get across it to safety in time.

The horse shied, rearing back from the approach to the narrow bridge. What the devil? Will fought to control the gelding, sawing on the reins until the animal stood quivering, its sides heaving and bloody foam covering its muzzle in the dim carriage lights. But it refused to move forward.

Lightning flashed, illuminating the wooden span. A sheet of water flowed over the planks, and the whole thing trembled and shifted in the current. In moments the creek would overtop its banks as well. No wonder the gelding balked.

Will knew he had to get them to the other side and to higher ground before the water swept the wooden structure away. He couldn't go back; the bridge over the other fork wasn't much sounder, and it was quite a distance in the other direction. If he did make it back across, they'd have to go miles out of their way to get to another bridge, and it likely would be washed out by the time they got to it as well. Either way, they could be stuck on the wrong side, maybe even washed away in the torrent. He had to risk it.

"We're going across." He peered into the darkness, making out the pale oval that was Nana's face. Just as well he couldn't see her eyes.

"Yes. God is with thee, William." Her confident voice carried above the roar of the wind and the drumming of the rain.

He handed her the reins. "I hope so. Hold him steady." He tugged a bandanna from his pocket and jumped down from the high seat. The wind buffeted his body and mud sucked at his boots. He grabbed the whiffletree in one hand, following it to the animal's head. Rain soaked through his clothing, chilling him to the bone as he looped one corner of the cotton square around the blinder on the left side. The horse tossed its head, pulling the cloth from his hand. "Damn." Jerking on the halter, he lowered the horse's muzzle and grabbed the other blinder, then managed to secure the cloth between, covering the spooked animal's eyes. It would have to do.

Hooking one hand through its chin strap, he clucked to the horse and started forward. His boots slewed sideways in the slippery muck, almost jerking him from his feet as the wind pounded his body, but the horse followed, as docile now as it had been reluctant a few moments before. Not so different from most people, stumbling blind ahead without a thought, as he had with Catriona.

He set one boot on the wooden plank flooring, wincing as icy water covered his toes, soaking through the leather and tugging him off balance. Leaning his weight on the horse's neck, he strode forward, securing his footing step by slow step. In the silence of a sudden lull the wooden framework creaked and the horse's hooves echoed with dull thuds on the submerged boards.

The wind returned with a vengeance, a wall of cold air slamming him against the gelding's broad side. The bridge swayed. His foot slipped and he went down on one knee, the current dragging him halfway under the animal. *Please, God, don't let him spook.* In his mind the frightened horse reared on his hind legs, dragging Will up into the air, clinging to the chin strap by one hand.

His feet scrambled for purchase on the slick, flooded planks. He pulled himself up, clinging to the gelding's rain-roughened hide. The bridge shuddered. Not much time before it went, not enough to be careful. He urged the animal to a fast walk, letting his own feet slip and slide as he stumbled forward.

His feet hit the sticky surface of the bank as the far end of the bridge pulled free of its moorings behind him, angling the span downstream. He slapped the horse's haunch and shouted in its ear. Seconds after the buggy wheels cleared the last plank, the structure collapsed in on itself, the explosion of sound rising above the constant howling of the wind as the bridge swept away in the swirling waters.

Water lapped at the narrow-spoked wheels. Will clambered back into the leather seat, the wind plastering his drenched clothing to him as he gathered the reins. He shivered and slapped the leather straps against the horse's rump, shouting at the animal above the storm. "Good work, boy. Now get us the hell out of here."

Chapter 31

Catriona finished spreading the old quilt over the horsehair sofa and walked to the parlor window, crossing her arms over her breasts and staring out into the blackness. Raindrops drummed on the roof, and the wind howled. No one had been in this room since Molly's funeral, seven months before. For a moment she thought she could still smell the flowers as she breathed in the damp, musty air.

She waited. At last a jagged yellow-white spear split the dark clouds, an instant of light spreading over the prairie for miles around.

Before the darkness returned, she narrowed her eyes and tried to make out the cotton field lying just beyond the pin oak marking Ian's grave. She shivered as thunder crashed and rolled overhead. At least the cattle were all bedded down safe in the corral, thanks to Joe. And she didn't have to worry about any nearby stream overflowing and carrying away the entire cotton fields. She told herself they were lucky, although she knew the hard rain could beat the small green shoots back into the dirt as surely as the flood waters. But until morning there was no way to tell if any plants would survive the storm.

The ceiling creaked above her head. The Andersons, upstairs in her room, getting ready to climb into her bed.

She didn't really mind. In fact, she'd insisted. Why should they spread blankets on the kitchen floor when she wasn't using all of her double bed?

A memory of Will stole into her mind, his strong arms around her, holding her against his naked body. She pushed the image away, concentrating instead on the Andersons and their plight. Putting them up in her room was the least she could do. How horrible, to watch all their crops swept away by the rising waters. She only hoped their house would be standing when the rain stopped, if it ever did.

Her wish wasn't pure charity. She didn't want to put them up any longer than necessary. It would take some time to shovel out the river silt and clean and dry things, but not near as much time as rebuilding.

She sighed and moved to the sofa again, curling up at one end with a book in her lap, although she wasn't sure she could read. Perhaps she should undress and try to sleep, but she knew it would be useless. Too many things weighed on her mind, not all of them caused by the storm.

Footsteps clattered on the porch outside. She jumped to her feet, grabbing up the kerosene lamp from the side table. More neighbors, no doubt. The waters must be rising faster than she'd thought. She raced through the kitchen on silent feet, but Sanapia already stood in the open doorway, helping two people inside.

Cat lifted the lamp, casting a wider circle of light on the newcomers. It took her a moment to recognize Will and Nana. "My God, what are you about?" Setting the lamp on the sideboard, she closed the outside door behind them and guided Nana to the stove. The woman's frail limbs shivered beneath her hand. "You're that wet." She glared at Will. "Are you *daft*, then, bringing her out in this?"

His lips thinned into a straight line. "The house stands too close to the water."

"And you could find no place closer?" Cursing his stupidity in her mind, she untied the strings under the old woman's chin and tugged the sopping wet cloak from the narrow shoulders, draping it over a high-back kitchen chair. Did he want his own grandmother to die of pneumonia?

A chill, withered hand touched her cheek. "Catriona, it

is not like thee to be unfair. William did his best, for thee as well as me." Nana's wheezing voice reached her beneath the noise of the storm.

"It is no matter now." Cat waved the argument away with one hand. "Sanapia, chafe Mrs. Bascom's hands and feet while I find her some dry things."

Sanapia grunted and led Nana to the glowing cookstove, her smooth face a mask to any who didn't know her, but Cat had learned to see beneath that calm surface. She could almost hear the woman expressing her disgust at the white doctor's impetuous disregard of the old one's safety.

After seeing Nana settled in a cozy chair, Cat flew up the stairs, remembering just in time to knock at her bedroom door. Wouldn't that have been a scandal, to walk in on the neighbors in each other's arms?

As she rummaged through the trunk and the wardrobe, she explained over her shoulder to the wide-eyed couple. The stack grew: one of Ian's red union suits, a pair of denim trousers, a warm flannel shirt, and dry socks. The boots would be too large, so she left them, pulling out a quilt and bundling it all together. She grabbed a flannel gown and wrapper for Nana, then added a pair of wool stockings and headed back down the stairs, bidding another good-night to the Andersons.

Back in the kitchen, she handed the gown and robe to Sanapia and asked her to show Nana to the sofa in the parlor.

The old woman took Cat's hands in her gnarled ones. "Bless thee for thy kindness." She turned and followed Sanapia, the glow of the kerosene lamp silhouetting them as they made their way down the hall.

Cat stood, waiting for her eyes to adjust to the dim light of the one remaining candle, then strode forward and thrust the bundle into Will's hands. "You can dress here. I'll sleep in Effie's room with her, and you can make up a pallet for yourself on the floor here."

"No need." Points of candlelight glittered in his eyes. "I thought I'd sleep in the barn." He paused, his voice softening almost to a whisper. "Up in the hayloft."

His words triggered a wealth of memories in her body. A warm ache tugged low in her belly, a delicious hunger swirling through her veins. She chewed her lip, fighting for control. It would be so easy to let go, to give in to his love, to allow herself to belong to him.

But no, he wanted too much—more than she could give up. She turned away. "I'll fetch you an oilskin to keep those things dry." She added a candle and some matches to the bundle in his hands, then rummaged in the press nearest the door. At last her fingers grazed the slick tarp. She pulled it out and handed it to him, avoiding his gaze.

He hesitated, then turned to the outside door. "Good night."

"Aye, good night, then." She balled her fists. It was all she could do to keep from following him into the rainy darkness. Instead, she leaned into the door, latching it against the driving wind.

She stood there a long moment in the warm darkness, shivering with desire. Even though she wouldn't let herself be with him, folded close in his arms, it came to her that she was glad—glad to have Will here and safe, to be able to scold him and fuss over him. His safety was one less thing to *fash* herself about in this long, dark, dangerous night.

Now, if only she knew how Geordie fared. She'd tried to talk him out of going into Dallas tonight. But, of course, he said it was the chance of a lifetime, to see a famous beauty perform on their own opera house stage, perhaps even meet her, speak with her. She hoped it turned out to be worth it.

Cat sighed and lifted the candle, holding it ahead of her as she tiptoed down the dark hall to Effie's room. Might as well go to bed, even though she knew there'd be no sleep for her until she counted all her loved ones safe under this roof. She only hoped her brother had sense enough to take a room in Dallas and stay there until the storm ended.

Blinking in the bright lights of the lobby, Geordie was happy to let the crowd carry him toward the outer doors; the sooner he escaped the throng, the sooner he could get on his way back to Arlington and home. Odors of damp wool and sweat surrounded him, mixed with the scents of toilet water and cologne. Bits and pieces of conversation swirled by, most centering on the poor quality of the acting and the beauty of the star.

The second act showed no improvement over the first, lacking even the unexpected drama of a woman fainting. But somehow it didn't matter to him. As he watched Mrs. Langtry strike poses around the stage, he kept remembering the sadness in her eyes when she spoke of her home. He'd looked behind the mask, something no one else in the audience could say.

His fingers itched to write the story. Of course, he'd have to be honest about the play and her acting ability, but he'd emphasize her grace and beauty. Not that it would make much difference to anyone but him. Mrs. Langtry would probably take little interest in a small-town paper like *The World*, and few of their readers could manage to get tickets to her next two shows, even if they had the money.

He glanced around him in the crush of bodies, recognizing several prominent Dallas citizens, all dressed in the height of fashion and expense. Although the audience was large, it was also very select; if he hadn't been a journalist, he wouldn't have gotten in. And this crowd wasn't any more likely to be interested in his opinion, so he might as well write the article to please himself, and be glad of the memories he could cherish.

The crowd spewed out onto the wooden sidewalk. Wind whipped the rain sideways, splattering the theatergoers as they stood beneath the opera house awning. Leaving behind as many as it took, a streetcar rang its bell and disappeared into the dark veils of the downpour, invisible in moments despite the frequent flashes of lightning. Huge drops thudded onto the street, turning it into a shallow river as the last hack drove off, the driver promising to return. Those left standing on the sidewalk muttered, shifting from foot to foot.

Geordie threaded his way through, glad he didn't have to wait with them. As he stepped out from under the awning, he turned up his collar against the torrent, but it hardly mattered. By the time he reached the livery stable, the rain had soaked through his clothes to his skin.

Shivering, he mounted his stallion and rode out into the darkness, the bright streetlights on each corner mere glimmers through the sheets of falling water. He had to rein in when a woman crossed in front of him almost beneath his horse's hooves, her Mother Hubbard floating out behind her on the wind. Lightning flashed overhead and crackled along the electric wires, exploding in showers of blue sparks like a Fourth of July celebration.

At the first intersection the wind tore his breath from his throat, almost drowning him with driven rain. A fire wagon raced east, its bell clanging above the roar of the storm. He couldn't imagine any kind of fire burning in this deluge. Must be a rescue of some kind, probably somebody stranded by high water. Somehow, he figured it wouldn't be the last such call of the night.

He lowered his face and urged his mount through the water rushing along the streets. He hoped the bridge would hold at least until he could get across. If it washed out, he'd be trapped in Dallas, maybe for days.

It might be safer to just stay here, turn around, and find a room in a hotel and wait out the storm. But the thought of spending the night in the city made him long for home and his own warm, dry bed. Besides, he still had to write his story about Mrs. Langtry. Her beautiful face swam before him. He ought to stop at the office, look in on Zeke, see how this issue was shaping up. And Cat and Effie might need him at the farm. No, he had to get back to Arlington tonight.

Wind buffeted him as he left the protection of the buildings along the river and approached the bridge. Lightning illuminated the swirling black waters of the Trinity, swollen almost to the top of its banks. The bridge swayed as the horse skittered across the slippery boards to the far bank. Another hour and they wouldn't have made it across.

Now he only had to worry about crossing Mountain Creek at Grand Prairie and Allum Branch this side of Arlington. He leaned forward and patted the stallion's withers.

"Come hell or high water, eh, boy?" The wind drowned his words as he squinted into the falling rain. They'd swim if they had to. He pressed his knees into the horse's ribs, and the stallion leapt forward, heading across the dark prairie. No matter what, he planned to make it home tonight.

Chapter 32

May 1888

Effie paced to the open window, leaning on the sill to enjoy the perfume of spring on the evening breeze.

Ida's voice followed her, halting after each word. "How —quickly—the—stubborn—air—"

She had to admire the girl's gumption, coming all the way out here, day after day. She didn't know what she'd expected a sporting woman to be like, but it certainly wasn't this hardworking, dedicated girl before her, sitting in Cat's parlor, reading from a primer.

Effie wondered what made a woman choose such a profession. She understood little enough of what went on at the Bon Chance, but it didn't seem a very happy life. Little wonder Ida was so set on learning to read, although she couldn't see how it would help much.

And no one could dispute that Ida was a dedicated student. Even right after the flood, when the washed-out train tracks and bridges closed the schools and kept everybody home, Ida had struggled on alone, without any help, puzzling out the words on her own.

She was already up to the fifth selection. Like most other students, Effie had always welcomed an extra holiday, no matter how much she liked her studies or her teacher. A few more weeks and another school year would end, and then it would be summer again. She could scarcely wait.

Ida stuttered over a word, then pointed at the page and held up the reader.

Effie left the window and settled beside the girl on Cat's horsehair sofa. "Half chiding."

The girl echoed the words, then drew in a breath and continued.

Effie returned to the window, listening to Ida with part of her attention, too restless to sit still after a long day of school. Beyond the barnyard stretched a swath of green all the way to the horizon. The rain had done that much at least, bringing lots of fresh grass for the cattle. Too bad it had washed away so many of the crops.

Her family had been lucky. Some of their cotton seedlings survived, but not the best plants. Still, even culls were better than no plants at all, or having to buy more seed on credit as so many farmers had been forced to do. That and late planting would cut their slender profits. Either way, most of them would sink deeper in debt in spite of the Alliance programs.

Still, the whole area had been lucky no one had drowned in all the high water. She'd been so relieved when Geordie finally showed up in the wee hours of the morning, drenched and covered with mud, she couldn't be mad at him. And in spite of the floods, Joe seemed to think they'd have a decent yield at harvest time.

Joe. She sighed again. He was so quick to notice some things, like a bloated steer or a break in the fence. But when she batted her eyelashes at him once, he asked if she needed some eyewash. And he just didn't seem to *see* her when she took him lemonade or asked him questions about his work. He was always polite, but he could have been talking to Geordie for all he noticed she was a girl.

Maybe Vi was right; she ought to ask her brother for his help. After all, he was a man, and besides, he was Joe's best friend. At least he could tell her if Joe ever talked about her and what he said. But every time she started to ask, something stopped her. There was no way he could think about her and Joe without being reminded of his feelings for Molly, and she couldn't stand the thought of making him relive that pain, no matter how frustrated she got.

If only she had someone else to turn to, someone who could give her advice about how to get his attention. Cat might help, but she'd be too embarrassed to ask. She'd probably just get some sisterly advice about taking her time. Besides, Cat was just so naturally beautiful, she'd never had to work at getting men to pay court to her.

Why, look at Doc Bascom, the catch of the county. At least a dozen young women would be happy to marry him, but he was crazy about a widow woman with two kids and a brother and sister to look after, to say nothing of trying to make the farm pay. The only reason they weren't married now was Cat's stubbornness about the Alliance. Effie pressed her lips together. You'd never catch *her* putting politics ahead of love. No, Cat wouldn't be a good person to ask.

A tapping sound broke into Ida's drone. The door swung inward and a small boy toddled toward them. Sanapia peered in. "Little boy hungry now. You feed."

"Thanks for watching him." Ida smiled up at Sanapia, then set the *McGuffey's Reader* on the sofa and held out her arms to the small boy. "Come here to Mama, you rascal."

Envy crept into Effie's chest as Ida lifted the baby onto her knee and undid her bodice. He chuckled and reached for the breast, leaning his head against his mother's shoulder, his eyes roving about the room as he suckled.

Ida leaned back. "Do you think he's too old to nurse? Hattie says I ought to wean him to a cup, but I'm afraid he might get the milk fever. I know your sister's a healer. Could you ask her what she thinks?"

Effie smiled. "Okay. She's still nursing Duncan, and he's only a few months younger."

Ida smiled. "Some of the girls say it ruins the bosom, but I don't care. I don't think men care much about that stuff anyhow, leastwise not with a—you know." She glanced down at her contented son. "I worry about little Arthur sometimes. Bringing up a kid at the Bon Chance, well, it just ain't right, you know?"

"Nonsense." Effie picked up the reader and set it on the

desk. "You're a good mother, and besides, he's too young to understand."

"But they grow so fast. It won't be long before he figures it out, and other kids can be so mean. It's bad enough being called a bastard, but being called the son of a sporting woman, well, he wouldn't have no chance to turn out decent." Ida's brows drew together and she sucked her lower lip in for a moment. "I've been thinking about saving up my money and taking little Arthur somewheres else. You know, get out of the life and make a new start. Maybe even marry and turn respectable." Ida's dark eyes sought hers. "If I learned to read real good, do you think I might ever be able to do something like that?"

Effie folded her arms across her chest. So that was the reason she tried so hard. Ida was even braver than she'd thought. "If that's what you want, I can't see any reason why not." She made a silent promise to help this girl any way she could.

Ida's eyes brimmed and she pulled the baby tighter until he squirmed against her. "Thanks, Effie. It means a lot, hearing you say that. And if there's ever anything I can do for you—"

Effie settled into Cat's best chair, an idea blooming in her mind. "Actually, there just might be."

Ida blinked, her eyes wide with surprise.

Leaning forward with her elbows on her knees, she searched for the right words. "You see, there's this fellow I like, but he doesn't even know I exist."

Ida giggled and held up a hand to stop her. "You don't need to say no more, honey, 'cause you come to the right person."

Cat reached high, pinching the long root hanging from the rafter to see if it was ready. A few more days of good weather and she could seal it in a jar with the others she and Sanapia had collected this spring.

Crossing her arms over her bosom, she tipped back her head and narrowed her eyes. The spicy scent of juniper branches mixed with the onion-smell of the iris roots in the warm air. Rows of herbs hung from the ceiling of her pantry—some flowers, some twigs, but mostly roots, all clean and ready to pack away for later use as soon as they were bone dry.

She could thank Sanapia for much of this, for showing her how to find the native plants, what parts to gather, how to clean them in running water and hang them to dry, how to prepare and use them to ease pain and cure sickness. She knew she had much to learn, but already she carried more remedies in her bag than ever before, combining the old knowledge with the new.

When she fingered a bunch of sneezeweed flowers, they crumbled to dust in her hands. Just right. She climbed onto the workbench and reached for the knotted string. Better to untie it than to cut it. Her fingers worked the knot for long moments until her arms tingled. If only she could reach an inch higher.

She eased herself up on tiptoe, swaying in the narrow space, her head near the whitewashed ceiling. Please let there not be any cobwebs clinging to her hair. Her fingernails tugged at the snarled strands until the knot loosened and unraveled. The flowers dropped onto the counter at her feet, releasing a cloud of dust. Damn! What a clumsy waste. Her eyes itched and her nostrils tickled. She grabbed a rafter as a sneeze convulsed her body, rocking the workbench beneath her. A smile tugged at her mouth as she sniffed and wiped the back of her hand across her eyes. At least the stuff lived up to its name. It was supposed to be great for stuffy noses and head colds.

The narrow pantry door swung open. Sanapia, she hoped, or Effie home from school early.

"Miz Macleod?" A deep masculine voice came from the kitchen.

Startled, Cat bent and peered through the doorway into Charlie Macune's handsome face. Her hands flew to her hair, smoothing it into place. "Hello. I was just untying—"

He stepped into the small room and reached up both hands. "Here, let me help you down." His hands closed on her waist and he lifted her to the floor. "The Indian woman told me where to find you. I hope you don't mind."

Cat tipped her chin down and smoothed her apron to hide her confusion. "No, of course I dinna mind." She gestured toward the kitchen. "Will you take a cup of coffee?"

His brows drew together. "Actually, if you don't mind, I'd rather talk with you here, in private."

She clasped her hands in front of her, wondering what he could want of her. "All right."

He touched one palm to the top of his smooth hair, the marks of his comb still visible among the dark strands. "There's been some trouble with the joint notes. I think I told you about the problems with the banks refusing to accept them as collateral?"

Cat nodded. Why was he telling her about this? She had no power inside the Alliance, or out.

"Well, last month I was forced to issue a business statement listing our assets and indebtedness." His voice slid over the words as if he'd practiced them, or said them the same way to several people. "It showed four hundred thousand dollars in debt and one million dollars in joint notes, but very little actual capital stock paid in." He turned his face away, cupping one hand over the back of his neck. "Some of our large foreign creditors are alarmed. We met with their representatives a few days ago, and we agreed to call upon the membership for an additional two dollars apiece in capital stock."

Cat cleared her throat. Two dollars! That was almost two day's wages. After the flood, many of her neighbors had gone into debt to buy more seed and replant their crops. "I see. And what is it you want from me, then?"

He turned to her and drew in a long breath. "The members respect you. You know how to rouse them to action, just like you did on Skye." His mouth tightened for a moment, then he continued. "I know this'll be a hardship to some. I want you to go out and convince them they need to do this."

"And if I don't agree?" She knew better than to suggest he find someone else. He'd need every lecturer he could find.

He shrugged. "If you can't persuade them, nobody can. And without this money the Exchange will close forever, just like the Grange co-ops all over the state."

Cat chewed her lip. What choice did she have? She believed in the Exchange. It was the farmers' only chance to buy and sell at fair prices. She sighed. "All right, then. I'll do it."

Will frowned at Sanapia. "What man?"

She shrugged, then held her hands apart, palms facing. "This wide."

He turned and headed for the house, leaving the Indian woman in the yard, arms folded, her gaze never wavering from the two small children toddling about. Some strange man inside the house with Cat—alone. Probably just a drummer trying to sell her something, or someone looking for an herbal remedy. Still, he didn't like the idea.

If only she'd spend more time working with him at the office and less time collecting herbs with Sanapia, this kind of thing wouldn't happen. He needed her help with patients more than the botanicals they'd collected. Perhaps it hadn't been such a good idea to send the woman here. But then, he'd had no idea she knew anything about local herbs. Leave it to Catriona to discover something like that.

His boot heels thudded up the steps and across the porch as he eyed the strawberry roan tethered to the railing. He swung the screen door open, then let it slam behind him. Let them know he was coming. He knew it was loco even to think she might want to be alone with another man, but he couldn't help himself where Catriona was concerned. And since the night of the flood, he'd despaired of breaking down the wall between them. He'd tossed and turned all night in her hayloft, hoping she'd slip out of the house and join him. But she hadn't, and he'd no idea how to get back into her good graces.

He stopped and listened. A man's voice drew him across the wide kitchen to the pantry door.

". . . arrange a schedule and purchase your train tickets. The members will put you up and feed you."

Will stuck his head through the narrow doorway. "Catriona?" The warm, dusty smell of dried roots and flowers tickled his nose in the small, warm space.

Cat's eyes widened. "Will, what are you doing here?"

"Mrs. Schoolcroft's in labor. I need you to assist in the delivery." He stared at the portly man in a dark, heavy suit. He didn't like his looks, not one bit.

"You remember Mr. Macune?" She lifted a hand in Will's direction. "And you know Dr. Bascom."

The man smiled. "Call me Charlie, Doc."

Will recognized the man, but it didn't relieve his suspicions much. He grunted and shook the beefy hand Macune held out, squeezing the soft fingers a bit too hard.

The man retrieved his hand, then sidled past Will and into the kitchen. "I have some other appointments, if you'll excuse me, Miz Macleod. I'll be in touch." He hurried out the door.

Will stepped into the tiny pantry. "What was that all about?"

Cat faced away from him, sweeping some yellow powder into an open Ball canning jar. A crumpled bunch of dried flowers lay on the bench in front of her. She answered without looking up. "He's head of the Alliance education committee. They want me to go on a lecture tour of the state this summer. I said I would."

"You said what?" Will couldn't keep the anger from his voice. "And just when will you have time? With the children and the farm and these damn herbs, you hardly make it to the office as it is."

She turned to him, lifting her chin and squaring her shoulders. Her eyes narrowed and her mouth thinned to a straight line. "What I choose to do is my business and none of yours. If you are not satisfied with the amount of time I can work for you, perhaps you should find yourself another assistant."

Chapter 33

June 1888

Excitement crackled in the air as Geordie made his way past the fighting cocks staked near the pit. The missing spurs on their left legs gave them an odd, unbalanced look. All around him men stood or squatted, some holding their birds, others drinking from glass whiskey bottles. Tobacco smoke hung in thick layers on the hot air, adding to the stifling odors of chicken droppings, unwashed men, and blood. God, how he hated covering cockfights.

Of course, it could be worse. He could be out bedding cotton in the hot sun with Joe, or home helping Effie and Cat with the kitchen garden. Still, he hoped they'd hurry and get this bloodbath over with so he could move on to the horse races at the fairgrounds.

He found an empty chair near the canvas tent wall, and brushed feathers and dust from the seat before he sank down onto it. When he pulled the notebook from his pocket, a folded piece of paper spiraled to the earth. He bent to retrieve it, opening it and smoothing the creases with his fingers.

Members of the Farmers Alliance of Texas:

Brethren: Grave and important issues confront us to-day. Unjust combinations seek to throttle our lawful and legitimate efforts to introduce a business system more just and equitable than is now prevailing.

His eyes skipped down the page.

. . . it is most earnestly recommended that a mass meeting be held at the court house in each county of the State on the second Saturday in June.

And Cat would be in Fort Worth at the Tarrant County courthouse, lecturing. No telling what might happen if the Alliance's enemies decided to make trouble with all those people gathered together. Much as he sympathized with the Exchange, he wasn't sure blaming the banks was the answer. It might stir the people to contribute their subscription money, and he was as sure as anyone that the banks sided with the merchants. But the truth was, the business was undercapitalized, and the fancy new Exchange Building here in Dallas wasn't helping their cause.

He folded the circular and stuffed it back into his pocket, then opened his notebook and searched for a pencil. The Grange newspaper kept attacking Macune, insisting he was incompetent and urging Alliance members not to invest in the Exchange. Not that it made much difference. Counties all over the state reported more new members each month.

The referee advanced into the pit, carrying a pair of scales. Two owners came forward, holding out their roosters for weighing. He knew if the cocks were more than two ounces apart, there'd have to be a rematch. Voices hushed as the man called out the weights. "Shawlneck, four pounds, fifteen ounces. Spooner, four pounds, fifteen ounces. A dead even match."

Geordie noted the names and weights in his book as voices shouted across the ring, laying wagers of five or ten dollars. The handlers attached the steel gaffs where the missing spurs had been, and held the two birds within pecking distance of each other to whet their appetites for blood. Most handlers penned the cocks away from their hens for two weeks before and didn't feed them the day of a match, just to make them meaner.

Geordie winced as these two beauties went after each other without much prompting. The Dallas Redquill had a ragged gill, but the red-ginger bird was perfect, with a high red comb. The slasher gaffs on their left heels flashed as they struggled to get at each other.

The referee held up both hands. "Get ready."

The handlers retreated and placed the birds six feet apart, facing each other across the ring.

Light glinted from the pocket watch in the referee's hand. "Pit your birds!"

The cocks rushed toward the center of the pit, pecking and clawing and beating their wings.

Nausea gripped Geordie as he glanced at the faces around him, mouths open, cheeks ruddy.

"Watch them shuffle!" A man next to him let out a high giggle. Other voices shouted encouragement to the fighters.

The gamecocks flapped in an ungainly tangle until the referee called the owners into the pit. "Handle."

Spooner's owner pulled a steel gaff from the cock's wing and carried him back to the line. Blood flecked his feathers, and his sides heaved in and out. No wonder, in all the heat and excitement. The owner bent and used his mouth to blow a stream of air over the red ginger, ruffling the feathers on his head and back.

After a moment's rest the owners returned the birds to the pit and the combatants came together again, half running and half flying amid the shouts of the crowd. Disgusted as he was, still Geordie found himself rooting for the wounded Spooner. After another flurry of wings and beaks, the referee again called for the handlers. This time Shawlneck's owner removed a two-inch gaff from the Redquill's back.

Someone to Geordie's left groaned. "He's got a rattle."

The bird's sides heaved and blood leaked from the wounded cock's beak. Spooner's gaff must have gone into his lungs. The handler wiped the head with a cloth, then thrust a finger into the bloody beak to help him breathe.

Once more the referee called the handlers to the lines, and the birds clashed. But this time Shawlneck gave only feeble resistance. In minutes he lay dead in the pit. His handler lifted the carcass and carried it from the ring, leaving red feathers and spatters of blood to mark his passage.

Around Geordie, men cheered, clapping each other on the back as the winners collected on their bets. Near the pit, two more handlers heeled their birds for the next fight.

The heat, the smell, and the violence weighed on him, churning his stomach with nausea. Shoving the notebook into his pocket, he rose and strode toward the tent flap. He'd get the names and weights of the other winners later, after the horse races. He'd seen enough to write his story, more than enough—a bellyful.

Outside in the bright sunlight, he breathed clean air and fingered the Exchange circular. The farmers pitted themselves against the bankers and the merchants in their own bloody match. He only hoped his sister had bet on the right side, for all their sakes.

With one hand on the old man's shoulder, Will guided him out of the office. "Mind what I said, now. Take that medicine every night before you turn in, and for God's sake, wear your hat when you go out in the sun."

The old man lifted the medicine bottle and nodded. "Sure thing, and thanks, Doc." He shuffled down the hall toward the stairs.

Will shut the door and trudged into his office, slumping down in his desk chair.

Lewis Price slouched in the other chair, his usual smile on his round face. "You look like you could use a drink, Doc."

Will grunted, the sharp odor of carbolic stinging his nostrils as he rolled down his shirt-sleeves and fastened the cuffs. He reached for the bottle in the bottom drawer and poured himself two fingers, then passed the whiskey to his friend. "God, I miss her."

The undertaker's smile slipped a bit. "Miz Macleod?"

Will nodded, then tipped the glass to his lips, letting the dark liquid burn a trail down his throat to his belly. "Damn, but she's a stubborn one."

He set the glass back beside the bottle and shut the

drawer, then swung his feet up onto the desk and leaned back in his swivel chair. "Of course, it's my own fault for pushing her, but when I saw her standing so close to Macune—" It wasn't until later he realized she'd been standing close to him only because it was a tiny room.

Lewis pushed the bottle toward him across the desktop. "Have another."

Will debated, then shook his head. "I still have house calls to make this afternoon." Maybe by closing the office at noon, he could finish up before sunset and sleep in his bed for a change, instead of in the buggy. "I'd have been out of here sooner if Cat had shown up."

Lewis snorted and reached for the bottle, pouring himself another shot. "It's just dumb luck she hasn't abandoned you altogether."

"Thanks." Will screwed his face up in mock pain. At least today she was close by in Fort Worth, instead of somewhere off in West Texas as she'd be next week. Still, she'd been gone the whole damn day.

"I mean it." Lewis sipped the amber liquor. "Not that I'm any expert on females, mind you, but what if she quits and you have another typhoid epidemic this summer, or another bout with the breakbone fever?"

Will rubbed his hands over his face. Lewis was right. He needed her help. Needed her, period. "Why didn't I just keep my mouth shut about the lecturing?" He'd backed down right away after Macune left, but the damage was done by then. They were growing farther apart instead of closer, and he had no idea how to remedy it.

Lewis cackled. "I've been telling you for years, you just ain't bright. Besides, you can't blame her for wanting the Alliance job. She gets a chance to travel, they pay her for her time, and she believes in the cause."

Will nodded again. "It wouldn't be so bad if she didn't spend so much time on her herbal cures." It didn't matter to her how unscientific it might be to take the word of an old Indian woman. She didn't see that medicinal substances had to be tested, proven effective. He'd heard it over and over at medical school.

Lewis wagged his finger. "Seems to me some of her medicine works pretty good."

Will poured himself another drink. "Oh, some of the stuff works all right." Like the snakeroot and the milkweed paste, but the rest was no better than snake oil or medicine show elixirs. "But I have real medicines that do the same things and take less of her time away from the patients."

Lewis just smiled and sipped.

Arlington was growing by leaps and bounds, with more people moving in every year. More people meant more sickness, but there was still only one of him. "Maybe Cat's right. I ought to hire another assistant, or maybe a trained nurse. Or better yet, another doctor. If I could build a hospital—" But unless his patients paid their bills, he'd never be able to afford it. Many of them tried, usually the ones who could least afford it. Of course, the ones with a little extra money seemed to forget about his bill until they needed his help again. Doctoring wasn't like banking; you couldn't foreclose on a man's health.

Lewis cleared his throat and set his glass to one side. "Seems to me a hospital might help Will Bascom the doctor, but what about the man?"

A loud banging echoed through the quiet rooms. He pushed himself to his feet and hurried to the outer door, glad not to have to answer his friend's question. An after-hours visit on Saturday could mean a real emergency or a false alarm of some kind.

He swung the door open and a man toppled toward him. Hands reached out from both sides to steady the fellow, who gave a low moan at the touch of his two partners, one young and one older. A layer of dirt and sand covered what was left of the man's clothes. They hung from his body in bloody rags, exposing great open wounds beneath. One side of his face was scraped raw.

Will motioned the men inside. "Put him on the table in here." He led them into the examining room. "Get those clothes off him." Rolling up his sleeves, he turned to the nearest cowboy. "What happened?"

Creases appeared in the younger man's forehead. "Horse

drug him a piece. Thought maybe one of his arms was broke too."

Lewis strolled from the outer office, wrinkling his nose at the bloody figure on the examining table. "Give me a call if you need me."

"I won't." Will grinned as his friend sauntered out the door, chuckling, then sighed and poured clean water into a basin. His house calls would have to wait a while longer.

Catriona forced herself to stand still in the hot sun on the courthouse steps, a smile plastered across her face. Her new corset itched beneath her breasts and sweat trickled down her sides. For a minute she wished she were back home with the bairns, or even in Will's office helping him with his patients—anywhere but here. What had she been thinking of, agreeing to speak to this huge crowd? She must be daft, indeed.

Not that she'd forgotten how important the day was, but why did she have to agree to speak? Wiping her sweaty palms on her skirts, she stared at the county agent, willing him to start the proceedings so they could get this over with.

Instead, he tugged his watch from his pocket and glanced at it for the twentieth time. She fought the urge to grab him and shake him. It must be noon or long past by now. What was he waiting for?

At last the man raised his hands for silence, then turned and introduced her, his voice echoing out across the sun-drenched square. A cheer went up as she crossed to the center of the stairway. She shaded her eyes with one hand. More than a thousand people swarmed at the bottom of the stairs, spilling across the surrounding grassy lawns. If they all paid their two dollars today— She'd just have to do her best to see they did.

"I'd like to read you a resolution printed in the *Southern Mercury* newspaper of two days past." Her voice quavered, but she lifted the newsprint and filled her lungs, determined to make her voice carry to every person present. "Be it resolved that we endorse our Alliance principles anew with tenfold vigor.

"Resolved, that we fully endorse the bold and worthy stand taken against the undermining efforts of the Dallas merchants and bankers.

"Resolved, that we, in support of our principles and institutions, will bear hardship, suffer privations, make common stock of what we possess, weather the storm of oppression through, and gain an honorable victory, or starve in the attempt."

After a moment of silence, a roar of cheering and applause almost deafened her. She folded the newspaper and tucked it into her bag, then held up her hands for quiet once more. Excitement coursed through her at the power she held in her hands. Instead of trembling with fear, her spirit rose to meet the challenge. Words flowed to her from some hidden source. "We all know why we are here. The banks have refused to grant loans to the Exchange on any terms or securities. And they are keeping the mails full and the wires hot to prevent any other bankers in any other cities from granting us loans."

The muttering of a thousand mouths rose up around her, but she raised her voice over them. "I think we are now taking the steps we ought to have taken at the outset; to create the needed amount among ourselves, independent of the bankers." Again, she had to wait for the cheers to subside. "It is time for each of us to realize that faltering now means an unconditional surrender. It means a perpetuation of discriminations which do now and have in the past deprived us of the just proceeds of labor."

Cat let the silence stretch for a long moment. "If we fail to rally to the standard, our children are slaves for the bankers and the moneyed monopoly." Her voice shook with emotion. "God forbid any Alliance man or woman in this state should falter at this time and surrender in the hands of the taskmaster." Her hand clenched in a fist and she raised it overhead. "Three cheers for the State Exchange."

Chapter 34

August 1888

Cat crossed off the last item and pushed the list back into her reticule. "And I'll need to order in some jute bagging for harvest time."

O. K. Frink pursed his lips and pulled an order pad from a drawer. "How many bales you reckon you'll have?" The smell of his witch hazel tainted the air as he leaned toward her.

She hesitated, hating to make the man privy to such information. He'd know how much cotton everybody grew for miles around. But then, he could figure it out by the orders for bagging. Most folks ordered from him, and nobody could do without. Once the cotton was picked and ginned to remove the seeds, it had to be baled and wrapped in bagging before it could be sold or shipped. She told him her estimate of this year's crop yield. Not so bad, considering the damage caused by the rain and flooding.

He scratched his pointy chin and scribbled on the page, muttering to himself. "Figure six and a half yards to the bale, at twelve and a half cents a yard."

She planted her clenched fists on the counter. "I'm sorry. Did you say twelve and a half cents? I pay in cash, not time prices, if you remember."

His ginger mustache twitched. "I ain't forgot. The price

jumped up from eight cents to twelve and a half this month."

She drew herself up, rage smoldering inside her. The man was a crook, no doubt about it. No wonder the store had so few customers lately. She'd only come here today for the few things the Exchange didn't stock. Well, it was not too late to go to another store. "Cancel my order, Mr. Frink. I'll take my custom elsewhere."

He shrugged and slid the order pad back into the drawer. "Suit yourself. You'll get the same price anywheres around." He leaned back, crossing his arms over his narrow chest and blinking his eyes. "Ain't you heard? The jute manufacturers formed a trust. They're holding all the bagging off the market." He gave a short nod. "It'll be twelve and a half cents a yard, if I can even get it."

Cat's anger cooled from a rolling boil to a simmer. She reached into her bag for her cash. "How much for just the groceries?"

He frowned, touching his pencil up and down the column of figures and moving his lips. "Two dollars even today, cash price." His mustache quirked up in a half smile. "What you wanna do about the jute? We're only talking about an extra thirty cents a bale."

"Thirty cents is better than an hour's wages for most folks. I'll do without before I pay that." The words sounded hollow even to her, but she couldn't give in to such robbery.

Frink giggled, a high, unpleasant sound. "Suit yourself, but you won't be able to bale without bagging."

Cat stacked the paper-wrapped packages of coffee and sugar in her arms and headed toward the door. She turned at the door and glared back at the plump little man. "Then I guess I'll have to find something else to use for bagging."

Effie giggled and pushed Ida's hands away. "That tickles." She enjoyed teaching the woman, and she wanted help with Joe, especially after the way he ignored her at the threshing party. But sometimes Ida embarrassed her.

The girl rested her knuckles on her hips and shook her head. "You're more skittery than a hog on ice today." Ida's faint scent of honeysuckle surrounded her as the girl pulled out the top of the corset once more, tucking the soft cotton lint around Effie's small breasts.

Cheeks burning, she looked down at her enlarged bosom.

Ida tugged the sides of the bodice together and fastened the buttons. "There. That oughta make him sit up and take notice."

"And everyone else in Tarrant County as well." Panic filled her at the thought of the stares and whispers next time she went to town. "I can't go anywhere like this. Everybody will know."

Ida laughed. "Know what? That you're coming into your womanhood?"

Effie leaned forward, her voice hissing out between clenched teeth. "Will you keep quiet? I don't want the rest of the family to hear this."

"Why not, if they're gonna know anyhow?" Ida's eyes crinkled, and the corners of her mouth twitched upward.

She flopped down onto the bed, glaring at her friend. "You're impossible today." She didn't see what was so funny.

"And every other day too, more'n likely." Ida tilted her head to one side, her eyes flickering up and down Effie's body. "He'll have to notice. He's a man, ain't he?"

"*Isn't* he, and I thought men didn't care about a woman's bosom. That's what you said about nursing little Arthur." She crossed her arms over her chest, then dropped them to her sides.

Bending, Ida clasped Effie's hands and pulled her to her feet. "I was talking about sporting women, not sweet young things that's never been touched." The girl tugged her toward the cheval glass in the corner. "One they know they can have anytime; the other they can only dream on."

Effie dug her heels into the braided rug and stopped. "That's exactly my point. It's deceitful, making him think I've got what I haven't."

Ida sighed. "Who's to say you won't grow some more? Besides, once he sees you're a woman and not a girl, he won't care no more about your bosom, 'cause he'll be all wrapped up in who you are and how lucky he is you like him. Now, come and look."

She let Ida pull her the rest of the way across the floor to the tall mirror.

The girl tipped the frame on its swivels so Effie's whole body reflected in the mirror, then took her shoulders and turned her sideways.

Effie stared at her profile in the mirror and realized Ida was probably right. The cotton only added an inch to her bosom, not enough so anyone would really notice, but it made her look more grown-up, more womanly somehow.

Ida's reflection winked back at her from the mirror. "If this don't get his attention, he ain—*isn't* normal."

The air reeked of sweat and hair oil in the summer heat. Geordie paced the width of the delegation, wishing the Texas Democrats would hurry up and vote on their party platform so he could get back to Arlington. Zeke hadn't looked so good that morning, but the old man insisted he go out and cover the story for the paper. He worried about his boss's health, but what could he do? Every time he tried to help with typesetting or printing, Zeke ran him out and told him to go bring back more news.

He'd be glad when all these conventions ended. First the Farmers, Laborers, and Stock Raisers in May; then in July, the Nonpartisans; then the Union Labor Convention; and now the State Democrats. And all of them went over and over the same issues—railroads, banks, trusts.

Nodding to one of the delegates, he turned and paced back toward the far side. He'd counted quite a few good Alliance men among the Democrats here. Even George Pendleton, the chairman pro tempore of the convention, was an ex-Granger who'd joined the Alliance.

No telling how long that would last. Sooner or later, the interests of the party and the Alliance were bound to differ, and the men riding the fence would have to jump to one side or the other. When the split came, it would cause some mighty rifts between brothers and long-time friends.

Like the rift between Cat and Will, although there was

more than politics keeping those two apart. Troubled hearts, unless he missed his guess. Although he could see both sides of their argument about Cat's work for the Alliance, he knew enough to keep his mouth shut and mind his own business. He just hoped they'd work it out soon. It pained him to see them both so miserable.

And what was ailing Effie lately? His little sister had acted mighty peculiar the last few months, ever since she started teaching Ida to read. A lot of the townfolk frowned on the idea of whores learning to read and write, and some had complained to Cat and anyone else who'd listen. Of course, his sister made no move to stop her, saying Effie had a right to do as she pleased with her free time. So Ida spent time reading with Effie at the farm almost every afternoon. He only hoped being around one of Miss Yvette's girls wasn't giving his little sister any ideas.

More than likely, Effie was just growing up. It was hard for him to think of her as a woman grown, even though she'd done a woman's work for two full years. Not that she was just hanging around the farm, waiting to get married, but he didn't want her to be an old maid either. He'd always thought she liked Joe, but he'd seen no sign of any courting, and that surprised him. After all, she was fifteen now, and a lot of girls her age were settled down, married with one or two kids. After all, look at Molly. She'd be just sixteen, and her baby almost a year old. And if they'd lived, perhaps another baby by now. He pushed the thought away and turned toward the platform at the front of the crowd.

Pendleton banged the gavel for attention, and the crowd quieted. "All the votes are cast, and the results are final. The platform of the Democratic party of the State of Texas is approved as written." A great cheer rose up as Geordie wove among the delegates, seeking a way out.

Now he could get back to the office and write the story. He smiled at the cheering and back-slapping all around him. They had a right to be pleased; it was a good platform, even though the railroad regulation planks fell a little short. If the Democrats wanted Alliance backing, they'd have to go further toward supporting a railroad commission in Texas in the next few years. But this was a good start.

He glanced toward the podium just as James Stephen Hogg shook hands with Pendleton. He'd been right about the state attorney general; the man was no fool when it came to choosing sides. It was no secret where the Alliance stood on railroad regulation. And the majority of voters in Texas now belonged to the Farmers Alliance.

Cat's eyes flew open, and it took her a moment to figure out where she sat. The horse's hooves thudded on the dusty road, and the sweet-rotten smell of a nearby creek perfumed the cool, dark air. The wagon jounced through another rut, knocking her against Geordie on the hard plank seat of the buckboard.

He grinned at her. "Sorry."

Laughing, she cuffed his arm. "You meant to wake me."

He shook his head. "Naw. Go back to sleep." He put both reins in one hand and pulled her head down on his shoulder with the other.

Cat leaned against him, grateful to him for driving the wagon. She couldn't remember when she'd been so tired. But it was worth it. The State Farmers Alliance had accomplished a great deal this week. Imagine, three hundred thousand members in Texas alone, and still growing.

She yawned, covering her mouth with her free hand. The government would have to take notice of that many voters, especially when they heard the new set of demands from the Committee on Industrial Depression. Most of the delegates endorsed the committee's recommendations for currency reforms and railroad regulation, although some still fought to keep the Alliance strictly a business organization.

She shifted on the hard seat, trying to find a more comfortable spot. Too bad politics wasn't the only squabble within the Alliance. The Grange newspaper had stirred up a lot of sentiment against Charlie Macune, calling him an incompetent and a thief. Some of the members actually believed the charges.

Charlie had done a good job of defending himself, though, and he'd turned over all the books to the convention leaders. They'd appointed a committee of five to get to the bottom of things, but she wondered just how objective those committeemen would be. The five men all owned large spreads and probably never bought anything on time.

Regular prices at the Exchange weren't much better than anyplace else. The ones who saved the most were the ones who went from crop lien to joint notes; they got everything on credit, but at cash prices. No, those five men wouldn't be at all impressed with the Exchange business records.

She rubbed one hand over her face. And that new editor for the *Southern Mercury* wouldn't be much help either. All he cared about was ad sales, near as she could tell. She just hoped he stayed true to the Alliance instead of printing what his advertisers wanted to read, or he could cost the Alliance a lot of members.

Silver moonlight cast shadows on the cotton plants lining either side of the road. The swollen bolls glistened, all but ready to burst. At least the counties were rallying around the jute-bagging issue. Every week more and more Alliances voted to boycott the jute manufacturers. Maybe a successful boycott would unify the membership again.

No telling how many farmers could hold out without bagging. With the drought the year before and the floods this spring, most folks needed to wrap their bales and sell them right away to pay their creditors. She wasn't sure how she could pay her pickers if she had to hold her crop for very long. If this boycott was going to succeed, they had to come up with something else to wrap their bales in, and soon.

She swayed against Geordie as he turned the wagon into the lane. Almost home. She hoped Will wouldn't expect her to be at his office very early tomorrow. A nagging ache forced its way into her body. She'd missed him these last few days, missed seeing him, working with him. But more than that, she missed the way they used to be, before she started lecturing for the Alliance. And even before that, before he asked her to marry him.

She pushed herself upright, clutching the plank seat with both hands. Perhaps she'd been wrong about him. It could be that he wanted her enough to take her on her own terms instead of as a piece of property. But if that was true, why had he not asked her again?

Chapter 35

September 1888

Effie wiped the back of her hand across her forehead and straightened, pressing her fist into the small of her back and breathing in the hot, dusty air of the cotton fields. Shading her eyes with one hand, she checked the angle of the morning sun. "It can't be more than ten o'clock, and I'm tired out already." Two more hours until dinnertime. She planned to stay in the cool shade of an oak tree the entire time, whether she got anything to eat or not. "I wish we could work before sunup or after sundown."

Ida tipped her face up and sighed. "Everybody knows you can't pick cotton unless the sun's shining on it."

The only good thing about picking cotton was looking forward to being done with it. She pushed the raw cotton down in her bag. "I hate doing this. Every year I swear I'll never do it again."

Ida's eyes twinkled. "Then why are you?"

"My sister can't afford to pay any more pickers until she can get something besides jute bagging. Mills don't pay money for cotton unless it's baled and wrapped." Effie shrugged. "So why are you here?"

Ida laughed. "You ought to know— You asked me."

"You could've told me no. Why didn't you?" She'd

turned the question over in her mind since they started picking at sunrise, and she really wanted an answer.

Ida's smile faded and she turned back to the cotton plant. "You done a lot for me, and I wanted to help out."

A grin stretched across Effie's face as she unslung the bag from her shoulder and held it out. "Here you go."

Ida giggled. "Better get yourself to work, girl, before that good-looking foreman of yours takes you to task."

Effie's gaze dropped. What a sight she must make in her shapeless green Mother Hubbard, her long hair tucked up beneath Ian's old black Stetson. She rubbed one long sleeve over her sweaty face, wishing she could bare her arms just this once. Catriona always insisted she cover her pale skin to prevent sunburn, but she'd probably end up covered with freckles anyway.

And a fat lot of good Ida's padding would do in this getup. Not that she needed it any longer. The girl had been right about that; her bosom had grown, even if no one could see it today. Too bad Ida hadn't been right about Joe noticing it.

Come to think of it, with her luck he'd likely pick today to want to pay her some mind. Maybe if she pulled her hat down low, he wouldn't recognize her. She glanced over at Ida. At least her friend didn't look too much better in a faded blue calico with a ratty old red bandanna over her hair.

Effie sighed and bent to work again, slinging the bag higher on her aching shoulder. The dried husk scraped her already sore fingers as she slid them inside a boll and pulled. The lock tore in two, leaving half the cotton stuck to the pod. "Damn!" She scooped the rest of the white fiber from the boll, scratching her fingertips again.

Ida stepped through the row and slipped her fingers into the middle of an open boll. "Like this." With a twist she cleared the whole pod in one swipe.

Effie shook her head. "Cat tried and tried to show me, but I just can't get it."

Ida cocked her head. "Same as I used to say about reading. Here." She demonstrated again. "Now you try."

She concentrated, taking her time and gathering all the

fibers in the middle. A fluffy white ball came out whole in her fingers. "Well, I'll be. Who taught you to do that?"

"I learned it from my daddy." Ida's face closed, and she stepped back through the row.

Curiosity churned in Effie's mind. This was the first time she'd ever heard Ida mention her family. She forced her voice to an indifference she didn't own. "What did your daddy do?"

Ida worked on in silence until Effie gave up getting an answer; it was none of her business anyway.

After long moments Ida's quiet voice drifted back between the dry plants. "Grew cotton, same as everybody else, and made lots of babies."

Effie chewed her lips. "Oh." She kept from adding a question mark with her voice, still pretending she wasn't much interested.

Ida moved in and around the cotton plants, always a few steps ahead. Although the girl never turned her head, her voice found its way back to Effie's ear. "We lived way out in the middle of nowheres, nobody else around for miles and miles. Mama died birthing the youngest, so Daddy said I was the mama now. There was five, counting the baby. I reckon I was about eleven then."

Effie waited, hardly breathing as the silence grew. She'd heard plenty of stories of hardship, but it never made the listening any easier.

At last the voice came again, roughened somehow. "When I got a little older, he'd get liquored up some nights and crawl into my bed." She gave a dry, harsh sound—part cough, part sob, part bitter laugh. "It didn't take long, and I really was somebody's ma. That first one died—a little girl—and I run off before there could be another." She punched the cotton down in the bag with her fist. "Almost starved until a madam took me in and made me a whore. It was better than living at home. Got beat up some, moved around a lot. Then I come to the Bon Chance. Been there ever since. And now I got little Arthur, and you done taught me to read some."

Ida's hands stopped, and her face turned toward Effie's. "I ain't never told that story to another living soul. I'd be grateful if we never spoke of it again." It was a request, not a demand.

Unable to trust her voice, Effie nodded.

Ida's knuckles whitened as she clenched her hands into fists. "I aim to change my luck, make a new life for myself and my son."

Effie stepped forward and touched Ida's shoulder. "You will." Dropping her gaze, she turned back to her work, letting silence fall between them again. There were worse things in life than having to pick cotton for a few days. Much worse.

Not for the first time, Will wished the town had another doctor, someplace else to send the patients he couldn't abide. He pressed his ear against the man's belly, holding his breath against the smell of vomit and witch hazel. Sounded just like a pot of chili bubbling on the back of a stove. Not a good sign.

He straightened. "There was red in it, you're sure?"

Frink nodded. "Right there in the mess I puked up, lots of it."

"And you didn't eat or drink anything red, no tomatoes or berries or watermelon, no red wine?"

Frink shook his head, his rust-colored hair scratching against the white linen cloth covering the examining table. "Nope, nothing like that, I swear." A sweaty hand caught Will's forearm. "What is it, Doc? It's a cancer, ain't it?"

Will struggled to keep from shaking off the man's touch. "Near as I can tell, it's an ulcer in your stomach." He lifted the man's hand from his arm, then moved away, rolling down his sleeves and buttoning his cuffs. "Have you had any problems lately, any reason to be upset more than usual?"

"Shoot, Doc, nothing but problems." The man's pointy face darkened. "It's these damn farmers and their damn Exchange. They about run me out of business with their joint notes, and now it's the jute boycott." His voice tightened. "Ain't my fault the bagging factories formed a trust." One hand went to the man's narrow middle, and a film of sweat covered his high forehead. "Jesus, Doc, can't you give me something for the pain?" The whine in his voice rasped at Will's patience. "My gut hurts something awful."

"Maybe someday medical science will be able to cure nerves and troubles, but for now all I can offer you is some advice." Will slid his arms into the sleeves of his jacket. "I want you to eat a bland diet, nothing spicy or greasy, and try to stay as calm as possible. Drink some comfrey tea; that might help."

Frink sat up, dangling his thin legs over the end of the table. "Say, Doc, there's something else I've been meaning to talk to you about."

Will sighed. He had other patients to see, and Catriona was too busy picking cotton to come in. At least she didn't go on any lecturing junkets during harvest season, but he still saw plenty of illness and more injuries. He tried to keep the impatience from his voice. "How's that, Mr. Frink?"

The thin red mustache quirked up. "Call me O.K., okay?"

Will bit into his lip. If this man didn't get to the point soon— "Okay. Now, what's on your mind?"

The man rubbed his narrow hands together. "You're looking mighty tired, Doc, and I think maybe you're working too hard." The tip of Frink's tongue swiped over his lips. "So I got to wondering how come you're the only doctor in town, and I figured out it's 'cause there ain't no hospital."

Will crossed his arms over his chest, wondering if the man could read minds.

"Then I figured if your accounts looked anything like mine, you could likely build a hospital if everybody paid you what they owed you. Am I right?"

Will nodded. This fellow was too smart for his own good, and a bit too nosy for comfort. "Go on." Might as well hear him out.

"Then it come to me." The man struck his forehead with the heel of one hand. "If I was to buy them accounts, why, you'd have your money all at once, like." The small eyes shone beneath rust-colored brows.

Suspicion crept through Will's mind. "What's in it for you?"

Spots of color appeared in the narrow cheeks. "Well

now, except for a modest fee, plus interest on the amount owed, I'd see it as a service to the community."

More than likely, a lot of his old customers were paying off their old crop liens with money saved on joint notes at the Exchange. But if Frink could add on what they owed on their medical bills, he could keep more of the farmers in debt and paying time prices at triple the going cash rate.

Still, which was more important: to get out of debt, or to have improved health care? He thought he knew what Catriona and the Alliance would say, but he wasn't sure himself. He strode across the floor and opened the door, gesturing Frink out into the hallway. "That's a mighty interesting offer, Mr. Frink. I'll give it some thought." He turned toward a half dozen others waiting outside. "Who's next?"

Chapter 36

Sliding his heels from the desktop onto the floor, Geordie leaned forward in his chair, unable to trust his own eyes. He skimmed the editorial in the *Southern Mercury* again, just to make sure. The official paper of the State Farmers Alliance was calling for Macune to step down, to "retire on his ear and his laurels, taking with him all the glories he has earned from his pet scheme—" Zeke had to see this. He stood and walked toward the door to the editor's office and poked his head around the doorjamb.

The huge desk gaped open, its rolltop lifted to reveal cubbyholes filled with slips of paper and envelopes. Zeke sat in front of it, his elbows propped on the ledger books and his forehead resting on his hands, his bald dome shining in the afternoon light.

"Zeke?" Geordie took a step inside. "You okay?"

The white-fringed head jerked up and the lined face turned toward him. Zeke looked even older and more tired than usual. His withered mouth turned down at the corners, and his voice held a gruff edge. "What the hell do you mean, sneaking up on me? In my day, a man could be shot for less."

"Sorry." He shifted from foot to foot.

Zeke hooked his wire-framed glasses over each ear. "Well, what did you want that was so all-fired important?"

He held out the newspaper. "The *Mercury*'s calling for Macune to resign. I just wondered if you'd read it."

"Blame fools, the whole damn bunch, and Macune's the biggest fool of all." Zeke pursed his lips. "Write it up. Anything else?"

Geordie shook his head. "Is something wrong?"

"Eh?" Zeke turned toward the desk. "Nope." He closed the ledgers with a thud and stood, rolling the curved top down and latching it. "I got too much work to do to stand around jawing with you." He tilted his head back, his eyes distorted by the thick lenses of his bifocals. "And you do too." He slipped a stained leather apron over his neck, tying it behind his back as he shuffled out the office door and into the pressroom.

Geordie trailed behind as far as his desk, slumping down in his chair and picking up a copy of *The World*. He leafed through, wondering what ailed his boss. Maybe the old man was working too hard. He'd kill himself with work if he didn't slow down. His gaze trailed over the columns as he flipped through the paper. Then he sat up and paged back to the beginning—news, editorials, features, fillers. But hardly any ads, not even many classifieds.

No wonder the old man was sweating over the books. A newspaper couldn't support itself without ad sales. Why, the bigger dailies devoted thirty percent of each page to display ads. His mouth dried, leaving the inside tasting of cotton. *The World* was losing money every day.

Dropping the paper onto the desk, he rose and made his way into the pressroom, determined to find out what was really going on.

Zeke bent over the press, his hands covered with black, poking a tool of some kind into the machine's guts. He spent more time fixing the press than running it. No wonder the old man looked so tired.

Geordie knew better than to ask him anything outright. Better to work up to it. "Broke again?"

Zeke squinted up at him and grunted.

"Why don't you just get rid of it and buy a new one?" That ought to get his attention.

"With what?" The old man shook his head, his fringe of white locks swaying.

"The money from ad sales."

Zeke straightened, then pulled the tool from the bowels of the machine and set it in his open toolbox. "You got something to say, spit it out."

Sweat dampened Geordie's armpits. "I just finished looking through yesterday's *World*. There aren't many ads."

"So?" The old man's narrow shoulders lifted in a shrug. "Sometimes you sell more ad space, sometimes less—that's the newspaper business." He wiped his hands on a grease rag.

"So, shouldn't we be trying to sell more?" He crossed his arms over his chest.

Zeke tossed the rag onto a composing table. "Who's this *we?* I sell the ads for this newspaper, and I'm doing just dandy." His bushy white brows drew together. "In fact, I was selling newspaper ads before you were born."

He sighed. "Oh, come on, Zeke, you know I didn't mean it that way."

The old man grunted again. "I don't have time to sell advertising, wasting my days kissing the backsides of a bunch of small-town, hayseed merchants."

Geordie uncrossed his arms. "Well, I've got time. I can go sell some."

"*No!*" The old man pointed a gnarly finger at him. "You stay out of my business." His sunken chest heaved, and he leaned against the edge of a table.

Geordie held up both hands in surrender. "Okay, I was just trying to help." He hesitated. Oh, hell. He didn't have anything to lose by giving it one more try. "Zeke, level with me. What's going on?"

The old man pushed out his lips and drew his eyebrows down over the bridge of his nose. "All right, if you must know." He unhooked his glasses from first one ear, then the other, dangling them from his fingers by one bow. "Some of our local merchants don't care for our stand on the Alliance programs, especially the Exchange."

Geordie's gut hollowed. *His* stand, not Zeke's. He licked his lips. "So what do we do about it?"

The old man's withered mouth curved up, and he chuckled. "Same as we been doing. Keep on giving them hell."

Without bothering to knock, Cat turned the knob and pushed the door open. "What's this I hear about discontinuing the joint-note program?"

Macune's mouth opened, then stretched into a smile. "Why, Miz Macleod, what an unexpected pleasure to see you. Won't you come in?"

She gritted her teeth as she took a seat and waited for him to close the door. Nothing irritated her more than being handled when she was angry. The sweetish-sick smell of old cigar smoke hung in the air. "Is it true?"

Macune sank down behind his desk, his mouth set in a grim line. "It was the board's decision, Catriona, and a wise one. The joint-note program created so much opposition from the outside and such confusion within the Alliance, they had to stop it."

Cat clutched her handbag in her lap, twisting the drawstring around her fingers. "But—"

He held out his hands, palms facing her. "The plan worked too well; we made a lot of enemies in the marketplace, enemies the Alliance cannot afford if it is to prosper." He placed his palms flat on the desktop. "What concerns me now is the need for some other system to furnish supplies to the membership."

Cat chewed her lip for a moment. "But the Exchange will factor cotton again this year?"

Macune pursed his lips, then gave his head a brief shake. "Opinions are much divided, but they decided to discontinue it as well."

A faint nausea twisted in Cat's belly. "What can we do?"

His broad shoulders lifted and dropped in a shrug, and his lips stretched in a thin smile. "The merchants lowered their prices in order to compete with us. We can hope they stay low for the next few years. As for selling cotton, we came up with a much better system. I'm sure the factors and agents will imitate it, since it's to their advantage as well."

He leaned back, his smile broadening. "There is good news though."

Cat untangled her fingers from her purse strings, trying to swallow her disappointment. She believed in those programs, had worked hard to get the Alliance members all over the state to believe in them, and now they were just gone, voted out of existence by men she hardly knew. "That would be a welcome change."

Macune leaned forward, his elbows on the desk and his fingers steepled together. "Altogether we took in fifty-eight thousand dollars in capital stock from our membership, thanks to you and the other lecturers." His eyes sparkled.

She managed a smile, but her mind came back to worry at the bad news, like a mongrel with a soup bone. "Charlie, I read the report of the Committee of Five in the *Mercury*. And the articles and letters attacking you. The editor is trying to get rid of you, make you a scapegoat for every problem the Alliance has."

He reached for a paper on a corner of the wide desk, then leaned forward and held it out to her. "I've answered them in kind." His voice rang with confidence. "This will go to every member in the state."

She took the broadside, glancing at the heading. The Alliance newsletter. Yes, that might do it. One thing about C. W. Macune, he could write convincing prose.

"The board won't put up with it for much longer." He rubbed his palms together. "It's starting to cost them members."

Cat slid the newsletter back onto the desk. "But, Charlie, if the Exchange doesn't sell cotton and doesn't take joint notes, what are we going to do with that acre and a half hall over on Market Street?"

"Well, we can still sell the same goods for cash." He smoothed one hand over his dark hair, his face splitting into a grin. "Besides, we'll need lots of room. I found a substitute for jute bagging."

The knot in Cat's middle relaxed, and she leaned toward him. "*Ach*, man, will you tell me, or must I drag it from you?"

He laced his hands behind his head and leaned back in

his swivel chair. "The Exchange bought that bankrupt cotton compress, and with it ten carloads of cotton bagging at seven and a half cents a yard. It's being unloaded on the New Orleans docks as we speak. I plan to ship a carload each to ten locations around the state to drive prices down."

Triumph leapt inside her, but she clamped down on it. "The price sounds right, but how does it compare to jute?"

"Superior in every way; fireproof, waterproof, dirtproof, and the mills can reuse it after they cut open the bales. This is going to start a whole new industry, create jobs for thousands of loom operators, cut insurance rates in half." Macune propped his feet on his desk. "And best of all, it will take another one hundred and twenty-five bales of cotton to make enough bagging, driving the price of cotton straight up."

Chapter 37

October 1888

Catriona wriggled her bare toes in the chilly water and bent to scrub the black soil from another thick tuber. Sanapia always insisted the medicinal roots had to be washed as soon as possible in running water. It did make things easier in the long run, getting the dirt off before it dried hard in the warm air.

The woman knelt beside her, her fringed skirts tucked up and her long gray plaits skimming the surface of the water. "Wash him good."

Cat nodded, then glanced at her companion. In spite of her gray hair, Sanapia was a fine-looking, strong woman. It seemed a shame she was alone. They were both alone.

And although everyone confided in the Indian woman, Sanapia rarely volunteered anything about herself. "Did you never think to marry again?"

Sanapia turned toward her, dark eyes narrowed in her smooth face. She shook her head, then bent to her work again.

Cat knew she should hold her peace, but the more she thought of Will, the more confused she became. Perhaps knowing about Sanapia's life would help her guide her own. "Why not?"

This time the woman stopped her work and sat back on her haunches to stare at Cat. "When white man kill all the buffalo, the people hungry, cold. Mothers and children go to the soldier fort, ask for meat to eat, hides to wear. Soldiers give rotten meat and dead man's blankets."

The woman turned her face away toward the trees lining the other bank. "My man, my babies sick. Bodies hot, spots all over. They die. Many of the people die." She shrugged. "No men of the people left for me to marry."

In the long silence, sadness engulfed Cat. What it must be like for Sanapia, having to live among strangers for the rest of her days. Cat knew how bad it was to lose a husband, but she still had her two bairns, her brother and sister, and others like her. And Will.

Forcing herself to turn her thoughts back to work, Cat breathed in the fresh smell of the creek, so different from the dusty scent of the drying grasses and leaves on either side.

Straightening, she tossed the clean root into a basket on the bank and wondered how much fire medicine they'd use in the next year. Sanapia swore by it for toothaches, burns, and fevers. They needed to gather all the herbs they could before winter set in. She reached for the last unwashed root and squatted to hold it under the crystal water. Since the healing powers grew stronger through the year, it made sense to pick things in autumn, when they hit their peak.

Otherwise she'd have chosen to stay inside with the bairns, taking her ease after a week of helping Joe supervise in the fields. At least they could afford pickers now since the cotton bagging came in, although she wondered if there'd be enough to go around. The manufacturers in New Orleans had asked the Alliance not to send for all the bagging they needed at once, ordering so many yards per month instead, so the mills could have time to weave more.

She'd hate to see any of the Alliance members resort to using jute, although there'd been some talk of reusing old bagging from years past, or even making some from straw—anything to keep from buying at these prices. She tossed the last root into the basket and followed Sanapia through the tall, dry grass to a stand of broomweed.

The Indian woman turned a still face toward her. "Get the tops, the flowers." Her hand went out, snipping a stem between fingers and thumb and dropping it into another basket.

Cat followed suit without even asking what the broomweed was for. Sanapia would show her when the time came. She let her mind drift back to cotton. There was concern over the six percent tare. The mills always subtracted thirty pounds from each bale to cover the weight of the boards and the jute bagging, but the cotton bagging weighed considerably less. That meant the growers stood to lose money on every bale unless the buyers adjusted the tare. If it broke the jute trust forever, it would be worth taking a small loss this year. It would be worth almost anything to show the businessmen of the world they couldn't cheat the farmers anymore.

But was it worth the loss of the man she loved? Her chest tightened at the thought. She'd missed Will this last week, even though being with him was a constant agony of desire—seeing him every day, working close beside him and not being able to reach out and touch his face, his hand. It had been a year this month since the argument in the loft, since they last made love.

Sometimes she looked forward to the lecture trips just to get away from the turmoil inside. At least when she traveled, they kept her too busy to think. Not like being at home. And when she'd explained about needing to be home to help with the harvest, he hadn't even blinked, saying he'd manage somehow.

She chewed her lip. Of course, in the past when he argued, she'd told him off right enough. Even if he wanted her to stay and help, he wouldn't show it now. And she couldn't bring herself to show him her feelings either, although she might as well admit to herself she still loved him, still wanted him, needed him. If only they could go back to the night in the loft, she'd agree to marry him right away and work out the differences later. She jerked a flower stem, scattering petals over the high grass. She knew now she wanted him back, but she didn't know how to let him know. And what if he no longer wanted her, except as an assistant?

Blinking back tears, she tugged another broomweed stem. If only Sanapia had an herb to cure loneliness and heartache. Or was it really only stubbornness and pride?

Geordie paused inside the doorway to let his eyes adjust. Despite the banks of windows to the south and west, the vast interior remained dim. The smell of oil oozed from the rows of farm equipment covering the brick walls and wooden floors. Bolts of cotton bagging leaned into a corner. So this was the new Alliance Exchange, the building so many members called the elephant. Around the great hall, several people stood in groups, talking in hushed tones, dwarfed by the immensity of the open space.

Although it covered only half the ground space of the Exposition Hall at the fair grounds, the Exchange contained as many square feet in its four floors as the Expo did in two. Whatever had possessed the board to build this behemoth?

A figure disengaged itself from a nearby group and came toward him. Smooth dark hair lay like a cap above the man's square face, and heavy brows and mustache guarded deep-set eyes and a narrow bow mouth. A thick neck and powerful shoulders widened to a stout girth. "Geordie Galbraith?" The man held out a meaty hand. "Charlie Macune. Your sister introduced us once."

Geordie clasped the man's hand. "I remember. Good to see you again, sir."

Macune released his grip and gestured at the room beyond. "So what do you think of our new place?"

"Mighty big." No sense mincing words, especially since Cat said Macune had been against the building from the beginning, although most of the members blamed him for its expense.

Macune slid his thumbs beneath his lapels, cupping his fingers inside the front of his dark wool jacket. "Yes, sir, that it is." The broad face turned toward Geordie. "Say, didn't your sister tell me you're a reporter for the—don't tell me—the Arlington paper, *The World?*"

Geordie nodded, impressed by the man's memory. "Yes, sir. That's right."

"There's somebody I want you to meet." Macune gestured toward the group he'd left minutes before. "Come on over here, son."

Geordie followed, his curiosity piqued.

Macune put his arm around an average-looking man. "This here's Milton Park, new editor of the *Southern Mercury*." He squeezed Geordie's shoulder. "Milt, meet Catriona Macleod's brother."

Park's face split into a grin as he pumped Geordie's hand. "So, the reporter. I've read your work. You've got a way with words, especially in your editorials. I'll just bet you're popular with the local merchants."

"No, sir, not very." He lapsed into silence as Macune introduced the rest of the party, all names he recognized from Alliance newsletters.

After a few minutes Park drew him aside. "How about a tour?"

Might as well. He hadn't made much sense of the conversation, coming into it in the middle. Besides, Zeke had sent him to do a story about the building, not to stand around discussing Alliance business. "Sure. Thanks."

Park led him toward the stairway in the northwest corner. "Only the first-floor walls are brick. The top floors are all wood, as you probably noticed from outside."

He'd also noticed the corner turrets and the high-domed roof. And the Chinese laundry and the saloon down the block. "Interesting neighborhood."

Park laughed as he mounted the stairs. "The city donated the land, and it does front on the railroad tracks, but I wouldn't want to make my home here." He winked. "Although there is a boardinghouse for ladies around the block on Jefferson Street, if you take my meaning. Takes some of the sting from the long hours I have to work." Park's elbow nudged Geordie's arm.

How convenient for the man—his own private harem next door. He fought the impulse to curl his lip. What would Park think if he included *that* in his article? He smiled at the thought.

The man stopped in front of a shiny wooden door, the

top half filled with clear glass. "These are the new offices for the *Mercury*." He fitted a key into the shiny brass lock and turned the doorknob. "Come on in and take a look."

Geordie blinked in the daylight streaming through the tall windows and gleaming from the shiny desktops in the first room. Typesetting equipment filled a second. He ran his fingers over a box of new metal type. "Where's your press?"

"We'll compose it here and pay *The Daily News* to print it. Works out cheaper in the long run, insurance and so on." Park leaned against a doorjamb, his arms crossed over his chest. "Think you could be comfortable here?"

Geordie jerked his head up. He couldn't have heard right. "Excuse me?"

Park uncrossed his arms and strode toward him. "I could use a man like you, Mr. Galbraith, somebody who stands behind the Alliance cause no matter what the price."

Geordie's heart pounded, and he cast about for something to say, an answer to buy himself time to take in the idea. "I heard the board issued a proclamation saying they wouldn't recognize the *Mercury* as the official Alliance paper unless they could have editorial control. Where does that leave you?"

Park smiled. "I *am* the board's editorial control. That's why our next issue will include a report of the Committee of Eleven, a report which will fully vindicate Charlie—Mr. Macune—and the Exchange of any wrongdoing."

"But what about the Committee of Five and their report?"

Park waved his hand in the air, dismissing the question. "In a few months time nobody will remember their report."

Geordie wasn't so sure, but he bit his lip and took in the room, trying to picture himself working here every day.

Park's smile broadened. "Any more questions?"

He shook his head. "I guess not. It's just— I have a job, and my boss has been good to me."

The man's face sobered. "And I respect that loyalty. I do need someone by the first of next year, but I'll tell you what." He put his left hand on Geordie's shoulder. "Let's just say if something happens and you decide to leave, I'd like first crack at offering you a job. Is it a deal?" He held out his right hand.

Geordie clasped it. "Aye, it's a deal." He knew this was what he wanted more than anything, to work for the *Southern Mercury*, the official newspaper of the Alliance. This was why he went into journalism in the first place, to make a difference in people's lives, to further the cause. But what was he going to do about Zeke?

Will heaved the almost dead weight of the boy's body onto the examining table, grateful for Catriona's help. "Let's clean off some of this blood and see what we've got here."

Cat had already turned away, gathering clean rags and soaking them in a basin of fresh water. She seemed different today, warmer, softer somehow. Or maybe she was just tired, trying to do too much.

He wanted to ask her how the children fared, and how the harvest was coming, but he didn't know if she'd take it as prying. Besides, with her shorter hours, there was never time. He rolled up his shirt-sleeves. If he could find some way to collect the money his patients owed him, he could pay her more, and she could give up traveling and lecturing. Not that she'd give it up even then; it meant something more to her than just a way to make money. He poured water into a basin and scrubbed his hands. For that matter, he wished he could marry her and take care of her so she wouldn't have to worry about selling enough cotton to make it through the coming year.

Will turned his attention back to his patient. The sick-sweet smell of blood and fear rose from the injured boy. One wide brown eye looked out of a mask of gore and bruises; the other had swollen shut, a mass of green and purple. A slow trickle of dark red seeped from both nostrils.

Will dropped into his bedside voice, calm and reassuring. "What's your name, son?"

"Edward Lee." His body jerked as Cat's gentle fingers sponged his eyes and nose. "It was just a corncob fight, Doc."

Cat's face tipped up toward him, one eyebrow raised in question.

Will pursed his lips to keep from smiling, remembering the battles fought in his youth. There was nothing like the excitement of stalking your enemy and beaning him with a soaking cob. "Like a snowball fight, but with corncobs."

Her face remained unchanged, waiting.

Must not snow much on Skye. He tried again. "After we pick and husk the corn, we strip off the kernels and dry them to make cornmeal. What's left are cobs."

She nodded, still sponging the boy's swollen features. "*Aye?*"

"The young men gather up the cobs and soak them in a livestock tank, and then they play war with them, throwing them at one another from behind trees or barns."

Her face clouded. "I *ken* what you mean now. And what do they fight for?"

He shrugged. "Just for sport, for fun. They mark out territories to attack and defend."

She turned her face toward the boy. "And the others, do they end by looking like this as well?"

Will answered, defending the game. "Not usually. Oh, a few bruises and scrapes, but nobody gets hurt bad." He glanced down at the boy. "Isn't that right, Edward Lee?"

"Sure, Doc. They bushwhacked me in the open, but they didn't mean nothing by it." His lower lip trembled. "Still, it don't feel too good."

Cat stepped away from the table, carrying a basin filled with pinkish water and heaped with bloodied rags. "That's the best I can do until he stops bleeding."

Will trailed his fingertips over the injured face, seeking broken bones or loose teeth, watching the boy's one good eye for signs of pain. As he put gentle pressure on the bridge of the swollen nose, the boy's body jumped. "Sorry, son. I have to see if it's broken."

His fingers probed the mass of cartilage and bone. "Okay, Edward Lee, we're gonna have to make a choice here, and soon, the way this thing's swelling. We can leave it as it is, and there's no telling what you'll look like or how well you'll breathe the rest of your days. Or we can leave it alone until it heals, then rebreak it and set it then, or we can set it now."

The boy bit his already split lip. "Set it now."

Will patted the boy's shoulder. "Good. Mrs. Macleod, could you hold him down for me?"

Cat moved behind him and clamped her hands on the thin shoulders, leaning forward, pinning the boy to the table with her weight. Her eyes met Will's, signaling her readiness.

His fingertips pressed into the swollen flesh, searching for the dislocated bone and gristle. Pinching with thumb and forefinger, he snapped the bone back into place.

The boy cried out, and strings of fresh blood and dark clots poured from his nostrils. Will reached for a clean cloth and swabbed up most of the mess. "I need some cotton lint."

Cat's long, graceful fingers held out a handful of clean white fibers.

Holding the broken bones in place, he packed the nostrils. "You'll have to breathe through your mouth for a while. Take this out of your nose tomorrow, and be sure not to bump it until it heals."

Edward Lee nodded. Will slid one arm under the narrow shoulders and sat the boy up, then ran his fingers over the skull. No bumps or soft spots.

Catriona held out a square of cloth covered with damp green leaves. "This is a comfrey poultice." She tied it over the black eye with a strip of clean cloth. "Keep it on for a few hours, until the swelling eases."

Will thought about protesting, then decided comfrey couldn't hurt. He remembered Nana using it on his bumps and bruises when he was growing up, and it always seemed to take away the pain.

The boy's split lips curved into a smile beneath his packed nostrils. "Thank you, ma'am." He held out a bloodstained hand to Will. "And thank you too, Doc."

Will clasped the thin fingers. "You know, son, the trouble with fighting is this: In order to have a winner, there's always got to be a loser."

Cat's voice surprised him, and he turned to face her.

"That's why it's important to be sure what you stand to win is worth risking the loss of what you already have." Her blue eyes sought and held his.

He wasn't quite sure what she meant, but he knew she was no longer talking about the boy or his corncob wars.

Chapter 38

December 1888

The coal-oil smell of ink rose from the newspaper in Geordie's hands. He raised his voice so Zeke could hear him in the back room. "A Wells Fargo and Company detective announced today that Black Bart, who robbed thirty-one Texas stagecoaches, several of them locally, has been located in northern California, robbing stages again."

The old man's bespectacled face appeared in the doorway. "Those fools have been chasing him for better than ten years. I doubt they'll ever catch him now." He stepped through the doorway, wiping his hands on a stained rag. "What else?"

Geordie flipped a page. "The usual screams of protest about the electoral college and the presidency. Hard to believe Cleveland's out and Harrison's in." He scanned the headlines. "Says here the auditor the Alliance hired has vindicated Macune. Oh, and the farmers are paying off their joint notes at the Exchange right and left."

Zeke sank onto a chair and removed his glasses, polishing the lenses with a red bandanna. "If Macune wasn't a crook, his plans should have worked. Not enough financial support from the membership's my guess." He hooked the bows of his glasses back over his ears. "May as well print them all." He blinked in Geordie's direction. "Hear tell the *Mercury* made you an offer."

Geordie turned his eyes back to the newspaper in his hands and shrugged, pretending indifference. Somehow, it didn't surprise him the old man knew. "Park said something about it when I wrote the piece on the new Exchange building."

"And what did you tell him?" The old man's voice held an odd, quavering note.

Geordie folded the paper back on itself, pretending to read, afraid of showing his disappointment. "I told him I already had a job."

"You know, George Galbraith, you've said and done some ignorant things in the past two years, but I've never known you to out-and-out act the fool before."

Geordie jerked his head up and dropped the paper on the desk, frustration kindling his sudden anger. "Listen to me, old man. I may owe you something, but you've no right to insult me that way."

Zeke's eyes sparkled and his face creased in a wide grin. "Owe me? You don't owe me. If anything, I owe you. The last two years have been the most fun I've had since I got into this business forty years ago back in Maryland." His smile waned. "But I'm too old to keep up with you." He leaned back in his chair and crossed his arms over his chest. "Hell, son, the only reason I stayed with it this long was to keep you writing until you got a better offer."

Geordie sank down onto the edge of his desk, struggling to make sense of Zeke's words. "But what about you?"

"I got an offer just last week from a young fellow wants to set this up as a print shop. And I got a married daughter back in Washington, D.C., keeps asking me to come live with her." Zeke chuckled. "Don't be a fool on my account, boy. Now, I want you to high-tail it over to the train depot and send Park a wire telling him you'll take the job." He leaned forward, planting his gnarled hands on his knees. "And get back here quick so we can get out the last edition of *The World.*"

Will breathed in the warm, spicy vapor rising from the mug, rolling the bittersweet taste of cinnamon and wine on his tongue. His gaze strayed again to Catriona's slender form, standing on tiptoe, touching a lit taper to the wick of each small candle on the tree. Circles of yellow light made a halo around her body in the falling twilight. He'd never seen her look so beautiful as she did tonight. His body ached with longing, and his fingertips pressed into the warm, smooth sides of the mug.

Later she would pass among the guests, handing out the wrapped packages mounded around the trunk of the tall spruce. He suppressed an urge to grab Cat's gift before she could open it and hide it somewhere. But what would he say? He pictured himself mumbling something about making a mistake. No, it was too late to change his mind. Now she would know he still loved her, and tonight he'd see her answer in her eyes.

He usually enjoyed Christmas shopping, but this year he'd agonized over his choices. All but one had been simple; bath salts for Nana, a postcard album for Effie, a mustache cup for Geordie, toys and sweets for the children. But he tried out a number of gifts for Catriona in his mind.

He rejected medical texts and a leather medicine bag as too practical and impersonal. And although he wanted something to remind her of their private ties, a lacy petticoat and drawers should be reserved for a husband to give to a wife—someday, perhaps, if his luck held. Then there were the ruby earrings, the string of pearls, the fur muff. He wandered through every store in Dallas until he found a set of ivory combs. When he'd imagined the lacy white ornaments against her black curls, he knew he had to buy them for her.

But why had he set them under the tree when he could have waited and handed them to her later, after all the guests left? He knew the answer—cowardice, the same that made him want to sign Nana's name beneath his own. Lucky for him she'd knit Cat an ice wool cloud, her gnarled hands clicking the large needles for weeks to make the fluffy shawl.

He tipped the mug, draining it of its last few drops, then moved through the crowd to the kitchen. From the pot on the back of the stove he dipped up more wine. A hand closed on his forearm.

"Does thee think that will help?" Nana's gentle voice shamed him.

For a moment he was a child again, caught throwing rocks at a jackrabbit. "No, but what will?"

The gentle pressure of her hand slid from his arm. "I am disappointed in thee, William. I thought I raised a stalwart man, one who always spoke his mind."

He stared down into the cup, knowing he had no answer for her accusation.

"Thee has been mooning over her all the day. It is time to tell her thee loves her." Her hooded eyes fixed on him, refusing to let him go.

But what if he told Cat and she laughed, or grew angry, or worse, pitied him? He lifted the cup to his lips and swallowed. No, he'd wait to see her face when she opened the gift. Then, if she smiled— "I will, Nana, I promise." He lifted his eyes to meet hers. "But not just yet."

"I can't do it. It's just too forward." Effie paced across her bedroom, clasping and unclasping her hands.

Ida perched on a corner of the bed, looking young and wholesome in a new dress of pale pink silk. "Well, if you can't, you can't. But he'll just keep ignoring you." She shrugged, then stood and turned toward the door.

"Wait." Effie held out one hand. "All right, I'll do it. Will you walk out there with me?"

Ida nodded. As they reached the doorway to the parlor, she dropped her voice to a whisper. "Walk over the way I showed you. I'll wait here."

Effie obeyed, swaying her hips and trying not to panic. Her heart pounded in her ears as she moved close enough to smell the faint sage and leather scent of his skin. "Howdy, Joe. How've you been?" She batted her eyelashes and looked up into his bright blue eyes.

He lifted a long-fingered hand, brushing a white-blond forelock from his eyes. "Miss Effie. Good party."

Effie chewed her lip, glancing back at Ida, standing by the parlor door. "You really think so?"

Two vertical creases appeared above his pale eyebrows. "Why else would I say so?"

Her heart pounding, she forced herself to giggle. "Silly me." She reached up and rested one hand on each of Joe's shoulders. "What do you think of our tree?"

Her gaze followed Joe's as he turned toward the tall spruce in one corner. Strings of popcorn, bits of bright ribbon and paper, and old Christmas greeting cards festooned its branches. Small candles glowed on the end of each bough.

His frown deepened. "I like it fine. I helped cut it and trim it, remember?"

"Yes, I do recall that." She pursed her mouth and smoothed his jacket lapels, then tightened his necktie. "Are you having a nice time?"

"Hmm? Yes, fine." His eyes connected with hers, as if seeing her for the first time that day. "Have you been dipping into the mulled wine?"

Her cheeks burned, but she managed a laugh. "What a thing to ask."

He shrugged, then took her hands in his, tugging them away from his chest.

She caught her breath, trembling at his touch.

Joe pressed her palms together and smiled. "Nice talking to you. Will you excuse me?" Without waiting for an answer, he released her and sauntered away toward Geordie.

Embarrassment and anger swelled inside her until she thought she'd choke. Turning on her heel, she stomped back across the parlor to Ida. "I don't know why I bother. He is so —so ignorant."

Ida tugged her into the hallway, her voice a loud whisper. "What happened? Tell me."

"He asked me if I'd been drinking wine." She stomped one foot on the wooden floor. "Ooo, for two cents I'd wring his neck for him. I ought to just give up on him and set my cap for some other boy."

Ida lifted one eyebrow. "Like who?"

She chewed her lip and peered around the doorjamb into the parlor. There *was* nobody else, at least no one who interested her, no one who made her palms sweat and her heart pound.

"You're right. I'm not gonna let him get away with this." Swinging around to face Ida, she clenched her fists, then planted one on each hip. "I'm gonna get him to notice me if it's the last thing I ever do."

Duncan careened against Catriona's legs, and she bent to scoop the lad up in her arms, savoring the sweet baby-smell of his black curls. She pressed her lips to his smooth, ruddy cheek.

The small, wiry body squirmed in her arms. "Down, Mama."

Laughing, she set him on his feet.

Without a pause he darted after Arthur, dodging in and out of the guests' legs. Reuben Williams toddled after, trying to keep up with the two older lads. Hard to believe Duncan was two years old today, with his own pursuits and friends. What would Ian think of his son now?

A tender sadness wrapped itself around her. The bairns' birthdays always brought back thoughts of their father, as they should. After all, he was the reason they were all here in Texas, and the reason she'd stayed and fought to keep the farm and to make a better life for them all.

So much had happened since Duncan's birth. She forced herself not to think of Will, but turned her thoughts to the Alliance. The movement had grown to a real force, first with the cotton-brokering program, then the joint notes, and now the jute boycott. The jute trust admitted they'd failed to make a profit this year, and the Alliance could take credit for that.

She crossed her arms and leaned against the door frame, grateful for a moment of peace in this busy day. The heat from the Yule log in the fireplace and the press of so many bodies warmed the winter air like sunshine. The sharp smell of spruce blended with the sweetness of spices, and voices rose and fell around her as her guests sipped mulled wine and chatted, waiting to open their gifts. Having a Christmas birthday party for her son was a good idea, but she was tired.

Thank God the harvest was finally done; all the bolls were picked clean, the cotton ginned and baled, wrapped in cotton bagging, and sold to the highest bidder in New Orleans with an adjusted tare. It looked as though she had enough cash to make it through another year without selling the cattle, at least as long as the cotton yielded the same amount and quality or better next season.

And even though the Exchange had dropped the brokering and the joint-note programs, they'd made a success of the jute boycott so far. She'd been relieved by the auditor's report, although she couldn't blame Charlie for resigning from the Exchange anyway to take up the post of National Alliance Chairman. Washington, D.C., would be better for him than Dallas, and he could carry on the work on a much grander scale there.

Perhaps with him gone, the local Alliance members could settle down and honor their pledges. Only a fraction had actually paid the money they'd promised. After the flooding in the spring, many members just didn't have two dollars to spare, but on her tours she'd seen stores and mills flourishing around the state with local Alliance support. She'd have to ask Geordie his opinion.

She glanced over at her brother, dipping wine into a cup for one of the young ladies. She knew he'd miss Zeke; the old man had been like a second father to him. But Geordie looked forward to his new job at the *Mercury* as well. Too bad he didn't show as much interest in the young women. He must still carry too many memories of Molly.

Somehow, Cat understood his reluctance. After all, look how Ian's memory could stir her still, after almost three years. Perhaps if she had waited longer before she gave her heart away again—

And Molly had been gone only a little more than a year. Of their own accord, her eyes scanned the crowd, fastening on a familiar figure seated across the room. Will held Duncan on one knee and Arthur on the other, bouncing them as they squealed in delight. She closed her eyes, remembering that bittersweet time right after Molly's death. It must be fourteen months since the night she and Will had argued in the hayloft, since he last held her in his arms. She wondered if she'd ever find her way back there again.

Betsy trotted toward her, her blond curls bobbing on her shoulders, not a bairn any longer, but a young lassie instead. Small hands tugged at Cat's skirt. "Mama, please, we want to open the presents now."

Duncan appeared at her other side, his two wee friends in tow. His mouth curved in a mischievous bow. "Pwesents now." Arthur and Reuben echoed him.

She laughed down at them. "All right, then. Here we go." They danced after her across the floor, telling everyone it was time. She scooped up a stack of packages, some in showy boxes with fancy cards, others in shiny paper or wrapped in old newspaper and tied with twine. Reading out the names one by one, she handed gifts around as her guests found seats or leaned against the wall. The air filled with the sounds of ripping paper and squeals of delight from the children, and more sedate thanks from the adults.

As she came to the few gifts bearing her name, she set them aside to open later, except for one small box covered in red velvet paper and tied with silver foil ribbon. She'd know that handwriting anywhere. She slid the small package into a pocket in her skirt, her heart quickening with excitement, wondering what it could be.

When at last she handed out the final gift, Cat sank onto an empty space on the sofa and drew the package from her pocket. She untied the ribbon, curling it around her finger and pushing the coil back into her pocket. She undid the fuzzy red paper, smoothing it over her lap, then folding it into a neat square. With trembling fingers she lifted the lid of the silver foil box.

Her breath caught in her throat, and her fingers traced the delicate carving of the smooth white ivory. She lifted one comb into her hand, surprised at its feather-lightness.

"Well, do you like them?" Will's voice held a question, a plea, a promise.

"Aye, that I do." Cat cradled the delicate comb in her palm, a tender warmth flowing through her veins. "They're lovely." A slow smile spread across her face as she looked up into his sparkling eyes.

Chapter 39

January 1889

Wind whipped across the porch, tugging at Catriona's clothing. She shivered in the sudden chill, remembering the storm right after Christmas, the strong south wind turning without warning to the west, blowing down buildings and storefronts all over town. And poor Mr. Putnam, losing his entire blacksmith shop that way. They were lucky they hadn't lost more than a chicken coop and a hayrick here on the farm.

Another gust blew up, carrying smoke from the cotton fields. Squinting, she turned toward the cloudy gray funnel reaching up into the broad Texas sky. Beneath it, half the field still stood, rickety brown stalks clattering together. Orange flames crept along the ground, leaving black stubble smoking behind. "In six weeks, tiny green shoots will cover those fields once more, only to be burned in turn next January."

Sanapia's fingers never faltered or slowed as they split dried mescal bean pods and popped the seeds into a basket. "The wheel of the year, he turns and turns."

Sighing, Cat bent to work again, grinding away at the small red beans. Gran had given her the old mortar and pestle back home on Skye, the hand-carved stone dish and grinder passed down through generations. If she closed her eyes, she could pretend the smoke came from a peat fire and the wind carried the scent of the ocean. A longing like a hunger filled her for a moment.

Life had been so simple, or so she remembered it. She knew who she was then, what she wanted, and what to do about it. Or did she really? It had taken her years to decide to marry Ian, but that was stubbornness on both their parts. And what kept her apart from Will, then, if not the same thing?

She tilted the mortar, holding it out and tapping it with her finger to make the ground-bean meal spill to one side. "Is this fine enough?"

Sanapia nodded. "Like white sugar."

Cat emptied the ground beans into a cloth bag and refilled the bowl from Sanapia's basket. Pressing the pestle down hard, she crushed them into red and white chunks.

She knew she cared about Will, loved him perhaps, wanted him as surely as she breathed. And he made it obvious he cared for her. She stopped grinding for a moment to reset the combs in her hair, wondering again what made him choose something so precious, so delicate for her. Did he understand her that well, to know how much his gift would please her?

Sighing, she whirled the grinding stone, pressing it hard against the sides of the bowl. It had been different with Will. With Ian she felt she had always known him. But with Will there was a part she never saw, a part turned away from her, held back. And what if she never had all of him, all of his love; could she be satisfied then?

Perhaps it was wiser, continuing on as they had for the past year, keeping each other at arm's length. At least then they didn't hurt each other, but she hated the very thought of pretending she cared for him only as a friend. Yet if they grew close again, and he asked her to marry him— That was the root of her confusion.

She added another bowlful of fine granules to the cloth bag, then hefted it in her hand. "Is this enough for one batch?"

Sanapia reached out her hand, weighing the bag in her fingers. She pursed her lips and nodded. "Boil him up until the water turns brown, then strain it through another cloth. Good for earaches."

The Indian woman set the bag aside and shook the basket of hulled beans. "Must be careful with these. Very strong medicine. Braves use them sometime for vision quests, but they make other peoples drunk or loco, then sleep a long time."

Cat nodded. "We'll store them on a high shelf in the pantry." If only she could hide her feelings away in a basket, high up where they couldn't hurt her. Or anyone else.

Will closed the office door, turned the skeleton key in the lock and straightened, listening. Faint music floated up the stairwell on the chill dark air. Grasping the handle of his black leather bag, he hurried down the stairs as night smells gathered around him. But instead of turning toward the livery, he strode toward Centre Street, then north along the wooden sidewalk, following the tinny sounds of a small brass band.

A large wooden wagon stood in front of the depot, its sides and wheels painted red and gold like a circus wagon. From the tailgate, a platform extended to form a sort of stage, where a tall man stood, dressed in a rusty black suit and straw bowler. Lanterns hung at intervals along the roof of the caravan, casting a circle of light over the small crowd gathered below. To one side sat three musicians in ragged band uniforms, their cheeks bulging in time with the out-of-key notes of a familiar tune.

Recognizing all the trappings of a traveling medicine show, Will let his curiosity draw him closer, edging his way through the crowd and arriving near the stage just as the band squeaked and squawked to a halt. The man on the platform took a step forward and held up a bottle. "Ladies and gents, may I present to you the only medicine you'll ever need to take again: Professor Hooper's Indian Vegetable Elixir, good for dyspepsia, diarrhea, dropsy, sick headaches, jaundice, disordered stomach, and a host of other complaints."

A man's voice called out from the back of the audience.

"How do we know it works?" Probably a shill hired to work the crowd.

Will turned to see if he could make out the owner of the voice, but it was too dark to say for sure which folks were locals and which ones strangers. He did catch a glimpse of that old reprobate Quincy, and Lewis Price gave him a sheepish grin.

The salesman on the platform continued without missing a beat. "I'm glad you asked that, sir." He set a glass tumbler on the rickety table in front of him and poured it half full of an evil-looking brew. "Do we have anyone here tonight in pain, suffering from a complaint the good doctors here in town haven't been able to cure?"

Another fellow stepped forward, waving a hand high over his head. Although he wore overalls and a chambray shirt like the local farmers, Will didn't recognize the tall, burly man with a red beard and bushy hair. He wasn't from the Arlington area, or Fort Worth or Dallas, for that matter.

The salesman motioned the volunteer up the steps and onto the stage beside him. "Now, sir, tell us your name and what ails you."

The big man crossed his arms over his belly and contorted his face. "Name's Rupert. I got me a colic, had it for years." He bent forward and let out a low moan. "Been to every doctor in these parts, and none of them done me any good."

Will crossed his arms over his chest. Most folks looked on medicine shows as entertainment, a pastime for whiling away the long winter months. But when they turned folks against their local healers, that could be dangerous.

The salesman patted the burly farmer's shoulder. "Here, my good man, try a taste of Professor Hooper's Elixir."

Rupert lifted the glass to his lips and poured the liquid down his throat, then wiped the back of his hand across his mouth. "Tastes powerful." After a moment his grimace smoothed to a grin and he straightened. "Why, my colic's all gone. I'm cured." He turned and enveloped the salesman's hand in his big paw, pumping the man's slender arm up and down. "Thanks, Professor, and bless you. How much is a bottle?"

"Only one dollar." The salesman held it up, the lurid label glowing in the dim lantern light.

Rupert dug in his pockets, then held out a handful of change and a crumpled greenback. "Shoot, give me two." He took the two bottles and hurried down the stairs from the platform.

"Anybody else?" The salesman's voice drew every eye to the stage. Those in the front of the crowd thrust their hands into their pockets or their reticules. Soon a hedge of arms lined the stage, each topped with a hand offering money. It seemed everybody wanted a taste of Hooper's Elixir.

Everybody except Will, who kept his eyes on Rupert sidling back through the crowd. Will's nostrils flared at the reek of alcohol as the man edged past him. Not too surprising; more than likely it was the main ingredient of their elixir.

Rupert continued on, nodding and accepting congratulations and encouragement from folks who'd witnessed his recovery. At last, when all attention returned to the stage, the man circled away from the crowd to the side of the wagon and crawled inside.

Will considered. He could make things difficult for the "professor" and his shills, but he couldn't prove they'd harmed anyone, or even cheated them of their money. For all he knew, their medicine might help folks, if only by making them believe in a cure. And even if he could have them arrested, the townsfolk wouldn't thank him for robbing them of their fun.

Perhaps just a word to the salesman about setting folks against their physicians, not that some of them weren't just as much charlatans as these snake-oil doctors. Hell, all a man had to do to graduate from some medical colleges was pay his money; he didn't even have to attend classes. But at least they'd be around tomorrow to take the consequences if they made a mistake. Professor Hooper's clan would be gone before sunup, or he missed his guess.

He shrugged. Folks would buy this stuff no matter what he said, because they wanted to believe in a cure-all. A doctor couldn't keep a man from being a fool any more than a lawyer or a banker could.

A shoulder butted against his upper arm, moving him sideways a few inches, jostling him against another man. He frowned down at the small man pushing his way to the front. "Well, well, Mr. Frink. You're not planning to buy a bottle?"

The man's eyes darted back and forth. "No, no, of course not." The tip of his pink tongue darted out, wetting his thin lips, then curving them into a smile. "I—uh—just wanted to get a better look at the show."

Will nodded. "Of course. How're you getting on with your camomile tea?"

Frink wiped his palms down the front of his jacket. "Fine, just fine." His small eyes narrowed. "Say, Doc, that reminds me." His voice lowered to just above a whisper. "What'd you decide about selling me them accounts?"

Will drew in his cheeks to keep from smiling. "Well, I can't say as I'm interested, but thanks for the offer." He held out his hand.

Frink pressed his damp palm against Will's, giving the faintest squeeze before he let go. "The offer still stands." He ducked his head in a brief nod. "Any time you change your mind, just let me know." He turned his face toward the stage. "Well, guess I'll be heading home. Excuse me."

Will placed a hand on the narrow shoulder. "I'm heading that way myself. Care for some company?"

Frink's Adam's apple bobbed. "Uh, well, I think I'll take in some night air, but thanks for the offer." The fellow lifted a narrow hand in farewell and slipped away through the mass of bodies.

Will threaded his way to the opposite edge of the crowd, then glanced back over his shoulder.

Frink's rust-colored head wove in and out amongst people's shoulders, headed once more toward the stage.

Shaking his head, Will let his mouth stretch into a smile as he walked back toward the livery. It was past time he started his round of night house calls, especially if he wanted to make it to Catriona's lecture at the old Grange hall.

Will slipped in through the double doors, pulling them closed and turning the knob with care so it didn't make any noise. The warmth of many bodies filled the large hall, along with the not unpleasant smells of assembled humanity—sweat, toilet water, leather, and damp wool. On silent feet he stepped to a seat in the very back row and settled down to listen.

He'd never been to one of Catriona's Alliance lectures, always using patients as an excuse. But after Nana took him to task at Christmas, he wondered if he'd avoided the meetings for fear of finding he'd been wrong, wrong about the Alliance movement and wrong about Cat's part in it.

Catriona's voice rose from the front of the hall, each word ringing clear even back where he sat. "We are not dead—"

A thunder of applause greeted her words, and she paused, a smile lighting her face. The pale tracery of ivory combs shone against her black curls, and a faint red glow warmed her cheeks. Even from this distance her dark blue eyes seemed to look into his soul.

Startled, he realized he'd missed much of her speech, lost in rapturous thoughts of her loveliness. He forced himself to listen to her words.

"We have been discouraged and halted, in doubt, not knowing what to think or where to move, for our building had been too rapid, like some huge undisciplined army rushing into conquest—" The conviction in her voice infused her sentences with zeal.

Will found himself wanting to agree with her, believe her words to be true. Glancing around him at the rapt faces of her audience, he realized he wasn't alone. Few orators he'd heard could inspire such attention. In fact, the only one in recent years was Attorney General Hogg. What a team those two would make.

Cat's voice soared toward a crescendo. "Many who flowed in with the tide rushed out with the 'I told you so's' and have made us weaker in point of numbers, but I hope better in point of love for the principles of our order." Again applause followed her words, and she smiled and held up a thin pamphlet. "Please turn to song thirty-four in your Alliance Songbook."

Around him, farmers and their wives stood, flipping pages. The man next to him thrust an open songbook into his hands. "I don't need it. Got this one by heart."

Will nodded his thanks as a fiddle squawked to life and voices rose around him. He didn't try to sing, but instead followed the lyrics with his eyes. The simple tune was called "Alliance Song," by someone named Alice B. Kent. Her four verses of short rhyming lines urged farmers to stand fast for their rights against monopolies and railroads.

After the final chorus a gavel banged somewhere, and Catriona's voice rang out. "Meeting adjourned."

Bodies eddied around him as he fought his way up the aisle. Mothers herded groups of children toward the double doors, urging them to wrap up against the cold night air. Men in overalls called across the crowd to neighbors about the farm implement show in Dallas or the price of cottonseed for the coming season.

As he neared the front of the hall, the crowd thinned. A group surrounded Catriona, men and women alike, shaking hands or waiting a turn to speak with her. Finally, the last one shook her hand and left her standing alone only a few feet away.

Cat turned toward him and stopped, her eyes widening. "Will, is there *aught* wrong?"

"No, I just wanted to hear your talk." A slow smile spread across his face.

"Oh." A faint reddish tinge crept up to her hairline, and she turned away, picking up her papers and reticule. After a moment she met his eyes, her voice light and self-mocking. "And what did you think, then?"

He put all his sincerest respect into his voice. "Very convincing. You've got a rousing way of putting things."

Her black eyebrows drew together. "I—uh—well, then. I'm that glad you thought so."

He took a step toward her. "Cat—" The words he'd held back so long tumbled out in a rush. "I was wrong. About the Alliance, about your work with them, about the lecturing." He swallowed, then went on. "I see now how important this is to you, no matter whether I agree or not." He held out his hand. "Can you ever forgive me for being such a fool for so long?"

Her lips trembled into a smile as her soft hand closed over his. A faint scent of sunshine and soap rose from her skin as her eyes smiled into his. "Aye, I can and I do."

Chapter 40

March 1889

Catriona held her breath to keep from gagging on the pungent odor as she passed the burnt feather beneath the woman's bloodied nose.

Pale eyelids fluttered, and a groan slipped between the split lips. The face contorted, then turned away from the smell.

Cat wrapped the feather in a cloth and put it back into her bag. "She's coming around."

Will lifted his ear from the woman's domed belly. "She's lucky to be alive, from the looks of it."

Cat lifted a dripping cloth from a basin of cool water and wrung it out. "And the bairn?"

"Can't tell much. I hear a heartbeat, and it gave a few kicks." He shrugged, rolling up his shirt-sleeves. "Might be better all around if she lost it."

Cat nodded, remembering the way the man's eyes shifted all around and his story changed from minute to minute. She'd seen it before, but not often, and seldom this bad.

"Silas?" The woman struggled to sit up, her eyes wide. "Where's my husband?"

Cat pressed the thin shoulders back against the bed. "In the next room, waiting. Now calm yourself." She nodded toward Will. "This is Dr. Bascom. I'm his helper, Catriona

Macleod. Your man called us in to see to your hurts." She sponged caked blood from the purpling flesh of the woman's face.

Will's fingers traveled up the woman's legs and arms. "No broken bones, near as I can tell. Where does it hurt?"

The woman's lips trembled and tears oozed from the corners of her bruised eyes. "Nowheres. I'm fine. I just want my husband."

Will patted the woman's shoulder. "We'll call him just as soon as I finish examining you, and Miz Macleod gets you cleaned up a bit." He glided his fingers over her skull, then held up a candle. "Keep looking into the light." He covered her eyes for a moment, then removed his hand. After a moment he set the candle aside. "Very good."

Cat dunked the bloody rag into the basin, then wrung it out to wipe off smears and spatters of blood covering the woman's arms and hands, as if she'd tried to shield her already bleeding face from further attack.

Will's fingers tiptoed over the bones in the woman's battered face, pausing when she winced and gasped. "Just how did this happen, Miz Ransom?"

The woman's pale eyes slid one direction, then the other. "I—I don't rightly recall." Her throat worked. "What did my husband say?"

Will's face turned toward Catriona's, an affirmation flashing from his eyes as his calm voice responded. "Oh, just that you were hurt and unconscious. What do you remember?"

Cat bit her lip. She hadn't believed the husband's story either. Another Ransom, probably related to Luke. Turning, she dug in her bag for a pot of salve. Funny how when she first started working with him, he questioned her about every medicine she brought in. Now he didn't even blink.

Mrs. Ransom coughed. "I guess I must've fell down. Yep, that must be what happened. I'm right clumsy lately, now that I'm carrying." One work-worn hand found its way to her belly. "The kid, is it gonna be okay, Doc?"

He frowned. "I can't say for sure. You really should be more careful." His eyes sought Cat's. "I'll go fetch your husband. You rest here for a while."

Cat gave a very slight nod and continued smoothing salve over the broken, bruised face after Will closed the door behind him. She kept her voice just above a whisper. "Did your husband do this to you? You can trust me. I won't tell him you said anything."

Tears spilled from the woman's frightened eyes. "No, you don't understand. He's a good man. It was my own fault." She winced as she wiped her wet, bruised cheeks with one rough hand. "It's like he said, I fell."

Cat kept her voice low, gentle. "He didn't say that. You did."

Panic edged the woman's whisper. "That's what I meant. Just like I said. Besides, it ain't none of your business."

Cat sighed, then touched the knobby shoulder. "You're right, Mrs. Ransom, it's none of my business. But think on this, then. A man who beats his wife will beat his child. Is that what you want?"

The woman's head turned from side to side on the blue striped ticking of the bare mattress. "You just don't understand."

The door swung open, and Silas Ransom sidled into the narrow room, twisting the brim of the old felt hat he carried. Lines appeared above his bloodshot eyes and at the corners of his narrow mouth. A sheen of dirt covered his unshaven cheeks, and he stank of old sweat and stale moonshine. "You okay, hon?"

"Fine." Sitting up, the woman waved away Cat's help and swung her legs over the edge of the rickety bed. "Just shamed to cause all this trouble." She stood, bracing herself on the bedpost, then stumbled to the man's side, leaning her battered face against his shoulder.

His arm went around her shoulders. "I want to thank you all for coming out and taking such good care of my Clory." He smiled and patted the narrow back. "Why, I'd a-sight rather lose my best team than my wife. What do I owe you, Doc?"

Sick inside, Cat gathered up her things and moved to the bedroom door.

Lifting his black leather bag in one hand, Will set his black hat on his head with the other. "Five dollars for the visit and a dollar a mile for the house call. Call it twenty-five."

The man's face froze, an ugly gleam in his rheumy eyes. "Ain't got that much in cash." His arm tightened around his trembling wife, her face still hidden on his shoulder.

Cat clutched her herb bag to her side, suddenly afraid for Will. Ransom looked capable of almost anything.

Will shrugged, his face a smooth mask. "Folks sometimes pay me in produce. Or you can send me the money whenever you get it." He turned and ushered Cat out the door.

At last, when they were in the buggy driving through the dark, chill night, Cat broke the silence. "Why would a woman stay with a man like that?"

Will turned a tired face to her, giving his head a brief shake. "I've been wondering the same thing." He paused, turning his attention back to the road. "My guess is he's got her convinced it's her doing, and he can't help himself, especially when he drinks."

A bitter taste touched Cat's tongue. "That's what she said—it's her fault, and he's a good man. Do you believe that?"

Will's brows and mouth drew down. "Of course not, but folks have a right to their own troubles. I learned years ago you can't save a drunk or a gambler from himself, and I guess that goes for wife beaters, and their wives too."

Cat shook her head and twisted the strap of her bag. "It's just not right, to drive away and leave her there. We owe it to her and her bairn to try to help them."

"Catriona, you can't help folks who don't want your help." He set his feet against the dash, and his voice thickened. "Besides, even if we could get her to admit it, there's no law against a man correcting his wife."

"Correcting? Is that what you call it? Next time he could kill her." She spat the words, angry at him even though she knew he spoke the truth.

"If he kills her, he'll hang, but until then he has a free hand." He hesitated, then turned to face her again, his voice gentle, pleading. "I don't like it any more than you do, but that's how it is."

"Aye, well it bears changing." Cat leaned back against

the leather seat and closed her eyes. She wasn't really angry with him, but with a world in which women had fewer legal rights than animals. In a country where stealing a horse was a hanging offense, she'd wager beating one was at least against the law.

"Hang on." Will's voice jolted her eyes open.

In the road ahead, a horseman waited, his rifle barrel gleaming in the moonlight.

Heart pounding, Cat clutched the sides of the seat as Will reined in the horse and brought the buggy to a halt.

"Doc, I reckon we'd better settle this right here and now." Cat recognized Ransom's voice.

"What the devil?" Will handed Cat the reins. "Stay low." He jumped from the buggy and advanced toward the horseman. "What's this all about?"

Ransom swung down from his horse. "I don't want to owe no man nothing." He held out his hand. "Here's a five, which is about a square thing, I reckon."

Will took the wadded greenback. "Now what?"

"Now, if you ain't satisfied, just get your weapon out of that there buggy and we'll settle it. I don't want no man to go away from my house dissatisfied, especially not you, Doc." Ransom's horse blew and sidestepped.

The reins dug into Cat's palms, and she held her breath.

At last Will's calm voice broke the silence. "I don't carry a gun, and if I did, I wouldn't fight you over my fee." He held the money up in the moonlight, then shoved it into his trouser pocket. "Tell you what: I'll call our accounts square just as long as I don't hear about your wife having any more *accidents*."

Ransom took a threatening step forward, then stopped and laughed. "Sure thing, Doc. I aim to take real good care of her, leastwise until the kid comes. Don't want nothing to happen to my own flesh and blood." The man climbed onto his horse, wheeled around, and rode off overland.

Cat dropped the reins and jumped from the buggy, running over the rutted track and throwing herself against Will's broad chest. "He might have killed you." If anything had happened to him— Tears welled up, and she trembled, pressing her face into his waistcoat and breathing in the man-scent of him. No, she'd lost Ian. She couldn't bear the thought of losing Will as well.

His arms tightened around her and he pressed his cheek against her hair, his voice murmuring in her ear. "There, there, don't cry, my love. I'm not going anywhere."

Chapter 41

April 1889

Geordie twisted in his seat to get a better look through the soot-covered window of the passenger coach. Outside, the South Canadian flowed wide and muddy beneath the trestle, and as far east and west as he could see, people lined the near bank on horseback, in wagons, buggies, hacks, and carts —every type of vehicle imaginable.

Camps had sprung up overnight, and now, as the hour moved toward noon, men and women visited back and forth, greasing axles and checking harnesses and saddles one last time. Voices rose in a deafening roar of singing, shouting, and argument. It reminded him of Independence Day and the Dallas State Fair all rolled into one. The excitement in the air almost made him wish he was there to enter "Harrison's Hoss Race," as the boomers called it, although he knew only the fastest and hardiest would win, and many would return without the prize of free land.

Across the water a swath of black edged the river for miles into the Indian Territory, where soldiers had burned the grass to clear the way for the settlers. Blue-coated cavalry men patrolled the far bank, keeping the settlers from moving in to stake their claims before the signal. As Geordie struggled to get his notebook and lead pencil out of his breast pocket, he looked an apology at his seatmate.

The boomer shrugged and crossed his arms over his chest, leaning back against the tall seat and closing his eyes. Probably saving up his strength for the hours to come, although how anyone could sleep in the hot, stale air was beyond him.

Men and women packed every inch of the car, and more sat on top, some even clinging to the windowsills and the cowcatcher, he'd heard. Geordie fingered his celluloid collar as sweat drizzled down his sides and back. The sun added to the discomfort as it rose in the sky, beating down on the metal car and cooking those inside. He'd long since stopped noticing the reek of unwashed bodies, and the breeze coming through the open window offered little in the way of relief. The red-clay dust blew right in, along with the black soot from the smokestacks. The firemen had orders to keep the engine standing, steam up and ready.

After sitting on the train all night for fear of losing his seat, Geordie longed to be able to stretch his legs, eat a meal, sleep in a bed. But he wouldn't miss this opportunity for anything—a chance to see a territory settled in one day.

He still couldn't believe his luck, having Park assign him to cover the opening of the Indian Territory to settlers. If only Zeke could share this excitement. Although Geordie liked Park, and he enjoyed the challenges of working for an official Alliance paper, he missed being the only reporter on a small-town newspaper. But most of all, he missed the old man. What would Zeke have to say about this? Imagine, two million acres, up for grabs to the first who could stake their claims to each one-hundred-sixty-acre parcel.

Of course, working for the *Mercury* hadn't been so bad, even if up until now the most exciting story he'd covered was the prediction of how many yards of cotton bagging the mills might produce. At first the estimates had been hopeful, but now the boycott looked doomed unless the jute manufacturers caved in soon. Whatever happened, it looked to be a bountiful year for cotton, with perfect weather so far this month.

Geordie fished in his pocket for his watch, tugging it out and flipping up the lid. Six more minutes. The roar outside diminished as folks jockeyed for last-minute advantage along the water's edge. Silence stretched out until he could hear the ticking of his timepiece as he counted down the final seconds.

Exactly at twelve noon, the cavalrymen fired their rifles into the air, the gunfire deafening after the long minutes of quiet. Then all hell broke loose as wagons surged forward into the muddy waters and the train crawled across the trestle, the engineers honor-bound to keep the speed equal to that of a horse.

Down below, one heavy wagon foundered in a sandbar just beneath the swirling surface. The driver leapt into the water, unhitched the horses, then swung onto one of the animals, swimming it into the current. As he reached the far bank, he urged his mount forward among the wagons emerging from the water.

Hordes of settlers spread across the blackened prairie without regard for common sense or safety, their humanity forgotten in their lust for land; some leapt from their horses to stake claims near the river, while others pushed beyond into grass taller than a man in some areas. Geordie watched from the train, horrified as more than one rider fell and died, trampled beneath the thundering hooves.

As the locomotive pushed farther into the territory, men jumped from the still-moving train, sprawling beside the track for a moment before they jumped to their feet and dashed off in search of homesites.

In the distance, yellow flames leapt beneath clouds of black smoke. A grass fire, probably started by a sooner to keep the settlers away from his claim while he hid in a nearby oak grove or a gully. Many who'd settled in the Indian Territory before the President's proclamation refused to give up their homes, even though Harrison had promised to evict them as squatters. Geordie didn't doubt they'd kill in order to protect their claims. It sickened him to realize how little some people valued human life, their own or others'.

At last the train ground to a halt. With a muttering roar of voices, men and women shoved one another aside, fighting their way through the crowded aisles, pouring out the doors and windows and scurrying away through the tall grass. In minutes Geordie found himself alone in the passenger coach.

He stood and stretched, shaking out his legs and walking up and down the deserted aisle, his notebook in his hand, fighting the disgust twisting his gut. For a moment he wished he'd stayed in Dallas, writing about crops and cattle. At the same time, he knew he'd witnessed a great event in the history of the West, an important one for the farmers who'd been crying for years for more farmland. But to take still more land away from the Indians, and to make it a contest, turning men and women into selfish brutes, clawing and fighting for land—

When the cramps in his leg muscles eased, he returned to his seat and marshaled his impressions. Time passed as he let the images spill onto the paper in the form of notes for the article he'd write later.

A pair of black-suited legs stopped beside him, and he looked up into the conductor's face.

The man's hair stood on end beneath his billed cap, and red edged his eyelids and threaded the whites of his eyes. "Not looking to grab yourself a homestead, eh?"

Geordie shook his head. "How soon until the next train going south?"

The conductor rocked back on his heels, sliding his heavy watch from his waistcoat pocket. "I reckon it'll be a spell. Likely catch a few other fares." He glanced out the window. "Some of the unlucky ones will want rides back where they come from."

Geordie nodded. He wished the man would get on about his business so he could carry on with his own. Maybe the train crew didn't have anything better to do until the disappointed settlers returned.

With a friendly smile the trainman replaced his timepiece, then leaned one forearm on the tall back of Geordie's seat. "A newspaper fella, eh?" He gestured to the row of open windows. "Ain't you interested in the people fighting and dying over claims? This race is only half the story; the rest is out there."

Closing his notebook with a snap, Geordie rose and faced the man. "I've seen a bellyful of fighting and dying in my lifetime. It's nothing I care to see again." He dug into the pocket of his trousers for a wad of greenbacks. "How much did you say the fare was back to Texas?"

Damn Joe Vanzee for laughing when she slipped out of the sidesaddle. Effie stomped across the yard, the muddy ground soiling the toes of her new riding boots. Was it her fault she'd learned to ride astride, and now, when she wanted to learn to ride like a lady, he treated her like a—like a—well, she didn't know what, but she hated him.

Lifting her skirts, Effie climbed the rickety back stairs. She had to get a grip on herself, or Ida would ask her what was wrong. She couldn't bear to reveal her clumsy failure, even to her closest friend. That's what Ida was to her now.

Tenderness filled her at the thought of how far the girl had come in so short a time, learning to read better every day, minding her grammar, working simple sums. She even wore modest dresses whenever she left the saloon. And Ida saved most of her pay now for the day she planned to leave the Bon Chance.

But the biggest surprise was how Ida could sense Effie's moods, understanding her feelings before she spoke of them. Must be something the girl learned in her miserable childhood. In any event, there was no hiding things from her, especially her frustrations with Joe. Come to think of it, this miserable spectacle was partly Ida's fault for suggesting she ask Joe for riding lessons.

Effie stopped just outside the door to catch her breath and smooth her skirts before stepping into the kitchen. Every afternoon without fail Effie found Ida sitting on the horsehair sofa in the parlor, engrossed in reading. But today the sofa stood empty. Surprised, Effie turned to survey the room.

The girl sat at Cat's desk, a quill pen in her hand and a sheet of paper lying on the green blotter. Her face tipped up for a moment, then she slid the paper under the blotter and set the pen aside, her cheeks bright with color. "Just practicing my cursive."

Effie smiled. "Where's the copybook?"

"I—uh, well, I was just making it up, like." Ida stood and circled the desk. "How was your riding lesson?"

Effie turned around, giving Ida a full view of the mud caked on the seat of her skirts. "See for yourself." Facing Ida again, she crossed her arms over her bosom and fixed the girl with a look. "So what kind of cursive practice are you making up—something I might help with?"

"Well—" The girl sat on the edge of the sofa and clasped her hands. "I was wondering if you might could show me how to write a letter." She sucked her lower lip into her mouth, the soft pink forming a tiny pillow in the narrow gap between her two front teeth.

More and more surprises—Ida writing letters. But who did she know? Her father, perhaps, but that hardly seemed likely. Perhaps little Arthur's father. In any event, she'd find out sooner or later.

Ida rose and Effie seated herself in the wooden desk chair, outlining the types of letters and their various parts as she jotted examples. "And then you leave a space and indent for the closing, something like 'With regards,' or 'Yours truly' "—she slid her eyes toward the rapt face of her friend—"or even 'Love' if it's to a beau. Then sign your name below. You know how to address the envelope?"

Ida's eyes met hers, and the sweet face blossomed into a smile as she nodded. "Thanks." One slender hand covered Effie's. "Now, what are we going to do about Joe?"

Will dipped his hands in a basin of clean water, then reached for a ball of soap and scrubbed his fingers, the pungent tang of lye filling the air. "You can sit up now, Vi." He dried his hands on the clean towel Cat held out to him. He smiled and nodded his thanks, then turned back to the patient. "I can find no sign of damage or disease to explain your symptoms. Perhaps there's some other reason you're having trouble sleeping. Is your bed comfortable?"

Violet Williams kept her face down, her hands smoothing the skirt over her lap as the silence grew. At last she lifted her eyes to his, a smile trembling her lips. "It's a bit difficult to discuss, something of a private nature."

Catriona cleared her throat. "Well then, I'll wait outside."

"No!" Vi swallowed, then continued in a quieter tone. "No, I'd be obliged if you'd stay. It'll be easier." Her thin fingers twisted the dark fabric of her calico gown. "It's about my husband. We've always gotten on so well together until—" She took a breath. "Until a few weeks ago when I found a letter in his coat pocket from some woman in Dallas, a young widow. It was a love letter." Her eyelids lowered, then lifted again. "We had a terrible row about it, I'm afraid, and I moved into the guest room that night, and I've slept there ever since—or should I say tried to sleep." A strangled sob escaped, and tears glittered on her cheeks. "I just don't know what to do. I love him, but I don't know how to make him love me again." She tugged open her reticule and pulled out a linen kerchief to wipe her eyes.

Catriona's gaze met his for a moment, then dropped away as she busied herself tidying the examining room.

Although he could guess where the problem lay, Will wondered again why folks expected an unmarried doctor to know how to cure their marital problems. How could he advise anyone, when he couldn't figure out how to win back the woman he loved? Since he apologized, they'd grown closer, but except for the confrontation with the wife beater, he hadn't been able to hold Cat, touch her, kiss her.

He rolled down his sleeves and sat on the edge of the desk. "Tell me, Vi, do you enjoy sexual relations with your husband?"

The woman gasped and her face crimsoned. "Why, Dr. Bascom, I don't know how to answer you."

Will smiled, using his most coaxing, soothing tone. "It's a simple question. Do you take pleasure in your marital relations?"

Lowering her gaze, the woman bit into her lower lip and shook her head.

He stood, pacing across the office. "When you and your husband are in bed—"

"Really, Doctor!" The woman sputtered and twisted her hands together.

He stopped and faced her. "Violet, you must answer my

questions as fully and honestly as possible, or I cannot help you. Do you understand?"

She nodded, pushing her shoulders back and setting her lips in a thin line.

"Does your husband kiss you?" He fought against memories of his lips pressing Catriona's.

She shook her head.

"Does he caress you, tell you you're beautiful?"

Again she swung her head back and forth in a negative answer.

"And have you told him these things would help you enjoy your relations more?"

"I—I don't know if I could. But do you think it might help?" Her lower lip trembled.

Will settled back on the desk, images of Catriona's passion flickering through his mind. "Listen, Vi, my guess is your man feels you don't want him, and this widow-woman does, just because she responds to him. If he felt like you wanted him and he could please you, I'm sure he'd forget her in a minute."

Vi pressed her lips together. "It just goes against everything I was taught and how I was raised."

He crossed his arms over his chest. "If it makes it possible to keep your husband, isn't it worth a try?"

A smile touched the corners of her mouth. "I see what you mean."

"The first thing you have to do is move back into your bedroom, and into the same bed."

She stood, her cheeks still pink, but her smile widening. "I'll do it. Tonight." She placed one soft hand on his arm. "Thank you." She turned and strode out the door, closing it behind her.

Catriona came across the room and stood in front of him, her eyes shining. "That was a kindness. You saved her marriage."

"Or at least gave it a chance." He lost himself for a moment in the dark blue of her eyes. His voice dropped almost to a whisper as he placed his hands on either side of her waist. "And what of us, Catriona? Do we have a chance?" He bent and pressed his lips against hers, the sweetness exploding inside his head as her arms encircled his neck and her body melted against him for a timeless moment.

Then she drew away, her hands pressing against his chest and her dark lashes shielding her eyes. Her soft words hung between them. "Aye, I hope we have a chance."

Chapter 42

May 1889

Effie's arm ached from the weight of the six-gun in her hand. She bit her lip as Joe's chest pressed against her shoulder blades and his callused hand steadied her wrist.

"Now sight along your arm at the bottle on the fence." His deep voice vibrated in her ear.

Trying hard to concentrate, she took a breath and wrinkled her nose. She should have trusted her own judgment about the cheap toilet water, but Ida had insisted it would drive him loco with desire. In the bottle it smelled fine, but once she put it on, it soured somehow. She hoped Joe hadn't noticed, since it was too late now to change her mind—about the scent or Ida's scheme.

After the awful riding-lesson incident, Ida had cooked up this new idea to get Joe's attention. All Effie had to do was ask Joe to teach her to shoot, and once he put his arms around her—well, so far, all he'd done was show her how to shoot.

Joe sniffed, then cleared his throat. "Now squeeze the trigger real easy."

She pulled the metal lever toward her in a smooth, slow arc. A deafening thunder split the air, throwing her backward into Joe. Slivers exploded from the wooden rail several feet away, but atop the post, the bottle still glinted in the sunlight.

The weight of the gun pulled her hand down as he released her wrist and strode toward the fence, running his fingertips over the splintered wood. "Not too bad." He combed his white-blond hair from his eyes and smiled as he ambled back toward her. He stood to one side, wrinkling his nose. "You try it on your own now."

Sweat dampened her armpits as Effie raised the heavy pistol to shoulder height, her muscles trembling with the strain. She sighted along her arm to the tiny bump of metal at the end of the gun barrel, lining it up with the empty whiskey bottle. She squeezed the trigger, wincing from the expected roar. The gun discharged, throwing her backward into the dust. There she sat on her aching backside, the six-gun still clutched in her hand.

Joe's laughter brought tears to her eyes, but she swallowed them and forced herself to smile. She probably did look a sight. She squinted toward the fence post. At least if she'd hit it, she could bear the humiliation. The bottle sat there, smug and untouched.

"Sorry I laughed, but you look pretty funny sitting there in the dirt. Reminds me of you riding sidesaddle." High-heeled boots crunched the dust beside her, and strong hands cupped her elbows and lifted her to her feet. "You hardly weigh as much as a feather. It's no wonder the kickback threw you."

Heat rose in her cheeks. The way he talked to her, she could have been one of the cowhands. Some women just didn't have the feminine wiles to win any man, and it looked as if she might be one of them. She ought to give up the whole idea and settle for being an old maid.

Joe brushed at the back of her skirt. "Next time brace your feet apart and flex your knees." He smiled down at her, then his nostrils flared. "Miss Effie, I hope you don't mind me asking this, but you haven't by any chance been using horse liniment, have you?"

All the months of frustration and anger welled up in her. Keeping the tears at bay, she threw the pistol down in the dust. Without a word she lifted her skirts and ran as fast as she could toward the house.

Geordie wished he could get the attorney general to commit himself as a candidate for the governor's race. Even though the election was still two years off, rumors were flying around the state about Hogg running on a railroad regulation platform. What he wouldn't give for a definite confirmation on that story.

With a sigh he stared out the kitchen window at the May sunshine. He enjoyed working at home on the weekends, even with all the noise and hurly-burly. It was the only chance the family had to spend time together. Maybe if he finished his work early enough, he could talk Cat and Effie into packing up a lunch basket and taking the children on a picnic.

He turned back to the notes spread out across the kitchen table. In response to the demands made at the jute-bagging convention, the New York and New Orleans exchanges had promised a tare adjustment for all those bales wrapped in cotton. That would cut down on the money lost on each bale, but cotton bagging was still scarce, and the price had doubled in the past year. What little of the cotton cloth wrapping the farmers could find cost them the same this year as jute bagging had the year before. He wondered how long the farmers would continue to support the jute boycott if it ended up costing them too much.

A gunshot from somewhere outside startled him until he remembered Joe saying something about teaching Effie to shoot. Why his sister wanted to learn to use a gun was beyond him, but he suspected it had more to do with the teacher than the subject.

Another shot echoed from somewhere along the fence line. He couldn't understand what was taking those two so long getting together, but it was only a matter of time. He knew just how difficult it was to dissuade his sister from any course once she'd set her mind on it. Either Joe had great powers of resistance or too little knowledge of women to realize fighting was useless.

Footsteps clattered up the steps and across the porch. Effie ran through the kitchen, red curls flying out behind her, her face a mask of pain. She was gone before the screen door banged shut behind her. The door to her bedroom slammed, followed by the sound of muffled sobs. A faint sour odor hung in her wake.

Geordie blinked, then rose and walked to the window just as Joe disappeared into the barn. What the devil? He paced down the short hall to Effie's room and tapped on her door.

"Go away." Rage and pain thickened his sister's voice.

"Effie, it's me. Let me in." He waited. At last the knob clicked and the door swung inward.

Red curls straggled around her pale tear-streaked face. Her lower lip quivered, and anger burned in her green eyes. "What do you want?" She spat out the words.

"Come on, Eff. Dinna bite off my head, then. I'm not the cause of your troubles." He let his accent slip back into Scots as he tapped her chin with one knuckle, but she batted his hand away.

"So I ask you again, what do you want?" Her fists dug into each side of her waist. Black dust clung to her calico dress.

"My own sister comes running through the house like the devil's after her, and she canna understand what I want. What did he do?"

She narrowed her eyes, then let go the door and flounced onto the bed. "Come in, then, if you must."

He stepped inside and closed the door behind him, then perched on the edge of a chair in one corner. "So?"

She crossed her arms over her chest, her hands still clenched in fists. "He insulted me. Asked if I was wearing horse liniment."

Geordie wrinkled his nose to keep from laughing. "So that's what I smelled."

She picked up a pillow and hurled it at him.

He ducked, then grinned at her. "I take it you aren't wearing any liniment, then?"

Her lips twitched. "It's toilet water." She heaved a sigh.

"It was Ida's idea. She's the reason I asked him to teach me to shoot." Her voice trembled.

Geordie waited, guessing there must be more to it, something about his friend Joe, if he wasn't mistaken.

Maybe he could at least get her to smile. "So what does that have to do with toilet water?"

Her face crumpled and tears welled from her puffy eyes. "Joe treats me like a child." Fresh sobs broke from her.

Poor kid. She must truly care for the lad. "And you'd have him treat you more like a woman?"

She nodded through her tears.

A germ of an idea stirred in his mind. "Tell you what. I think I have a plan that'll make Joe sit up and take notice."

Effie pushed herself up and twisted toward him. She wiped her tears with the back of one hand, leaving a muddy streak across her cheeks and nose. "Tell me."

He laughed. "First things first. I think you might want to wash your face."

Catriona paused on the doorstep and slid her hand inside her cloth bag, fishing for the small jar as Will strode down the porch steps. She turned to the distraught mother hovering beside the open door, pressing the glass container into the woman's hand. She pitched her voice low. "Smear this on a cloth and wrap it over the rash." Without waiting for a reply, she turned and hurried down the stairs. Yellow light spread across the dark ground, guiding her footsteps toward the waiting buggy.

Resting her palms on Will's shoulders, she avoided his eyes as his hands closed on her waist and he lifted her over the tall wheel into the buggy. She settled herself on the tufted leather seat, smoothing her skirts and taking slow breaths to calm the pounding of her heart. He'd have a right to be angry if he found out about the medicine, but she couldn't just leave that poor woman with four itchy young children and no remedy. It was his own fault really; when he'd told the woman there was no cure and to just keep the itchy patches clean until they healed over, she'd tried to signal him, but he'd ignored her.

Will circled behind the two-wheeled rig and climbed in beside her, stashing his leather bag beneath the seat. Without a word he shook the reins and clucked to the horse.

The buggy sprang into motion, pressing Cat back against the seat. Good. He must not have seen. She leaned her head back and closed her eyes, breathing in the soft night air. Wildflowers perfumed the darkness, blending with the green smells of the tall grass lining the dirt road. A warm wind caressed her face.

"So what was in the jar anyhow?" Will's voice cut across her reverie.

She swallowed. "Broomweed jelly, for the rash."

"Does it work?" He kept his face forward and his voice toneless.

She studied his profile in the dim light. "Sanapia swears by it, and it canna hurt." Her words hung like a veil in the darkness between them.

"No, I reckon you're right. It can't hurt." He turned, a smile softening his handsome features. "Have I told you tonight how beautiful you look?"

A tender warmth stirred deep inside her as she returned his smile. "Are you seducing me, then?"

He chuckled. "What if I am? Am I having any success?"

Lifting her chin, she met his gaze. "I canna say. Perhaps you'd best try me and see."

As they approached a line of trees following a narrow stream, Will slowed the horse to a walk, turning in among the cottonwoods. He hauled on the reins, and the buggy creaked to a stop. Turning, he pulled Catriona into his arms.

She melted against him, her lips seeking his with unexpected hunger. An aching emptiness grew inside her. It had been so long. She slid her arms around his neck, her palms smoothing the soft hair on the back of his head, her fingers recalling every precious plane.

After long, dizzying moments, he drew back, his eyes locking hers in a silent embrace. She sat bemused and trembling with desire as he clambered down over the wheel.

He reached up for her and swung her to the ground. His hands lingered on her waist and a smile flitted around the corners of his mouth. Then he turned and lifted a carriage robe from beneath the seat and slung it over his shoulder. His warm, strong hand closed around hers, and he gave a gentle tug. "Come."

She followed him under the dark canopy of the leafy branches and beside the rock-strewn creek bed, the wet mystery of its scent surrounding her as she picked her way through the dark. All at once they emerged into a small clearing carpeted with grasses and wildflowers, glowing in the bright moonlight. Will spread the carriage robe and she sank down, tipping her head back and drinking in the cool splendor of the stars. "Ooo, it's that lovely." She lay back, cupping her hands behind her head.

Will stretched out beside her, his fingers reaching to smooth her hair and caress her cheek. He bent over her, his face a dark blur shutting out the stars as his lips brushed hers. She lifted her mouth to his, her lips parting, drinking in the sweetness of his kiss. Her arms encircled him, pulling him atop her, her senses hungry for the weight of his body pressing her down into the soft bed of grass.

She closed her eyes as his kisses moved to her neck and one of his hands slid inside her bodice, cupping one breast beneath the stricture of her corset. Longing flamed through her as she slid her fingers down his back and beneath the waist of his trousers, pulling him against her.

Will moaned, and his breath rasped against her ear as he tugged her long skirt up around her waist and loosened her bloomers. With a long, trembling sigh, he stroked down her waist and belly. She gasped as his fingers slid between her thighs. Pleasure radiated through her as she lifted her hips, melting with her need to have him inside her. She fumbled with his fly, her hands clumsy with desire. At last she released the smooth hardness of him, her fingers caressing and encircling him, guiding him inside her.

Will's mouth closed on hers in a tender, savage kiss as he entered her, filling her completely. A lovely itch of pleasure built at the base of her spine. She rose to meet his thrusts, a warm sweetness spreading through her veins, possessing more and more of her until she trembled in a silent explosion of ecstasy.

Above her, Will tensed and cried out, then collapsed on

top of her, panting. She slid her arms around his chest, holding him against her, savoring the tang of their lovemaking on the warm, sweet air. She drifted, unwilling to think, to risk somehow breaking the spell of this magic time.

After long, precious moments, he groaned and rolled to one side, curving his body around hers, his lips soft against the skin beneath her open bodice before he pillowed his head on her breast. "Catriona—"

She placed her fingers against his lips to silence him. "Hush, my love. Please dinna say it. Only let this be enough for now."

Chapter 43

June 1889

Joe rested his forehead on Bertha's hairy side, his hands squeezing and pulling in easy rhythm. Streams of white liquid hissed and rattled, hitting the sides of the tin bucket at his feet in foamy spurts. The sweet smell of fresh milk overlaid the dustiness of hay and the reek of manure in the warm barn. He usually liked milking, especially at sunup, when the world was new and private.

But lately, every time he got off by himself and quiet, all he could think of was Effie. Memories plagued him. The feel of her soft, pale skin as he supported her gun hand. The warmth of her arm alongside of his, his chest pressed to her shoulder blades, the back of her skirt sloping away from her slender waist just inches in front of his fly.

He closed his eyes against the tightening in his groin. He'd give anything to get rid of these thoughts and imaginings, wondering what she'd look like with her copper curls all hanging down around her shoulders, in her nightclothes —or in nothing at all. All cream and roses, he'd wager. A beautiful woman.

He shook himself. No, she was just a kid, his best friend's sister. Why, she wasn't even sixteen yet. Of course, when his sister was fifteen— Sadness gripped him. Best not to think about Molly or her little boy.

A horsefly buzzed around his head and he let go of the teat to wave it away. Bertha sidestepped toward him, and he steadied the bucket with his feet, then went back to milking, his stubborn thoughts returning to Effie once again.

He winced as her face flashed through his mind, her green eyes cloudy with tears and her soft cheeks bright red. He could have ripped out his tongue after the words left his mouth. Whatever was he thinking of to say such a thing to a young lady?

Bertha's tail slapped his shoulder, leaving a green smudge of fresh manure on his shirt-sleeve. He was one to talk. It never crossed his mind to wonder what he smelled like to her.

He lifted his head, rolling his tight shoulders. But that was the problem. All these years she'd been growing up, and he was too thick to see she wasn't a kid anymore. And now that he finally saw it, it was too late.

A fly buzzed near his head, but he ignored it, pressing his head into Bertha's rib cage. The whole blamed thing was loco. The cow lowed and sidled toward him, knocking one back foot against the bucket. He grabbed the tin pail just as it tipped, sloshing milk over one hand but keeping most of it from spilling into the dirt. Darn persnickety critter. Just like a female.

He wiped his wet hand on his shirtfront. Well, there was nothing to be done about it now. Effie hated him, that was sure. He'd seen it in her face every day for the past month. He squirmed inside. Not that he faulted her for feeling that way.

He pounded Bertha's haunch with his fist to get the blamed cow to move over again. But Effie had to take some of the blame too. After all, what was she trying to prove, dousing herself with scent when he was teaching her to shoot? And the stuff *did* smell strong, just like liniment. Hell, since that day, every time he walked into a livery stable and smelled that smell, he got all stirred up just thinking about her.

• • •

Geordie glanced at the wall clock and shuffled the papers together on his desk. If he left now, he could get home in time to help Cat decorate the barn for Effie's birthday party. As soon as he'd explained the plan to her, she'd insisted on helping. A smile stretched his lips. Effie knew what she wanted. Which was more than he could say for poor Joe. He didn't even realize he was being set up. Of course, it was all for the lad's own good as well.

Standing, he rolled his sleeves down and fastened his cuffs, glancing about the *Mercury* newsroom. He raised a hand in greeting. "Harvey, don't forget about tonight."

Elsen cocked his head. "This sister, she look anything like you?"

Geordie shook his head.

The man grinned. "Lucky girl. I'll be there."

Guy Willborn spoke up from the desk next to Geordie's. "Me too. I can't believe an ugly fella like you could have a good-looking sister."

Geordie laughed. "Well then, you'll be surprised tonight to see I've two, one older and one younger."

Old white-haired Ezra Speers popped his head up. "How much older, and is she married? Does she wanna be?"

"Not that much older, old-timer." It had taken him months to get used to the casual insults these Texans found so amusing, but he'd grown to accept their ribbing as a token of esteem. A good thing they didn't take their joshing seriously, or they'd end up shooting it out in the streets. He slid his arms into his sleeves and started toward the door.

Just as he reached it, it opened, spilling a young messenger across the threshold, his face red and his shoulders heaving. The lad must have run the whole way from wherever he'd been hired.

Geordie took the narrow shoulders and guided the wheezing youth to a chair. "What is it?"

"The jute-bagging trust—" The lad gasped for air and his throat worked.

This could be important, must be for them to send a runner all this way. "Aye, what about them?" He fought the urge to shake the poor kid.

"They lowered the price to nine cents a yard."

Geordie let go the bony shoulder, and the boy fell back, his narrow chest still heaving. "Then the Alliance has won." He pushed through the other reporters crowding around the messenger and hurried back to his desk, shrugging off his jacket as he went. Cat and Effie would have to manage without him for another hour or so. This story was just too big to give up, and it wouldn't wait. He grabbed his notebook and pencil, scribbling his opening paragraph.

"What are you doing, Galbraith?" Park's voice pulled him from his task.

He smiled up at his boss. "Writing about the Alliance victory over the jute trust, sir."

Park hitched up one trouser leg and perched a hip on the corner of Geordie's desk. "I believe that's a bit premature, son."

Geordie dropped his pencil and stared at the man. "How's that? They've dropped the price. The boycott's a success."

Park crossed his arms over his chest. "Then you tell me, what's to prevent the trust from raising the prices again next year, or the year after?" He shook his head. "No sir, we called this boycott to destroy the jute trust. There's just too much to be gained by substituting cotton bagging, and too many cotton mills to ever have to worry about them forming a trust of their own. That's why Chairman Jones turned down their offer to lower the prices a month ago."

Geordie leaned back in his chair. "But won't that end up costing the farmers more, what with the six percent tare and cotton bagging so scarce, and the prices going up?"

Park stood and placed a hand on Geordie's shoulder. "That's where we come in, son. It's our job, *your* job, to convince our readership it's to their advantage to keep on boycotting jute, that it'll save them money in the long run."

Geordie chewed the end of his lead pencil. "Aye, but will it really?"

Park smiled down at him. "We better hope so, hadn't we, son?"

• • •

Will sipped the cool applejack, savoring the mild bite of the fermented cider as he tapped his toe in time to the fiddle music. He hadn't been to a barn dance in years. Cat and Nana had done a darn good job of decorating, too, carting in armloads of wildflowers to pretty up the stalls, raking and scrubbing to get the animal smell out.

He'd been worried about his grandmother's health of late. She seemed more fragile than before, and she got winded whenever she exerted herself. Someday soon he might have to face life without her. He glanced toward the corner where she sat, tapping her toe to the fiddle music. His worry melted away. Right now she looked as young as Effie, as if she could live forever.

And he'd never seen the guest of honor look so beautiful. Imagine, little Effie, sweet sixteen already, her coppery curls piled high on her head, her green eyes bright and her cheeks flushed. Except for her coloring, she could be a younger Catriona. Little wonder every time he caught a glimpse of her tonight, a swarm of handsome young men surrounded her, many from the neighboring farms, and a few from as far away as Dallas.

Something warm leaned against his knee. He glanced down, then placed his hand on a halo of golden curls. Rosy cheeks dimpled, and a chubby arm wrapped around his leg, the sunny face turning back toward the dance floor. He'd wager she was supposed to be up at the house with Sanapia, in bed if he judged aright by the long white nightgown she wore.

A tenderness kindled in his chest, and a twinge of guilt. Betsy would be four years old soon, if she wasn't already, and he'd bet good money she didn't recall her father. And Ian had never gotten to see Duncan, hadn't even known of Catriona's pregnancy when he died. It was such a shame to miss the wonder of these children. He couldn't imagine loving them more if they were his own.

He'd wished they were his more than once. After all, wouldn't Ian want them to have a father? And would he have wanted Cat to live alone? He tried to put himself in Ian's place. If the situation was reversed, he'd like to think he was a big enough man to want her to remarry. But he hated the idea of sharing her with another man even after he was dead. Hell, he had enough trouble as it was, sharing her with the ghost of her dead husband.

As if she'd heard his thoughts, Cat bustled over, her mouth turned down but her eyes alive with mischief as she scooped her daughter up in her arms. "Elizabeth Jennet Macleod, what are you doing out here? Sanapia was that frightened when she found your bed empty."

The child placed chubby hands on each side of her mother's face. "Please, Mama, I want to watch."

Will cleared his throat. "Can't hurt to let her stay up a bit longer, seeing as how she's already awake."

"And you"—she turned her smiling face toward him, her eyes alight with mock disapproval—"hiding her away like this. Why, you ought to be ashamed, leading this poor child astray." She kissed Betsy's pudgy cheek. "Now say good night to Dr. Bascom like a good girl."

A pudgy hand thrust out toward him. "Good night, Doctor."

He grasped the tiny fingers. "I'd be pleased if you'd call me Will." He held her wide blue eyes with his as he bent and brushed his lips across her dimpled knuckles.

Betsy giggled. "Mama, he kissed me, right on my hand."

Shaking her head, Catriona pursed her lips. "I swear, Will Bascom, you spoil these children rotten. If anybody asks, I'll be right back, just as soon as I can get this hellion back into bed."

She swept away in a swirl of skirts, heading toward the open barn door and almost bumping into Joe Vanzee.

Joe stopped beside Will, hands stuffed into his trouser pockets and his pale brows furrowed. "Howdy, Doc." The young man crossed his arms and leaned his back against the wall, his angry face turned toward the middle of the barn, where the dirt floor had been cleared and swept for dancing.

Will followed his gaze, wondering why Cat's foreman looked like a bear with his paw in a trap.

Couples swung around the floor, following the voice of the caller and the sweet sounds of the fiddle. Effie's red hair shone like a beacon, bobbing and weaving among the other dancers, her face glowing as she threw back her head in laughter. She must have danced every dance, even taking a turn around the floor with his old friend Lewis, and once he saw her in Quincy's arms as well. He glanced again at Joe. Perhaps that was the problem.

"The birthday girl seems right popular tonight." Will kept his tone mild as he took a sip of applejack.

"Too darn popular, if you ask me. Every time I get close to her, one of those coyotes heads me off at the pass." Confusion and frustration vied in Joe's voice. "This song's finally winding down. 'Scuse me, Doc." The kid pushed off from the wall, his long strides covering the distance across the barn before the last note died.

Effie stood in the center of the floor in a circle of young men, sipping a cup as one of them talked and gestured. Just when Joe reached her, they all burst into laughter. Will couldn't make out any of the words exchanged, but as the fiddle struck up a new tune, one of the young men stepped forward and bowed to the copper-haired beauty. She shrugged and set her hand on the offered arm, gliding onto the dance floor and leaving Joe standing with clenched teeth and fists.

Poor Joe. Will felt just as frustrated when he couldn't get Cat to talk about their future. Every time they were alone and he tried to ask her, she refused to listen, putting him off. He wanted to ask her to marry him now, not waste any more months or years apart. But maybe she needed more time, time to get over her grief, time to let go of Ian's memory. Or was he just a coward, afraid to ask for fear she'd turn him down again?

Effie squeezed her partner's arm as he escorted her away from the makeshift dance floor, murmuring his thanks. "I should be thanking you, Bob."

He grinned, then sobered. "It's for a good cause, but I hope you can square it with Mariah later. She's mad as hops at me right now."

Effie smiled and waved to her old friend, but the lass scowled and turned her face away. "And me, too, by the look of it." She hadn't even considered this particular result of her brother's plan. "I'll have Geordie speak to her. It'll go down easier coming from him." She patted his arm, and he hurried off toward his sweetheart, to try to mend fences no doubt.

She caught sight of Geordie and had to struggle to keep herself from rushing over to him. Instead, she excused herself from the circle of young men waiting to ask her to dance, then took her time greeting the folks crowding the barn. And as she made her way across the dirt floor, her eyes kept returning to Joe, standing slouched against the wall, his mouth turned down and his arms crossed over his chest. She'd never seen him so unhappy.

She forced herself to smile at the two reporters standing next to Geordie. "'Scuse me, but could I borrow my brother for a minute?" Without waiting for an answer, she tugged him to one side, keeping her voice low. "You've got to stop it. I can't stand to watch him suffer anymore."

He patted her hand. "There, there, he'll survive. Are you sure he's had enough?"

She punched his shoulder. "I thought you were his friend, but you're enjoying this, aren't you?"

He winced at the blow, then grinned. "Aye, I believe I am at that. And have you forgotten? He insulted your perfume."

"Toilet water. Besides, he was right. It did smell sort of like liniment." She planted one fist on each hipbone. "Come on, Geordie. My feet are tired."

Placing one palm on his chest, Geordie heaved a noisy sigh. "All right, then, but I think you're letting him off too easy. Don't blame me if he takes you for granted later." He headed toward the makeshift stage, where the caller and the fiddler stood drinking from tin cups.

Effie smoothed her skirts and touched her palms to her hair, then sauntered in Joe's direction, watching her brother from the corner of her eye.

Fiddle music squealed through the air, and the caller's voice rose above the hum of voices. "This next dance is ladies' choice. All you gals grab your favorite fellas for the Texas Star."

Taking a deep breath, she strode across the open space

and tapped Joe on the shoulder. "I hope you haven't promised this dance to anyone else."

He swung toward her, eyes wide and mouth open. Pressing his lips together, he shook his head. "Nope, I'm not spoke for yet."

She smiled into his blue eyes. "Would you care to dance?"

"Yes'm, I'd be honored." His throat worked. "Uh, you smell right pretty tonight." His cheeks reddened, and he turned his eyes away.

Anger teased her for a moment, but then she had to stifle a smile. It must have cost him something to say that. It almost amounted to an apology, probably as close as he was likely to come to one. "Why, thank you, Joe."

He turned toward her again, a smile lighting his handsome features. He brushed a sheaf of blond hair from his eyes, then held out his arm. "Shall we?"

Chapter 44

July 1889

Cat set aside the sheaf of papers and stretched, enjoying the morning sunlight and the perfume of wildflowers in the clearing. What a pleasure, sitting outside to work on her lecture for the afternoon. In some ways, camp meetings reminded her of Skye, where the crofters did as much work outdoors as possible in the summer after the long winter hours crouched inside their smoky black houses.

Here at Village Creek, the folks pitched tents or slept in the backs of their wagons, and the women clubbed together to cook meals and wash dishes and clothing. Guilt nibbled at her pleasure. Although Sanapia contributed more than enough for the whole family, she ought to be helping the others with chores as well.

Especially as Effie was no good to anyone after her birthday. Joe had gone to Geordie the next day to ask for permission to court her. Since then, the lass had spent every spare minute sitting beside him on the porch at home, talking. Every now and again he'd reach out and take her hand, and she'd pull it away and shake her head. And since the camp meeting started, more of the same. Her sister had learned the power of telling a man no and making him wait, and she wasn't likely to forget it soon.

Even if Cat wasn't helping the other women with camp

chores, she wished she could at least go with Will to call on the ill or injured. She smiled, happy just knowing he was nearby, and grateful he hadn't insisted on talking about anything serious just yet.

She dreaded more talk of marriage, knowing how he felt about her Alliance work. And her own illegitimacy. She wondered sometimes how the *laird* got on, and her half sister. There were some people from Skye she didn't miss, after all. And neither her brother Fergus nor her cousin Malcolm mentioned Rory or Bridget in their letters. Not that either man had any more use for the laird and his one legitimate daughter than she did.

She wanted to savor her time with Will without thinking about what it meant. And from past years she knew he'd be too busy to think about much this week as well. There seemed no end to the mischief young lads could get into here in the woods, everything from broken bones to bellyache to the itch. And a few of the older folks needed care as well.

She sighed. Much as she'd rather spend her morning with Will, she hadn't any other time to write her speeches. And after all, that was the purpose of the camp meetings, to let the farmers know what was going on and what it meant to their lives.

She picked up the stack of handwritten papers and leafed through page after page of new business and old business, looking for the platforms adopted. It was good of Alliance President Evan Jones to provide minutes of the Eight-Hour Convention and the Freight-Rate Convention, both held only the week before. Pressure was building for the coming election year, and she intended to make sure the farmers understood how to cast their votes in their own best interest.

A shadow fell across the pages, and she looked up into a sad-eyed face. "Aye, and can I help you, then?"

The man pulled a battered hat from his head and licked his lips. "Miz Macleod?"

She nodded.

"The other folks said I should talk to you." He twisted the tattered hat brim in his hands. "I brung a whole wagon full of watermelons to sell to the folks here, and three nights running some of my biggest and best disappeared, and I don't know what to do about it."

Cat set the papers aside. "Do you have any idea where they went?"

He scuffed a toe in the dirt. "Well, ma'am, I hate to call any man a thief, or any child neither, but I seen some of the bigger boys poking around thereabouts just after sundown. It was too dark to make out their faces or tell just who they was."

Cat crossed her arms. "I see." Although she could guess who the culprits might be, she must be careful not to accuse the wrong lads for fear of offending their parents, but this man deserved to be paid for his produce. If only there was a way to catch them at it, or, better yet, let the thieves punish themselves. A slow smile spread across her face as an idea began to take shape. "If you'll give up one of your melons, I believe I can get you your money and see you don't lose any more."

Will cradled the heavy watermelon in his arms as he ducked through the opening. He knelt and lowered it to the ground, then smiled up at Catriona.

Her whisper cut through the dim air as she fastened the tent flap behind him. "Are you sure no one saw you?"

He nodded, pitching his voice low to match hers. "Hand me my longest scalpel, and have the decoction ready."

"Aye." She chuckled, her eyes twinkling in the lantern light as she handed him the razor-sharp instrument. He'd never seen her like this, so full of mischief. She never ceased to amaze him, and each new facet of her he saw intrigued him even more.

Steadying the melon to keep it from rolling, he worked the thin blade into the dark green skin, following the natural indentations to better disguise the cut. The sugary smell of ripe watermelon filled the small tent as he cut, keeping the incision as small as possible. He removed the square of rind and set it aside to use later as a plug, then dug out the soft red pulp until he reached the heart. "Ready."

Cat handed him a glass bottle, still radiating warmth from the preparation of the clear liquid inside.

He held the top to his nose, wrinkling it at the faint almond odor. "What's this?"

"Wild cherry cordial." The corners of her red mouth twitched. "After this, they'll think twice about stealing a watermelon."

"What'll it do to them? No, never mind. Don't tell me." He chuckled as he tipped the bottle up, pouring the contents into the narrow hole a bit at a time, letting it seep into the sweet red flesh before he replaced the green plug of rind. "There, as good as new." He held up the bottle, still half full. "Is that enough?"

Chuckling, she nodded. "Aye, for ten men." She corked the top, then replaced the glass flask in her bag.

Will hesitated, not wanting to anger or insult her. Still, he had to be sure. "It won't do them any real harm, will it?"

Cat crossed her arms over her chest and shook her head. "It should wear off in a few hours, but until then they'll wish they were dead."

Clutching her herb bag over one shoulder, Cat lifted the door flap and ducked inside, holding her breath against the sudden sharp reek of vomit inside the tent. In the circle of lantern light, a young lad writhed and moaned on a pallet on the ground, while a man of striking resemblance stood by, watching.

Will knelt beside the patient, his hands pressing into the lad's abdomen. He looked up as she entered. "This lad has terrible pains in his belly, and he's running from both ends."

Cat struggled to keep a sympathetic look on her face. She hated to see anyone suffering, but it served the lad right, stealing another man's food day after day. She fastened her eyes on Will's. "And did you find the cause, then?"

His eyes narrowed the tiniest bit, and he leaned over the lad. "Gus, did you eat or drink anything after your supper tonight?"

The boy's gaze slid toward his father. "I don't recall."

Will's face tipped up and he squinted in the bright light

of the lantern. "Well, Mr. Ransom, I can't help much unless I know whether this is food poisoning or a fever—hell, it could even be typhoid."

Cat coughed to cover a smile at his cleverness. That ought to scare the lad into a confession.

Ransom's brows drew together, and he hunkered down at the head of the pallet. "Best tell the doc what he needs to know, boy."

The lad crossed his arms over his belly, his eyes sliding first right, then left. "I et some watermelon just after dark."

"And where did you get this melon?" Ransom's quiet voice rasped across the night air. "You didn't have no money to buy no melon."

Cat shivered at the faint edge of cruelty in the father's tone, her sympathy growing for the ailing lad.

"From a wagon, Pa." The lad's throat worked. "The old man, he give it to me."

The father stood, undoing the buckle of his belt. "And just why'd he want to do that, I ask you."

"I—uh, I done some work for him." Gus's eyes filled with unshed tears. His voice was tight with real fear. "You gotta believe me, Pa."

"You stole it, didn't you, you sniveling little bastard?" Eyes blazing, the man jerked the leather strap from around his waist, grasping both ends in one hand. "I'll beat you till you can't stand up."

Cat swallowed against the disgust knotting her stomach, sickened by the man's brutality and filled with regret for her part in this charade. No wonder the name sounded familiar; it was the same last name as the man who beat his wife. They must be brothers or cousins.

Will rose, his most charming smile stretched across his handsome face. "Looks like that's hardly necessary, Ransom. The boy's had punishment enough by the look of him."

Ransom's eyes narrowed, and he slapped the belt against his thigh.

"Tell you what—" Will stepped toward the man. "I got some good sipping whiskey in my tent. Let's you and me take a walk over there and have a taste to settle our nerves. I think Miz Macleod can handle Gus." He put his hand on the man's shoulder and steered him toward the open tent flap.

Ransom's face turned back over his shoulder. "Ought to let you lay there in your own stink." Then he ducked his head and stepped through the doorway.

Will paused, the canvas flap in one hand. "I'll be back in a few minutes. You'll be all right?"

She nodded. "Aye. Go on." The tent flap fell behind him as she rummaged in her bag. At last she pulled out the bottle she wanted and knelt beside the moaning lad. "Here we are now. Can you sit up?"

He nodded and struggled upright, propping himself with both hands. "What is that stuff?"

She smiled. "Bilberry tea. It'll soon set you to rights." She held the bottle to his lips. "Here, take a few swallows. Not too much now, or it'll come back up."

He relinquished the bottle and lay back. "Funny thing, watermelon never made me sick before."

Avoiding his eyes, Cat stoppered the bottle and set it beside the boy's pallet. "Perhaps it was tainted."

The lad's nose wrinkled. "Could be, but it don't matter none. This has put me off the taste of melon permanent."

"Aye, well, you try to sleep a bit now. And take a few sips of this each time you wake until your insides settle down."

The lad nodded and closed his eyes, one hand clutched around the glass bottle.

She turned down the wick, dimming the light of the lantern to a dull glow, then slung her bag over her shoulder and stepped outside. She breathed deep, relieved to get away from the oppressive odors and tensions of the Ransom tent. With a father like that, no wonder Gus had the devil in him. The idea of anyone beating a child or an animal—or a woman—sickened her. Thank God Will had been there to divert the man's anger.

The faint sweetness of blooming coneflowers blended with the creek smells and the hint of juniper on the warm night air. Moonlight dappled the dry leaves at her feet, its milky whiteness lending magic to the grove as she stood beneath a pin oak, waiting for him. She leaned against the trunk of the tree, its scratchy bark pressing into her back and shoulders through the cotton of her dress. Too bad all men couldn't be so kind and gentle.

"How's our patient?" Will strode toward her through the clearing, moonlight flickering over his lithe body as he strode beneath the canopy of branches.

Warmth surged through her at the sound of his voice. "A wee bit more comfortable, with perhaps a taste of regret. He's not likely to steal any melons again soon." Standing on tiptoe, she brushed her lips over his cheek. "And the father?"

Will slid his arm around her waist and chuckled. "I left him sipping at my whiskey bottle. I doubt he'll remember any of it in the morning."

"Let's hope not." She shuddered in his embrace. "That poor lad."

Will nuzzled her hair. "The boy's not without blame in this, remember. But let's not talk about the Ransoms." He released her, then clasped her hand and tugged. "Come."

She followed him along the path to the creek, content just to be alone with him in the warm darkness. At the water he turned upstream, holding aside branches and helping her pick her way among the rocks until they reached a wide backwater. She'd never seen the swimming hole at night, its smooth surface reflecting the light of the full moon like a mirror.

Will turned and drew her into his arms, his lips soft and warm against hers.

She melted against him, her passion rising to match his own. They'd been at the camp meeting a week, and this was the first time they'd been together without a hundred pairs of eyes watching everywhere they went. She hadn't realized how hungry she was for him until this moment.

He drew back, a grin lighting his handsome features. "Care for a swim?"

Her heart raced at the thought of sliding into all that silky water, washing the dust and sweat from her skin, and Will beside her, his naked body gleaming in the moonlight. "But what if somebody comes? They'll know."

His smile dimmed. "What if they do? Catriona, I'm not

ashamed to be in love with you; I don't care who knows it." He stepped away and slipped out of his jacket, hanging it on a willow branch and unbuttoning his shirt. "I'm going in." His words hung in the air as he stepped out of his trousers and waded into the pool.

She hesitated, then her fingers flew to the buttons of her bodice. In moments she was beside him, the tepid water slipping over her bare skin like gentle fingers. She waded out until the water flowed past her shoulders, her toes finding solid footing among the smooth stones on the bottom of the creek bed.

Will swam toward her, then dived, his buttocks glowing white in the moonlight before they disappeared after the rest of him.

She started when hands touched her beneath the water, then relaxed as they caressed her, smoothing the planes and contours of her body.

At last his head broke the surface inches from her face. With one hand he combed back his wet hair, rivulets of water trailing down his cheeks and ears. "Catriona, I—"

She leaned toward him, silencing his lips with hers, her arms encircling his neck and her body pressing against his. The cool silkiness of the water made his skin warmer, the hair on his chest rougher.

His hardness pressed into her belly, sending shivers of desire up her spine. Cupping her buttocks in his hands, he lifted her against him so that her breasts broke the surface of the water.

With a low chuckle she wound her legs around his waist, then arched back as he bent to take one nipple into his mouth, sucking it and flicking it with his tongue until she moaned aloud. Then he fastened his lips around the other, his tongue sending delicious jolts of warmth through her body, kindling a hunger between her legs.

She leaned forward, pouring her longing into a breathless kiss as her body slid down along his, his hands still cupped around her thighs. Under the water she rubbed her thumbs across his nipples, then sent her fingers exploring the hard planes of his chest. Her hands smoothed the sleek muscles beneath his arms and across his back, then down to his narrow waist, pressing into the soft flesh of his buttocks. Wet black curls plastered against her shoulders as she clung to his neck.

He moaned in her ear as he lifted her, then guided her down onto him, rocking her. His gentle thrusts filled her, sending waves of pleasure radiating through her body, each one stronger than the last. She strained against him, flames of bliss spreading through her veins, consuming her until she gave herself up to them in a shuddering groan of completion.

He kissed her neck, then carried her toward a grassy spot at the creek's edge. Kneeling, he lowered her to the ground, her legs still locked around his waist. He hovered over her, his face hidden in darkness.

Cat caressed the tight muscles of his back as he thrust inside her again, his slow rhythm building to a frenzy. With a low moan he collapsed into her embrace, leaving a gentle kiss on her shoulder before he lay still atop her. Beyond his shoulder her eyes drank in the sight of the stars sprinkled overhead, a million candles flickering in the warm darkness. If only there was no one else, no world full of work and worry to pull them apart. If only this moment could last forever.

Chapter 45

Joe's stomach churned as he peeled back the green hull of one of the swelling cotton bolls and pointed it out to Miz Macleod. "See there, that's a boll weevil." He flicked the disgusting bug onto the ground and squashed it with the toe of his boot, then released the pod and swept one hand out, indicating the acres of cotton spreading around them. "These pesky things are all through the fields."

She crossed her arms over her chest. "And how much will we lose because of these weevils?"

He tilted his head, calculating. "You'll be lucky to make one bale for every fifteen, twenty acres."

Her dark blue eyes widened, and small red spots appeared in her cheeks. "And can we do nothing, then?"

He dropped his gaze to the ground, then looked away from the dead bug toward the horizon. "Well, yes'm. Come December we can burn the stalks right as soon as we finish harvesting. That might help keep them from coming back next year." His eyes slid back toward her for a moment.

Her jaw tightened. "So you're telling me there's nothing we can do to save this year's crop?"

He scuffed dirt over the smashed bug with his toe, then planted his heel over the tiny grave. "No'm. Nothing now." He turned to face her. "And that's my fault, Miz Macleod. If

I'd a noticed them sooner, we coulda tried to pick them off by hand when the plants was smaller." He cleared his throat. "By the time I saw them, it was too late."

"Dinna blame yourself. You couldna know." She took a slow turn around, her eyes narrow in the bright sunlight. Only the distant lowing of the herd disturbed the quiet countryside. "Damn!"

Joe scratched the back of his hand, waiting as the minutes stretched out. "Ma'am, what're you gonna do?"

She turned toward him. "I canna say." She turned her eyes away and stood silent for a long time.

Joe held himself still, not wanting to disturb her thoughts. If there was any way to save her farm, Miz Macleod would find it.

Birds twittered in the tall grass beside the field, and in the distance Old Domino bellowed after a heifer.

At last she spoke, her voice rough with sadness. "Joe, how much could I get if I sold the cattle?"

Startled, Joe's eyes strayed toward the herd, some of the finest cattle he'd seen in this part of Texas. Over and over he'd heard Miz Macleod say how they were her dead husband's pride and joy, and that she'd never let them go, no matter how broke she got. It was a shame to sell them, especially for the rock-bottom prices the Fort Worth Stockyards offered. "Five dollars a head." He knew the price only too well. His family had just sold ten head for enough money to get by until harvest time. "Of course, they're offering three times that in Pueblo."

"It's the only thing left to do." Her lips set in a thin line and her brows knitted. "We'd best find a way to get them to Pueblo."

Joe shook his head. "But the railroad will charge you the difference in freight."

Her eyes held his in a level gaze. "Not if we drive them overland." She turned and headed back toward the house.

It was a loco idea, but he knew better than to argue. Miz Catriona was just like her sister. Once they set their minds to something, there was no talking sense to them. If one of them said she was gonna do something, it was a sure bet she'd do it, no matter what anybody else said.

• • •

Will smelled the old man before he saw him. His nose wrinkled at the reek of sweat and stale whiskey as he stepped into the dim room from the bright sunlight of the porch. He wanted to know just why Quincy sat at Catriona's kitchen table, sipping from a cup and looking just as comfortable as could be.

Cat and Joe stood on either side, bending toward each other over the table, pointing at something and talking in low tones, so engrossed none of them looked up when he entered.

Quincy leaned forward, his finger stabbing at the large square of paper. "Iffen you was to drive north on the old Western Trail through Injun Territory, then west across the Public Land Strip, you could catch the Goodnight-Loving just across the New Mexico border and follow it right to Pueblo. That way you got good trails, plenty of water, and you bypass most of the fenced range too."

Will's shoulders tightened with suspicion.

Cat turned to Joe. "What do you think?"

One long-fingered hand brushed hair out of the boy's sober face. "I reckon he's right, 'specially about the water. The Staked Plains due west of here are mighty dry."

She nodded. "That's what we'll do, then."

Will cleared his throat.

Her dark blue eyes turned toward him, and her lips curved into an inviting smile. "I didn't hear you come in." She stood and moved toward the stove. "Have a seat. I'll bring you some coffee."

He strode toward the table, nodding to the two men. "What's this?" He studied the crude drawing of Texas and the surrounding states.

"Map of cattle trails." Quincy's gnarled hands rolled the heavy paper into a tube and tied it with a leather thong, his face averted.

Will took the cup Cat offered, covering her hand with one of his. "What's this all about?"

She turned her face up to his. "The weevils have ruined the cotton. We'll be driving Ian's cattle overland to market in Colorado." Her tone held no hint of doubt, no room for argument.

Will released her hand and let his breath out in a slow stream. "And what's Quincy got to do with it?"

She turned away from him and made her way back to her seat. "He's hired on as trail boss, with Joe as his second. I mean to drive the chuckwagon myself."

"I see." Will lowered himself into the straight-back chair. He didn't want to make the same mistake again, forbidding her to do anything. They'd come too far for that. He couldn't bear the thought of being apart for another year, or perhaps for good. Clenching his jaw to keep from saying more, he put the cup to his lips, hardly tasting the hot, bitter brew.

Quincy stood. "There's only one more thing, Miz Macleod. The last few years, most of the drovers headed up north to the open range in Montana and Wyoming, or else out to the Panhandle to work them big ranches. We're gonna need some men."

The lovely smooth span of Cat's forehead wrinkled, and her white teeth pressed into the soft flesh of her lower lip. "Aye. Well, we're not the only ones hurt by boll weevils this year, or the only ones who'll need to sell cattle to survive." She turned to her young foreman, her brow smoothing as she spoke. "Joe, get everybody you can to come here tonight, young boys, old men, widows—anybody who can ride a horse astride." Her forearms crossed on the tabletop, each hand cupping an elbow, her eyes alight with excitement. "I'll get you your cowboys, Mr. Quincy. Is there anything else?"

The old man dragged the toe of one boot across the wooden floor, then his whiskered face split in a gap-toothed grin. "I reckon not." He tapped the rolled-up map against one palm, his face turning toward Joe. "Let's you and me ride out and get a look at them beeves." He swung around, holding out a hand to Will. "Nice seeing you, Doc."

Will shook his hand and waited until the two left. When he spoke, he forced his voice to stay level. "Have you thought about this? What about our patients?"

Cat wrapped her hands around her coffee mug. "I've spoken to Sanapia, and she's agreed to help, if you'll have her. She knows everything I do, perhaps more."

"And your children?" He struggled to keep his face neutral.

"I've hired Ida to stay with Effie and the bairns. She's been looking for a way to get wee Arthur out of the Bon Chance, and Yvette's agreed to let her go." She smiled and reached out her hand. "Geordie can manage the farm, and Effie can help. The grain's all in, and I'll be back in time for the cotton harvest, such as it is. You do understand." Her voice held a pleading note. "I have to do this."

He squeezed her hand, weighing her words. In a way, he did understand. Without the money from her cotton crop, she'd have to go into debt to someone like Frink, and he knew how much Ian's farm meant to her. "But can't you send Joe and Quincy? You don't have to go."

"They're good men, but Quincy's old and likes the bottle overmuch, and Joe's too young to ride herd on the cattle and an old drunk as well." She paused and tilted her head. "Would you trust those two alone with *your* cattle all the way to Colorado?"

He shook his head. "But there must be another way."

Placing her palms flat on the table, she pushed herself up with a sigh. "If there is, I dinna *ken* what it might be." She gathered up the coffee cups and turned away toward the sink.

He sipped his coffee again, his thoughts roaming over the possibilities. If he had the money, he could just give it to her, buy the herd from her or something, but where could he get that kind of cash? Hell, he was lucky to have enough to live on the way his patients paid their bills. The thought triggered a memory. Maybe there was a way to resolve this after all, but he wouldn't say anything to Cat until he knew for sure. No sense getting her hopes up if it didn't pan out.

The afternoon sun cast shadows against the weathered plank sides of the chuckwagon. Reflecting on the success of their hasty meeting, Catriona counted the tied-up bedrolls stacked in the front. The men all swore they'd be ready to depart the next morning, and there were that many. It must be the lure of the trail, or all the stories of the old cattle drives. With more and more barbed wire fences going up across the range, and the railroads pushing across the country, the long drives were a thing of the past even before she came to America with Ian. This part of Texas wasn't likely to see many more cattle drives like this, and these men couldn't resist one last chance at adventure.

Whatever the reasons, even with the cattle from all the surrounding farms making up a decent herd, they'd added twice the riders they needed. But it was just as well so many had volunteered, since most were old men or young boys, and few had ever driven cattle any distance. Joe and Quincy would need all the hands they could get if they wanted to make it to Pueblo without losing half the herd. And cattle left dead on the plains earned no one any money.

At first she'd been sick at heart when she thought of selling Ian's cattle. But she realized he'd rather have her sell the herd than lose the farm. What good were cattle with no land to graze them on? And now that she'd grown used to the idea, she was almost looking forward to the excitement of the trip herself.

She twitched at the skirt tangled between her legs as she climbed down from the high seat, irritated by her own clumsiness. As much trouble as they were, she knew she'd be glad to have these bloomers when she needed to ride astride. In order to get used to them, she'd decided to practice wearing the puffy breeches beneath her old chambray dress.

She circled around the wagon to the chuckbox sitting in the rear. Standing on tiptoe, she reached up and unlatched the hinged lid, letting it down to form a worktable. The faint smells of coffee and lard surrounded her. She couldn't resist tugging at a white ceramic knob, opening one of the many compartments and poking among the contents one more time.

When Quincy had shown her how to stack everything inside to make the best use of the space, he'd confided that he'd hired on as a cook once, but couldn't take the ribbing. Small wonder the men complained of the food, with nothing but white flour, cornmeal, and beans available. She hoped to do better by adding fresh greens and herbs gathered along the trail.

"Cat?" Will's voice spun her around.

She smoothed her skirts, wondering if he'd notice the lumpy britches under the chambray. She forced herself to smile. "Aye. And what do you think of my kitchen for the six weeks coming?" She pointed at the chuckbox.

"I'm hoping that won't be necessary." His mouth quirked up in a smile.

She crossed her arms over her chest and set her jaw. She'd been waiting for this, expecting him to argue, to try to persuade her not to go, telling her to leave it to the menfolk. "And how's that?"

He tugged an envelope from his inside breast pocket and handed it to her. "Go on, open it."

She turned the packet over and lifted the flap. A stack of greenbacks crowded the narrow space inside. She closed it and handed it back. "I canna take charity, even from you."

His smile froze. "What charity? I want to buy your herd."

Why did he have to make things so difficult? "You have no land. Where would you pasture them?"

He shrugged. "I'll sell them in Fort Worth."

"At a loss?" She shook her head. "No, lad. I already told you, no charity."

His lips thinned. "Then I'll rent pasturage from you." He thrust the packet toward her again.

She ignored it. "And what of the others? Have you enough to buy them out as well?"

His eyes narrowed. "What others?"

Her stomach clenched into a knot. "My partners. We've rounded up close to a thousand head. Are you ready to buy them all as well?"

His eyes flashed. "You're right. I can't afford to buy them all. But you could sell me yours, and let Quincy drive the rest of them north."

She stared at him. "If that's all the better you think of me—"

"I'll tell you what I think of you." His voice rose over hers, drowning out her words. "I think you're a stubborn, mule-headed woman, and I won't let you do this."

She clenched her fists. "You canna stop me, and if you dinna know more about me than that, I've nothing left to say to the likes of you." She turned her back to him, slamming the compartments shut and closing the chuckbox lid with a bang.

A gentle hand touched her shoulder, and Will's voice breathed in her ear. "Please, Cat. Take the money. I love you. I want to marry you."

"Marry me?" She pushed his hand away and whirled to face him. "So that's what you've a mind to buy, then, a wife." She touched her forefinger to her chest. "I'm no for sale."

His shoulders sagged, and he placed the envelope back in his pocket. "I'll just keep this in case you change your mind."

Cat clenched her teeth. "That willna happen."

He opened his mouth, then closed it and shook his head. Without another word he turned away.

She crossed her arms and stood trembling as he walked back to his buggy, the setting sun outlining his dark body with gold.

Clambering up, he clucked to the horse, and the buggy leapt forward in a cloud of dust.

Cat leaned her head back against the lid of the chuckbox, holding back her tears.

Chapter 46

August 1889

Catriona shifted her weight from one side to the other as she headed the oxen north from Doan's Store. After two weeks of driving the chuckwagon from sunrise to sunset, jolting over rutted tracks on the hard plank seat, bruises covered her backside. Her arms ached from holding the reins by day and hefting the huge pots in and out of the wagon each evening and morning. And her feet hurt from walking the hot sands to give her sore buttocks a rest.

Odd how a land so flat to the eye could hide so many potholes and gully-washes. Such emptiness ought to include silence and peace, not the constant dust and noise of the herd surrounding her now. Just ahead the Red River spread wide in the hot sunshine, all treacherous sandbars and swirling eddies, according to Quincy.

She shuddered, remembering the near tragedy at the Brazos when the cattle started milling midstream and ended up spread out over the far bank for two miles. It had taken half a day to round them all up. At least none of the riders had drowned, and they didn't lose any cattle, but even then, a score of men turned back for home that night, complaining of hardships and privations. No one could dispute their claims, since they were all true. Still, the best men hung on, and Quincy had drilled them and their horses for hours before declaring them ready to leave the Brazos and head north once more.

A hot wind carried the stink of cow manure and parched grasses over her, drying her skin to a sticky tightness. She coughed and blew her nose, turning the red bandanna black with inhaled dust. Of course, that was nothing compared to the dust storm they'd driven through three days out of Fort Griffin.

She squinted toward the treelined banks just ahead. At least the air near the river held a bit less grit, and swimming the cattle might even kill the stench for a bit. The smell of her own sweat reminded her how long it had been since she soaked in a hot bath. Perhaps she could find a way to get clean before they left the river altogether.

The oxen plodded down the gentle slope toward the ford, their hooves making sucking noises in the wet sand. Catriona kicked off her brogans and clambered down, the soles of her feet drinking in the soothing chill of the riverbank. The spoked wheels of the wagon sank into the gritty surface, and the great haunches of the gelded bulls bunched and knotted as they pushed on toward the water.

At the river's edge Cat gathered her clumsy skirts around her and climbed onto the slow wagon, no longer worried about showing her bloomer-covered limbs beneath. Shading her eyes with one hand, she scanned the flowing water for ripples on the surface that told of the shallowest passage, then headed the oxen in at an angle, leaving Texas behind and crossing into what remained of Indian Territory after the boomers settled the Oklahoma Territory the spring before.

She recalled Geordie's stories and was glad she'd missed that brutal stampede for land stolen from the Indians just as the acres where her farm now stood had been stolen from the Comanche, Sanapia's people, decades earlier. That they were almost all dead and gone by the time she arrived did little to ease her sense of injustice, her unease at owning someone else's land. Not that she had time to wrestle with those ideas just now.

Around her the hands whistled and yipped, wheeling their mounts to keep the steers bunched together and headed toward the far shore, the best swimming horses leading the way. The far shore drew nearer as the ox team held their slow, steady pace. They walked in the shallows and swam the depths, the water-tight wagon box floating behind. Catriona leaned back, relishing the fresh air and the suddenly smooth ride.

Somewhere near midstream the wagon wheels jolted onto a hidden sandbar, throwing her forward with a jerk. She caught herself with both hands as the oxen pulled ahead for several lengths until the chuckwagon slowed, then ground to a stop. The near ox bellowed, lowering his head and straining against the oxbow.

"Damn!" Stuck in the middle of the river, and nobody near enough to help. Besides, the drovers had their hands full with the herd. She'd have to get the wagon free by herself. After she tugged all the supplies and pots and pans forward in the wagon box to get as much weight as possible over the front wheels, she climbed down beside the team.

Water chilled her feet and legs, sending shivers through her body as she lowered herself to her thighs, then to her breasts before her feet sank into the silty riverbed. Holding on to the traces, she waded through the murky flow until she reached Samson's head. Grabbing the wooden **U** hanging beneath his wattles, she leaned her weight toward the far shore. "Come on, lad, pull."

The longhorn blinked his pink-rimmed eyes and blew warm breath from his damp black nostrils, then surged toward her, bellowing when the weight of the stranded wagon held him back. Cat urged him forward again and again, turning her head every now and then to see if any of the men had noticed her plight and decided to rescue her. After the first few days of "ma'ams" and gallant assistance with every chore, she'd managed to convince the hands she could hold her own. Now they expected her to behave as any man would, getting the wagon unstuck on her own.

Taking a deep breath, Cat grabbed one of Samson's longhorns and looked him in the eye. "Now then, lad, this time's the one." She let go and grasped the oxbow on either side of his head and faced him, then leaned all of her body weight backward. "Pull!"

Seconds passed, stretching to minutes while the ox

snorted and heaved against the yoke. At last, with a great creaking groan, the wagon lurched forward.

Before she could rejoice, Cat's long skirts tangled around her legs and she lost her footing, dropping beneath the swirling waters between the longhorn's great hooves. She held her breath and let go of the yoke with one hand, struggling to untangle the wet cloth clinging to her ankles as the current turned her this way and that, bouncing her against the animal's broad chest. Somehow she managed to get her feet under her again and thrust her head above the surface.

Water streamed from her nose as she coughed and spat, clinging to the ox with both hands as he carried her ahead across the current. After a minute she patted his massive shoulder. "Brave lad, Samson." She pulled herself hand over hand back to the wagon and up into the seat.

Cat pushed her streaming curls back from her face and grabbed the reins, her breath rattling in her chest as she guided the ox team through the shallows and onto the far bank. She pulled them to a halt and stood on the seat. So this was Indian Territory. By Quincy's reckoning, they were two thirds of the way to their journey's end. On impulse she unhooked her wet skirts and stepped out of them. The damned things had almost gotten her drowned.

Joe's voice hailed her as he brought his stallion alongside. "You okay? I saw you fall, but I was too far away to help none."

"Aye." She shook her hands, spraying bright droplets of water into the air. "I was wishing for a bath today." As a strange expression settled over his features, she followed his gaze to the wet bloomers clinging to her legs. "If you value your health, Joseph, dinna say a word."

"No'm." His lips twitched upward, and he covered his mouth, coughing, then waved a hand in the air. "Damn dust." Tipping his hat, he wheeled his mount and trotted away.

She lifted the sopping skirts from the seat and leaned over the wagon's high sides to wring out the water, then tossed the wadded garment far to the back, away from the bedrolls. For a moment she stared at her bloomers, the heavy brown cloth stuck to her legs, revealing her contours to all the world. Then she sat down on the hard seat again, lifted the reins, and clucked to the oxen. Proprieties didn't matter much right now, not near enough to risk her life. By God, if she was going to have to do a man's job, she might as well dress like one.

Geordie blinked and covered a yawn with his free hand, wincing at a fresh blister on his palm. He'd written late into the night to meet his deadline at the *Mercury*, then headed out at sunup to cut hay before he hurried to the opening ceremonies of the State Farmers Alliance convention.

Weariness ached in his back and neck and he closed his eyes, wondering how Catriona fared with her cattle drive. His sister never lacked grit, he had to give her that, although sometimes he questioned her common sense, especially when she turned down Will's offer to buy her out. But then, without her stubbornness she wouldn't be Cat, and he'd be grubbing in the ground on Skye with a footplow instead of writing for a living.

Still, it bothered him to see Will so miserable. He'd asked Sanapia how they were getting on, but she just grunted and went about her business, even though Ida and Effie did a splendid job of caring for the house and the bairns. They'd both make good wives someday. Too bad he couldn't feel toward Ida as he had toward Molly. Although he enjoyed her company and found Arthur bright and mannerly, he just couldn't see himself married, to her or anyone else, for that matter. He'd just about resigned himself to a bachelor's lonely life.

He opened his eyes with a start, realizing the opening address had begun while he catnapped.

"—the last year has been the most trying and critical period in the history of our order—"

He tugged his notebook from his pocket and found his lead pencil, jotting down as much as he could of Evan Jones's speech.

"—sore trials, disappointments, heartaches, dissensions, disintegration, and desertion." The speaker paused, sipping from a glass on the podium.

Geordie scribbled the words he recalled, playing them back through his mind.

"A period that threatened the very existence of our order and its business enterprises, and tried the very souls and patriotism of our membership—" The president of the Texas State Alliance paused, letting each delegate relive his own experiences over the past year.

Geordie's memories uncoiled at the president's words. The State Alliance had suffered several setbacks and blows since the high hopes of the year before. The faces around him reflected his own frustration.

Jones cleared his throat and went on to call for a redirection of strategies away from the merchants and middlemen and toward the supply of currency, blaming it for "the necessity of credit or mortgage," and "all the oppression of our people," and ending with a ringing cry for "just and intelligent legislative reformation."

The crowd rose to its feet, stamping and cheering. So, the Alliance leaders had abandoned all their other economic programs to concentrate on the currency issue. He wondered what his sister would have to say about that.

The rapid trilling of the twin brass bells on her windup alarm clock drew Catriona from the dark, comforting arms of sleep. Curbing an urge to smash the timepiece, she silenced its annoying clatter and sat up. Of their own accord, her fingers twisted the brass key, rewinding hidden springs to keep the black hands turning a tick at a time through another day.

Another three weeks to Pueblo. Halfway there. She pushed her tangled hair back from her face and gazed over the wagon's high side at the North Canadian River, its pearly-gray surface two shades darker than the sky in the glow of false dawn. In a circle around the glowing embers of the banked campfire, the cowhands lay rolled in their shakedowns. Around them, shapeless humps lay scattered across the prairie like boulders, only the smell of manure and an occasional stirring to give any sign of life. God, but she was sick of cattle.

A snatch of song floated to her from the far edge of the herd. She recalled her turn at watch, the slow pacing of the night horse beneath her as she sang Gaelic lullabies to soothe the bedded beasts. She had to admit there was a freedom in these open spaces, riding beneath the stars, her experienced cow pony heading a stray back into the herd. Too bad she'd been too tired to enjoy it. She could only imagine what it must be like for the men who drew the last two-hour watch just before dawn. She yawned and shivered in the morning chill. Not much worse for them than for her.

She tossed off the tarp, scattering drops of dew across the wagon bed, pulling her arm back in beneath the soogans, glad of the warmth of the thick quilts as she struggled into bloomers and one of Ian's old shirts. Getting dressed lying down was tricky enough, let alone doing it beneath the covers, but it was the only privacy the chuckwagon provided, and the only protection from the damp cold mornings as well. Dressed at last, she used the cover of darkness to relieve her bladder behind the wagon and wash her face and hands before the wrangler roused himself to gather in the remuda.

She lit her lantern and stoked the fire with wood she'd collected along the trail the day before. After she filled the five-gallon coffeepot and hung it from the pot rack over the fire trench, she busied herself slicing steaks from the side of beef in the back of the wagon and stirring up dough for biscuits.

When she'd filled the row of Dutch ovens with meat and shoveled hot coals over the baking sourdough, she set out the cups and plates on the worktable along with what Quincy called "reloading" tools—knives and forks. As the first rays of the sun peeped over the flat horizon, she pulled a covered dish from the chuckbox. She'd spent a pleasant half hour the day before picking wild goose plums, and she meant to give the men a special treat for breakfast. Around her, cowhands roused themselves and crawled out of their bedrolls, spooling the blankets inside their waterproof tarps and dumping them near the chuckwagon to be loaded up later.

"Morning, Miz Cat." Quincy's grizzled face appeared at

her shoulder. "If you ain't a sight prettier than the last trail cook I knowed." His stubbled cheeks split into a grin.

She flashed him a smile but kept on working. No matter how good or bad her food tasted, it had to be on time if they were to make their fifteen miles today. And somehow, today she planned to find time to sit and read the newspaper Joe had found for her at Camp Supply two days before—a *Fort Worth Gazette*, no more than a week old.

Wiping her hands on her apron, Cat turned toward the men clustered around the water barrel, splashing handfuls of cold water over their faces and passing around the common towel and comb. She pressed her thumbs and forefingers in a circle around her mouth, opening her hands outward to guide her voice. "Come and get it before I throw it out."

The men lined up, each helping himself to a tin plate and cup before he moved to the fire, their voices quiet as they speared steaks and biscuits with their forks and took their places cross-legged on the ground to eat.

Cat speared herself a piece of meat and a biscuit and rescued a few of the sweet, ripe plums, setting her plate aside to eat later. Climbing onto the plank seat of the wagon, she rummaged beneath the sacks of flour and beans for the slick feel of newsprint.

The rising sun cast long shadows across the pages as she savored the sharp smell of ink and devoured the news from home, reading aloud to herself. "Henry Bowlin, a respectable Arlington farmer, found out today that his boy had stolen a neighbor's (Morris Putnam's) horse and sold it in Fort Worth, where he was arrested for horse theft." She knew Henry, knew how he doted on his son. Poor man, he must be torn between his love for his son and his sense of right and wrong.

In the distance a lost calf bawled for its mother until a deeper lowing answered it. She wondered what Betsy and Duncan were about at this hour, no doubt still asleep in their beds. No matter how much she trusted Effie and Ida, she longed to know they were safe and well, to hold them in her arms again. And poor Geordie, trying to run the farm and keep up with his job at the *Mercury*. She should be there, but she knew she needed to be here as well. Damn the railroads and the stockyards, and damn the boll weevils most of all.

One by one the hands finished eating and dropped their tinware into the roundup pan to soak. Still quiet, the men sought out their horses and rode out to rouse the bawling cattle.

With a sigh she turned back to the newspaper. "One half million bricks were transported from Arlington today to Fort Worth to build a stove foundry." She wondered how long it had taken the brickmakers to shape and fire that many bricks.

As she turned the page, her eyes lit on a London by-line. "The Cotton Exchange here today took a firm stand against cotton bagging. As it is well known that Britain is the largest single market for cotton produced in the United States, experts agree that New York and New Orleans exchanges may soon follow suit, at the least in refusing to adjust tares for bales wrapped in materials other than jute."

Her jaw clenched. It made sense. After all, jute was a very important product of the British Empire. To accept cotton bagging, they'd be harming their own market. But for the farmers of Texas it meant one more blow against their struggle for economic freedom; for every step forward, the world forced them to take two back.

"Damn!" With great care she tore the column from the page, careful not to rip any article she hadn't yet read. Folding the rest of the *Gazette* into a neat square, she tucked it once more beneath the heavy cloth sacks of dry goods, then clambered down over the wheel, the strip of newsprint fluttering like a flag from her hand. She strode across the now-empty camp toward the fire trench and squatted close enough to warm the knees of her bloomers.

She held the ragged scrap of paper in the flames, watching the orange flames lick upward, leaving nothing but brittle black crepe where moments before words had been. As the flames seared her fingers, she dropped the last corner into the fire, watching it melt to nothing in the fire's red-orange heart. A wave of darkness settled over her. Perhaps Will had been right after all; this battle was too big for the likes of her.

Chapter 47

September 1889

Hands knotted together in her lap, Effie squirmed on the buckboard's high seat and craned her neck to squint along the railroad tracks toward the east. Anticipation surrounded the depot, filling the late afternoon with electricity. Crickets called from the dry grass, and the faint reek of coal smoke hung in the hot, dry Indian summer air.

Her eyes slid toward Geordie. He slouched on the seat beside her, leaning his forearms on his widespread thighs, the reins loose in the limp hands hanging between his knees. Sometimes his composure annoyed her. She turned back to the tracks. Where was the train, and why was it taking so long to arrive?

A small hand patted her arm. Betsy's gray-blue eyes narrowed. "Auntie Eff, how come Arthur had to stay at home? Doesn't Mama want to see him too?"

Effie caressed the golden curls. "Of course she does. But Arthur's mama thought it would be better to wait there. Your mama will see him when we get home."

Betsy's light brown eyebrows wrinkled, and she put her arm around her small brother's shoulders. "Well, Duncan and me don't think it's better."

"*Whist*, now. You must be patient. The train will be here

soon, and then we'll take your mama home, and you both can play with Arthur until bedtime."

Betsy flattened her lips together, then nodded and tugged Duncan toward the tail of the wagon box.

Trouble was, she agreed with the lass. No matter how tired Cat might be after the long trip, Effie wished Ida had agreed to come along, if only to keep her company and help her calm down. Cat's telegram had just given the day and time she'd arrive and nothing more. Anything could have happened to Joe in the last six weeks out on the trail. And the men who'd come back early had complained of the hard life and the wild cattle towns along the way. She'd heard tales of the way cowboys lived, gambling and drinking and shooting up towns, and the women— Maybe she should have been nicer to him before he left, not so coy.

Pressing her fingernails into her palms, she glanced back at the bairns playing on the wagon bed and wondered just how they would take to their mother's return. After all, Cat had been away six weeks, and that must seem very long to two small bairns. No doubt Betsy was old enough to be left with someone else, but Duncan seemed confused about who Catriona was, almost as if he'd forgotten her. A steam whistle shrieked in the distance. Well, he'd remember soon enough.

Duncan and Betsy cheered and clapped, jumping up and down in the back of the wagon as the locomotive chuffed closer, belching black smoke from its stack. The engine noise deafened Effie as the train slowed, gliding to a stop beside the depot. The mare shied and snorted, but Geordie grasped the reins and kept her from bucking or bolting. Effie climbed down over the spoked wheel and lifted the children out onto the platform, enclosing one small hand in each of hers.

"Arlington!" The conductor's voice rose above the hissing of the steam as the engineer bled the brakes.

Catriona grabbed up her carpetbag as the door of the coach opened. The car attendant set a heavy wooden box in front of the open door for a step, then took her bag, swinging it out and setting it beside him before he offered her his hand. She lifted her skirts, awkward after so many weeks in bloomers, and stepped down onto the platform, swaying with the odd sensation of standing still. "Thank you."

She reached for the heavy bag, lifting it with ease. Compared to the pot rack and the pots and pans in the chuckbox, the heavy bag weighed no more than a feather. She shaded her eyes with one hand, the long horizontal rays of the late sun making a world of silhouettes.

"Mama!" Betsy's voice rang out, and a small body raced across the wooden planking, curls streaming out behind. Thin, wiry arms wrapped themselves around Cat's thighs. "Oh, Mama, you're home."

Tears pricked at Cat's eyelids as she knelt and gathered the bairn against her. "There's my bonny lass."

Duncan strode forward, his lips set and his dark brows drawn.

Cat smiled. "And who might this fine lad be, then?"

Betsy giggled. "Oh, Mama, that's only Duncan."

Cat widened her eyes. "Why, and so it is. He's grown so much I hardly knew him." She reached for his hand and gave it a grown-up shake. "How do you do?"

A smile twitched the corners of his mouth, and he walked closer into the circle of her arms.

Cat held them tight against her. God, it had been so long. "I missed you."

Effie smiled down at her, her narrow fingers worrying the cord of her reticule. "And we missed you. Are you ready to go?" The lass grabbed the handle of the carpetbag, groaning as she hoisted it from the platform. "The wagon's this way." Effie's copper curls gleamed in the late afternoon sunlight.

Cat had forgotten just how lovely her sister was. No wonder Joe could talk of little else the past six weeks, poor lad. She stood, scooping the two bairns up, one on each hip. They squealed in delight as she followed Effie back across the passenger platform.

At the wagon Geordie gave her a peck on the cheek and lifted the bairns into the wagon one at a time before he handed his sisters onto the high seat.

Cat winced as she settled onto the hard plank, but her bruises had healed a bit on the long train ride through Kansas and the Oklahoma Territory. She held on as Geordie backed the horse away from the platform and headed into the narrow street. Cat grabbed the seat, then glanced up as they turned the corner and passed Will's office. All dark. He and Sanapia must be out on house calls already.

The sick emptiness of regret washed over her. If only— But no, she'd relived every moment of their last argument over and over again these last weeks, never finding anything she could have said to change the outcome. Still, she couldn't deny her love for him. She longed to see him, but dreaded it at the same time.

"Cat?" Effie's hand squeezed her upper arm, her eyes wide and color rising in her cheeks. "How's Joe?"

A smile tugged at her lips. At least someone had reason to be happy about a man. "Seemed right enough when I left him. He and Quincy headed south with the rest of the hands, bringing home the horses and the wagon the same day they put me on the train in Pueblo." She couldn't help teasing her sister a wee bit, holding back the words she knew the girl wanted to hear. "They'll be back in three weeks time, give or take a day or two."

Effie nodded, chewing her lip in silence for a moment as the outskirts of town rushed past behind her. "Did he—did he say anything about me?"

Cat laughed. "Aye, and precious little else the entire trip, to the point the other men threatened him if he didna cease."

Effie's smile blossomed, and her green eyes shone.

Geordie cleared his throat. "And the Pueblo Stockyards, did you get what you went after?"

Cat reached into the carpetbag and pulled out a bundle of wrinkled green bills, holding them up in front of two pairs of wide eyes. "You might say that."

Smells of coffee, tobacco, and molasses surrounded Will when he stepped through the doorway of the general store. A cowbell clacked as the door swung shut behind him. Frink's narrow face tipped up. "I'll be right with you, Doc."

Only one customer waited at the counter, a thin, rangy woman in a dress of patched chambray. She glanced at Will, then back at Frink's fingers. The merchant bent over the counter, totaling up her bill, his thin reddish mustache twitching as his lips moved and he touched the pencil to the paper. "That'll be seven fifty today, Miz Ransom."

She must be paying time prices; seven fifty was a lot of money for the few small items stacked on the counter. Her name sounded familiar, but it took Will a moment to figure it out. This was the mother of the young watermelon thief at the camp meeting.

The woman's thin lips pinched together. "Best put it on account, Mr. Frink."

The man's small eyes glittered. "Certainly. And by the way, how's the harvesting coming along?"

She hesitated, then bobbed her head again. "Fine, sir, just fine." She marked an **X** on the bottom of the bill Frink held out to her, then handed it back and turned away.

"Good day to you, ma'am. And my best to your husband and son." Frink smiled after her, though the warmth never traveled from his lips to his eyes.

The woman hurried toward the door without a reply, clutching the bag in her arms.

"Well, Doc, what can I do for you today?" Frink crossed his thin arms over his narrow chest, the empty smile still glued to his lips.

"It's about the accounts—" Will paused.

Frink's small eyes widened, and he held up one palm, gesturing for Will to wait while he scurried after the Ransom woman, bolting the door behind her and hanging a closed sign on the door. "Let's step into the back room if we're gonna talk business."

Will followed the small man to a curtained opening at the back of the store. Smells of stale food and unwashed linen closed around him as Frink pulled the curtain aside and ushered him through the narrow doorway. Sunlight glowed from the tiny room's one window, dimmed by a heavy layer of dust and cobwebs. Food crusted the pots and pans stacked on a small woodstove in one corner, and dirty dishes littered a rickety table. Frink motioned Will to a seat on a small wooden bunk covered with tousled gray sheets and ragged blankets, then sank down on the room's one chair.

Will eased himself onto the bed, wondering why a man would choose to live in such squalor. His eye fell on the large safe against the opposite wall. Perhaps that explained it. He'd seen men ruled by many demons, passions for strong drink or poker or sporting women, but Frink lived for money —to get it and to keep it. Pity edged the disgust roiling in his gut.

Frink's mustache quirked up, and the man's most charming voice rolled out of his smiling mouth. "Now, what's this about the accounts?"

Will pulled the envelope from his pocket, the same he'd tried to hand Catriona before the cattle drive. "I want to buy them back from you." He lifted the flap and fanned the greenbacks. "It's all still here. I haven't spent a dime."

Frink's small eyes fastened on the bills, and the tip of his tongue rimmed his mouth, but he shook his head. "Well now, those accounts ain't for sale. You understand, they're worth more to me than I paid."

Will ground his back teeth together. He should have expected something like this. "How much?"

Frink's eyes narrowed as they flickered from the money to Will's face. He named a figure.

Will clenched his fists to control the anger raging through him. "That's three times what I sold them for."

Frink shrugged. "Take it or leave it. I already told you I don't want to sell."

Will stood, towering over the small man. "You know I don't have that much."

Frink jumped up and backed toward the doorway to the store, then stood trembling in front of the curtain, his arms crossed over his narrow chest. "You don't mind leaving by the back door, do you, Doc? It's probably better for both of us if our dealings ain't common knowledge."

Will turned the black ceramic knob and jerked open the battered door, slamming it behind him. He stood in the alley for a moment, letting the quiet morning shadows surround him. How could he have been so stupid? He should have known Frink only wanted those accounts to keep the farmers in debt; that way he could charge them interest and triple the prices of their supplies.

Frink was a menace, but the man had been right about one thing—the fewer people who knew about this, the better. He could imagine what Catriona would say. Not that there was much chance she'd ever want anything to do with him again anyhow; she'd made that clear enough before the cattle drive. Still, her opinion mattered to him more than he cared to admit.

Catriona lifted her hand from Reuben's forehead and turned to the lad's mother. "How long has he had this fever?"

Violet Williams chewed her lip, answering in a soft voice. "Two days. I called just as soon as I heard you'd returned."

Cat bit back angry words. Some folks put off calling a doctor because of superstition or ignorance, but she'd never known Vi to be one of them. The woman must have had a good reason for taking such a risk with her son. Cat gentled her tongue. "Why did you not call Dr. Bascom then?"

Vi closed her eyes for a moment before squaring her shoulders and lifting her chin. "We hadn't enough money, and we couldn't afford to go any deeper into debt." Dark smudges deepened her eye sockets, and her brown hair fuzzed around her head, making her pale skin even whiter. Vi probably hadn't slept since her son took sick. "I'm afraid I don't know when we can pay you."

Anger and impatience crept into Cat's voice. "And since when is money to be considered when a bairn is ailing?"

Tears glittered in the woman's eyes, and a slight bitterness edged her tired voice. "Since the good doctor sold his accounts to Mr. Frink. We'd all but paid off the crop lien, but now, with the bills for Reuben's birth tacked on, we're in debt almost as deeply as before."

The words hit as hard as any blow. Sold his accounts? Will? And to Frink? Her mind refused to make sense of it for a moment. He had no reason she knew of. True, some of his patients couldn't pay on time, but enough did to cover his office expenses. And those who couldn't pay in cash brought him chickens and vegetables. He wasn't about to starve or go broke.

The small lad on the bed moaned, and Cat set aside her confusion to concentrate on getting him better. "What has he eaten?"

Vi's brows drew together. "Not much. I've been giving him well water. He'll hardly take anything else."

"It may be tainted. Best put some branch water on to boil." Cat reached in her bag for dried purple coneflower and snakeroot. "Have you any dried bilberries?"

The woman nodded. "I put up as many as I could. What is it— What's wrong with my son?"

"Near as I can tell, it's typhoid."

Violet swayed, and her voice dropped to just above a whisper. "Is he going to die?"

"Not if I can help it. Now go and fetch me that water in a teapot." She kept her voice calm and confident.

Vi hurried out toward the kitchen and the creek just beyond.

Cat rolled up her sleeves and measured out dried herbs into a small cloth bag for the tisane, her eyes straying again and again to the stricken lad.

He stirred and moaned, then opened his eyes. "Mama?" His voice creaked like an old man's.

She shushed him, caressing the small round apple cheek. What if it was too late, and she lost him? No, she had to believe he'd survive. And no matter what else happened, she'd see to it Will Bascom regretted the day he sold out his patients to a weasel named Frink.

Chapter 48

October 1889

A confusion of smells swirled through the stuffy air as delegates sidled past Geordie on their way out the door. He frowned down at his notes, trying to make sense of the words he'd scribbled during Macune's speech.

An arm fell across his back, and he found himself squeezed in a viselike grip. "Young Galbraith, I thought it was you." Macune's broad face beamed, and his mustache curved up into a smile.

Geordie cleared his throat to hide his consternation. "Sir, what a pleasant surprise. I had no idea you'd remember me."

Macune chuckled. "Nonsense, boy. I haven't been gone so long I'd forget my old friends." He stroked his mustache with thumb and forefinger. "So what'd you think of my plan?"

Geordie swallowed. "To be perfectly frank with you, sir, I'm not sure I understand all of it."

Macune's thick brows lowered. "Well, son, put simply, there's only just so much money." He slid his thumbs under his lapels, his fingers curving into the front of his jacket. "Every year in the fall, money gets tight and prices go down. So what happens to the farmer?"

Geordie tapped his lead pencil on the notebook in his hand. "Well, he has to sell his cash crops for low prices."

Macune nodded, his eyes alight. "Exactly. Then, every spring, money loosens up. And what does that mean to the farmer?"

Geordie pursed his lips. "Prices rise, so he has to buy seed and supplies at a higher cost."

Macune clapped him on the shoulder with one large hand. "So my subtreasury plan would mean putting more currency out there in the autumn to keep prices from falling when the farmer sells, and removing some of the greenbacks in the spring to keep prices from rising when he buys."

Geordie nodded, scribbling the words in his book. If it worked, the plan sure would have helped Cat this year. Joe's estimates of the cotton crop had been pretty close to right, and with the cost of the cotton bagging and the six percent tare, it was a damn good thing she'd driven the cattle to Pueblo. "Thank you, sir. I believe I understand it better now."

"My pleasure, son, but enough of this talk. What do you think of St. Louis?"

"I'm not really sure what to think. It's big, that's for sure." Geordie glanced around the echoing hall.

Macune's elbow nudged his shoulder. "Wait'll you see Washington, D.C., and New York City." One eyelid flickered. Was that a wink, or just a twitch? "Say, how's that lovely sister of yours? A shame, a woman like her living without a husband, but I bet she's remarried by now."

He shook his head, and opened his mouth to speak, but Macune continued.

"No? If I was there—" He gave his head a little shake. "Never mind. I've been reading your work, young man, and I like what I see. You're going places, mark my words." He clapped Geordie on the shoulder again. "Will you excuse me, son? I've got to talk to a few other folks." He winked again. "I'll be in touch."

Geordie stared after him. Did he mean it, or was it just his way of being polite?

• • •

Effie wrung her hands and paced the plank floor of the porch. What was taking him so long? It had been an hour since she saw him riding beside Quincy in the chuckwagon, headed down the lane toward the corral with the extra cow ponies tethered to the tailgate. What if he'd changed his mind on the way back from Pueblo? What if Quincy had talked him into stopping with some sporting girl along the way? What if—

She glanced in through the kitchen window, where Ida leaned over the kitchen table, writing another of her private letters. As if she heard Effie's thought, Ida raised her head and lifted one eyebrow.

Get a hold of yourself, lass. Effie nodded, then took a deep, calming breath and walked to the wooden bench Ian had built to sit on in the evenings. Funny, sometimes she could hardly remember her brother-in-law's features at all, but his presence stayed clear in her memory no matter how long he'd been gone. If he were here, she knew he'd be able to ease her mind. She sank down on the hard wooden seat and folded her hands in her lap. Yes, that was better. It wouldn't do to let Joe know how nervous she really was.

Footfalls rounded the corner, and there he stood at the bottom of the steps.

She sat quite still, her heart pounding as she drank in the sight of him after two long months.

His face glowed with scrubbing, and water darkened his white-blond hair, the marks of the comb still showing. He wore a clean shirt tucked into his denim trousers, and the toes of his boots shone with fresh polish. "Effie?"

She rose and walked toward the steps, forcing a calm smile to her lips, then held out her hand, the gracious hostess greeting a guest. "Joe, welcome back. It's so nice to see you." She gestured to the bench behind her. "Would you care to sit a spell?"

He hitched up his trousers. "Well, I been sitting for the last two months, either in the saddle or in the wagon. What I'd relish is a nice long walk."

Warmth stole into her cheeks, but she hoped he wouldn't notice. "That would be lovely. I'll just fetch my bonnet." She forced herself to take her time walking across the porch and through the kitchen door, then answered Ida's questioning look. "Going for a walk." She raced down the hallway to her room and pinned the new straw hat in place. She glanced in the cheval glass at her reflection, hoping he'd like the way she looked, then hurried back through the kitchen and out the screen door. "I trust I didn't keep you waiting too long."

"No'm. And may I say it was worth the wait? That's a right pretty hat you're wearing." He climbed the stairs and crooked his elbow.

She slipped her hand under his arm, appreciating the warmth of his skin and the hard plane of his arm muscle beneath his shirt. He smelled of lye soap and leather, with a faint undertone of horse. A gentle warmth tingled through her body as he guided her down the steps and out across the fields.

Copper and tan prairie grass glittered in the warm sunlight, tugging at her skirts as they waded through fields dotted with late asters and goldenrod. A goldfinch circled overhead, then landed a few feet away to peck at a loose spray of switch grass, its stem heavy with seed.

She fought down panic as the silence between them lengthened. She slid her eyes toward him, but he walked on, his face closed. She cast about in her mind for a clever remark, but it had to be intimate as well—something to encourage him and hint at her interest without seeming pushy or wanton. But, dammit, she *felt* wanton! In misery she held her peace.

At last they reached a stand of oak trees on a slight rise. "Care to sit?" His pale eyes flickered over her face.

She nodded and sank down beneath the tree, tucking her skirts around her ankles as she drew her knees up to her chin. She wondered why he'd changed his mind about sitting in the short time since they left the porch.

He rubbed his palms on his pant legs, then hunkered down a few feet away, picking up an old acorn and rolling it between his fingers, his eyes averted. "I missed you." She almost didn't catch his quiet words.

Her heart thudded in her ears. "And I missed you." She paused. "I really am glad you're back."

His face lifted and his gaze met hers, a hint of a smile around his lips. "You are?"

She nodded.

He rose and came toward her, kneeling at her feet. His words poured out in a rush. "I went loco out there without you. I thought about nothing else. And then one night it hit me—this is love. I'm in love with you, Eff. Will you marry me?"

A voice inside her head shouted *yes, yes, yes,* but she bit her tongue and took a deep breath. She'd waited too long for this moment to spoil it by agreeing too soon. She curved her palm along his smooth cheek and relaxed her lips into a tiny smile. "I need some time to think about it."

The sip of hot coffee turned bitter in Catriona's mouth as she gazed out the kitchen window at the buggy wheeling into the drive. She thought Will had understood when she told him she could no longer work with him. Even though little Reuben survived his bout with typhoid, she couldn't forget what Will had done by selling his accounts to Frink, and how close the wee lad had come to death.

After setting the cup down, she strode out onto the porch and closed the door behind her. She told herself she wanted to keep the chill wind from blowing through her house, but she knew it was also to protect her family from hearing another confrontation with Will. No matter what he said, she'd not back down and change her mind, no matter how dire the emergency. She pressed her lips together, rehearsing her words in her mind.

The buggy pulled to a stop a few paces from the steps, kicking dust into the air. Will leapt over the tall wheel and took the steps two at a time, his auburn hair frowsy and his face haggard.

Cat's throat tightened at the panic in his eyes, her speech forgotten.

His voice rang hollow in the morning air, like an icy

wind blowing over a grave, his words simple, without apology or explanation. "It's Nana. I need your help."

Fear leapt from his eyes into her heart, tightening her chest. She swallowed, then nodded. "I'll get my things." She hurried to the herb pantry, shouting for Sanapia to mind the bairns until she returned. She grabbed up her bag and a shawl on her way back to the porch.

Will waited at the buggy to lift her over the wheel, then clambered in and slapped the horse's rump with the reins.

Cat fell back against the seat as the fields flew by on either side, the brown grass dotted with dried stalks of wildflowers and shrubs blackened with frost. Icy wind tingled her nostrils as she studied Will's profile, trying to understand how she could have been so wrong about him, how she could have loved him, trusted him, shared herself with a man who would conspire with the likes of Frink to enslave his patients for a few dollars—Judas and the twenty pieces of silver.

She swallowed salty tears and turned her thoughts to the work ahead. She didn't even know what ailed Will's grandmother, but it must be serious for him to ask her for help. Nana Bascom had come to mean a great deal to Catriona. If there was anything she could do, any way she could help the old woman, she would never hesitate, no matter what Will might have done.

He urged the horses on, the buggy wheels eating up the miles to Will's childhood home. Only his skill at the reins kept them on the road. At this speed, all she could do was cling to the seat and hope they didn't meet anyone coming the other way.

Cat studied the old farmhouse as it grew closer, wondering what it must have been like for a young boy, losing his parents and coming to live here with his grandmother. She could never doubt his love and concern for Nana, or the old woman's love for him. He'd told Cat how his grandmother had sold off the farmland years before in order to pay his way through medical school.

She wondered again why he still stayed here whenever he could get away from the office, why he didn't sell it and buy something more convenient. The house was too small and too far from town to ever make a good hospital. It could be Nana who wanted to stay out here, or perhaps he'd never really been serious about his dream, or about anything else he'd ever said to her.

She clutched her bag as he rounded the corner into the drive and hauled on the reins to stop the horse at the foot of the front steps. As he reached to help her from the buggy, she held up one hand to stop him, her eyes seeking his. "I want you to understand, Will Bascom, I'm no doing this for you; it's for Nana I'm here." She almost regretted the bitter words as they fell from her mouth, but he had to understand where she stood.

His eyes registered pain, but his mouth firmed into a thin line. "That doesn't matter now. Come on." He lifted her down, then grasped her arm and half-led, half-dragged her through the door and up the front stairs. "It's dropsy. She's had it before, but never this bad." He tugged Cat through an open bedroom door, taking her shawl and setting her bag on a table near the bed where the old woman lay.

Ignoring the faint scent of camphor and mildew in the bedclothes, Catriona leaned her ear against Nana's fragile chest. There, between the short gasping breaths, the old woman's heart thudded, a rapid and irregular beat.

Nana's lips moved, but no words came out. A cough racked the thin body, making the veins in her wrinkled neck stand out. Cat's hand traveled over the swollen belly and legs, the same as Gran had described so many years before on Skye.

After finishing her examination, Catriona moved to the doorway and beckoned to Will, waiting until he stepped past her into the hall. She closed the door behind them with a soft thud. The big old house lay quiet, the air still and heavy with the faint scent of decay.

Will's brow knotted, and the corners of his mouth turned down. Fear darkened his hoarse whisper. "All I know is to give her opium for the pain. But that won't help much." He swore under his breath. "If only I had something to strengthen her heartbeat, make it more regular."

Cat bit her lip. She knew of a heart tonic, but it was not without danger. "I—I have something that might help."

Will's eyes widened and he clasped her shoulders. "Then what are you waiting for?"

She held up her hand. "If she's too weak, or if she takes too much, it might stop her heart altogether."

His shoulders sagged and his face grayed. No matter how they argued, Will had meant something to her once, and it hurt watching him struggle with this difficult choice. Without the tonic his grandmother would die. But the medicine might kill her as well.

At last he spoke, his voice weary. "If we stand by and do nothing, she'll die. At least this way she has a chance." Tears glistened in his eyes.

Taking a deep breath, Cat nodded, then turned and opened the door, striding toward the woman on the bed. She reached in her bag for the small stoppered bottle of heart tonic. Digitalis, Gran called it, for the foxgloves it came from. She set it on the bedside table and her medicine spoon beside it. "Help me sit her up. It'll make it easier for her to breathe."

Will brought extra pillows and lifted the narrow shoulders so Cat could prop them behind the bony back. As he settled the old woman against the bolster, her eyelids flickered open and she croaked out Catriona's name.

Cat took the gnarled hand in her own. "Don't try to talk. Does sitting up help?"

The old woman nodded.

"I've brought some tonic, an old family receipt." She smiled, careful to keep the concern from her voice. No sense adding worry to the woman's discomfort. "It tastes horrid, I'm told."

The corners of her wrinkled mouth turned up, and her hooded eyes sparkled.

Cat pulled the stopper from the small bottle and poured dark liquid into the silver spoon, then slid it into the old woman's open mouth.

Nana wrinkled her nose as she pursed her lips around the spoon, and she shuddered as she swallowed.

Cat stoppered the bottle, then held it out to Will, warning him not to exceed the proper dosage. "I'll stay until she's resting easy."

He nodded, his haunted eyes turning back to the form on the bed. "What do we do in between?"

She settled into a rocker near the window and pulled her knitting from her bag. "Nothing we *can* do but wait."

Chapter 49

December 1889

The final bang of the gavel reverberated through Catriona's head.

"Sold!" A cheer went up from a group standing near the back, people she recognized from Alliance meetings. At least they'd kept it in the family.

She closed her eyes for a moment against the tears pricking her eyelids, almost wishing she hadn't come. After all, what had she hoped for? She'd known there was no way the Alliance board members would come up with the money to pay their creditors and save the Exchange. Still, it took a moment to sink in. It was over, truly over, never to be again.

Something about the sheriff's auction reminded her of a funeral. Perhaps she'd forced herself to watch the sale of the Exchange Building to the highest bidder because it would help her believe all her hopes for the financial programs were truly dead and gone. Like Ian, like Molly and her bonnie wee son.

Geordie had tried to explain the new National Alliance programs, their demands to Congress. She understood most of them, especially the commerce commission and freight rate railroad planks. And now, with rumors flying that Jim Hogg would run for governor on a railroad regulation ticket, that much might become a reality.

She liked the sound of Macune's new subtreasury plan, although she found it hard to understand how it could help the poor farmer as much as the joint-note plan or the cotton exchange. She only hoped Macune was right, but she wondered how long it would take the new bill to pass both the House and the Senate. And what about now, today, this year? Folks like the Williams family needed help to keep their farms and to raise healthy bairns.

Will's part in their problems still rankled, but she had to be honest with herself and admit how relieved she was to be able to see him, spend time with him, even if it was only when she went to check on Nana's progress. They'd been lucky. Gran's heart tonic had worked. Of course, Will's grandmother was a strong woman, and he'd given her the best of care, moving his office to the house so he could be nearby if she needed him during the day and hiring Sanapia to stay with her while he went on house calls at night.

A hand tapped her on the arm.

Cat turned and nodded to an Alliance member, reaching for his name—Ramsey, Randall?

The man smiled, showing gaps where teeth had been. "Miz Macleod, me and the boys just want to thank you for all you done for the Exchange. We ain't gonna forget." He shoved his hands into his overall pockets and rocked back on his heels, his eyes flickering over the room, everywhere except in her direction.

Cat struggled to think of something appropriate to say. *Congratulations* or *good luck* refused to leave her lips. Perhaps a question would be safest. "And what is it you plan to do with the building now?"

The farmer pulled his hands from his pockets, rubbing them together palm to palm, and his eyes lit from within. "We got all kinds of plans for keeping her going. We're gonna change her name to Alliance Commercial Exchange. Ain't that purty?"

Cat nodded, wishing for some excuse, some way to get away from the man. Not that she didn't wish them well. She did, but she felt as if they were dancing on a lover's grave.

"And we're gonna offer stuff like the big stores do, you know, like when you buy a wagon before a certain day, you get a chance to win a sewing machine, or for every ten dollars you spend, you get a chance on a new cookstove." The man's eyes shone. She couldn't manage to share his delight at the group's cleverness and business sense.

"How interesting." In desperation she thrust out her hand. "It's been lovely chatting, but I must get home."

The man's huge paw crushed hers. "I hope you'll still be one of our regular customers, Miz Macleod."

"Yes, well, thank you." She hurried out the doors and down the steps, then turned around for one last look, her sadness a lump in the pit of her stomach. She knew she could never bring herself to come here to shop again, Alliance Commercial Exchange or no. It would never be the same.

She straightened her shoulders. It was only a building, after all. The Alliance was more than that; it was people, poor people fighting for a just cause. This was just a setback. The members would never give up until this country was free of those who preyed on the poor and the weak.

Cat stepped aside to let Will brush past on his way out of Nana's bedroom. The faint man-scent of him stirred something inside her, but she steeled herself against it and moved toward the bed. "And how is my patient getting on today?"

Nana's withered mouth curved up and her hooded eyes sparkled. "I think thee must tell me." Her voice had lost its croupy, liquid sound.

Cat leaned her ear against the narrow chest, listening to the strong, steady beating of the old woman's heart and the clear passage of air in the lungs. She raised her head and gave Nana a bit of a smile, then lifted the hem of the old cotton gown and felt the withered legs. Good. The swelling was almost gone. She palpated the woman's belly through her nightclothes. Soft, with the organs near normal size again. She tilted her head. "Quite good. You've been following orders, then." She lifted the bedclothes, smoothing them over the old woman's lap.

"We Friends are strong believers in common sense. What does it profit thee to call a healer if thee does not heed her good council?" Nana dug her elbows into the mattress and wriggled upright against the bolster. "I only wish thee would take mine."

Cat's brows drew together, and she chewed her lip. "And what advice might that be, then?"

One gnarled hand caught hers and held it until she looked into the old woman's eyes. "William belongs with thee."

Cat tugged her hand away and gave her head a wee shake. "I dinna think so."

"Thee are much too harsh with him." The old eyes held hers.

She kept her tone soft, even. "I know he is your grandson, but I canna forget the people he hurt."

"And does it not matter that he did it for thee?"

Cat's heart pounded in her chest. "For me?" The old woman must be mistaken; she was ill, confused.

Nana drew her lips together and nodded. "Did thee never ask thyself where he got the money he offered for thy cattle?"

She sank down on the bed beside the old woman and shook her head. "I dinna think to ask." She swallowed. If what Nana said was true, he'd sold his accounts to buy the cattle, to keep her from driving them across country. "That still doesna make it right." Her voice sounded weak in her ears.

Nana's face softened. "He sees that now." She patted Cat's hand atop the counterpane. "But did thee know he has tried to buy back the accounts from that money changer?"

She hadn't known, hadn't guessed, or even let herself wonder about it. Her righteous certainty sank in her belly like a stone. "And?" Her voice quavered just above a whisper.

"And the man refused to sell them back for less than three times what he'd paid for them. William had no choice but to keep the money." Nana laced her withered fingers together and rested them on her chest just above the folded-back bedclothes. "He plans to buy land to build a hospital, but so far he has found nothing at the right price."

Cat nodded. Still, it made no sense, selling the accounts

to buy cattle he didn't really want, trying to buy them back from Frink when he needed the money for a hospital. Her mind reeled with confusion. She needed time to think, to sort this all out. "But why did he do it in the first place? I dinna ask him for help."

Nana shrugged, her gentle old voice caressing Catriona's ear. "Sometimes love makes people do very foolish things."

Warmth crept into Cat's cheeks. Was the old woman talking about Will, or about her?

Nana reached out and touched a gnarled finger to Cat's face. "Could thee grant a sick old woman a boon? Give my grandson one more chance."

Will shifted both reins to his left hand and touched his chest to reassure himself the note from Catriona still snuggled in his breast pocket near his heart. Even through his heavy coat the paper gave a muffled crackle.

Please come for Sunday dinner at one o'clock.
Catriona

The words echoed in his head as he unbuttoned the wool greatcoat and tugged his pocket watch from his vest. Almost one now. Leaning forward on the tufted leather seat, he urged the horse into a trot, then worked his gloves off, one hand at a time, his sweaty palms drying in the icy air. No woman had made him this nervous since he left Arlington to go east to medical school.

Hope and despair roiled in him. Ever since Cat found out about his dealings with Frink, she'd refused to meet his eye, to talk with him, to work with him. Not that he blamed her; he'd been downright stupid not to figure out what Frink was up to. And he knew some of his patients thought twice about calling him now, even for serious problems.

Why, he wouldn't have blamed her if she'd turned him away when he'd come to ask her to help with Nana, but he was grateful she hadn't. If it wasn't for Cat's heart tonic, he doubted Nana would still be alive. And now that his grandmother grew stronger each day, he knew it wouldn't be long before Cat would stop visiting the house, and then he'd have to learn to live without her again, unless—

He didn't dare hope she'd changed her mind. After all, the situation remained the same. Frink wouldn't sell the accounts unless he got back triple what he'd paid, and Will just didn't have that kind of money. But what else could the invitation mean? A small spark of hope kindled inside him.

He slowed the horse to turn into the drive, admiring the house Ian had built as he drew near it. Smoke curled up from both chimneys, and in each of the three gables one tall window reflected the weak winter sunlight. It was a fine house, the kind of house Catriona deserved, just as Ian had been the kind of man she deserved.

No wonder she had twice refused to marry him. There was no way Will could measure up to her memories, plain and simple. He'd been crazy ever to imagine he could, even for a minute.

Why, she'd probably invited him here because she felt sorry for him, and wanted to tell him they could be friends again. Or maybe she wanted to talk to him alone about Nana.

He reined in, walking the gelding to cool him down. It was too cold outside for man or beast, let alone a horse hitched to a buggy. After he led the roan into a vacant stall, he wiped down the rough winter coat and forked fresh hay into the manger.

Trudging across the hard-rimed mud of the yard toward the kitchen door, Will wondered at the quiet. Everybody must be inside because of the cold, or maybe they'd decided to start eating dinner without him.

As he mounted the steps, the door swung open and Cat stepped outside. He'd never seen her look so beautiful.

Black curls haloed her smiling face. "Come in out of the cold, then." Her sweet voice held a note of intimacy, or did he imagine it? She held the door open and ushered him into a kitchen redolent with smells of roasting beef, then held out her arms for his coat and muffler.

His eyes drank in the sight of her as he shed his outerwear.

She wore a simple dress the same color as her China-blue eyes, its high neck and fitted bodice clinging to her body. Her hand brushed his as she gathered his greatcoat to her bosom, and sensuous memories engulfed him. "Please have a seat. I'll just hang this in the hallway." She turned away, the back of her skirts swaying with each step.

Get a grip on yourself, partner. He settled in an armchair, casting about for something to say. "So where are the children today?" Silence lay over the house, except for Cat's heels clicking back toward him from the hall.

She swept through the door and smiled, tilting her head to one side. "I sent them all to a play party, with Sanapia as a chaperone." She laughed. "Not that Joe and Effie need one. She holds him to one kiss a day, poor lad."

She folded her strong, slender hands together, her skin white against the deep blue of her skirts. "I'm that glad you could come. The dinner willna be ready for another hour, but I hoped you might give me some business advice."

Disappointment smothered the last embers of hope. So, that was the reason. He forced a smile to his lips. "Sure, what do you want to know?"

She sank down onto a footstool near his knees, her skirts spreading around her. His eyes blurred. She looked for a moment like a giant-size bachelor's button, black in the center, haloed in blue. Bachelor, that's what he was, and doomed to remain one. He knew now if he couldn't have this woman for his wife, he'd go to his grave unmarried.

She leaned forward, her elbows on her knees and her chin in her hands. "I understand you've been searching for land for a hospital, so you're familiar with prices and property values."

He nodded. "I've looked some." Nana must have told her. "Why?"

She lifted her shoulders in a slight shrug. "I've thought of disposing of part of the farm, a few acres. What do you think it would be worth?"

He leaned back in the rocker, trying to mask his surprise. After all she'd been through to keep the farm together and free of debt, it made no sense for her to part with any of it unless she needed the money. This might be the chance he'd been waiting for, to help her, and to make his dream come true at the same time. Her property would be the perfect location for a hospital—far enough from town for peace and quiet and plenty of fresh air but near enough to be convenient for patients. He cleared his throat. "Well, that would depend on which acres."

She rose from the low seat, her skirts floating down around her slender ankles. "Come upstairs with me, then. You can see the very spot from the window."

He followed her up the narrow stairway, mesmerized by the swaying of her skirts and the faint woman-musk rising in her wake as she led him into a bedroom. When his gaze fell on a battered cloth bag hanging from a hook in the wall, he realized it must be Catriona's own room. It was like her, beautiful but simple and honest.

She beckoned him to the window and pointed. "Down the drive and toward town, there, where the pecan grove stands." Stepping away, she settled herself on the bed near the high, carved headboard, her skirts spread across the log cabin quilt. "And what do you think, then?"

"I think I'd like to buy it, but I couldn't offer as much as someone else." He named a price, offering all the money he had. It wouldn't leave him anything to build with, but at least it would be a start. "Will you sell it to me?"

She shook her head. "No, I canna."

He turned away, the sweet taste of hope turning to ashes on his tongue. So, that said it all. She'd sell to someone else, but not to him. He stared out the window at the small grove of pecan trees glistening in the winter sun.

In the distance a bull bellowed, a deep roar of desire. A heifer answered, the higher, lighter bawl of a coquette.

Cat pleated the cloth of her skirt with her fingers, afraid to say the next words. So far, her plan had worked so well, but what if he didn't want her after all? What if she made a fool of herself after telling him no twice? She drew in a deep breath. "I canna sell it, because I plan to give it to my husband as a wedding gift."

He turned to her, his mouth open and his eyes wide. "Husband?" Pain colored his deep voice.

She bit her lip and shook her head, trying to keep the

trembling out of her voice. "He hasna asked me yet, but I was hoping he might this afternoon."

Understanding lit his eyes as he strode toward her and dropped to one knee beside the bed. Reaching up, he took her hand in his and gazed into her eyes. "Catriona Macdonald Galbraith Macleod, would you do me the honor of becoming my wife?"

Tears filmed her eyes, and for a moment she couldn't breathe. A smile spread across her face, and she reached out one hand to caress his cheek. "Aye, and gladly."

Chapter 50

Catriona clung to the seat of the buggy, her ivory lace veil whipping the tufted leather behind her as the countryside blurred past in the winter afternoon. An icy wind numbed her cheeks and fingertips as she burrowed deeper under the carriage rug and gazed at her new husband, unable to control her chuckles of delight.

He looked about twelve years old, bundled up in his greatcoat, hunched forward over the reins, urging the roan to higher and higher speeds as they hurtled down the road from the church to the farm. He'd told her about the old frontier custom of giving a prize to the first person to arrive at the wedding feast after the ceremony. Getting married in Texas wasn't so very different from weddings on Skye, with their *creeling* and *bottling* traditions. Here the people held races and something called a *shivaree* instead. It sounded like fun in a hurly-burly fashion.

She tugged the rug up over her nose, breathing in the faint smells still clinging to it from their lovemaking along the creek last summer. Her body tingled at the memories of their pleasure. She was looking forward to her wedding night.

"What the—?" Will hauled at the reins, bringing the

horse to a rapid stop, the gelding's neck arching as it sidestepped and blew.

Cat sat forward, wondering why they were stopping. They still had almost a mile to go before they reached the farm, and the others were close behind.

A thick rope stretched across the narrow country lane, with two burly young men each holding one end. The smaller of the two spoke up. "Afternoon, Doc. Gus Ransom, remember?"

Cat nodded, remembering the lad's face. The young watermelon thief from the camp meeting.

The lad nodded his head toward the other youth. "This here's my partner. We heard you was passing this way after your wedding and we wanted to offer our congratulations."

Will nodded. "Thanks. Now, if you wouldn't mind lifting your rope, we'll be on our way."

Gus grinned. "Well now, Doc, we'd like to oblige you, but I'm afeared we'll have to charge you some toll to cross here."

A faint thudding of hoofbeats drew Cat's attention out the buggy's back window. In the distance a buckboard rattled toward them, coming fast. It must be Effie and Joe, trying to beat them home.

Will glanced behind him, and a devilish smile lifted the corners of his mouth. "Tell you what. I'll pay you double if you'll stop that buckboard coming down the road and keep them here, oh, say five minutes or so."

"Sure thing, Doc." Gus held out his hand as Will dug in his trouser pocket.

The other lad laughed aloud. "Hey, it's Joe Vanzee and his girl. This is gonna be fun."

Will dropped a handful of silver into the outstretched palm, and the two boys dropped the rope, letting the horse pull the buggy across before they tightened it to waist level again.

"Giddap." Will snapped the reins and the roan pulled away.

Cat leaned back, her happiness complete as she looked forward to the afternoon and evening ahead. Sanapia would have the wedding feast spread by the time they arrived. But instead of sitting at the head of the table through three seatings of guests as she and Ian had on Skye, the folks here would serve themselves and balance their plates on their laps barbecue style, laughing and talking as they all ate at once.

And then they'd strike up some fiddle music and dance, with a caller's singsong voice reminding everybody what the steps were. And later, after their guests went home, she and Will would climb the stairs, and for the first time since Ian died, a man would sleep beside her in the tall bed.

"Whoa." Will reined the horse in at the steps and vaulted down out of the buggy. He reached across the seat and scooped her into his arms, then carried her up the steps to the front door and turned the handle.

Cat's arms closed around his neck and she snuggled against his shoulder, breathing in the man-scent of him as he swung the door wide and carried her across the threshold into the front hall. He set her on her feet, and she kept her arms around his neck, pressing her body against his.

He smiled down at her. "Howdy, Mrs. Bascom."

"I love you, Mr. Bascom." She stood on tiptoe, pressing her lips against his.

His arms tightened around her, and his tongue darted into her open mouth.

Cat poured all the hunger of the last months into her kiss, her heart beating and her breath coming in short gasps.

"Let's have none of that in front of the guests, now."

The voice startled Cat, and she pulled away to stare.

Lewis Price stood in the doorway of the kitchen, chewing on a fried chicken leg, a grin across his round face. "Can't you two wait until later?" The undertaker winked. "Say, what's my prize for getting back here from the church first anyhow?"

With trembling fingers Will undid the last button and took one step back as Catriona lifted the embroidered white nightgown over her head. She stood beside the bed, her body glistening white in the steady glow of the kerosene lamp. Black curls tumbled over her shoulders, all but hiding the glory of her breasts.

He drank in the sight of her narrow waist and smooth belly, the elegance of her slender legs, the dark mysterious triangle of her womanhood. His groin tightened. He'd never seen her nude except by moonlight. "God, but you're beautiful."

Her eyes blazed at him and her soft lips curved upward in invitation. She held out her arms.

He opened his shirt at collar and cuffs, then tugged it over his head in one motion. His fingers fumbled at the buttons of his fly, then he stepped out of his trousers and gathered her warm body to him, unable to believe the softness of her flesh against his. He sought her parted lips, covering them with his, savoring the sweetness of her tongue.

She sank back onto the bed, her arms encircling his neck, tugging him down atop her. The doeskin softness of her belly welcomed him as she lifted her pelvis, rocking against him.

The door shivered on its hinges and the air exploded with the sound of a fist banging on the wooden panel. "Hey, Doc, open up."

Will froze, closing his eyes for a moment and wishing his tormentors to an eternity in hell. He leaned down and kissed Cat's forehead in apology, then raised his head and lifted his voice. "What is it?"

Voices jumbled together outside the door, then one rose out of the chaos. "Medical emergency."

Will groaned and pushed himself to his feet. As he struggled into his trousers, Cat tugged back the quilt and slid beneath it, her mouth twitching and her eyes filled with laughter.

He padded barefoot to the door and turned the knob, bracing his body so it could only open a few inches.

"Shivaree!" Bodies crammed the small hallway outside the bedroom door, some with faces blackened by charcoal and many with pants and shirts turned wrong way around and buttoned up the back. A din erupted in the hallway. Cowbells clanged, pots and pans banged together, and outside in the yard a shotgun blasted away. Will was glad Nana and the children were miles away tonight, safe and sound at his childhood home.

One blackened face leered at him, the halo of dark curls identifying the owner as his friend Lewis. The two lanky minstrels behind him could only be Geordie and Joe.

Will tried to push the bedroom door closed.

Lewis wedged his body into the opening. "We've come to drink to the bride's health."

Will wrinkled his nose at the faint smell of alcohol on the man's breath. Lewis seldom drank, and when he did, he made it a habit to pretend to be more affected than he was. "Haven't you had enough?"

The man grinned, white teeth and red gums gleaming in the blackened face. "Never!"

Again the revelers burst into deafening noise.

Will dug in his trouser pocket, bringing out a handful of greenbacks and handing them to the plump undertaker. "You already drank up every drop of spirits in the house tonight. You'll have to go to town."

Lewis turned to the crowd, waving the wad of bills in the air.

With another cheer the men vaulted down the stairs and out the front door, their footsteps shaking the house with as much noise as a cattle stampede. How in the world had they assembled in the hallway without a sound?

He closed the door and turned the skeleton key in the lock, then leaned against it, smiling down at Catriona where she lay all tucked up in the bed. Outside, the hoofbeats of several horses thundered away. They were gone, at least for the moment, and now he could be alone with the woman he loved.

Cat laughed and beckoned him toward her. "Husband, come to bed." She turned back the covers, giving him another glimpse of her naked beauty.

Desire stirred in him, the shivaree forgotten. He slid between the cool sheets, reaching for his wife's warmth beneath the heavy quilt. His hands traced the smooth perfection of her breasts, his fingers teasing the nipples to hardness. He bent and sucked first one, then the other, surprised at the familiar sweetness of her flesh, her quiet moan feeding his own passion.

He kissed the softness of her belly and nuzzled the moist triangle of her most feminine secrets, his tongue savoring the delicate flavor of her womanhood.

She moaned and lifted her hips. Her fingertips tangled in his hair, caressing his scalp. "I canna wait any longer, love."

A shock of delight coursed through him as she spread her thighs and welcomed him. He moved inside her, his pleasure building to the brink of delicious madness as she tightened around him.

Catriona lifted her hips, straining against him. She gave a long, sobbing moan, her body rigid in his arms for a moment until she sank beneath him into the bedding, a sigh escaping her lips.

He lay perfectly still, savoring the spasms tightening like tiny fingers around him.

After a long moment her legs encircled his waist, her heels pressing into his buttocks.

Only then did he release his hold on his passion, thrusting inside her on a rising crest of hunger, burying himself in her body, becoming one with her for an eternal moment of ecstasy. He gasped and settled atop her softness.

Her arms cradled him against her breasts, her fingers caressing his back with gentle strokes.

Closing his eyes, he reveled in the satisfaction pulsing through him. He'd waited for this moment for so long, to make love to Catriona, to take her as his wife. The words of the wedding ceremony echoed in his head. *To have and to hold, from this day forward.* To hold, but not too tight. This was one filly who did better without a bit and a bridle.

Loud banging roused him from half-sleep. He rolled to one side and lifted his head, pitching his voice to carry across the room, a touch of irritation edging his words. "What is it now?"

"Just me again, Doc." Lewis's raucous voice filtered through the closed door. "We didn't want you to get too lonely, so some of us boys come back to serenade you. We sent a couple of fellas on to town to bring us back some rotgut so's we can toast you all in proper style."

Cat chuckled against his shoulder.

First he gave her a mock scowl, then aimed his voice toward the door, good-natured sarcasm edging his words. "Thanks. We appreciate your concern." He lay back on the pillow, pulling his wife against him as loud voices and gunfire erupted outside their bedroom window and pots and pans clanged together in the hall.

Cat snuggled up close, her head on his shoulder, her fingers making lazy designs in the hair on his chest.

He was glad she didn't mind the boys having their little fun with the shivaree. It really didn't bother him. Nothing could bother him right now. All that mattered was Cat's happiness, and that she was finally his wife. He kissed the top of her head. He knew he'd love her for as long as they lived. And somehow he was sure no matter how many times they made love, he'd never stop wanting her.

Cat lifted the glass high, the light of the kerosene lamp shining through the amber liquid. Her eyes scanned the faces around her—Effie and Joe, Geordie and Ida, Will and Nana—her family. "To the year that's near done, and the one that's coming."

Other glasses clinked against hers before she lifted it to her lips. The smoky tang of Talisker stung her nostrils and trailed fire down her throat all the way to her belly. The last bottle of whisky she and Ian had brought from Scotland. Somehow, opening it for New Year's Eve seemed fitting.

Fergus and Jennet would be celebrating Hogmanay so many miles away on Skye, likely drinking the same spirits. Their last letter had announced the arrival of another bairn, a wee lassie named Catriona, for her. The crofters' struggles with the lairds continued, but she'd no doubt her brother and her childhood friend were happy together. She sighed, knowing there was little chance of ever seeing them again, but she'd no regrets about her new life, her new home, her new husband.

She squeezed Will's arm. "This last year has given us all some surprises." She turned toward Effie and Joe. "I wonder what the next will bring."

Joe shuffled his feet and turned to Effie. Color rose in the lass's cheeks, and one elbow prodded the lad's ribs until he spoke. "Me and Effie, well, uh—we're getting hitched come June."

Cat set her glass aside and took her sister by the shoulders. "I'm that happy for you, lassie." She touched her lips to her sister's glowing cheek.

"Thanks." Effie's eyes met hers for a moment before she turned to accept congratulations from Will's grandmother.

Each time she saw Nana, Cat marveled at the health glowing from the old woman's face. Now, since Will had moved to the farm, Sanapia had asked to live at the Bascom place, and the two spent their days gathering and preparing herbs for Cat and Will to use. Useful work made a powerful tonic for them both, and much as Cat missed Sanapia, she realized how well the women filled each other's lives.

Geordie lifted his glass. "A toast to a fine couple." He pounded Joe's shoulder with his fist. "I guess this makes you my brother now."

Joe managed a sheepish grin and touched his glass to Geordie's, then took another swallow. "And what about you? Ain't it about time you got married?"

Her brother's face clouded for a moment, and Cat guessed he was remembering Molly. Then Geordie grinned. "Ah, misery loves company, eh?"

Effie planted her hands on her hips and glared.

Cat laughed and leaned her head against Will's shoulder, taking comfort from his nearness and the faint scent of carbolic clinging to the wool of his jacket.

Geordie's face sobered. "Truly, Eff, you know I envy you both." He lifted his glass in her direction and sipped. "Actually, I have some news as well." He tipped his face down, his gaze directed into the golden liquor. "I've taken a job with the *National Economist* in Washington, D.C. I leave tomorrow."

Cat drew in a sharp breath, joy and sadness churning inside her as her congratulations joined the others. She was happy for her brother's success, and now he'd live near old Zeke Timmerman again. She knew he'd come back to Texas to visit, or perhaps one day she and Will could go to see him.

Still, she would miss her brother. Since their mother died so many years before, she'd helped raise him, and she loved him almost as her firstborn child. But all mothers went through this, and it had only just begun. Someday soon it would be Betsy, then Duncan, then— She nuzzled against Will's shoulder. Perhaps she and her new husband would have more bairns in their future.

A silence fell as the old mantel clock struck three quarters of the hour. Only fifteen minutes until the new year, the beginning of a new decade. Ten years before, she hadn't met Ian yet, had barely known Texas existed. And now it was her home.

Ida cleared her throat and took a step forward. A red spot burned on each of her cheeks. "I know me and little Arthur ain—aren't really part of this family, but we couldn't love you all any more if we was." She turned the glass in her hands. "What I'm trying to say is we'll miss you all." She licked her lips. "See, I got this fella's name from one of those mail-order-bride places, and we've been writing now for most of a year, and I told him all about me, and what I been and done, and about Arthur, and—well, in his last letter he asked me to marry him and come live in Oregon, and I wrote back and told him yes."

Cat laughed as Effie squealed and grabbed Ida by the shoulders, dancing her around the room. As Will bent to kiss the lass on the cheek, Cat let go of his arm and slipped through the parlor door; she'd wish Ida happiness after the excitement ebbed a bit. She hurried through the kitchen and across the yard to the barn. Just enough time before midnight to check on Bossy and her newborn calves.

The door creaked on its leather hinges as she stepped over the threshold, breathing in the warm smells of hay and manure.

Bossy lifted her muzzle, jaws circling as the cow turned her liquid brown eyes toward Cat. Two bull calves jostled each other, bumping their heads against their uncomplaining mother's side, each one with its mouth attached to a teat and a ropy tail curved up over its back.

Cat patted the cow's haunch, then bent to examine the twin babies, both fine, healthy animals. Old Domino had outdone himself this time. Ian would have been proud of his prize bull, siring two babies at once from one cow. She was glad she'd kept him and the six milk cows. At this rate he'd replenish the herd in no time. She stood and stretched, a deep sense of contentment rising up in her as she walked to the door.

Once outside, she leaned against the tack-room door, huddling in her shawl against the chill of the night air, savoring the peaceful scene spread before her. Stars arched from horizon to horizon against the black dome of the sky, and tall prairie grass waved silver in the moonlight.

From inside the house came the faint sounds of voices and laughter. Faint strains of "Auld Lang Syne" reached her through the door, the words echoing in her ears. Her mind wandered back through the years to the first day she'd seen Ian on the Isle of Skye, standing in the kirkyard in his tall hat and strange clothes. Sometimes it seemed she'd loved him forever, even before they met. And he had given her not only his love, but his children, his land, and in the end his life.

A dark figure separated itself from the wall and stepped toward her. "Thought I might find you out here." Will handed her a glass, its contents glistening in the moonlight as he hummed along with the tune coming from the house.

The words echoed inside her head. *We'll take a cup of kindness yet . . .*

He put his arm around her waist and lifted his glass, touching its rim to hers with a gentle clink. "To the past."

Quiet joy flowed through her as she shook her head. The past was gone, something to be cherished and stored away, like Ian's clothes folded in the old trunk. Something to take out and look at every so often, not to wear like a shroud of mourning every day. She turned to Will and smiled into his eyes as she lifted her glass. "To the years ahead."

Historical Note

In 1892 James Stephen Hogg was elected governor of Texas with strong backing from the Farmers Alliance. The platform included his promise to pass legislation to regulate the railroads, a promise he kept later that same year.

The National Farmers Alliance joined forces with the People's Party in the 1890s. The resulting Populist movement generated countless political reforms during the twentieth century to the benefit of farmers and other working-class people.

The Knights of Labor was later reorganized as the American Federation of Labor (AFL).

Glossary

Key to language abbreviations:

Sc=Scottish
T=Texan
Fr=French
L=Latin
C=Comanche
D=Dutch

Ach—(Sc) an exclamation
Aught—(Sc) anything
"Auld Lang Syne"—(Sc) old long since, traditional New Year song
Aye—(Sc) yes
Bairn—(Sc) baby
Bekwinatsu—(C) swelling medicine
Boll—the fruit of the cotton where the fibers grow
Boll Weevil—an insect that eats the fiber in a cotton boll
Bonny—(Sc) pretty
Boomers—(T) settlers in the Oklahoma land rush
Braxy—(Sc) old, full of fat
Breakbone Fever—a painful tropical fever spread by mosquitoes (also known as dengue)
Canny—(Sc) clever
Canna—(Sc) can't
Cashrom—(Sc) footplow
Cher, Chérie—(Fr) dear, dear one
Clamjamfree—(Sc) mixup
Cotton Bagging—cotton cloth used to wrap bales of cotton for market
Counterpane—a bedspread or quilt
Daft—(Sc) crazy, stupid
Dengue—a painful tropical fever spread by

mosquitoes (*see* Breakbone Fever)
Dinna—(Sc) didn't
Drouth—archaic spelling of *drought*, lack of water
Fash—(Sc) upset
Greit—(Sc) cry
Hogmanay—(Sc) New Year's Eve
Hurly-burly—(Sc) commotion
Ja—(D) yes
Jute Bagging—hemp cloth used to wrap bales of cotton for market
Lad, Laddie—(Sc) boy
Lass, Lassie—(Sc) girl
Loco—(T) crazy
Morbus Strangulatoris—(L) diphtheria
Non—(Fr) no
Nought—(Sc) nothing
Oui—(Fr) yes
Receipt—archaic for *recipe*
Remuda—(T) a herd of cow ponies
Reticule—an old-fashioned drawstring purse, often beaded
Roundup pan—(T) a pan full of water for dirty dishes
Shakedown—(T) bedroll
Shivaree—(T) wedding night hazing, usually very loud
Soogans—(T) heavy quilts used in cowboy bedrolls
Sooner—(T) settlers entering Oklahoma Territory before opening
Whist—(Sc) hush

About the Author

For Stephanie Bartlett, researching the connection between the nineteenth-century agrarian movement and the labor movement in the United States "really opened my eyes." Discovering the real West from a woman's perspective also fascinated this "cultural busybody" as she reconstructed the daily lives of European immigrants in Texas during the late 1800s.

A second generation Oregonian who loves to travel but has never lived anywhere outside her native state, Stephanie Bartlett claims to require mountains and green trees around her in order to feel at home. She moved from the mid-Willamette Vally to the southern part of the state in 1981, where she now makes her home with her husband, Mel, her daughter, Ariel, and two cats, Magic and Baby.

FANFARE